THE LAUGHING MAN CHRONICLES

THE SPINNING SISTER

ROBERT J BARLOW

The Spinning Sister

A copy of this publication can be found in the National Library of Australia.

ISBN: 978-0-6482930-6-4
Also available as an e-book

Published by Ouroborus Book Services
www.ouroborusbooks.com

Cover by Sabrina RG Raven: www.sabrinargraven.com

The Spinning Sister

Robert J Barlow

A train pulled up at a suburban station, painted in black and red. It wasn't supposed to stop there; it wasn't supposed to stop anywhere at all. It wasn't supposed to, in the strictest terms, exist in this reality or any other. Even assuming it had, as most things have, a right to its existence, it should not have stopped here.

Breaks that weren't supposed to operate squealed, doors that weren't supposed to open opened and two people got out. You may assume, following this theme, that they were doing things they weren't supposed to, and you would be correct. One wasn't supposed to be here, and the other wasn't supposed to leave.

The one who wasn't supposed to leave was a tall. red-haired woman in a floor length dress, plainly making a game but ultimately doomed attempt to keep it out of the dirt. She seemed to be focusing on it with the intensity of someone who absolutely didn't want to be focusing on something else – perhaps the trail of blood coming off the back of her dress and shoes, or the body part she had to kick out of the way.

The man who wasn't supposed to be there at all was small. He wore black leather pants and a hooded jacket, with no shirt or shoes. The hood was down, exposing his plain, freckled face and short, blond hair. He sung to himself as he walked, his face split in a grin, and appeared to be bopping to an entirely different tune than the one he was singing.

'Hidihidihidihi,' he sung. 'Hidihidihidihi.

Hodihodihodiho.'

'You know that is supposed to be a call and response song, don't you?' She looked at him, raising an eyebrow.

'I may be less than absolutely clear on what exactly that means,' he replied, before returning to his song. 'Hodihodihodiho.'

'It means.' She spoke through gently clenched teeth, breathing deep. 'That when you sing it, you're supposed to sing to an audience, and have them sing the other half back.'

'Oh really?' He thought about that for a moment. 'Ahh. Then you will sing with me?'

'No, I will not,' she snapped, seemingly determined to be nothing less than absolutely clear on the subject. 'I do not sing. Ever.'

'Oh.' The man who wasn't supposed to be there considered this for a second as he crossed a street. 'Then I suppose I have to do both parts myself.' That decided, he tipped his head back and sang again with renewed vigour. 'Heedyheedyheedihee.'

'Have you considered,' she interrupted, raising one finger to interject, 'not singing?'

'I consider all kinds of things,' he replied and, again having responded in a manner he deemed adequate he returned to his song. 'Heedyheedyheedihee.'

'I think I am beginning to hate you,' she said through gritted teeth. 'Which is admirable, considering that I have only known you for seven and a half minutes, and you recently saved my life.'

'Really?' He stopped, all cheer gone. He looked at her, his teeth beginning to sharpen and his body beginning to grow. 'Because my deep and abiding personal respect for you, and my hope that we may one day become friends was the only reason I didn't leave you on the train.'

'Oh, silly.' She gave a shaky, unconvincing laugh and patted him on his steadily swelling shoulder. 'Silly man, I was joking, as firm friends do! Play ribaldry, making fun, that's all.' Her voice was brittle, like it could shatter at any moment.

'Oh.' He grinned, his teeth suddenly returning to those of a normal human. 'I apologise. I don't have many friends. I don't know what it is about me. Perhaps I'm just odd. Is it the lack of understanding of the rules of singing?'

'Possibly.' She raised her eyebrow. 'Or it could be the fact that you kill people.'

'Only when I have to!' he protested.

'You had to break into a moving, interdimensional prison?'

'I mean,' he paused, 'I was paid to. So that counts.' She folded her arms and stopped moving. He thought about that for a moment. 'Does that not count?'

'I'm afraid not.'

'Well you may be right,' he considered. 'Perhaps my tendency toward murder is something of an obstacle to my ability to make friends and influence people.'

'I don't know about making friends.' She looked at him for a long moment and gave the ghost of a smile.

'You seem to be able to influence people well enough.'

'Oh!' He smiled. 'You think so?'

'I mean, aside from murder one of the few things you're known for is your ability to influence people.'

'I mean you aren't wrong.' He stroked his chin and thought. 'But I don't think that's the same as being friendly or personable.'

'That is the case,' she agreed. 'So where are you taking me?

'Somewhere safe.'

'Somewhere safe.' When she repeated it, her voice was marred by suspicion. 'Somewhere safe can mean a lot of things. Technically the train I was just on is somewhere safe, but I wouldn't want to stay there.' She thought about that for a long moment. 'Or at least it was somewhere safe, before you arrived.'

'Well I mean it's not anymore, but it...' He thought about it, putting his hand over his mouth. 'Oh no, you think I'm kidnapping you! I'm so sorry! That's so rude of me, if you didn't want to be my friend anymore I would understand.'

'No, no its fine.' She paused. 'But you have kidnapped people in the past. That's part of how you influenced other people remember?'

'That is the case,' he admitted, thinking about it carefully. 'But not you! I respect you, admire you even! I'm only going to keep you where I take you tonight, and if you don't like it there, you may go, unharmed and with no risk of recapture. You may consider your retrieval a token of my high personal esteem for you.'

'Thank you.' Her voice still had a certain 'waiting for the dagger" quality.

'No problem!' He smiled. 'Happy to help!' After a moment he returned to his song. 'Radiradiradirah!' Soon they arrived at a derelict house, walked inside and disappeared into the basement.

The train pulled up at its next scheduled stop and officials from both the Lost and Legion entered. It was one of the few places in all the dimensions where there could be no hostility between the members of the two groups who thought the world was about them. The train was one of the things too important to be tampered with. Prisoners were only placed here with the consent of both sides, and both sides guarded and inspected it.

'Was this you?' The Lost representative's name was Princess. She wore street clothes, with a tiara perched on her head as the only clue that she was slightly strange. That and the fact that she was currently dispassionately contemplating a severed hand.

'I suppose that question means that wasn't you.' The Lord of the Code was the Legion's liaison, a tall man with hooded eyes in a white suit. He looked at her from under the brim of a snap brimmed fedora.

''Fraid not your lordship.' She stepped inside.

The train was full of signs of violence. Blood spattered the walls, windows, roof and floor. Bodies, and pieces of bodies lay in every direction. Laser burns, impact craters, punctures and slash marks ripped through the metal. Half the seats were gone, ripped out, blown up or simply destroyed. Princess adjusted her tiara and thought for a moment.

'Well.' She nodded at it all. 'Shit.'

'That is the limit of your insight thus far? Profanity?' The Lord sighed, looked mournfully at his shoes and pants, and walked onto the train. 'Any idea what happened?'

'From what I can tell.' She picked at an acne scar on her face as she thought. 'Most of the prisoners were killed as well, in their seats no less. They were locked in, didn't even get the chance to fight. Whoever broke in killed them before they got loose or let the guards do it. This wasn't a prison riot, it was a massacre.'

'With a side of snatch and grab.' Code pointed to the one seat that had been opened. 'They killed all the guards, and all the prisoners bar one.' Code looked at her. 'Why are you smirking at me?'

'I saw something you missed,' she explained. 'It wasn't a they, it was a he, or maybe a she.'

'I'm sorry?'

'Look at the gunshot patterns, and everyone who was killed was either killed by friendly fire or punctured by what looks like, sharpened body parts? Whoever did this beat these people to death with their enhanced body, and it was only one.'

'Well.' He thought about that for a moment. 'Shit.'

CHAPTER ONE

'You are being watched.' The creature across from Adam looked like a panther, with glowing green eyes, its paws making the slightest noise as the claws nicked the ground. The piece of the Elder God known as the Laughing One watched him as he moved with it, the two of them stalking each other, Adam's own claws, long and green, hung low in his hands.

Adam didn't watch its feet anymore. He'd learned that lesson the hard way during his early training bouts, they could move too fast and it lied with them. He watched the creature's centre mass; if it leaped at him he'd spot it in the shoulders. He could cover that.

'People usually are.' He turned suddenly and lashed out a feint. The panther jumped back, giving ground to keep its face safe. 'There's you, and the other one, wherever it's lurking. He's not all that chatty, is he?' He didn't look up at the set of yellow eyes that he knew were above him, watching from a secure location. The Laughing One had constructed all of this for him. He was standing in the middle of a stone circle, with ashes and dirt in the middle. Around them was a ring of trees where the other one was watching from. He knew that stepping into the trees was a mark of failure, a sign that he needed the cover to work in. The other one watched from there. It rarely drew his attention during his day to day life, only speaking up when it had something to contribute.

'No indeed.' The Laughing One sounded amused

by the whole thing, as usual. 'You will discover that is has uses soon enough. Especially since it once partnered with a Legate of the Eternal Flame. It is strong, it is clever, and you would be unwise to ignore its judgment once rendered.'

'Unlike you.' Adam fell into a fighting stance. 'Who tends to talk a lot and say nothing.' With that the two of them engaged. The Laughing One leaped across the empty fire pit. Adam ducked low and scythed his foot into the ashes, spraying them into the creature's face. He took a step forward, drew back his claws and slammed them into the blind creature's throat.

'Ahhh. Point to you.' With that it reappeared on the other side of the pit. The scenery blurred, shifted, changed and now Adam was standing atop a rocking, wooden barge over roiling water. The Laughing One moved too quickly for Adam to mount any kind of offensive, so he just jumped backwards into the water.

'Goddamn that's cold!' His entire body seized up for a moment until he managed to adjust. The salt water was freezing but Adam might be able to fight in the water and it wouldn't be. Somehow, even under the water, breathing through the mask, he could hear the Laughing One's voice in his ears.

'Yes, unlike myself, who tends to speak off the absolute point of the topic, which you also just did in this case I may add. Now, as I was saying, someone is watching you.' It was standing still on top of the barge as he swam underneath it. It knew he couldn't swim forever and was content to watch him with its teeth and claws bared. As soon as he broke the water it'd strike.

'Do you have any idea who's watching me?' It shook its head half a centimetre, unwilling to take its eyes off him.

'I know a few things, but not much.' It considered for a moment. 'I know its intention is not entirely benign. Perhaps it means to use you, perhaps it means to kill you, perhaps it means only to watch you. It's hard to know without knowing more about it, but whatever it is, it watches you with active intentions.' It took Adam a moment to realise active intention meant it wasn't just watching him to see what it could see.

'Are there any more of those damn bug things in me?' He made a move to the side and the Panther turned slightly. It had him dead to rights, he'd have to think of something. 'And if there was, would you know it?'

'I would not,' it admitted.

'I would,' the voice from the sky spoke. The form of the creature was a white owl with bright yellow eyes, still noticeable despite the bright daylight. 'You have none.'

'Still, the fact remains.' The Laughing One pushed him back onto topic. 'You are being watched.'

'Yes,' the creature confirmed from the sky. It never said more than it needed to but once it started, if they were lucky, it would open a dam and the creature would manage to force out as many as a dozen words within the space of a few minutes before it fell silent for another few days.

'Do you guys know anything else about it? Do you know where they can watch me? At home? At the carnival with Annabelle?'

'Yes,' they replied in perfect unison and Adam almost took the chance to strike when the Laughing One's eyes flicked up to the owl, but the attention was too fast.

'All the time?'

'No.' In unison again.

'Most of the time, but not always,' the Laughing One clarified. 'It doesn't seem to depend on where you are. They seem to be able to observe you wherever you are, and I cannot isolate a pattern as to when.'

As it spoke Adam swam under the platform they'd been fighting on, hoping the creature would wait for him to climb up from the other side. What he actually did was lash out to hack at the bindings holding the raft together. As it fell apart he lunged up, only to feel a set of bright white teeth lock around his head. It apparently hadn't been nearly as surprised as Adam had hoped for.

'Point to me.' The world shifted again, and this time they were standing across from each other in a pure white room, no obstacles or gimmicks.

'Okay.' Adam returned to the conversation. 'What do we do about this?'

'Keep our eyes open for now. Follow every lead we find and wait until the observation gets too close. Let them show themselves. Wait until a limb or an eye pokes out from behind their little hidey holes.' The green light in its mouth shined into a grin. 'When they get complacent, when they begin to slip.'

'Strike.' The creature's wings had blades on them, short but sharp, and as Adam turned to look at it the wings tore through his throat, it flared its wings and its claws bit deep into the Laughing One before it could react.

'Point to him.' The panther's voice was wry.

As Adam awoke he reflected that it was always going to be strange to sleep in a cocoon, no matter how big it was. Adam and Annabelle weren't nearly at the point where they would consider moving in together, but they were officially comfortable crashing at each other's places now. This experience was considerably stranger for Adam than Annabelle, considering that she slept in a hammock made from spider silk that she turned into a cocoon every night with webs from her hands.

Still, he had to admit it was softer and cosier than his sheets had ever been, and it was actually surprisingly comfortable once you got used to the idea that you were hanging from the roof rather than sitting on the floor. The two had grown close trying to save the world together and had been getting closer ever since.

He unwrapped his arm from Annabelle's bony shoulder, the spider by adoption not stirring in the slightest. Her hair had decided it wanted to be orange and green now, a combination which didn't feel like it would work but the black lines between the two kept them separated and didn't clash too much. He rolled out of bed and the second his feet hit the floor her eyes sprang open.

'I don't understand how me physically moving you doesn't wake you, but my feet hitting the ground does.'

'Because if you're close enough to move me without approaching me you're someone I want here, so there's no need for me to wake up.' She rolled out of bed, grabbing a dress that hung off a piece of the webbing that held their little nest in its position high above the carnival Annabelle called home.

'You know.' He pulled his pants on and yawned; he'd been sleeping in his coat and mask, as the two pieces were where the Presences lived, and he wanted to be able to speak to them. 'This whole spider kingdom is all well and good, but where do you get laundry and stuff like that done? I haven't seen a washing machine since I showed up here. I mean, finger-wiggling, magical whimsy is all well and good, but I'm starting to stink.'

'Don't really know.' She thought about it for a moment, then shrugged. 'The servants must do it. I can have them cleaned for you if you need me to. It shouldn't be a problem.'

'Right. Because you have servants.'

'Yes, indeed I do.' She nodded. 'You don't really get this whole "I'm technically a queen" thing I have going on, do you? Technically I could order anyone in this place to do anything I wanted. I won't, I wouldn't, because that would be a really crappy thing to do to them and they're my friends, but I could. I earned the dreams of this carnival, and that's earned me a good many liberties over the decades.'

'How old are you?' Decades? She's been working here for decades? That was, more surprising than it should have been.

'Older they you think.' She rolled her eyes. 'And no, I'm not going to give you a real number because it'd just bother you. I am, intellectually, emotionally, and physically somewhere in my mid-twenties. Can we just leave it at that?'

'That's a common thing as well isn't it, people just being tremendously different ages to how they seem?'

'It happens sometimes,' she admitted. 'For some of us it depends on the variety and potency of the magic, and the time we spend on worlds where time is wrong but most of us don't age right. Sometimes faster, sometimes slower, sometimes not at all, but you can trust everyone think and feels about as old as they look.'

'Except when they don't?'

'Except when they don't.' She pointed to him and smiled. 'You're starting to catch on.'

'Yeah.' He smirked. 'Give me a few more years and I might develop the first clue as to what I'm doing.'

'God, I hope not.' She shuddered. 'People who know what they're doing too much end up like Xavier or that big tattooed bastard in the cloak.'

Dating Annabelle was every kind of strange. Going

from place to place; sometimes spending time on the normal plane of reality, some on Annabelle's and some on places that were neither. They'd go out to dinner at a normal restaurant one night and dancing with things that looked more like demons than Adam was comfortable with the next. They would stay in and play video games and three days later meet up and spend the night eating and rehearsing with the interdimensional carnival folk. Some of those weren't human and some may not have even existed as far as Adam could tell. There was a seven-foot man who always wore white that no one acknowledged, who ate, performed and rehearsed with everyone else without hearing or speaking a single word. Adam spoke to him once and he seemed mortified, so he shut up and left him alone like everyone else.

The strangest part was that she seemed to be as fascinated with his world as he was with hers. Doing something as mundane as going to the movies and getting Chinese food seemed to delight her, while she often found the strangest adventures boring.

All things considered, it was a weird status quo, but there it was. She was smart, charming, a freaking circus performer, which was awesome, and she was pretty much his match at everything. The circus people liked to play gambling games of varying tools and complexities, including some stuff that was outright magic, and Adam, with the powers of the Laughing Man could learn to do just about anything they could do quickly enough to make him a match for them, but Annabelle seemed to have some hyper learning of her own.

He'd made friends with a couple of performers, though the clowns didn't seem to like him all that much. Annabelle assured him that they treated everyone who wasn't one of them like that. They mocked him endlessly, made a point of making jokes out of him and messed him around but apparently that was no less than normal for a new person. The fortune tellers avoided him religiously, but a ringleader named Kayla and a giant strongman named Cole were friendly enough and he managed to get close with Scarlett. The spider woman had taken him across the borders between worlds once when he had needed to speak to Annabelle. She was quiet around him at first, but she warmed up quickly and revealed the quick-witted spider woman underneath.

The circus served massive family meals out of seemingly nothing that decorated the table at any time of day for anyone who wanted to sit down whenever they felt like it. There was usually at least someone at the table, and something laid out for them if it wasn't a show day. The motley crew engaged each other loudly, calling for one person or another for stories, songs or to pass something. Kayla told the dirtiest stories he'd ever heard, regardless of context, and with alarming regularity. They were bad enough that Adam even had to walk out of the room a couple of times. It felt like being part of a big family, which was an experience Adam had never had before. For most of his life it had just been his mum, dad and him, then it had just been Mum and him, then, after a few terrible life choices it had just been him.

Annabelle and his friends got along well enough, the few he still had. He hadn't exactly been close to any of them even before he started disappearing for weeks at a time and now he found it harder and harder to relate to normal people whether he liked it or not. He was busy, he had things to do, and while he was off in another world friends had turned into acquaintances without Adam noticing. No great loss he supposed, if he was willing to be rid of them without even noticing how special could they have been? He still had his housemates, Alex and Nick had come to expect him to be interesting when he was there and absent when he liked. Besides, money for groceries and rent came in and the couple were low stress. That was the benefit of having friends who were happy in and of themselves.

He was just finishing pulling the coat back on over his clothes when Scarlett's head popped over the bottom of the cocoon they lived in, accessible only by climbing a ferris wheel when your car was at the top. He smiled and waved, and she flashed a bright grin.

Scarlett did have one impediment to being her friend, and it was something that Adam, with his own neon grin, felt hypocritical for judging.

Her teeth dripped venom when she smiled. Which was frightening.

'What is it, Scar?' Annabelle smiled back at her friend,

seeming to have no vestige of awkwardness to the fact she was still mostly naked in front of her friend.

'Someone is looking for you,' she informed them. Annabelle rolled her eyes.

'Who wants me now? Do I have ambassador stuff to do that I forgot about?'

'Not you, both of you. I mean he said he was looking for the F-wit with the claws and the colourful spider B, but obviously he didn't bleep either of the words like I did.'

'Oh.' Annabelle smiled. 'How'd that go for him?'

'We spent an hour tormenting him about which particular colourful spider B-word he wanted. We did a whole parade thing, showing him just how many of us there were. He didn't get intimidated or anything, so sucktacular, he just got more and more angry. Dude has a real potty mouth.'

'Who says potty mouth, in this day and age, and who says sucktacular at all?' Adam questioned.

'I do.' Scarlett poked her tongue out at him. 'Anyway, the girls were considering trying to take him down, but we'd prefer to handle it peacefully if possible. We'd win, but we'd lose some sisters and…' Her voice picked up tempo further and further until Annabelle pressed her forehead against Scarlett's, then kissed her on the nose.

'Relax, just breathe sweetie.' Her voice was soft and affectionate. The two of them were very physical, as Annabelle was with most of her family. 'I understand perfectly. I'll be down to negotiate soon.'

'I just don't want you to think...' Annabelle kissed Scarlett's forehead again.

'I would never think that. I know you'd fight for me if I asked you to, and you know I'd never ask unless there was no other choice.' The two hugged and Scarlett waved to Adam, smiled, and took three steps before she jumped off the web like a bungee jumper, the thread falling off her back. She stopped at the end of the thread, reached her hands down, and rolled onto the ground.

'Show off,' Adam grumbled. Annabelle let out a peal of laughter.

'Says Mr 'wears his bright green glowing claws in public',' She teased.

'Touché.' He nodded. 'So, do we have any idea who this guy is?'

'If it was just me I'd have a good dozen possible enemies on the list, but you being involved, him swearing at us and not being Pan narrows it down so far it comes out the other side.'

'I don't know what that means. You made that saying up.'

'Could be anyone.' She grinned and tossed her brightly coloured hair. 'Come on, hold on tight to me and we'll take the short way down. It'll give us time to have breakfast before we meet this guy, so I don't get hangry.' She paused and pointed at him. 'What's rule number one of interdimensional relations?'

'Never negotiate while hungry. You make dumb choices or threaten to eat people.' Adam rolled his eyes. 'Which I am straight up telling you is not an applicable lesson if you're not a spider.'

'Incorrect,' she declared. 'It's just harder to act on if you're not a spider.' The hug tightened, and the thick band of spider web coiled around them. Annabelle mimicked Scarlett's movements and jumped them off the side of the alcove. Adam had never really been afraid of heights, and the apprehension he did have had been killed of necessity by the spider realm, as everything floated in a void here.

Still, freefalling while counting on your girlfriend's grip strength to keep you from falling for eternity would have been the fright of his life if not for the Laughing One; the Presence on his face kept him calm. Unlike Scarlett, Annabelle flipped them over in mid-air, allowing them to land on their feet, with a little less elegance than the red backed woman had.

The man waiting at the entrance was taller than Adam remembered, but other than that he fit the memory to a T. Cheap, poorly fitting brown suit, messy brown hair, sharp yellow teeth that he barked at Adam. He sat on an old but comfortable looking couch, his fists clenched so tightly that his body almost vibrated. From his hands came long brown claws that tore into the soft cloth.

He was the Dread Bear.

And Adam had recently gone along with a plan that involved someone stealing his identity.

CHAPTER TWO

'What are you doing here?' Adam looked at the large man, who stared back at him.

'You know, that's a good question.' What he'd heard from the imposter was an accent that sounded vaguely Scottish and abnormally deep. What he heard from the genuine article was a voice so deep that it rumbled, causing a primal fear to rise in his stomach. He rose to his feet and Adam looked up, the imposter had been shorter as well. 'I have one of my own if you don't mind. What, the hell happened, while I was asleep?'

'I think I can answer both of your questions.' Annabelle raised her hand in surrender. 'If you wouldn't mind being calm for just a moment, Dread, I'm sure we can discuss this like reasonable adults.'

'Not feeling all that reasonable,' he snarled, and Annabelle met his eyes. Where Adam had been uncomfortable, Annabelle seemed stony calm.

'It's the only way you're getting any answers. If you attack us, my sisters will attack en masse. Perhaps you'll win, perhaps you'll lose, but by the necessity of your actions, the talking part will be over, and you won't get any answers from us.'

For a moment his muscles appeared to swell, almost doubling in size in front of them, and began to cover himself in thick brown fur, before returning to his "normal" two meters in height. He turned and walked toward a kiosk, ignoring the fact it was unmanned. 'I'm getting a hot dog.' He began to prepare himself one, reaching into the boiling water with his bare hand. 'You've got until I finish it to explain this to me before I do something someone else will regret.'

'Okay.' Annabelle looked at him for a moment, then, ignoring the need to converse, began to prepare the two of them food as well. They began to scarf down carnival hot dogs, which were still just on the fun side of gross. The Dread Bear had one in each hand and was making a horrible mess of the food as she spoke to the two of them, turning to Adam first.

'This is the Dread Bear. Once known as Ursas, though I'm getting not anymore.'

'But didn't that guy turn out to be...'

'He did indeed turn out to be a shapeshifter mimicking the shape of the Dread Bear.' She continued to speak even as the facts dawned upon Adam and he felt a dread rising in his stomach. 'This however, is the genuine article, who was impersonated while he was sleeping. He has apparently woken up and is, if I'm not altogether mistaken, not pleased by the fact he was being impersonated in his sleep.'

'Understated.' Food sprayed from his mouth as he spoke, and Adam looked away, his own appetite gone. 'But essentially accurate.'

'The being that we knew as Ursas was another person, pretending to be the Dread Bear for the purposes of espionage. The real Dread has worked for the Legion for most of his long life.'

'With.'

'With the Legion for most of his long life and, as a bear must, has hibernated now and again. During that time, he was taken advantage of, which is a big no-no for bears for various reasons. He's come to us for answers, which,' she turned to the bear, 'I'm afraid to say we don't have.'

'Try harder,' the big man rumbled through his food. Adam decided it was time to step up make things clear.

'All right.' He spread his arms. 'Let's start with a few obvious things. One. I'm not going to tell you who the shapeshifter was. He saved our lives and that counts for a lot. If that's not negotiable, we can throw down right now.' The table slid back as the Dread Bear got to his feet, his claws growing long and gouging into the wood. 'Though obviously I'd prefer we didn't.'

'Talk fast spider girl.' The Bear pointed at Adam. 'Your boy's about to get you both killed.'

'That's not the important issue now, is it?' Annabelle smiled at him, seemingly still completely calm. 'Yes, it's bad that someone got the information, but isn't the more important question how he got it? Who on your side sold you out? You trusted them to protect you and they either screwed you or screwed up. Either way, isn't that the real problem?'

'It's one of the real problems.' He rose and headed back to a stand, then returned to them with a pair of sticks with meatballs on them. 'I want to know what happened and how it happened. All the parts with my copy in 'em. Now.'

Adam looked at Annabelle, watched her nod and burst into an explanation of what had happened during his first adventure. His journey for the Laughing One, the piece of an extra universal entity that granted Adam his power. He related the negotiation with the Legate, the strange leader with the faceless white mask, and his sidekick Ursas, who had later been revealed to be another bear hidden inside his form by magic. He spoke of some of the stranger things that had happened, and the real Dread Bear laughed, spitting everywhere when Adam revealed he had torn off another man's arm.

'Least he didn't completely let my name down.' He wiped his mouth with the back of his hand and gave a contented grunt. Adam launched into an explanation about obtaining his Presence, his fight against the lightning throwing brat Lady Raiden and his meeting with the King's Man. The emotionless robed sociopath who had brainwashed him. He talked about his betrayal of his friends and uncovering the plot of the ancient and powerful demigod known as the King of Eternal Flame and how Adam and the traitor, who called himself Ursas, had cut down the Legate and defeated the god.

After the story had finished the Dread Bear thought about it for a moment. He spat, got to his feet, turned around and walked off. Adam made to get up, either to follow him or leave, even he didn't know, but Annabelle reached out one hand and held him in place.

'I wouldn't leave just yet.' Her tone was quiet and completely emotionless, her face still stony. 'Wait until he comes back, if he'd not back in five minutes we'll go.' She held his hand and he did his best to pretend to be calm. Sure enough, a couple of minutes later the sizable bulk of the Dread Bear came back into view.

'Here's how I see it,' he commented, pacing back and forth in front of them, seeming to be ranting to himself. 'I'm going to fight someone. Gonna tear 'em limb from limb, eat the pieces. I'm gonna hunt down their friends and allies, everyone who dared to defend and offer them shelter.' He turned to them and put his hands on the table in front of them. 'Which would normally include the two of you since you're between me and that shifter of yours. The only reason I'm not tearing off on a rampage is that spider girl has a point.'

'And you'd almost certainly die if you do that here. Outnumbered a couple of hundred to one and all,' Adam interrupted. He had no idea why he'd said that.

'Seriously?' The Bear looked at the two of them. 'Do you have no idea when to shut up?'

'Not really,' he admitted. 'I'm doing my best.'

'Do better,' he advised. 'So, here's what I can do for you. You help me find the real culprit and I don't take it out on you.'

'What do we get out of it?' Annabelle asked. Adam wasn't sure whether to admire or admonish Annabelle. He came there with threats and she was negotiating.

'Other than your intact bodies?' His claws bit into the table again, the wood cracking and shifting. He closed his eyes and took a moment to think. 'Fine. Since I trusted my security to the Legion and they failed, you may consider this my official audition for your little crew. Find who sold me out, deal with them, or put me in a position where I can deal with them and I'll consider switching my allegiance.'

'Deal.' Annabelle was across the table with one hand extended before Adam had even thought about it. The Dread Bear wrapped it in one of his own massive mitts and they shook.

'Did you just volunteer me for this?' Adam mumbled up at her.

'Sorry darling but this is a standing order. Any opportunity to get one of the great beasts on our side must be taken, up to and including all reasonable prices and measures with a very broad definition of reasonable. Tracking and smacking down the sell-out is something we'd have do to anyway.'

'Why? Aren't they on our side?'

'If they're willing to sell out the other side for a price, then we can't be sure they won't do the same to us.'

'And if I don't want to do it?'

'Then I'll do it.' She shrugged. 'I'd prefer to have you along for the ride dear, but I'll do it without you if I have to.'

'Yer mumblin' like I can't hear you.' He looked at them. 'You're holding my hand. Stop both of those things.' Annabelle let go of his hand and he started cleaning his teeth with one claw. 'I'll lend my support if you need it. As long as you don't expect me to do any social shite. If I show up it's for violence, understand?'

'Do you have a name?' Adam looked away from him. God this man disgusted him. 'I mean I can go back to calling you Ursas.'

'Name's dead.' It was that simple to him. 'You can call me Konstantin, if you have to call me anything but Dread. Ursas is his name now. It's not mine.'

'Okay.' Adam studied him for a few long moments. 'You aren't any kind of sane at all are you?'

'You really oughta watch your mouth.' The newly named Konstantin reached into his coat and pulled out a small piece of paper with some numbers on it. 'All right. We've got a deal. Take my number, call me if you need reinforcement and let me know if you have any leads. If you don't get this done before I start to lose my temper the consequences of that will be on yer own heads.'

'The consequences being a rampage?'

'Rampage.' The snarl turned into an ugly grin and he studied his own claws. 'Yeah. I like that word. Rampage, there's going to be a rampage.'

'Okay.' Adam shrugged and nodded, trying to stay relaxed. 'Operation redirect the rampage, take one.' He ran his hand across his forehead and took a breath. 'I'll give you a call when necks need stomping.'

'If there is nothing else.' Annabelle got to her feet and turned, delivering a line over her shoulder. 'Enjoy the carnival. If you're looking for work, we can probably find you something in the house of horrors.'

'Well fuck you very much,' Konstantin said but was laughing as he turned to head out of the Carnival.

CHAPTER THREE

'You were supposed to kill the entire train.' The man in the plague doctor mask's voice was curt and cold. 'I told you, all of them needed to die. Is that such a difficult concept?'

'You told me there were a few specific targets.' The long-haired man sighed. 'I didn't see the point in massacring an entire train to kill a few men.'

'And yet you did.' The voice rapidly progressed from curt to frustrated. 'So, having accomplished that task in every meaningful way you chose to leave a single survivor, jeopardising an otherwise absolutely certain security grid.'

'Well, how do you know that was how it went down?' He pointed at the screen with a sudden delighted expression on his face. 'Perhaps I was in a desperate situation and only by freeing and promising not to kill one of the prisoners did we manage to overpower them all together.' He plainly thought this was a very persuasive argument.

'Very well.' He paused a moment. 'Was that how it happened?'

'It was absolutely not,' he admitted. 'Everyone else was dead when I let her go.'

'Then why, oh why, did you let her go?' They had reached the end of frustration and gone all the way to anger. He leaned forward, revealing the glowing green lights behind his eyes. 'Since the reason you presented has been revealed to be entirely false?'

'I liked her,' he admitted, sighing softly. 'She was nice, steadfast and dangerous! Always grew up rather admiring her.' He looked at the ground, running his hand through his hair awkwardly. 'I mean she was my idol until I surpassed her, and I still hold a certain level of sentimental appreciation. Couldn't bring myself to do it.'

'You are a professional killer.' The voice was a guttural growl. He rose to his feet and the world behind the screen began to crackle with power. 'Part of the reason people hire professional killers is their lack of inclination to get sentimental!'

'Yes, well.' He scratched his head for a long moment and then shrugged and smiled. 'Oops?'

'What?' Now he was yelling. This didn't seem to affect the strange man.

'Well I'm not certain what else you expect me to say really. Mistakes were made, a person who should have been killed by another person was not. A body was not dropped and as a result of that a loose thread was not cut. If you wish to find someone else to hunt the woman in question down to kill her I have a few recommendations, all of whom are entirely capable.'

'Well that would seem unwise.' He pointed out. 'I mean after all if you hire a man to kill someone and then they fail to do so it would be rather foolish to hire them to do the same again.'

'Very well.' He'd returned some of his calm, speaking through gritted teeth rather than shouting. 'Are you ready to begin cleaning up the rest of the loose ends?'

'Yes indeed!' He clapped his hands excitedly. 'More lovely murders.'

'Is there anyone else around here you respect too much to kill when you are paid to that you would like to tell me about before I do the hiring?'

'Not that I can think of.' He took a long moment to consider it. 'No, I'm pretty sure there aren't, and if there are I'll be sure to tell you when you suggest them, so you can have someone else kill them before I get the chance.'

'Tell me, since you're so invested in assisting us, where exactly did you put Miss Devereaux?'

'It's very rude not to call someone by their assumed name you know,' he scolded, folding his arms.

'I am not concerned with politeness, I am concerned with the young lady's current location.'

'Oh, that's not something that you need to worry about.' He smiled. 'She's no danger to you. I put her somewhere safe and she won't be leaving until long after this whole business is completed.'

'All the same, I would like to know her location.' His arms were folded, his entire manner speaking of terrible retribution to be laid against this madman.

'Yes, well, wanting isn't getting I'm afraid.' He smiled. 'If you want her found, you'll have to find her.'

'It would seem I will,' he growled. 'Then listen closely Six. If you should make any more mistakes you will be declared a liability. You will be added to the list of those who need to be removed.'

'Oh?' The boy named Six didn't appear to move

from his seat, and yet he was in front of the screen, his body twice its size, his limbs longer and his eyes sharper. 'And who will you send to do that? Who in your deck will be sent to trump Six?'

The voice was silent and Six looked at him, tipping his head to each side. Then, with a noise of satisfaction he stepped away and moved, calmly and slowly back to his seat, and picked up the paper on the table. He looked it over, smiled, waved, and headed out of the room. 'An information broker, two Lost foot soldiers and a chosen of the Legion.' He muttered to himself, chuckling. 'Might even take me a whole week.'

Once he was gone the man in the plague doctor mask, which was, in fact, his actual skull, counted to ten.

He then proceeded to break everything in sight. The table was reduced to splinters, the walls smashed, the equipment, including the screen he was communicating with, were broken into pieces no bigger than a centimetre. He swore consistently for a good long time then took a moment to breathe. Then started swearing again for a few minutes longer.

As he calmed a spectrum of colours began to appear around him, red, yellow, green, purple, orange, blue. The seven of them glowed in different colours as the skull faced man looked at them.

'What do we do sir?' they spoke as one.

'We will adjust.' He smiled. 'That's what we do. Have the mirror twins acquire their artificer. The poor man wants to end the world anyway, he may as well do some good before he dies. How goes the search?'

'Several weaknesses have been located, but none of them optimal. We need nothing less than the single weakest point in the dimensional wall.'

'I am aware of what we need!' he bellowed. 'Go find it!'

He needed to watch his outbursts. So far, he'd managed to restrict them to people who could afford to have seen them, but it was only a matter of time if he continued to lose his temper. While there was more leeway among his own people than the Legion he couldn't develop a reputation for being unprofessional. He was powerful, but not powerful enough that he could afford to antagonise people.

Not yet anyway. If this was successful, his own people would fall over their boots to attend to him no matter his temperament.

'So where do we start?' Adam looked over at Annabelle. She'd had preparations to make, so they'd spent a few hours at the Carnival before they head out to get to work. 'Can we count on Xavier and Pan? Or any of the others?'

'It's a distinct possibility.' Annabelle thought about it for a moment. 'A possibility we shouldn't look into too hard just yet. I'll run down some leads, with your help of course. I'll need you to watch my back and we'll bring in the others as we need them.'

'Again, I have to ask, why?' She and Pan had offered him a passing explanation last time he'd asked the question, it had been something to do with adventures and problems belonging only to certain people.

'Basically, because until we know something's going to end badly for us we don't want to add ingredients that might make it go wrong. For now, it's you, me and Konstantin, new participants will be added when things go wrong, when they're put in our path on the web, or when we need them.'

'Okay.' He thought about it for a moment. 'So, I shouldn't go see them for training?'

'Oh, you absolutely should,' she countered. 'You sorely need training. Besides, we want to give them every chance we can to end up on our side. There's no evidence to suggest sustained proximity leads to desirable partnerships, but if someone's gonna get stumbled in I'd prefer it was Pan.'

'Stumbled in?'

'What it's called when you suddenly just end up part of an adventure.'

'You don't want Xavier?'

'Where Pan goes, Xavier goes.' Adam remembered the two of them. Pan, the giant mohawked soldier who was absolutely dedicated to the Lost, one of the two armies who fought for control over the world behind the scenes, to the extent that he was even named the Lost Soldier.

Xavier was his, something. He was lashed to Pan by some nebulous threat of blackmail, so the two of them were almost always together. They fought together, lived together, and seemed to assume they'd die together. In their last adventure the two of them had joined up with Annabelle and a couple of others to guide Adam to the elder god piece called the Laughing One. They both scared the crap out of Adam, but they seemed to know what they were doing, which was something Adam couldn't say for himself.

Over the last months Adam had been training with Pan, taught to manage his Presences, the Laughing One, who lived in his mask, and the other, who lived in his coat, which he currently only called 'the other guy', the creature not having given its own name yet. He was getting stronger, faster, and learning to use his other gifts. Primary among them was the eyes the Laughing One gave him, the ability to locate weak points in his opponent's bodies, which had lately extended to just about everything.

He was slowly but surely learning how things worked, and if he knew how it worked, he could eventually figure out how to work it. With Xavier's help he'd been slowly developing a fighting style all his own. He still mostly fought with the powers the mask gave him, aiming stabs and heavy slashes toward weak points, but lately he'd been learning to predict attacks and use the ability to his advantage.

Other than making his weapons and body a little stronger he had no idea what the owl did. He'd been assured that as he came to understand the creature he would gain more of its power, which was annoying given the fact the damn thing rarely spoke.

'In that case, I have training today. Do you think you could start chasing down leads on your own? Or will you need to wait for me?'

'I'll come with you.' She wrapped her arm around his. 'You need me to get you back to your world, and I can drop a few lines into the water as we go.'

The two of them took a rather roundabout journey to the place they were to meet for training; Annabelle made several stops along the way. She stopped at the café, ordered everything on the menu, and then left without eating anything or paying. Once she walked into a kindergarten and got into a bareknuckle fight with a boy of perhaps six, while the crowd cheered, smoked, gambled, and engaged in heavy cursing at her. The boy beat her handily three times in a row before she managed to push him to a draw. She fed a pack of stray dogs and won a drinking contest with a small crowd of green men. Adam's role, throughout all of this, was to stand behind her, not talk all that much, and learn what he could, and, of course, to detect any cheating or subterfuge not done by Annabelle.

'That was the last place.' She wiped her forehead and grinned.

'Okay.' He looked over at her. 'I have a few questions that are all basically the one question and all essentially consist of *what the hell?*'

'I told you I was running errands,' she replied. 'I was putting lines in the water, planting seeds of various forms of information gathering.'

'So, was I supposed to help you fight that one kid?

I mean, you were fighting a kid, but he also completely wrecked you three times, so I wasn't sure.'

'No, it's cool.' She flashed him a smile. 'He and I are old friends, and he's in his mid-forties.' Adam paused and looked at her in what was no doubt a familiar way, blank incomprehension.

'For some reason that's even stranger to me than if you'd said hundreds.'

'Well that's between you and the therapist you don't have.' She smiled and ruffled his hair. 'The dogs and the gremlins are probably our best hope if I'm honest, but if all it costs are a few bruises I'm happy to turn over the stones.'

'So how are you still sober?'

'Because the gremlins are, to a one, complete idiots. They don't know the difference between vodka and water and they're so used to being the ones doing the cheating they don't bother to check me. All I am right now is hydrated.'

'So those things are gremlins? They're real?'

'They are. There are a few creatures from their worlds that can live in ours. Some places in our world anyway. Now come on.' She punched him in the shoulder. 'You have training to get to.'

'We're being watched.' The voice just burst from his lips. 'I didn't say that; the other half did. I've been observed on and off for a while now and apparently, it's active. He noticed.'

'All right.' She nodded and got out of the car. 'Just keep talking to me like everything's normal.'

'Is everything not normal?'

'It is absolutely not.' She kept herself sounding vaguely cheerful. 'You head to training babe. I'll see if I can tail you and catch whoever's watching.'

With the appearance of blissful ignorance and actually feeling out of his depth, well, slightly more out of his depth than usual anyway, Adam made his way to training.

The place Adam trained was just above a skate centre, a piece of nineties nostalgia that hadn't changed a single aspect since Adam was a ten-year-old. He swore it still had the same music set, the same announcer, even the exact same script. Above the building was a small studio covered in workout gear and crash mats.

'Why is it the Legion gets giant glowy corporate headquarter style buildings and we have to do with a tiny room that smells like foot sweat?' Adam complained as usual. Not that he could smell it anymore, the Laughing One wouldn't allow it, but he still knew.

'Each side has members of a range of circumstances,' Pan replied. 'We have palatial estates in Las Vegas, Tokyo, Hong Kong and Dubai. We even have a place in Melbourne that would blow your mind. It just so happens the man running your show favours a more Spartan environment. So, suck it.'

'If it helps,' Xavier spoke from the couch he lay on, trailing a bottle of wine from the fingers of one hand, 'I find it every bit as distasteful as you do.'

'Then it is fortunate that your misery fuels me.' Pan picked up a medicine ball from the rack and whipped it as Xavier's face. Xavier turned slightly and extended his leg, blocking the ball with the sole of his bare foot. He rose, placing his foot on the ball as it hit the ground. 'So, are we ready to begin training yet? Or do you two have more bitching to do?'

'One more thing first.' He paused. 'One more thing in general, not one more thing for me to bitch about. I'm being watched you see, by something external to me. Not all the time, but it doesn't seem to matter where I go or what I do, they can keep an eye on me. Just in case it bothers you.'

'It does.' He scowled. 'It's not all that strange, but it's annoying.' Pan cracked his knuckles with a loud pop. 'Xavier, run him through your part while I make sure we're not being observed, okay?'

'As you say.' Xavier slugged back his wine and took off his bright red coat, one sleeve cut off and stitched to cater for his missing arm. He pulled the sword from his cane and began to pace around Adam. 'Shall we dance?'

'Looks like.'

For the next hour Adam stretched, blocked, twisted and whirled at Xavier's whim, led by the nose, through technique after technique. He knew Xavier was going easy on him, he went easy on anyone he was training beside, otherwise he'd just beat Adam too badly for him to learn anything. Still, the one-armed man moved faster than Adam would have believed possible if he hadn't seen it.

The Laughing One's power slowed the way Adam perceived the world, but even then, he couldn't find a way to put the Red Gentleman, as Xavier was known, onto the back foot. As they practiced Pan made his way around the room, drawing symbols on the walls, chanting strange little tunes and observing them both. Now and again he would throw some piece of criticism or advice Adam's way, which would change Xavier's fighting style slightly.

When Pan eventually took over the training the exhausted Adam was permitted to relax. The first half hour of his training was weakness isolation, taking the time to pick holes in things and have his Presence reach out to put weakness in a mystical defence and strike them. He knew that, with the small amount of their power he'd accessed Adam was weak in a brawl, but the Laughing One's ability allowed him to locate the weak points and strike there. That made Adam dangerous, but not powerful. Pan was tough, but his shield could be broken if Adam knew exactly where to aim.

He rarely did, and it often ended in painful and humiliating defeat.

The remainder of the training was meditation, trying to make deeper contact with his Presences. The Laughing One was easy, he was kind of a brat, and a bit of dick sometimes, but that was easy enough to understand. He just wanted a laugh. The problem was the owl. Ever since he'd taken it from the Legate of the

Eternal Flame the strange little creature had been distant. It was obviously powerful, and clever, but it rarely said more than ten words.

'It might be easier if you let it set the terms of your next meeting.' Pan placed a massive hand on Adam's shoulder. 'It's obviously not comfortable opening up yet. No doubt it was either loyal to, or hated, its last owner. So, either it's going to be slow to trust, or slow to trust you. It might help to let it take the initiative, since its pervious partner obviously didn't. Make it clear that you're very different to the last guy.' Adam shuddered to remember the Legate. That guy had done everyone he could to always be in control, so this might be a way to distance himself.

Anything that made him different form the Legate had to be a good thing.

He lay down, most people meditated sitting but Pan said it wasn't a big deal. Apparently being comfortable was the most important thing. He closed his eyes and did his best to concentrate, but this wasn't what he was good at. His mind didn't go quiet easily.

'So how do I do this?' He was alone with Pan, and he felt his mind extending. Xavier had gone elsewhere; his energy made a new person trying to connect to spirit almost impossible. He had too much emotion and energy for anything else to get in. Pan was very different, his energy was simple and consistent, a heavy, slow pulse that filled the room was a comforting rumble.

'Just think about speaking with him, like you

would with either of them normally. Think about going to somewhere to communicate, like you do to begin the training that I taught you. The only difference is this time you can't put any judgment or expectations on it. Just go talk to him. He'll put himself onto the scene if you let him.'

'All right.' Adam closed his eyes and had been laying there for about ten minutes when the creature appeared. This time it wasn't an owl, or a mask or coat. This time it wasn't a training ground, or the usual dark room in which he chatted with his Presences.

This time he was sitting in a dressing room, slightly cramped and with too much gear in it, sitting at an overloaded desk and looking into a mirror. Instead of his own face, the mirror displayed a white expressionless mask.

No. It seemed expressionless at first, but it wasn't. It wasn't just any mask, this one showed all the subtle facial tics and changes of any human face. As he noticed this its lips crept upwards in a slow smile.

'You always wanted to perform,' it told him.

'Yeah, I did.' He nodded, shifting a few things from the desk as he watched the mirror. 'Never had the talent for it though.'

'You had talent. What you never had was desire. You wanted it, but never enough.'

'Fair enough.' He smiled at it. 'So, I have to ask, how much do you know about me?'

'Not as much as I would be comfortable with,' it

admitted. 'It is as if I were plucking things out of a stream as they pass me, anything that seems…' its smile grew wider, 'shiny.'

'Part of which was my idle acting desire?'

'My last partner was an actor before he learned the name of the king.'

'That guy was an actor?' he spluttered. That was so unreal, the idea that this weird, twisted creature who had tried so hard to keep his composure and then lost his mind, had been a person? With dreams? Aspirations? A job?

'His name was Andrew McCann, and learning the name changed him significantly, as it did you.' Adam remembered and winced with remembered pain.

'That is the most screwed up thing ever.'

'Close.' it admitted. 'I too had no choice but to serve the king. Yes, Andrew was once an actor of stage and screen, much as you briefly dreamed of being.'

'Weird.' He studied it. 'So, what's your deal?'

'I am not altogether certain I have a deal as such.' The mask appeared thoughtful. 'I keep my own counsel, listen more than I speak, and dislike most beings. Is your true question how you would go about gaining my power?'

'I don't know.' He thought about it. 'I mean power would be ideal, but if we're going to be living in the same body for the rest of our lives I'd rather we learned to get along. Learn some measure of trust and mutual respect, but yeah, I'm not going to pretend I don't want your power. That's why I got you in the first place, and it's why I'm keeping you around. Sorry.'

The face seemed to be thinking for a few moments, then smiled a little and nodded.

'Seems fair,' the mask agreed. 'Very well then, here is what I want from you in exchange for some of my true powers. Keep your eyes open, pay attention and try to see beyond what those around you can see.'

'Okay.' Adam considered this. 'What are you babbling about?'

'If I tell you that it will rather defeat the purpose of the exercise.' It smiled at him. 'Question what you have been told, believe only your own eyes and not even those, until you are certain you have watched closely.' With that the face winked.

'What is it with you Presences and masks?'

'That has nothing at all to do with us.' How did a floating face shrug? However it went about it, it managed. 'You see us as masks, garments or animals and so we are. If you wish to change how we seem to you, change your perception of yourself and us.'

Adam laughed at that. Of course, everything was shaped by his own crazy ass mind. Why couldn't it have been something more reliable? 'So, does that mean you're going to talk more when we're training now?'

'I'm afraid not.' The mask shook. 'I speak when I have something to say, or when it otherwise profits me to do so. I needed you to understand me a little, and now you do. Thus, I may now return to my silence.' Suddenly its hollow eyes opened wide and its voice was sharp. 'Roll left!' he bellowed, and Adam was back in the world.

The blade aimed at his head was moving slowly, his gift allowing his perception of time to speed up and slow down the world around him. He moved without thinking, rolling sharply left like the owl had said. Dammit, he'd forgotten to ask its name again! He rolled again and again, pulling himself to his feet and engaging the rest of his power.

This time he felt a little different, his eyes took in every detail of his attacker in seconds, from the missing teeth he displayed as he opened his mouth in shock, to the tear in his right, black leather glove as he spun a large, gleaming blade in the hand. He had long red hair, dark eyes, and freckles on his face. He wore a singlet, torn jeans and trainers, and showed nothing special other than the blade itself.

Pan was on the ground, still in his calm meditative position, and Adam yelling for his attention didn't wake him up. Xavier was standing outside the room, with a bemused look on his face. His knife probed against the doorway as Pans own wards glowed to keep him out.

Adam looked at the unkempt man and flashed a smile under the mask. The white coat with the owl inside it felt comfortable on his back in a way it never had before. It had always been heavy, or fit wrong, or just been too warm. Now, it felt like it belonged with him.

'All right, ugly.' He grinned and spread his arms, the long green claws glowing, his black mask grinning bright. 'Come at me. I'll have your arm off at the wrist and we can skip right to the interrogation.'

'You're pretty cocky for a kid,' he spat.

'You're pretty ready to throw down for a guy who tried to kill me in my sleep.' Adam was perfectly happy to keep talking and goading him until Pan and Xavier could get into the fight. The man with the knife looked at the big man on his left and realised there was going to be a problem soon, then lowered his knife and charged.

Adam identified the fact before it came, he slid low and kicked out at one knee, hearing a soft crack as his boot hit it. It made the big man sprawl, but in seconds he was back on his feet and ready to engage.

The green lights that indicated opportunities flashed a killing blow, showing the angle the claws could slip into under the ribs and through the heart. At the last second Adam slipped the claws back in, and shifted his aim a little, punching him just right to knock the wind from his lungs. As he struggled for breath Adam slipped a claw neatly across his leg. The big knife swung too close and Adam retreated.

'Why can't I analyse his pattern?' he asked the creatures in his head.

'Doesn't have one. He's slashing truly wildly. I would guess he has no training at all, just a freakish speed and a desire to kill you.'

It was almost funny. Yesterday Adam would have found this almost insurmountable, but he felt almost completely confident.

'I am He who Watches the Flames.' He heard his own voice, calm, dispassionate. 'You may call me Watcher.' And Adam's eyes were suddenly even better. He could see the thick muscles on the assassin's arms tightening, and the cloth bunching as he readied his good leg to launch. He stepped in and placed all six claws into the blade's path. He used one to slow the weapon, and caught between the claws of the other, the gleaming blade thudding into the glove.

Adam pulled the claws back from his free hand and landed one, two, three punches into the man's face, before driving a knee into his solar plexus, and knocking him backwards. The green points lit up all over the man's throat chest and legs as they squared off.

'I could have killed you fifty ways by now,' he growled.

'Yeah maybe.' The big man grinned back, wiping his hair from his face. ''Cept you don't have the stones for it, do ya? All I gotta do is get you once.' He charged again, the wild swinging even faster this time. Adam watched him carefully, picked his moment, and slammed his claws into the blade arm, letting his claws gouge deep into the limb. He spun sideways, turned, and slammed his elbow into the side of his head.

This time the assassin stumbled for a moment, then flashed an ugly grin, tossed his knife into his other hand and rushed right back into the fight. The knife slipped through the Watcher's armour and Adam winced in pain as he pushed his opponent back, letting him go with a kick to the slashed knee.

'Like I said,' he spat. 'You don't have the stones for this, kid. Just lay down and let me end the big one. Tell you what, once I do, I'll forget you were ever here.'

'Piss off,' Adam replied, quite eloquently he thought. All he had to do was get the other arm, if this guy couldn't hold a knife then there wasn't an issue. Go for the disarm, and if that had to be more literal than he'd otherwise like, he could always just have Mercy patch the man up.

This time Adam charged, swinging his clawed hands straight at the left arm. The assassin held him off with the blade, and Adam winced as an incredibly strong knee slammed between his legs. His Presences could numb the pain some, but a force five knee to the balls still put him down.

The big man drew the knife back and Adam only barely managed to block the blow, his hand knocked away against the floor. Ugly drew back and thrust the knife for his heart, the claws on Adam's own off hand only just managing to block the blade. The knife began to bite into the material of the glove as Adam held it, lashing out with his off hand. Dammit, he should have trained more about not panicking. He missed, and missed, and missed, cutting pieces off his assassin even as the bade went harder toward his chest.

Then there was a sudden crack, and the pressure was gone.

'Sorry Adam.' Pan tossed the assassins body across the room. 'He was using some kind of mind mojo to keep me down. Took me longer than I'd like to realise you weren't in the meditation with me anymore, and a minute or so longer to get out.' He picked up the knife, then scowled and tossed it onto the ground. 'I hereby abandon this Presence and renounce my position as its owner.' He looked at Adam. 'Once someone's killed, their killer gets the Presence, but you can abandon it if you want.'

With that Pan turned and slammed his fist through a wall.

Adam thought about saying something but was distracted by Xavier moving with almost blurring speed toward the knife. He picked it up, and it changed to a set of boots, which he made a face at and tossed to Adam.

'I hereby gift this Presence to you.' Adam caught it and held it for a second. It was so angry, so hungry, it ripped and tore and snapped at his mind, wanting to take a piece out of the world. Adam dropped it, but he held his head.

'What do I do? Make it stop!'

'Say 'I hereby abandon this Presence'.'

'I hereby abandon this Presence.' The feeling in his head was gone.

'That... is disgusting.' He spat on the ground. 'What's its deal?'

'You're incompatible.' Xavier looked at him. 'Horribly incompatible it seems.'

'Incompatible?' Adam looked at Pan, but the big man ignored him, wearing out a punching bag with furious intent. Xavier cleared his throat for attention.

'What is the highest number of Presences you've ever seen a person with?'

'The big creepy bastard had four.' He nodded. 'The King's Man.'

'The average member of our world has two, and he had four, yet he was very different to you. Why, I wonder, is there such a small distinction with such a large difference? And why, since you and I both have two, are we not equals?' He smiled wider. 'And why, pray tell, did I not stab Lady Raiden in the chest and take hers, bringing me up to three? Or take this man's? I've killed dozens of people with presences in my time, and I've still only the two? Why is that?'

'I don't know the answers to any of those questions and you know it,' he grunted.

'Compatibility!' Xavier declared. 'Sometimes the powers do not fit, sometimes the personality doesn't. You must live with these things in your head and they must live with each other. Sometimes powers double up, making them worthless, sometimes you can't imagine what they can do well enough to use them. Sometimes they can't or won't work with each other or can't or won't work with you. You can force it of course, but that will hurt both you and them, while adding very little.' Xavier looked at Pan for a moment and paused, like he was deciding whether to say something.

'Go ahead,' Pan grunted.

'In extreme circumstances you can cause yourself

permanent consequences, including death. We need to make sure we can work together or remove a Presence when we can't.'

'If we don't, bad things happen,' Pan grunted.

'Okay.' Adam nodded. 'So, what are we gonna do with this?' He pointed to the knife.

'Run it through the hands of our friends, all the people we know and like, then all of the people who are on our side. Then we go further and further if we must, until we can give, sell or trade it to someone who will make use of it that pleases us.' Xavier took a cloth out of a drawer and wrapped the knife in it.

'Annabelle first,' Adam insisted.

'I've no objection to that.' Xavier nodded.

'Settled then,' Pan spoke from his spot. 'Your girlfriend gets dibs, but if she says no then I get to decide what to do next.'

'Deal.'

'Good.' Pan pointed to the door. 'Then you should go relax.'

'You killed that guy.' Adam pointed to the assassin and Pan shrugged.

'He did try to kill us in our sleep. My options were limited. Couldn't be sure he'd be able to be knocked unconscious, but I'm yet to meet someone who can walk off a broken neck.' He thought for a moment. 'You know what, let's get you a drink and somewhere safe to relax for a few hours. My boyfriend has a nice place and he's been on me to invite people around.'

'You have a boyfriend?' Pan rolled his eyes and

scowled as Adam spoke.

'You literally cannot be surprised that I'm gay. You are not allowed. My being gay literally saved your life once.'

'No.' He shrugged. 'I'm surprised you're in a relationship. You have a partner who's okay with you bailing on him for weeks on end to go to another world?' Pan seemed far less bothered by the fact Adam couldn't believe he was in a relationship.

'He knows the score.' He smiled. 'His family has provided funding for the Lost for generations. He works for an ad company. They let him have a week off or so whenever I get back into town, but he's a hardcore workaholic and sleeping alone never bothered him. I know it's a little odd, but it works for us.' He smiled. 'Besides, he's a great cook.'

'I have to meet anyone who could survive a relationship with you.' Adam smirked.

'Don't be rude about Jeremiah,' Xavier scolded, holding out one finger like he was warning a child. 'He's a darling. Hurt him and I'll be upset.'

'Understood.'

Jeremiah and Pan lived in the centre of the city, in a building with glass almost everything. The walls were plain cream, and all the furnishings were marble and steel. They reclined in leather armchairs while Jeremiah, a young, blond man who had welcomed every one of Pan's friends with a hug he obviously meant, procured food and drinks for them all.

'It's amazing to see you all!' he said earnestly. 'Pete so rarely brings people around, except Xavier of course, how are you dear?' The two of them embraced and Xavier nodded, taking his hat off and putting it on a hatstand which was doubtless there just for that. 'I'm Jeremiah St Croix.' It was hard to tell whether he was Australian or British.

'I'm Adam Westbrook,' he replied. 'This is Annabelle, whose last name I just realised I don't know.'

'As in Adrian Westbrook?'

'Who's that?'

'Ah. Asked and answered I suppose.' Jeremiah nodded. 'Adrian Westbrook is an investment banker, one of the biggest in the country. He's a colleague I respect and admire.'

'Okay, good to know.' He shrugged and looked at Jeremiah for a moment. 'So, you're one of those stick up the ass, "I know a guy" types. So, how'd you end up with a guy like Pan?'

'I don't exactly think of myself as a–'

'His family has worked for mine and a few others for generations,' Pan interrupted. 'He's a rich boy among rich boys, but he's not an asshole about it. He's one of the good ones, which means he's only a prick on a very bad day.'

'For generations?'

'We weren't always ad me.' Jeremiah took the talking back, glaring at Pan who had opened his mouth. 'What I am is what we call a supplier. I am not Lost, I have no magic of my own, but what I do have is a knack for making money. I work for a number of Lost agents, supplying them with the mundane things they need to save the world.'

'I was wondering how you guys keep jobs when you have to disappear for weeks at a time.'

Jeremiah thought about that for a moment, making calculations in his head. 'About thirty percent of the money that your people make comes from work. You either take jobs that are fly in fly out and allow you to keep appointments, or that let you keep transitory hours. Singers, bands, authors, freelancers, that kind of thing. Another thirty percent comes from investments and the things you steal from the Legion and people who unknowingly support them. The rest is from suppliers like me. We fund your exploits and fight our own less literal war against the Legion's people in the same industry.'

'So, suppliers screw each other over too?'

'We do, yes. It's important that's you have what you need and it's just as important that they don't. I fund Pete, Xavier and about a dozen others you don't know about. If you need I'll probably also end up funding you.'

'Not you?' Adam looked over at Annabelle from where they cuddled up on a chair. She shrugged, her hair and clothes now a vibrant shade of purple.

'No. On the odd occasions I feel the need to spend too much time outside my family's home dimension I work tech for a few bands. If we don't need to rely on suppliers, we leave them be. It's not good to drain resources like that.'

'Which is of course, nonsense.' Jeremiah threw up his hands. 'I have more than enough resources for a few more charges. I'm more than rich enough!'

'Don't let him fool you with this domestic act,' Pan gently teased his partner from the living room. 'He had the housekeeper tell him where everything is and prepare food ahead of time, so he could be the perfect host.'

'Peter!' Xavier scolded. 'We are his guests and you shouldn't question how he prepares for us!'

'You have openly told people that you wanted to murder them, while talking about them like they aren't here, inside their own home, which they invited you into.'

'Also, they were monks,' Adam added. They had been an odd bunch of people, and difficult to deal with, but the brightly coloured monks had never raised a hand against them.

'That was different?' Xavier protested.

'How?'

'I know the rules and choose not to obey them. The other players at the table may hate a cheat, but worse by far is a man who tries to play the game with no idea of how. You should know the rules, so you may know the correct ways to break them.'

'Xavier. Please stop acting like an ass,' Jeremiah scolded, returning with drinks.

'There are ways these things are done is all I'm saying,' Xavier grumbled.

'Does anyone but you agree on what exactly

those ways are?'

'Ignorance is no excuse for bad behaviour.'

'Do you remember how I told you a minute ago to stop acting like an ass?' Jeremiah quirked an eyebrow and Xavier nodded, taking his drink and nodding his head obligingly.

'People keep telling me that, and I'm never quite sure what it means I should do.'

'In this case, shut up and drink. In fact, extend that to all situations.' Annabelle motioned to the ridiculous, fruity, umbrella drink in Xavier's hand. He also had a glass of whiskey on the table, and he seemed to alternate between the two.

'I shall.'

'So, Adam, tell me what your story is.' Jeremiah leaned toward him with a smile. 'I've heard about Annabelle before but never you. You seem delightful.'

'I am delightful,' Adam agreed, much to the eye rolls and smirking of everyone else. 'I'm new.' He proceeded to relate the story to Jeremiah, who seemed more interested in his role than impressed. Still, he was appropriately sympathetic and cheerful at the right points and listened to the rest with attention. When he was almost done Jeremiah interrupted.

'I was wondering when a polite time would be to mention the whole "what happened to your severed arm" thing.'

'I fed it to a bear!' Xavier declared cheerfully, then regaled Jeremiah with the story of his long con that involved feeding his arm to a bear spirit. It hadn't slowed him down much, as he was almost as good with one hand as he had been with two.

They talked about their interdimensional journey, and Adam's meetings with the spider queen Widow and the strange Knight of Mirrors. They told him about how Adam had been kidnapped, and the final show down between the Legion's forces and Adam's ragtag group.

'Well that is just about the strangest thing I've ever heard of, and that's not a low bar to leap considering my associates.' Jeremiah put down some snacks and smiled over at them. 'So, what are you up to now?'

'Well, you know the bear that we cheated?' At this point Xavier and Pan were alert, their eyes fixed on him. He looked at Annabelle, wondering if he should go ahead with this and she nodded. 'Well he's apparently really pissed someone told Ursas he was asleep. He's now informed me that if we don't find out who sold the info he'd lose his temper and take it out on everyone involved. The exact word he used was 'rampage'.'

'Actually, you said rampage. He just agreed with you.'

'Adam,' Xavier scolded. 'Stop giving our enemies ideas.'

'Anyway,' Adam cut through what they were saying. 'He said if I found out who sold the info the Dread Bear would consider joining us.'

'We aren't selling out our own,' Pan rumbled.

'No, we aren't.' Adam nodded. 'Look the way I see it if he goes off on his own he's going to kill the information broker, and everyone they sold to just in case, and probably also me just to round out the pack. If we can say with absolute certainty that this guy isn't selling it to anyone else, I can't tell him the jobs done.' He looked at Pan. 'There's some magical whatever we can do to make sure someone doesn't pass out information, right?'

'Yes.' Pan wasn't happy about it. 'There is something to be done to ensure that silence, once guaranteed, is ensured.'

'And I can help as well!' Xavier declared, finishing his drink.

'How?'

'I think you may have forgotten the part where the entire betrayal was my idea. I'll take you to Billie and you can tell her the circumstances. I'm sure she'll be willing to be reasonable, and if not, we can always threaten to murder her.'

'Xavier!' Jeremiah snapped. 'I won't have that kind of talk in my house!'

'I apologise.' Xavier raised his hands. 'We definitely don't actually murder her. I promise. Absolutely no real informant murders. Is it food time now?'

'If you can't be polite then food time is never.' Jeremiah folded his arms. Xavier responded to this by falling to the ground with his hand over his face.

'I sincerely apologise!' he stated. 'I beseech, I grovel, I beg!'

'I have a very good cook.' Jeremiah revealed, winking at Adam, then pulling Pan out of the room with him. The two of them returned moments later with what looked like an entire pig carved and sliced, along with about a half dozen side dishes. He laid them out and the five of them tucked in. Jeremiah ate like a normal person, and at first Adam thought there was no way they were going to finish everything laid out in front of them.

Then they all kept eating, and eating, and eating. Long past when Jeremiah had given up, Adam wasn't even full, and by the time he was done the other three of them were still firmly in stride.

'How the hell do you three eat so much?'

'You never noticed how much you can eat?' Pan looked up at him through a mouthful of pork.

'I hadn't.' Now he thought about it, Adam hadn't eaten more than two meals a day for most of his life. Now he was snacking regularly and hadn't skipped breakfast in his home dimension since he'd met the Laughing One. 'Now you bring it up though.'

'We eat a lot, drink a lot and don't sleep much.' Pan pushed away his fourth plate. 'The more we engage with our Presences, and the more power we gain, the truer that becomes.' He filled a fifth plate, though slowly and less enthusiastically.

'Xavier has a bigger appetite than any man I've ever seen, and I've known professional weightlifters,' Jeremiah pointed out. Now that Adam noticed the Red Gentleman had polished off more of the food than Annabelle and Pan combined.

'Why is that? I mean you have more Presences than

he does, and you're bigger.' Pan paused, swallowed and replied.

'He's had his for longer.'

'How long?'

'Longer than your ancestors can remember,' the strange man replied for himself. 'Longer than the language you speak, and the trees that made the wood of this table.'

'Is he for real?' He looked back at Pan, who shrugged.

'Almost never, but he is old. He's been around longer than anyone I know. Every time anyone asks him he gives an answer like that.'

'Very well. I shall give you a clue.' Xavier smirked. 'The civilisation into which I was born has the word "ancient" in front of it now.'

'So, you're like, a couple of thousand years old?'

'Who can say?' he replied airily.

'You could,' Adam pointed out. 'Right now, if you wanted to. Wouldn't even be hard.'

'Yes.' Xavier looked at his fork, appearing to ponder this situation. 'I suppose I could. So, what do you plan to do once this nonsense is over?'

'I need to train.' Adam had decided this a while ago. 'Properly, somewhere safe, where I can start out. There has to be a school or something.'

'There is.' Pan locked eyes with him, suddenly deadly serious. 'But you may not survive it, it's only for the strongest among us. It's less like a school, and more like a hostile environment in which you learn by existing.'

'The Lost doesn't have enough organisation to make a proper learning institution,' Jeremiah cut in. 'You have a few places that work to raise us to greater strength. I went to one during my transfer.'

'What happens there?'

'You survive.' The big man said simply. 'and people attempt to point you in the right direction. You find the lessons that suit you. When the right thing happens and you've had enough you can go, when you give up, you can go. That's up to you.'

'Sounds like fun.'

'Prepare to be surprised,' Pan smirked. 'But yeah, some of the best and worst people I ever met were in that place.'

'Okay.' Adam slapped the table and made to get up. 'Let's get to it.'

'No!' Jeremiah blurted. 'You don't go off on mystical garbage tonight. Tonight, you eat dessert, make pleasant conversation and sleep in our guest room. Then you can go off and do whatever you like tomorrow.'

'I don't exactly like doing this you know.' Adam clarified. 'It's more of a thing that happens to me than.'

'His house. His rules,' Xavier commented.

It was actually rather nice. It was strange to end up watching a movie on the couch and drinking with people who fought monsters and killed people, but Jeremiah enforced normality with a very civil iron fist, and they managed to spend the night. They watched TV, drank, swapped storeys and he and Annabelle spent the night together.

Adam wasn't wearing his mask this time, so of course he couldn't sleep for a few hours, which was an issue Annabelle didn't share. He felt like a freak when he realised he'd been laying there staring at her for what must have been half an hour. Eventually, remembering some advice he got from a shrink. Adam got up and took a walk around the house.

'Hey.' Pan was sitting out on the balcony, laying back on his recliner chair. He wore black pants but no shirt or gloves and the tattoo, usually on his head, now roamed freely across his body, spiralling into strange patterns.

'Hey. What's the deal with that tattoo?' he asked, keeping his eyes on it as it danced around his bicep.

'Man, it's past midnight. You gotta ask the heavy questions now?'

'What else are we gonna talk about?'

'You like football?'

'Not really.'

'Yeah me neither.' He sighed. 'The tattoo is a Presence, just like any other.'

'Lie.'

'Huh?'

'I'm doing this new time saving thing where instead of doing the boring parts of a conversation I just say lie when someone lies to me, then they either tell the truth or let it go. Everyone wears Presences, they're removable, even Annabelle uses some form of dye in her hair for hers. Yours is a tattoo, permanent.

Like the King's Mans.'

'Right.' He thought for a moment and then shrugged. 'It's a long story, but I'm eventually going to have to tell you part of it, might as well do it now. Something went weird when I bonded with my third Presence. The gloves are linked, and they're awesome, two of the most powerful Presences in the world. Then I got the third, and suddenly things went weird.'

'Weird how?'

'Not telling you that part. Anyway, now I can take the twins off whenever I like, but the Mother of the Lost here and I are stuck together forever. No Exit style.'

'No Exit?'

'Old play,' he explained. 'Set in hell, where all hell involves is being stuck in a room with a bunch of people you hate, unable to sleep or blink or leave.'

That actually did kinda sound like hell.

'What's her ability?'

'The thing I did with the gargoyle. In addition to the baseline of making me stronger and faster et cetera she also lets me contact, communicate and integrate another Presence, taking on its knowledge and abilities. It only works while we're both willing, and it's painful for both us, but we can do it.'

'No one's ever told me everything their Presence does before.'

'Close enough to it anyway.' Pan closed his eyes and smiled. 'Call it a bond of trust.'

'So, you can't sleep either?'

'I can,' he spoke up. 'And I will, once Jeremiah's

completely out. After an hour or so he sleeps like the dead and my thrashing and screaming don't bother him.'

'Nightmares?'

'Like you would not believe. So, you're an insomniac?'

'If you believe my mother I haven't slept well a single night of my life. The Laughing One changed that lately, if I put on the mask I can go out like a light, but it bugs me to count on it too much. I like myself.' That was a lie. 'Or at least I like the idea of who I am.' Truth. 'The Laughing Man might be tougher and cooler than me, but he's also scary as hell, cackling like a lunatic like he does when I get scared. Seems to think me being scared and in pain is funny.'

'He's a mean mother, no doubt about that.' Pan clapped Adam on the back and Adam winced. Even without the gloves the Lost Soldier was strong. 'I think you're right. It's a good idea not to keep him on too much. We change a lot, and it's best to keep it gradual.'

'So, there's no way not to change?'

Pan laughed at that one.

'There's never a way not to change man. You move house, you change. You fall in love, you change, you fall out of love, you change more. If any person changed their name and appearance today and spoke to themselves from three years ago they wouldn't guess who it was. If you want a major life choice not to change who you are you are thoroughly SOL.'

'That simple huh?'

'Simple, yes.' Pan pulled out a cigarette and lit up. 'Easy, no. You should keep the change slow, keep it calm. There's no reason to go Laughing before you need to.'

'So I guess it's the start of another adventure, or whatever else you want to call it.'

'Not at all,' Pan chuckled, smoke coming out of his mouth and nose. 'It started when you met the bear. By the time you know you've started, it's already too late to turn back.'

Chapter Four

Adam managed to get to sleep without the mask eventually, climbing into bed beside Annabelle and keeping his eyes closed until the world faded away without him. When he woke up it was somehow without hangover or issue, and to a crowd full of eager Lost who were going on an adventure to meet a woman Xavier knew called Billie. She was apparently out in the middle of nowhere, so Pan took his giant abomination of a truck up a mountain into the country.

He drove like he wanted to die, taking tight corners at full speed on roads that were barely big enough for all four wheels. He charged up the mountain with a smile on his face and Adam eventually managed to enjoy the scenery, once he realised he wasn't about to die in a fiery wreck.

The mountains over the city were gorgeous. The light in the sky, the forests leading up to the city met his eyes and shifted with Pan's insane pace. A half an hour of climbing the mountain, with roars of the engine, Pan pulled up at a peaceful campground.

'So, is this where we'll find Billie?'

'This is not where we'll find Billie.' Xavier contradicted. 'Pan and I will find the path there; it's what he does best. Billie is hard to find at the best of times. She's a paranoid little bunny rabbit and she never leaves her own place. There aren't many ways to find her in the dark and, without both of us, it'd be impossible. She's secure in her little hidey hole, and no one gets in if she wants to keep them out.'

'But you can?'

'She'll let me through, she trusts me. Which may be something of a mistake unless things go horribly right.' He seemed fundamentally unbothered by the idea of betraying his friend.

'Okay. So where do we go?'

'We don't go anywhere yet.' Pan was smiling as he pulled out a large bag of camping supplies, without many words he began to put up tents and unload food that looked like they'd be there a few days. 'We relax and wait until things start to seem natural, then we go.' So, for the second night in a row the group sat down and made good company of one another as best they could. They drank and traded stories. Adam even got the feeling that they were doing their best to keep the stories mundane so that he could make a meaningful contribution to the tales of embarrassment, ridiculousness and romance that they were telling.

They might as well not have bothered; the whole group still had a good deal more experience than he did.

'Compared to you guys it seems like I haven't even lived,' he admitted.

'Don't butt into that, kid.' Pan put his hand on Adam's shoulder. 'We might have a few more stories but we also have a lot more pain, and a lot more distance. The world will tell you that everyone's having a better time, that everyone has more purpose, but none of us really know what we're doing.'

'I do,' Xavier refuted.

'Except apparently him, but he's so badly fractured from the world that sometimes I'm not sure he knows his own name. I wouldn't be too quick to believe him.'

'Xavier.' Adam remembered. 'Don't you have something for Annabelle to try on?'

'Indeed, I do!' Xavier nodded. 'I was distracted by not caring very much.' After a moment's rummaging in his magic hat he pulled out the knife they'd received from the assassin, dropping it on the ground in front of them.

'Where'd you get that?' Annabelle went down on her knees and examined it with a curious eye, sending a spider to crawl across the weapon.

'From an assassin.' Adam nodded. 'We've all tried it out, and it didn't work for any of us. I made Xavier give it to you next.'

'Sweet of you,' Annabelle mumbled. She reached out one finger and gently ran it across the side of the weapon. The two of them began to glow, and the spiders began to swarm over her body. Her eyes went wide, and she stroked the weapon almost sensually. 'Hungry,' she said in a strange, singsong voice. 'So hungry. Wants so much.'

The three of them looked at each other awkwardly as Annabelle ran her hands across the weapon, her teeth bared and eyes bright, a smile on her face. She let out a noise of pain, shook a little as her colours began to glow. Then, with a sudden groaning pull the weapon split in two, turning from one large blade to two small curved daggers. In the middle of each knife was a hole, a hollow channel in the exact centre.

'Oh.' Her voice was different, the calm with an undercurrent of desire, hunger, aggression. 'That is interesting.'

'And the spider got her fangs.' Xavier's voice was quiet. 'Well done, beautiful.'

Annabelle flipped her knives in her hands, spinning them over her wrists and into her hands. A black liquid began to flow out of the end of the blades. She pointed at Xavier and Pan with them.

'Begone, darling boys. I have appetites to satisfy.' The two of them looked at each other meaningfully, then stepped away from the fire, heading off in opposite directions.

The knives slipped away into her belt, and she approached Adam, running her fingers across his collarbone.

'When I picked up that thing it was,' he paused, 'too hungry. It wanted everything, all at once, right now.'

'It still does.' She leaned close to him, pressing her lips into his neck. 'But it works for me. Maybe it's the spontaneity and desire I need.' Her fingers ran through his hair.

'The guy who had it first,' Adam pushed against her gently, pushing her away from him a little, 'he was crazy with it. Couldn't take care of himself.' He was scared for her. He didn't want her to lose it.

'It's okay.' Her voice was tender. 'It fits with the other one. It fits perfectly. I don't understand how I spent so long without it.' She ran her hands through her hair. 'Gods, I've been collecting resources for so long, putting things in place for when I needed them. The Carnival could make us so much stronger, I should–'

'Hey, hey.' He reached out one hand and cupped her cheek. 'Maybe take a minute and think things over before you decide to uproot your people and deploy them like a military?'

'Right, you're right.' She thought about that for a moment. 'I'm here to protect them, not rule them. Still, they could be doing so much more! We all could.'

'Okay.' He stroked her face. He didn't know what to do about this, something in his gut was churning. Annabelle always seemed to be in control. It was weird watching her like this. 'Of course, we could, but there's not much we can do about it right now.'

'You're right.' She put her hand on his chest. 'But there is something I can do right now.'

A part of Adam wanted to push her away again. She was being strange, aggressive, not her usual well thought out self. Everything with her seemed so planned, but, all of a sudden, here she was.

Still. He wasn't made of stone.

Adam spent the next day training, meditating and practicing with Annabelle and Xavier. Annabelle was more skilled, and Xavier was just better but Adam was improving quicker and quicker. He was learning to anticipate Annabelle's moves, and was getting closer and closer to not being beaten as he danced and leaped away from the spiders. Xavier almost seemed beatable from time to time, but every time he had, he'd stepped up his game a dozen degrees and did that thing where he seemed to blur and reappear elsewhere with terrifying speed.

It was exhausting, and once again Adam reflected on the fact he seemed to be dealing with people he had no hope of beating. He could beat Annabelle with her whips, but she still had dozens of spiders she wasn't using. A couple of people could actually fight with and hope to beat would be helpful.

It was while he was meditating that the Watcher got his attention.

'They are watching you, now, not from far away,' the soft voice rang in the back of his mind.

'What?' He made to get up and start a chase, but a blast of pain wracked his head.

'Stay still,' Watcher scolded. 'Keep your eyes closed and act as if nothing has changed. Continue to meditate whilst I detect the life around us.'

'Finally ready to start cooperating, Watcher?' The Laughing One sounded even more amused than usual.

'Finally, something occurs that is worthy of my cooperation.'

In front of Adam's closed eyes, the world started to reshape itself in green, pulsing like a cold war era radar. Trees, plants and rocks began to form around him, their outlines were blurry, but they were there.

'Why am I not opening my eyes?' he asked. 'So, I can see worse? Is this some kind of challenge? Because this is not the time.'

'I am aware.' The Watcher's voice was cold. 'I am looking for things you do not ordinarily see. These things are irrelevant to me. Movement, even the smallest movement is highly relevant to me.'

'Okay.' He nodded. 'What do I do?'

'Anyone or thing that moves, that so much as breathes deeply or wiggles a toe will be recognisable to me. Our target is not currently moving, so we shall provoke that movement. Stay still, stay calm, and when I say so rise, spin around and hurl the branch by your left hand as hard as you can at the Red Gentleman. When you do, it will inspire reaction and you will need to move with due haste.'

'Understood.' Adam tried to seem relaxed as the Presences tightened his focus, and Adam got ready.

'Now!' Adam whirled and sprang to his feet. He took the branch in his left hand and hurled it, as hard as he could, end over end at Xavier. The Top Hat Man tossed his sword in the air, took the hat from his head, cut the stick in two with the brim and put it back on his head.

'Go! Now!' There was a light behind Adam's eyes, the radar going off. Someone who had breathed in and twitched suddenly. Adam took off as fast as he could, dancing through the scrub, his footprints placed by

71

his faithful Laughing One.

Xavier let out a small noise of objection then followed with his usual terrifying speed.

'Red.' The voice coming from the trees was slightly familiar. 'I will drop him where he stands if you step in. This is his business, you should take a walk.'

'Touch the boy and you will spend the rest of your very long life in paralysing agony.' From Xavier's tone he may as well have been commenting on the weather as he walked back toward the camp.

'Two hundred and thirty-seven,' the voice spoke.

'Huh?'

'That's how many times I could have killed you since the first time we met. You know, I was not expecting you to beat me fair and square as you did. You are impressive, not as impressive as you think you are but impressive nonetheless.' With that the assailant stepped out of his hiding place. 'I was expecting to put you dead to rights, issue my threat and have you give up the mask, but things don't always go as planned.' He shrugged. 'If I was there to kill you, you would have died.'

Adam had seen this man once before. The man had tried to snipe him from across the street while he slept in his house once. After a brief but terrifying battle, Adam had broken the man's gun, and the assassin had returned the favour by informing Adam that if he didn't surrender, he would never be safe again.

'You!' He raised the claws and made ready to square off, only for the pale man to raise his weapon and drive Adam to his knees with a sudden, bone shattering, organ shifting, blood-boiling pain.

'Laughing Man!' he screamed in his head. 'Why aren't you killing my pain?'

'I am!' The Laughing One was plainly alarmed. 'You aren't in a quarter of the pain you ought to be!'

After a few paralysing seconds the switch flipped and the weapon, the white sonic rifle that the pale man wielded, ceased its humming altogether. Adam straightened back up and shook off his pain the best he could.

'Yes.' His voice was dispassionate. 'Me. Now back to that number, two hundred and thirty-seven. In your sleep, as you made love, as you trained and fought. All that time I followed you, watching through the scope of this very gun and all that time I could have killed you, over and over and over.' He shook his head and chuckled.

'So why didn't you?' Adam's voice was a ragged growl of pain and hate

'Because.' He slowed down his speaking as if he was trying to make sense to a small child. 'Things are more complicated than you think. I am Legion, you are Lost. If it were that simple I would have killed you over and over. They are not, I have not, and I shall not.'

'Okay.' He took a deep breath. 'Did you send the knife psycho?'

'That particular plan was excellently crafted and executed terribly at the key moment. My flaw, if I have one, lies in quite the other direction. They wasted all that time cutting you off from any help or support, waited for the perfect moment and then sent that madman.' He shook his head and sighed, one hand on his face. 'You don't perform surgery with a rusty scalpel no matter how skilled a surgeon you are.' He sighed and shook his head. 'I apologise. That's off the point. Merely a personal gripe.'

'Understood.' He nodded. 'What do you mean it's not that simple?'

'There are Lost who are a good deal more likely to kill their own kind than mine, and for reasons of my own I have been protecting you since.' He thought about it. 'Since the first time I shot at you, in my own way.'

'I almost got my throat slit!'

'And yet something in the magic keeping you asleep failed at the last moment, allowing both you and the large man to wake up.' He tapped himself on the head with the barrel of the gun. 'You are welcome.'

'Why are you defending the other side? After you tried to get me to give up the mask I mean.'

'My motive involves keeping you safe. The easiest way to do that, was giving up what would have made you a target, you stupid child.'

'I'm not much younger than you.'

'Not objectively anyway.' He scowled. 'You could have lived a long, happy life, where people like me didn't gut shoot you. You, however, had to… what's the term?' He paused, thinking about it for a moment. 'Screw around, and now we have this.'

'All right.'

'I am not asking you to think my way, but I am asking you to think. Something is about to happen, I don't know what, but the way you choose to react will tell a lot.'

'Someone tell me what the hell is going on!' he demanded of the world in general.

'I can tell you this.' He paused, cocking his head. 'There has been a way things worked for a long time. Some people, on both your side and mine, want to change that established order in very different directions. The kings, queens and the things that lie beyond are taking an interest and some of us are tired of.' He stopped suddenly, looked around, swore in a language Adam didn't understand and set off running.

'What?'

'Said too much!' he shouted over his shoulder. 'Have to go! I will protect you and speak to you when I can! Until then, seek change! The Lost say they are agents of change, but what have they done differently?' And then he was gone.

'Okay, this cryptic bull is unacceptable,' Adam grumbled, setting off after the strange, pale man at a run. This time he'd follow him wherever he went. He'd follow until the tracks ended and then he'd follow further. The mission didn't matter anymore, he wanted answers!

All the determination didn't help much when there was no way to make good on it. Adam followed the tracks to where the man disappeared and searched the area as thoroughly as he could. Once he came up empty he called Pan and Xavier over and they all searched together. Even Annabelle's dozens of spiders spread out through the forest to aid in the search. For hours the four of them wandered the forest until well into the darkness, searching for a clue.

'This is a waste of time.' Pan scowled. 'The dimensional barriers are weak here, that's why we came here to start with. He could have gone anywhere.'

'Hardly a waste of time,' Xavier countered. 'The young man learned attention to detail, tracking and wilderness survival. Failure is not the same as wasted time.' He smiled and shrugged. 'As it is we were taking a chance. In the meantime, I have found the beginning of the path.'

'Just then?'

'Several hours ago.' He smiled. 'But you were all so enjoying your search and I wouldn't want to interfere. Besides, once I know that Billie is here she'll welcome us at any time, and I've been keeping track.' With that he pointed his sword. 'Peter. This is unlikely to be easy even with her permission. You will all need to keep your eyes peeled. Threats will likely come from anywhere at any time. Likely we will not know where the threats are until they are already sprung.'

'Heads on a swivel, got it.' Pan nodded. 'Adam, behind me, Annabelle, behind him. Gent, you lead. Anyone who says or does anything stupid or out of order, is going to be smacked in the mouth.'

Xavier looked at the others for a moment, then closed his eyes and cut a hole in the fabric of the universe. Pan grabbed the sides of the cut and clenched them in both hands, ripping at them with all of his strength. 'Go.'

Xavier went on the path first.

When Adam came through he'd expected a dark forest, something discrete, quiet and threatening, but as they stepped through, the threats weren't so quiet.

'Pan!' he called. 'Why are people shooting at me?'

'I have no idea.' Pan grunted, a rain of arrows bouncing off his skin as he made his way up a rocky path. 'Xavier! Why are people shooting at him?'

'I told you this wouldn't be easy!' Xavier called. He did that thing where he almost blurred and came to rest in hiding. The area was an old battleground. At the top of a hill was a large wooden fortress with a group of archers stationed at the top. In front of them was a ramp. There were a series of barricades that lead up to the ramp, but they were few and far between. 'Now, Peter, let me remind you, do not run straight into arrow fire and hope you don't die!'

'Right.' He nodded. 'That's not a plan.' He moved to a barricade and rested behind it, taking a few deep breaths. It was ten meters from Adam, who still hadn't stepped through the portal. 'Laughing Man! If you don't move your arse the portal will close, and you will be stuck there.'

'Which will make you slightly more useless than

you already are.' Xavier appeared to be wondering whether or not he could get there by hat without getting shot.

'Annabelle.' He turned to her. 'Are you gonna be okay?'

'Of course, I will.' She was already wrapping her skin in silk, the white strings taking on the green of her dress and hair, and then pushed past him and set off at a sprint. As she moved she swirled her bright colours. The arrows went through her clothing as she moved, but they didn't hit her mass.

Adam took that chance to move while she had all of their attention. He split into another direction as he moved for Pan's barricade. As he watched the archers, the green lights indicating where the arrows would land grew brighter and brighter as he jumped, whirled and moved between them. The ones he could avoid he did, the others he blocked with gauntlets or cut away with the claws that sent them swirling away from him.

'Please try not to get hit too often.' The Laughing One's voice was soft in his ear. 'The gauntlets will reform if they shatter, but it will take a while.'

'Yeah, well, my options are limited.' He jumped behind the barricade, Pan already three barricades ahead of him, and scowled down as he noticed a nick on his side. 'I'm already hit guys! I don't know what to do!'

'Toughen up.' Pan looked back at him. 'All right everyone. I'll move first and the rest of you go from barricade to barricade after me. If we're all moving at once they won't be able to isolate any of us.'

'All right. Three, two, one, go!' And they all set off, Annabelle's distractions and Xavier's blurring speed drew fire. Pan took five or six shots as he moved and ignored them completely. Adam, for his part, stayed low and started moving from barricade to barricade, focusing on his objective as he passed Annabelle.

'Hit,' Annabelle grunted, flexing her arm as she sat behind her barricade. Adam turned back and moved back to her barricade, he had to help her!

'She is better equipped to handle being under fire than you are,' the Watcher's calm voice reminded him. He hesitated for a moment, wondering whether to return to his barricade or go to hers. As he tried to think he felt a shock of pain running up his leg. The arrow in it drove him to the ground and he started to try to crawl toward the barricade. Arrows started to land all around him, some bouncing off the Watcher's coat, the arrows only scratching his skin rather than slamming into his organs.

He tried to keep moving, tried to ignore how screwed he was if he had to crawl the rest of the way. He had to focus on getting to safety, getting to Annabelle, and trying not to die.

Then a pair of hands were behind him, grabbing him with ease and pulling him, tossing him behind the barricade.

'Thanks.' Adam expected to hear Pan's voice.

'You are an idiot,' Xavier spoke through his teeth. 'Annabelle with an arrow wound is an issue. You with an arrow wound cripples us. Both of you with arrow wounds makes this next to impossible.' He yanked the arrow out and Adam screamed until he'd run out of breath. 'Even I am not fast enough to carry us both. How on earth are we supposed to get up that ramp with people shooting at us while you're like this?'

'How am I supposed to know? I'm not Pan! I can't just walk through them.' Actually, now he thought about it… 'Hey Pan, I've got an idea; get back here a sec!'

'Kay.' Pan ran back to them, then brushed the arrows out of his back, seeming more annoyed than in pain. 'Oh damn, you're both hurt. How'd that happen?'

'Annabelle was shot because she was unlucky. Adam was shot because he is stupid,' Xavier clarified. 'Do we have any ideas other than retreating?'

'No. Options are limited,' Pan growled.

'Okay.' Adam nodded. 'I'll redeem myself for doing something stupid that hurts me by doing something stupid that saves everyone. Pan, can you pick up one of those barricades if it's lashed together?'

'Easy.' He shrugged.

'Then do your usual thing. Annabelle can you tie the barricade together, then to his arms, so he can lift and move it?'

'Easy enough.'

'All right.' He looked at Xavier. 'Once we get up close can you throw your hat and get the bow guys?'

'Almost certainly.' Xavier put his cane in his belt.

'Okay then!' Adam clapped his hands. 'That

conveniently means I don't have to do anything except hide behind Pan. Okay, break!'

Annabelle began to spin her hands, the silk pouring out of her skin and making its way around the barricade, then spun it around Pan's hands, putting the entire structure at one easily lifting point. With a grunt of effort Pan pulled the entire construction out of its base. Annabelle hurriedly bound the rest of the barricade together.

This path was slow and painstaking, with grunts of effort every few seconds from Pan.

'Raise it a little,' Adam called as the trajectory became clear. 'Lower, and to the left.' He slowly but surely coached Pan's entire way up, using the Laughing One's gift to figure out where Pan had to block next. Once they got to the bottom of the structure Pan held the barricade in place.

Xavier took off his hat, said something quick, flourished it and threw.

'Got two!' He looked up over the barricade. 'The other two lost bowstrings, so we have a few minutes.'

'Why didn't we hear anyone dying?' Adam wasn't sure why he was asking.

'Did you really want to?' *Good point.* 'Spinning Sister, if you wouldn't mind setting our dear Peter free? Quickly please!' Annabelle tapped the silk strings and they fell apart, letting Pan free. The big man pushed through the door, and as they walked past, Xavier's sprung around the back of the barricade.

The creatures he had killed were losing form before Adam's eyes. What had been a quartet of archers were now four things that appeared to be made of putty, steadily losing shape.

'What are those things?'

'They are thoughtforms.' Xavier shrugged. 'They only have power or substance in their own world, and once that world has been broken they disappear. Billie makes them for security.' He looked around. 'Usually there are a good many more of them. Perhaps the invitation counted for a lot.' He headed down a path toward a small, stone cottage, in the middle of a forest, neither of which had existed before.

'So, Billie's in there?'

'Certainly.' Xavier looked at them. 'Be ready. She is… a lot.'

Adam pushed open the door with one hand, looked inside, then turned, lowered his mask to clear his mouth, and threw up.

'Well, this is awkward.' The man inside the room was small. He wore a hooded jacket and leather pants, and had short blond hair peeking out from under the hood. He was bare handed and covered in blood. 'You were supposed to show up after I left. This is a huge mistake on my part and I couldn't be sorrier.'

Tipped back on a chair with her back against the wall was what Adam guessed were the remains of Billie. She was in bloody chunks against the wall, her organs strewn liberally in various directions.

'Six!' Xavier slipped into the cottage and pushed

Adam out of the way. The stranger braced himself for attack, only to be wrapped up in Xavier's one arm. 'How are you, my darling? Faring well I trust?'

'Uhhhh.' Adam looked at the two of them as they pounded each other on the back. 'What's going on?'

Xavier straightened his coat and turned, the smile still lighting his expression, and smiled at the rest of the group. 'Everyone, this is my dear friend, Six. We grew up together, best of pals and bosomiest of buddies. Six, these are my allies, the Lost Soldier, the Carnival Queen and the Laughing Man.'

'A pleasure.' He raised one blood drenched hand and smiled at them like nothing was wrong. 'How are you all?'

'Well...' Adam looked at the others, wondering why he was talking. Annabelle was holding her head with one hand, looking more disappointed than angry or surprised, and Pan was... Pan was standing still as usual, but one of his hands was clenching and stretching, the leather of his glove creaking softly. 'You just killed the person we came all this way to see and I'm slightly scared for my life.'

Pan began to advance toward the assassin. The LOST tattoo on his head glowing, and his muscles swelling as he moved.

'Not a good idea, Soldier,' Xavier called. 'Six is something of a problem if he should choose to be.'

'I really am absolutely very sorry.' Six looked at the group of aggressors, sitting on the table with a look of sorrow on his face. 'If I had known Xavier, or you others, needed to talk to her, I absolutely would have killed her later.' He thought about that for a long moment. 'Actually, that doesn't make a lot of sense does it? If you're only killing someone so they don't talk letting them talk to anyone rather defeats the purpose. So, I suppose I'm not sorry?' He appeared to seriously question this assertion. 'That's probably not important now the deed is done. Yes. I am Six.'

'Six of what?' Was that an actual question he'd just asked? Why had that been the only thing he could think of to ask?

'Six of Nothing.' He laughed, clapping his hands excitedly. 'Good question, very good question. I usually get such boring questions like "what are you doing in my house?", "Why would you do this?", "Is that a head?" Very boring questions to hear all day. Also, isn't it rather obvious when something is a head?'

'Okay.' Adam thought about that. 'But why did you kill her?'

'Urgh!' He rolled his eyes and stomped his foot. 'Fine. I killed her for the same reason all the Reds kill people. Because someone else told me I had to, just like he does.' Six flicked one hand at Xavier, who nodded. 'We get the job, we do the job and in our own way our interests are furthered.' He hugged Xavier suddenly, with great enthusiasm. 'And for so long our dear Gentleman has been out of the loop. So very long. Working off some obligation or another.'

'I am truly sorry.' Xavier bowed.

'We understand, of course we do! How could we not after all he's done for us?'

'Thank you.' Xavier rolled his eyes, but he was smiling. 'If you could perhaps elucidate on why you felt the need to kill my dear Billie? While it does solve one of our problems, in fact, it solves our biggest current problem.' He looked at the rest of the group. 'In fact, why do we care about this at all? Billie is dead, leak plugged, you can go report back to the Dread Bear and tell him the mission is accomplished!'

'Okay, that's a fact, but it's not exactly the issue here!' Pan snapped at them. 'We have a lunatic assassin out here following some agenda we don't understand. That's a thing we usually investigate. It's a thing we're going to investigate!'

'And I'll help!' Six of Nothing declared.

'Okay, time out! Time out!' Annabelle clapped her hands. 'Time the hell out for just a second. Just… I need a moment to get this straight. We come all this way to find information, only to find out that the informant has been assassinated and our assassin is offering to help us get to the bottom of the people he was hired to kill!'

'That is a succinct, accurate and insightful summation. Well done.'

'Okay.' She nodded. 'Putting aside how insane that sounds for a second, you can just tell us who hired you, and why.'

'Well, actually, I can't,' Six began.

'He means that literally,' Xavier interrupted. 'Not

entirely anyway, not while he's working. Once he's started he won't be able to break the rules.'

'What do you mean?'

'His mouth will literally not say the words and his body will not make the movements.'

'I can't tell you who, but I can tell you why!' He thought about it. 'Well I can tell you most of why.'

'Oh?'

'Well, yeah. They said something when I wasn't listening about...' He thought about it for a moment. 'Preserving the sanctity of the binary, holding the independents accountable and getting rid of complications.' He shrugged.

'You mean you heard them when they thought you weren't listening?'

'No. It was when I really wasn't listening. I can hear things without listening you know, most people can.'

'The binary.' Annabelle looked at the three of them. 'They said those exact words, preserve the sanctity of the binary. What else can you tell us you did?'

'Those exact words.' He knocked his knuckled on his head. 'I can't tell you what exactly I did but I killed a bunch of people for upsetting some people, then I killed a few informants and now I have a few more people to kill and then a master plan will take place, but I won't be a part of it.'

'Any idea what that master plan may be?' Apparently, Annabelle was in charge of this interrogation, which made Adam quite happy.

'No. They don't trust me because I let one of the

prisoners go. They're only going to send me to kill the people only someone of my qualifications can kill, because there aren't many of those.' He grinned and clapped his hands excitedly. 'I can take you to Claire! That's a good idea, I'll do that. That's helpful, I like being helpful.'

'I'm sorry, this can't be allowed.' Pan loomed over him. 'I will have to ask you to come with me. I can't allow you to kill any of my people.'

'You won't be able to beat him,' Xavier chimed in.

'I'm sure you'll tip the balance.' Pan scowled. 'Blackmail, remember?'

It was true, Pan was holding something over Xavier's head to ensure his cooperation. As far as Adam could tell without it the strange dandy would otherwise be a violent madman, his desire to hunt down a nebulous group called the Kings completely unrestrained. While that seemed like it would be just what Pan wanted, given that the Kings seemed to work for the Legion, but apparently homicidal madmen weren't good for the "organised war" thing.

'As in physically can't,' Xavier protested. 'It's beyond my abilities. I can't fight another servant of the Ladies.'

'Who are the Ladies?' Anabelle queried.

'They own Xavier, and his entire little crew of merry psychos, which apparently includes that guy.' Pan pointed at the strange man named Six of Nothing. 'Who I'm pretty sure I now have to fight.'

'Okay!' Annabelle raised her hands. 'I get that

insane urge I really do, but can you wait until he gives me the location before you try to fight him?'

'Seems fair.' The word LOST now blazed with light on his head, his muscles four times the size they had been. 'Would you mind?'

'Sure.' Six stepped up and explained his friend's location to Annabelle. 'See, Claire was someone I was supposed to murder but didn't because she's my friend. She might be a good lead for you.'

'Not to look a gift horse in the mouth, but why are you helping us?' Adam asked, they glared at him.

'Well the Gentleman is currently on your side, and I should be helping him. Also, I really hate the people I'm working for. A lot.'

'But aren't you working for them because the Ladies told you to.'

'I mean I am.' He appeared to be musing, then pointed to Xavier. 'He's obeying you and the Ladies want him to. Is he consistently cooperative and helpful?'

'He is not.'

'Exactly. So, the spider lady knows where she is, and I hope she'll be ready to help.' He turned to Pan and cracked his neck from side to side. 'So, you wanna fight me now?'

'Sister, slow him down, I'll take him on. Laughing Man if you find a weakness go for it.'

Annabelle lashed out with her webs, only for the long-haired man to effortlessly jump out of their way, kick off a couch and disappear through a wall.

Pan approached the wall and tried to push through it, to no avail. He drew back one big hand, smashed his fist into it, and made a completely unhelpful hole in the wall.

'Well I don't know about all of you, but that seems to me like it went quite smoothly. I met an old friend, the girl we wanted not telling tales is dead. All in all, I say we did a good day's work.' He smiled, straightened his hat and headed back the way they came.

'Okay.' Annabelle looked at them. 'Team plan. Pan gets a team together and goes to save those people that guy is killing. Adam and I go and find this Claire lady and see what she knows. Okay? Break.'

'Wait, Annabelle, we...'

'Break!' Annabelle took Adam's hand and lead him out of the strange place, down back the road where they were shot at. There were already new archers on the ramparts, but they didn't shoot at them as they made their way down the path and back to the park.

'What's going on?' Adam asked.

'We need to go. Come on, we're not taking the car, we're going my way.' She tugged him into the darkness.

'Through the web?'

'Yes indeed.' She bent down into the dark and ran her hands through the dirt. 'Come on sweetie, I need you to come out now. Normally I'd be nicer about this, but we don't have time.'

'What's going on?'

'Not right now!' Annabelle snapped at him. 'We

need to go find some help, someone we don't know too well, someone who isn't on either side.'

'Aren't we going to go find that Claire girl?'

'Yes, we are, once we have some security.'

He thought it over for a moment, and a lightbulb popped into his head.

'Well, I know someone who's already kind of involved and not on either side. Bad side, he is the guy who just threatened to kill us.'

'Literally anyone would work for me right now!' She reached down into a hole in the ground, took a couple of deep breaths and pulled as hard as she could. She came away with a fistful of web, which she started to pull hand over hand. As she yanked on it, the ground cracked open, the web ripping stone and dirt away.

'What do you want?' the ornery male vice spoke. His voice was deep, and he sounded tired. Slowly and painstakingly a brown furred spider crawled up over the lip of the hole. He was ugly even by spider standards, with spiky hairs and a truly hideous face, but in front of their eyes he turned into a well-groomed young man in brown slacks and a collared shirt. He straightened his shirt and looked at them bleary eyed.

'Hey, Leaper.' She waved.

'Hello, Annabelle.' He smiled. 'What the hell are you doing here and what do you want?'

'Rude.'

'You bring trouble. What do you want?'

'I need a quick ride back to the Carnival.' She held out her hand. 'And I'd prefer if none of my aunts or uncles found out I was here.'

'Why on earth would I want to do that for you?' He wiped his bleary eyes. 'You wake me up in the middle of a nap and ask me for a favour? And who's this guy?'

'That's the Laughing Man.' That meant he was a friend, but not one she wanted to trust with his real name. 'LM, this is Leaper, he's one of my many cousins.' She smiled, turning back to Leaper. 'He's my boyfriend, well, kinda, and he's helping me do a favour for our people. So, come on, do your part and help us out!'

''Fraid that's a no can do little cousin.' He wiped his eyes and smiled at them. 'I'm very close to sorry, but you know my father will be furious if I let you go without talking to him first, and I'd rather have you hate me than have him be disappointed in me.'

'Seriously?' Annabelle rolled her eyes. 'Your entire side of this family sucks. All right, take us in to him, but if this goes bad I swear to mother I am going to have you eaten.' With that the two of them headed down the string.

'Your threat is noted and will be responded to appropriately.' He nodded, heading down the line.

'Can you really have a person eaten?' Adam whispered to Annabelle as the two of them walked through the web. He barely needed to steady himself anymore, as long as he kept his eyes straight ahead

91

and didn't try to rush things the web was more than thick and sticky enough to keep him stable as they moved.

'I mean I probably could.' She thought about it. 'Yeah. If I really put my mind to it, I could have someone eat him.'

'Really?' As they returned to the spider world, Leaper turned back into a brown furred spider who crawled through the webs and showed them the way to a giant interconnected web.

'I said I could, not that I ever would!' She whisper-snapped at him. Adam looked out into the horizon and watched the spectacle that unfolded.

Adam had seen a lot of cool things in the spider world: he'd seen the Black Widow's pleasure garden and the Carnival. There'd been forests on the webs and entire villas supported by white lines. So it was strange to see someone's lair as being a simple, if extensive, spider web. The web was filled with a giant black spider, who moved with languid motions, reaching out to manipulate the webs. As they watched, he reached out with one leg, puled heavily on the string and another spider appeared in front of him as if summoned by magic. Which he almost certainly had been. The two of them had a short conversation, and the other spider sprinted off into the darkness.

'So that's my uncle Trapdoor.' Annabelle pointed to him. 'He never moves, but he has a literal and metaphorical web that means he'll never need to. Case in point.' She rolled her eyes and stepped out onto the web, taking Adam's hand and pulling him with her. The giant spider reached out one leg and the web launched her over to him.

'Annabelle, darling.' He spoke softly, his own voice tainted by a clicking, crackling sound. 'What are you doing blessing us with your presence?'

'Just passing through, Uncle.' She smiled and curtseyed to him, her voice warm.

'You've been avoiding a lot of the family lately. Is something wrong, dear?' It seemed like a loaded question, but Annabelle visibly relaxed.

'Nothing is wrong, Uncle. Well, nothing until yesterday anyway. I have a new boyfriend, and a lot of work with the Carnival. Aunt Widow hit on my boyfriend before we started dating, so that's also really awkward. I'm having some interpersonal issues and I don't need any more cut ties or strained relationships.'

'Oh, I understand, dear.' His voice sounded sad. 'You don't have time for your family anymore.'

'It's not that; you're always so dramatic!' This was so weird! They were just like every other family. She took a deep breath and closed her eyes. 'Which is not to say that you're wrong. I really should make more time for my family, but it's not as if I'm the only one not putting work in here. Everyone knows where I am, and they can come visit me whenever they like. I'm not saying that I'm not in the wrong, but I'm not the only one.'

The giant spider gave a sigh like a gust of wind. 'Perhaps you're right, dear. Too many of us have become too sedentary, and a night out at the Carnival might be nice for some of the family. We've spent so long stuck in our webs and our ways, letting all you youngsters to the hard work.' Annabelle had warned Adam once that this creature was one of the most dangerous of her whole family. He didn't seem dangerous, he seemed like a tired old man regretting becoming tired and old.

'Does that mean you might be ready to leave your web, Uncle?' The laughter that came out of the giant body was like boots crushing glass.

'I'm afraid not, darling. I'm too big, old and powerful to head to even the outskirts of the webs anymore. They will collapse under my feet.' He settled himself. 'This is my final location.'

'Alright.' She smiled at the big spider and sat down in front of him. 'So, I need to tell the family something, but I also need to make sure no one on either side of the war hears about this. Others may say what they will about you, but your only loyalty is to the spiders, so I can trust you to distribute the information.'

'I thought you were one of the ones on the side of the war?' His head twisted to the side. 'Aren't you bringing a Lost boy down here for exactly that reason?'

'He's not been Lost nearly long enough to have any loyalty to them, as for me, everything I do I do for the good of our people. I just have a very certain idea of what is best for our people.' She focused up. 'And right now, there's a group trying to wipe us out.'

'What?' Adam and the spider said in unison.

'What do you mean wipe us out?' The spider rose up on its legs, venom dripping from his teeth.

'There's a group out there that we just found out about, who want to wipe out everyone who isn't a part of the binary, who doesn't owe any allegiance to the Legion or the Lost. That's all the people in the pocket dimensions, the Wild Ones, the Independents, the Neutrals and…'

'The Great Animal Spirits.' His voice became louder, and colder, coming to life with anger. 'That's a bold idea. Attempting to reduce entire worlds to nothingness. Very ambitious. How will they do it I wonder?' He was pulling on the strings, and a number of terrifying looking spiders were heading in to him, then heading immediately back away. Adam got the feeling this guy was about to take out his frustration on a large number of people.

'We don't know for sure.' She bit her lip for a moment, deciding what to say. 'All we have, as leads go, is an escaped prisoner we're looking for, and the knowledge that one of the Ladies' killers is looking for them.'

The spider rustled for a moment, thinking. 'That is odd. The Ladies are independent entities in and of themselves. Why would they support an attempt to wipe them out?'

'Perhaps they've finally taken sides against us.' She

shrugged. 'Perhaps they've got something else planned, and perhaps they're a pack of raving mad bastards who think it'd be funny to set the world on fire.' Annabelle sighed and threw her hands up. 'I don't know, Uncle, all I know is we're running out of time before something goes wrong and we lose people.'

He paused for a moment and almost all of Annabelle's body tensed. Finally, he ponderously turned and fixed all eight eyes upon them. 'You will come to the next family gathering, yes?'

'Absolutely.'

'Absolutely.' The giant spider thought about things for a moment and he pulled a few more strings. 'I know a few people who may be of some assistance. They won't be our people, but they'll be people to be counted on, people who owe me. They have inspired my wrath, and you may call upon my people when you need them.'

'Yes, Uncle.' She nodded.

'Now where can I take you?'

'My Carnival, if you don't mind.'

'Of course, sweetheart. Now tell your young gentleman that he can stop panicking. I may be something of a nightmare to some of our lesser companions, but I have no intention of eating him, so he can unclench.' Adam smiled under his mask and tried to relax. It didn't work, but he held out one hand anyway, trying to be brave.

'Nice to meet you, Sir.' He realised that the smile

on the mask grew brighter when he smiled. The giant spider reached out and placed one massive leg on his hand, Adam shook it as best he could.

'Good boy.' He sounded almost pleased. 'A little courtesy goes a long way. Now you may go.' He flicked a leg and a long series of strands launched out into the ether. 'Follow that path and you shall reach the Carnival. Get what you need and get to work. You can get a ride on one of the simpler relatives.' He waved another leg and a giant spider crawled up the web to the newly formed lines. Annabelle climbed up the side of her giant brother, then trailed a web down for Adam. She webbed them into place as the massive creature began to scuttle away.

'He didn't seem so bad.'

'If you ever come here without me he'll eat you,' she replied. 'He probably would have done something unpleasant to both of us if our mission wasn't important. Trapdoor likes to eat people who bother him.'

'I'll keep that in mind.'

'But yeah,' she smiled. 'Real stimulating conversationalist.'

When they returned to the carnival chaos was reigning, customers were fleeing from the front gates in every direction, other than a crowd who thought what was going on is part of the show. They saw the Dread Bear, at his full ten massive feet of fur covered beast, brawling with a trio of large tattooed men. The cast of most of the carnival was gathered around the three of them, chanting.

'Bear fight! Bear fight! Bear fight!' the performers chanted.

'What the hell is going on?' Annabelle snapped, grabbing one of her performers by the shoulder and pulling him over.

'It's a bear fight.' He pointed at the bear fight.

'Okay.' She took a breath. 'Why is there a goddamn bear fight in my carnival? Actually, better question, if you're going to be having a bear fight at my carnival why it is distracting from the show rather than being a part of it!' She clapped her hands and whistled, pushing her way through the crowd. 'Scarlett?'

'Yes, Boss?' Scarlett jumped over the heads of the crowd. Scarlett was naturally a spider, but right now she was a tall, thin, dark skinned woman with a red birthmark that ran from her chest to her neck. She had been tossed over the head of other people and landed on her feet in front of Annabelle.

'What the hell is going on?'

'What's going on is that you left me with a giant pissed off bear man!' She flung out her hands. 'He didn't leave! We thought he'd leave! We told him to leave and he ignored us! As time went on we tried to force him to leave, and he started a fight. He almost killed a dozen patrons and like three of the clowns. So, we tried to put him to work, but he can't do anything other than fighting!'

'So, have him work security.'

'We tried that!' She looked like he was about to

start tearing her hair out. 'He ended up more of a danger to the crowd working security than he did as our enemy! So, we just started to try to keep the mad bastard entertained.' She looked tired, her eyes hollow.

'And you settled on people fighting him?'

'I mean, yeah, mostly. The strong men like it and some of the other performers kind of use it to blow off steam. The only problem is we can't keep him on a stage, so he's been pretty much tanking our bottom line. The rampaging bear is pretty much nightmare scenario number one for normal people at a carnival. Guests have been bleeding off fast.'

'Oh no, no, no, no!' Annabelle took a deep breath and tried to relax, walking over into the middle of the fight and throwing webs onto the bear. 'That's enough! The four of you stand down right now!'

'Bleed and die!' the giant bear screamed.

'Konstantin!' Adam took a deep breath and accessed the Presence, letting the mask speak with as much authority as it could. 'We're done! Now stand down and quit acting like a child!' Konstantin turned on him, his jaws wide.

'What did you just call me?'

'I told you to stand down.' He pointed at the big creature, walking just out of his arm's length. 'I told you I'd get the job done if you'd keep yourself under control. I got the job done, but I see you haven't managed the basic instruction of 'don't break anything', something a literal child can do. Somehow it seems like I was given the harder job and yet you were the one who screwed up.'

'I oughta rip your goddamn arms off,' he snarled, taking a step forward. If Konstantin didn't buy this, he didn't have a hope.

'You ought to do your damn job.' With any luck that perceived authority would give him enough pull to make the big creature think. 'Now, do you want to hear how we solved your problems, or do you want to throw a tantrum?'

Konstantin looked at him for a long moment, then took a step forward, his breath was hot and foul in Adam's face.

'Do not move.' The voice in his mind was quiet and calm. 'A step forward he will take as aggression. A step back he will take as submission. Either way, very bad for you.' So, Adam forced a smile to make his mask glow and kept the rest of his face cold. He didn't draw his claws, didn't take a step forward or back.

'Work or tantrum, big man.' He kept his voice calm and thanked god for the vocal distortion that happened naturally through the mask. 'Can't have both.'

Konstantin roared. This time it was right in Adam's face and it was loud enough and forceful enough that he had to do all he could not to take a step back. He tried not to breathe and hold himself steady as the big creature turned away.

'Work it is.' He tossed his head and turned back into his normal form, a large man with a torn brown coat and a sour look on his brutish face. He flexed his muscles, looked at Adam and headed to the nearest seat, collapsing into it. 'What'd you do?'

'Well the saleswoman's dead, so there's that. Your leak of officially plugged. Your imitator will not have the resources to mess with you next time you sleep.' Konstantin thought about that a moment, scratching his jaw.

'That was easier than I expected it to be.' The big man picked his teeth with one claw.

'And in doing so uncovered a plot to kill you, Annabelle and almost everyone you know.'

'Aha!' He clapped his hands and laughed. 'That's where I thought we'd end up. All right, I'm in.'

'Ummm.' That was unexpected. 'Okay. You don't want to hear details or anything?'

'Will there be violence?'

'Almost certainly.'

'Are we hunting people?'

'I mean,' he thought about it, 'people are hunting us, so we're going to have to hunt them back.'

'Got all the information I need.' He shrugged. 'Where are we goin'?' He seemed to ignore his own question, cracking his neck each way and walking off in a random direction.

'I need to talk to Annabelle first.' Adam corrected. 'Take five and don't break anything. I'd rather not have to reconsider your use in this situation.'

'I already don't like you.'

'And I absolutely don't care as long as you do what you're supposed to.' Adam turned away and took

Annabelle's arm, letting her lead him away from the main carnival and up to the ferris wheel that would take them up to the place they slept, Annabelle's hidey hole. 'I need to talk to you about... everything. The independents, the binary, the animal spirits whatever. I need some more details. I need the next step on this drip feed of information you've all got going on. Also, you need to tell me why we had to get away from Xavier and Pan.'

'Okay.' She put a hand on his shoulder, seeking for calm. 'I've explained to you, and you've observed that the whole Legion Lost thing isn't the end of it. There are dozens of other factions in the worlds, with their own ideas of how worlds should be run. Some of us want a role in the making of the world, others just want to be left to our own stuff and be left alone. The animal spirits are part of that. Each animal has a counterpart in the other worlds, just like humans, and when a human being in our world matches well enough with an animal spirit in another world they become something that's more than both.' She thought about that for a long moment, deciding whether to part with another piece of information. 'That's what happens to most of them anyway, I'm a little stranger. Anyway, the point is the binary refers to the simple two side struggle between Legion and Lost. Chaos and order, but since no order is perfect, and true chaos doesn't exist, there are plenty of other factors that stabilise the worlds.'

'And that's what these people are trying to get rid of?'

'Yeah. The complicating factors. They want to reduce the world to a simplistic state, but they don't understand that the world isn't simple, and it shouldn't be. They're trying to generate a status quo that simply cannot hold.' She sighed. 'But since I assume reasonable discourse hasn't historically worked with people like that, we have to use our own people. No one with a state in the Legion or the Lost. Which absolutely includes Xavier and Pan.'

She wasn't wrong. Pan was called the Lost Soldier for a reason, and Xavier fought a personal war against the King of the Eternal Flame who, from what Adam knew, was basically a Legion god. While Xavier was part of the nebulous 'servants of the Red Ladies' he pretty much still worked for Pan for now.

'Aren't I a member of the Lost?'

'The fact that you had to ask that question makes me pretty sure I can trust you.' She smiled, taking her hand in his. 'You're a good guy, and you seem to care about me. Plus, I've known you a while and you don't seem like a secret fanatic, so I'm going to ask you for help.'

'Does that mean I shouldn't have invited a random bear?'

'No. We need all the help we can get.' Annabelle pulled off her orange and blue dress, even pulling the colour out of her hair to replace them with a simple purple and black. After a moment's careful thought, she tapped the knives with her fingers, turning one pure black and the other vivid purple. Adam thought about getting ready himself, then realised he didn't exactly need much and just packed some of their extra food and clothes into a bag to take with him.

Konstantin has already been stalking around the entrances and exits of the carnival, just about ready to lose his temper all over again. As they made their way down, each of them acknowledged him with a nod on their way past, and he fell into step.

'Where we going?' he grunted.

'Thought you said you didn't have any more questions?'

'Yeah, push me.' His voice moved through the register of "grunt" into "snarl". 'That's a good idea. Where are we going?'

'We're picking up an escaped prisoner.'

'Oh.' He thought about that for a moment. 'Dead or alive?'

'Alive. We're just picking her up. I have every expectation that she's going to come with us willingly. There are people who want her dead and we need to know why, and presumably stop the next people who are coming to kill her.'

'Boring.' the giant whined; Adam rolled his eyes. The bear man was like a big child. 'So how do we get there?'

'Go back into the centre world and walk a few blocks.' Annabelle chuckled. 'The crazy guy straight up stashed her in a suburban home and left her there. She's been sleeping on a completely mundane university student's couch for the last few days.'

'Hiding in plain sight?' It wasn't a bad idea, because it made her anonymous. It also had an additional effect: anything from any other world used in front of people who had nothing to do with it created catastrophic consequences. Apparently, the spirits who kept people company weren't big on having their comfortable ignorance stepped on.

'Or he's lazy and doesn't give a damn, one of those two things. Either way they haven't got their hands on her yet, maybe not even their eyes.' It was a few more minutes before they got to the end of the street, finding a blue, suburban house up on posts to avoid flooding. With no other idea of any better way to manage the situation he climbed the stairs and knocked on the door.

A bleary-eyed young man with long hair and no shirt answered, rubbing sleep from his eyes.

'What?'

'Hi. We're looking for Claire?'

'Who's Claire?'

'The girl who's been sleeping here for the last few days?' He turned to Annabelle. 'Are you certain you got the right place?'

'Oh her.' He sounded more amused than bothered or upset. 'Yeah, she's in the shower. She'll be out at... I don't know, she'll be out whenever.'

'She's been in your house for three days and you haven't learned her name?'

'There are a lot of random girls who come in and out of the house. I gave up on learning the housemate's girlfriends' names until their fifth or sixth time here.' He wiped his eyes, grunted and pointed into the living room, turning away and going into the bedroom by the hall.

'We just need to talk to her about–'

'I don't care, just get her out of my house!' The bedroom door closed, and they were left in some stranger's living room. The three of them sat down on a worn-out futon and waited for Claire to come out.

Claire, as it turned out, was a tall thin woman in red, with long red hair halfway down her back. She wore a long red dress and heels that seemed more suited to a ballroom than a living room.

'Hello.' She smiled at them, raising one hand. 'Give me a moment to get something form the kitchen and I'll happily sit down and chat with you all. I assume Six's people sent you.'

'Oh, no,' Adam reassured. 'I mean he told us where you were, but he's not who sent us here. We're hoping to figure out what the people who went after you are doing and–' Konstantin almost blurred as the big man moved past the couch, leaping off a coffee table to take the knife she threw into his own chest. The futon shattered under his weight as he landed, letting out a grunt of pain as the weapon landed in soft flesh. The bear rose to all fours, then charged, lifting the mess covered table with one hand and hurling it at her head. As she readied herself to throw again, he launched himself over the counter, landing on both her and the table and pinning her under the wood.

'Listen carefully.' His deep voice now boomed around, filling the room. 'I need to know what you know about the people trying to kill me, who also tried to kill you. If you don't answer, completely and honestly I'm going to tear your head from your shoulders and paint the walls in your blood.'

'Well then, I understand.' Her voice was calm, even cheerful, for a person who was currently pinned under a table by someone four times her size she'd just thrown a knife into. Annabelle got to her feet, reached under Konstantin and pulled the knife from his guts, to be rewarded with a dull grunt. 'What would you like to know?'

'Why he had to hide you would help.'

'Well, I was on a moving prison into which that lunatic broke and killed all the guards and inmates within, bar me. Apparently, he's a fan of mine.'

'Moving prison?' Adam chimed in. 'What's that?'

'It's a train,' she explained. 'It never stops moving, through time and space, and dimensions. It never stays in one place, it never belongs anywhere, and it never stops unless the driver stops it, which he does for a sum total of two reasons. One, to pick up a prisoner and two, if a madman finds a way to break in, kill everyone inside and stops it by force.'

'So, he stopped some kind of Lost train for mass murderers?'

'No, all the prisoners on that train are there for the same crime. The one crime the Legion and Lost agreed needs to carry a life sentence.'

'Which is?'

'Treason.' She smiled form under the table. 'We all betrayed our own side and pursued our own interests over the war.'

CHAPTER FIVE

They took a moment to get Claire out from under the table, and left, thoroughly ignoring the protesting trio of people who actually lived in the house, taking her by the arm and leading her over to a nearby bench. Konstantin held her arm in one massive hand, not allowing her to so much as take a single step away. After it became clear to him that she wasn't going to run away, he sat her down at a bench and pulled off his shirt and jacket, letting Annabelle bind his wound with her silk.

'So, the Lost have a train where they keep the people who screw them over?' Adam asked.

'No.' She shook her head. 'It's both sides: people who betrayed one side and didn't get the protection of the other. Some joined the indies, some just screwed their side over and left, and some tried to burn the world down. Whatever it was, the deed committed was judged to be beneath the contempt of both sides. You can't be put there without the consent of both the conductors. One Legion, the other Lost. Given that the sides hate each other, and one will usually applaud anything that hurts the other, you can imagine what anyone on this train might have done.'

'And this guy killed them all?'

'All the guards, the driver, the conductors and all of the prisoners but one. Though the prisoners' part wasn't hard because we were all trapped in our seats.'

'So, what did you do?'

'None of your godsdamned business,' she snapped, showing her first piece of fire since they met. 'Anyway, that hooded psychopath decided he was willing to let me go. He said he was a fan of mine, and that he hated the people he was working for.'

'Okay.' Adam raised his hands and smiled, cutting into the conversation. 'Claire, do you have any idea why Six of Nothing wanted you all killed?'

'Seems pretty simple to me.' She smiled. 'We're the ones who have no allegiance to the Legion or the Lost, and we don't have the kinds of limitation the independents have to live with. I'm entirely local to this dimension, with no need to sacrifice to live here. I don't like either side, since they locked me into a train seat and left me to die, so I'll happily take you to who or where you want to be.'

'Except we have no particular idea of where to go.' He looked at the bear man, the spider woman and the fugitive. 'Do any of you have a plan beyond trying to hunt down the assassins?'

'No, not with our current resources.' Claire thought it over. 'We need a Lost member and a Legionnaire, someone who can walk our paths or theirs unrestricted. There are doors that you just can't walk through without a member of the right allegiance. So, unless you have one of the Lost in your back pocket we're rather limited.'

'I'm Lost.' Adam raised his hand. 'The Laughing Man. Pleased to meet you.'

'Then we'll have to go to the seats of power of both

sides and hunt down the people involved. We'll have to find out exactly what they intend to do. We'll have to go deep into both sides to explore and gather information.'

'Wait a minute. There are strongholds and headquarters and stuff?'

'Of course, there are.' She glared at him. 'We won't exactly be welcome there, since we're new, but if we keep our heads down and don't make a fuss the Legion shouldn't be a problem for us. They're pretty certain that no one who isn't with the Legion can get in because they can't, unless they're with one, and all the Legionnaires who aren't loyal to the Legion are.' She motioned up and down herself.

'So, unless they realise you're a traitor you're good?'

'Until they realise,' she corrected. 'If we're very lucky we might get out beforehand, but I'm going to be on the run by the end of this little charade.'

'Okay.' He nodded. 'One on each side then. Where do we start?'

'We need to find the Legion's local place of power.'

'Oh, that? I know where that is.' He smiled. 'They know me there, they want to kill me there.'

'Okay.' She nodded. 'Then we just need to sneak in and wait for a thunderstorm.'

Luckily thunderstorms during a Brisbane spring are pretty much guaranteed to happen every few days. The city had become a game of elemental tag as parents, businessmen, children and teenagers tried to avoid getting wet, their attempts all the funnier for their futility. Adam had joined the dance as well, holding his white coat over his head and moving determinedly forward. Annabelle had spun herself an umbrella out of, what else, spider silk. The rain didn't seem to stick to Claire at all, falling around her feet without touching her. Konstantin just kept his head down and grumbled as he moved, displaying that Ursas's vast variety of curse words was true to form with the man he'd been imitating. The smell wafting off him was like wet dog, multiplied by dozens.

They stopped off for a snack before heading out, and Claire was suitably mortified by the horrifying spectacle that was Konstantin putting anything near his mouth. Members of the public, who had committed no sin worthy of such a thing, recoiled in shock and horror as the big man shovelled fried chicken into his mouth, bones and all.

Trying to feed the four of them had been a task, but the food court had just about managed it. Claire took a single bite of her sushi before handing it off the Annabelle and declaring she wasn't hungry and was ready to go. In the end when Konstantin asked for more money Adam refused, just to stop him taking up all their time.

The Legion's headquarters hadn't changed much since Adam's throwdown with the local Legate. The building was still ultra-modern, and the walls and floor were still naturally pure white, lights bathing the room in colours that had alternated as time went on. The last times Adam had come here everyone had known what it had been for, and none of them had questioned him. Now, with the mask in his pocket and accompanied by the other, things were less streamlined. As they walked up to the elevators they were stopped by a young lady in a suit with a "customer service" smile on her face. She waved the four of them over. Claire held Konstantin by the collar of his shirt and dragged him forward with her.

'Do you have an appointment, Miss?' she inquired.

'No. I do not have an appointment. I was not aware I needed to ask my inferiors for their permission to return home. I need to use the lightning room, you are currently in my path and I ask you now, politely, to remove yourself from it.'

'I'm sorry.' The smile didn't slip a molar as she reached under her desk. 'You are required to fill out the C-23-5 request form and…' Claire tapped Konstantin on the shoulder and he stepped forward, picking the young woman up with one hand. Claire took the forms and began to fill them out.

'Do you know who I am?' he growled in her face. She didn't recoil at all.

'I'm afraid not, Sir.'

'I am the Dread Bear. Currently under contract to the local Legion. My contract has recently been rendered void. That bothers me. Let me go back so I can check in.'

'I'm afraid the forms still need to be–'

'Done.' Claire handed the form over. 'Now,

may we go?'

'Yes, Ma'am.' They headed past the receptionist, moving for the elevator.

'Why'd you bother scaring her if you were planning to fill out the forms anyway?'

'Because now she wasn't watching me lie. Some of their people can see deceit. Harder to see while they're busy being terrified. Putting my own name on the forms would have raised alarms, so I had to pretend to be someone else.'

She hit a series of buttons on the elevator, then tapped to the side of four buttons, all of which started to glow.

'Seriously?' Adam complained. 'We had to go through a spider web and I almost got turned into her aunt's love slave.' He poked Annabelle, who scowled at him. 'And all you guys have to do is sign some forms and take and elevator? That's completely unfair.'

'Life is unfair.' Claire shrugged. 'Besides, proper procedure is pretty explicitly one of the small number of perks to our system. It can be slow and frustrating at times, but we do get a few advantages.'

'I'm pretty sure it's "they" for you now.' Annabelle took the jab Adam was going to. 'You're not exactly a good soldier anymore.'

'Shut up.' She stepped off the elevator and out to the roof, holding her arms wide. 'Everyone join hands and don't let go, no matter what happens. Travelling by thunderstorm can be risky if you don't know what you're doing.'

'Okay.' Adam took her hand in his and looked at the others. 'What do we do?'

'We just wait for the lightning bolt.'

'Wait, wait, wait!' He released her hand and jumped back. 'Lightning? Like we're actually going to be hit by a bolt of lightning?'

'Yes, we are.' She nodded. 'It's the Legion's favourite method of transportation. Fast, efficient and with no concern for the safety or wellbeing of individuals.'

Annabelle sighed and pointed to Konstantin. 'I'm not holding his hand.'

'This is juvenile,' Adam sighed. 'Stand between me in Claire then.' He rolled his eyes and took her hand in one of his own, pulling her over to them. He placed one hand in Konstantin's massive mitt, which engulfed and almost crushed his own. Claire joined hands with the other two and flashed them a smile. 'Alright, everyone, this is going to hurt a little.' The smile turned to a smirk. 'And then it's going to hurt a whole awful lot.'

The sky above them crackled one last time, and then there was a light that was so bright it blinded him. His body began to shake and rock as the lightning ran up and down his spine, his hands locked into a tight grip with the others. He wondered for a second why she'd bothered to tell him not to let go of the others, he couldn't have even if he wanted to.

Of course, once Konstantin's grip tightened on his

hand he realised it was still going to take all of his attention to keep his grip. He felt his fingers crack under the pressure and thought for a moment about trying to force his digits out of his new ally's grip. He didn't allow his hand to tear free though, resisting the urge and calling on the power of the Laughing Man to dull his pain.

Then the actual lightning pain kicked in and he gave up on the idea of dulling it. Every nerve was on fire, he was in so much pain he could barely think, barely sense, in so much pain that the very concept of pain left his mind and became an all-consuming white noise. Stars appeared in front of his eyes and buzzing filled his ears. He wasn't sure if it was taking all his will to stay conscious, for the simple reason that he wasn't sure he was still conscious. Breathing was occurring, somehow, barely, because he could still smell a few things, mostly metal and burned flesh.

Then the world around him went blank. He could detect nothing but a soft ringing in his ears and he wasn't entirely sure whether or not his eyes were closed. He could still smell the metal, though not the burned flesh and thanked any gods you cared to name for that.

'Laughing One? Watcher? You there, guys?'

'We are always here,' they replied immediately.

'Do I have any massive burns or anything?'

'No.' The Watcher took charge of the conversation. 'You are entirely uninjured, though you may wish to take a moment and centre yourself before you open

116

your eyes. What you see next will likely come as something of a shock to you.'

'Even by the current standards?'

'Even that,' the Laughing One confirmed. 'This will be more personal.'

Adam took a deep breath, tried to centre himself and slowly opened his eyes.

In front of him were people who were both very familiar, and very strange. He knew that Konstantin was called the Dread Bear but now he really looked the part. He was a massive, black furred, hulking monster with dried blood matted to its fur and coating its wicked claws. Its teeth were long, jagged and pointed and they finally looked right in its face. It looked at them for a long moment, then turned on its heel.

The woman beside him was red from her head to her toes, her hair was white, and her skin glistened like the carapace of a red insect. Her eyes were black, and a whip slung from her hip. She had a sword across her black and regarded the others in the room with an expression, as if she was wondering how much they'd be worth at market. He could only guess that this was Claire.

Annabelle looked like, Annabelle, but so very different. She wasn't in her usual colours, rather she was the colours. The colours in her hair, clothes and skin all danced and shifted as she stood in place. They were everywhere, in her eyes and on her skin. Spiders made of crystal danced around on her and within her, playing and exploring. He felt like he could stare at her forever and never get bored.

'You okay, Laughing Man?' the red skinned woman spoke softly.

'Are the rest of you seeing this?' He looked at his own hands, they were black, with claw holes in the fingers.

'Yeah.' Annabelle put her hand on his shoulder. 'You're kind of creepy looking.'

'I mean, thanks?' He looked around, moving from people to scenery. 'Any mirrors on anyone?'

'Why would we have mirrors?' He acknowledged with a nod that his question had been stupid.

They were in a city, laid out in a simple grid pattern. He knew it even as he cast the most cursory glance. The buildings alternated between black and white. People, in various states of human and strange moved in orderly lines and queues. Some gasped and gaped in every direction with wide open eyes and smiles or shock on their faces. He guessed they were new, like him. Those who minded them took them by the hands and led them into the lines in which they fit. They moved from blocky lines of straight up buildings to a series of spired and domed halls, all by some order Adam couldn't begin to understand or recognise. He just had this strange niggling voice in the back of his head telling him that he should screw it up in some way. That he should tear down a building, or start a fight, or at least change a sign or scuff something. He needed to.

'Resist the urge, babe.' Annabelle put her hand on his shoulder. 'It's fine. I know it feels wrong to you,

Legion strongholds always feel wrong to the Lost and vice versa They want to fix us, and we want to break them, but if you can't hold it, if you break or mess with anything they'll know you don't belong here and you look freaky enough as it is.'

'Seriously? I look that scary?' He smirked. 'I'm used to being the least scary one in the room.'

'Because you absolutely aren't going to let this go, I'll help you.' Claire approached him and touched his head. Suddenly he could see through the eyes of Claire, the Devil Driver, the Thrice Cursed. Suddenly he was looking into one of the many eyes of a creature. It stood, its skin completely black, barely humanoid, encased in a strange gleaming cloth. The only exceptions were a series of eyes that opened and closed on his body. Some glowed, some were slitted like a cat, and some simply were the eyes of a human being. Across its face was a glowing green smile, and lines of the same green ran up its arms.

'What the hell?' he spoke, and he saw the strange thing's smiling face move. 'Holy crap, is that me?'

'It is,' Claire replied.

'Yeah. That's about as creepy as I'm gonna get.'

'I'm bored.' Konstantin had already left, scouted the area, primarily by falling into a few lines with a lot of pushing and shoving. 'I checked the area, there's nothing interesting here. Let's go.'

'All right.' Claire waved her hand at them, a smile on her face. 'Come on, follow me and do as I do. Don't talk to anyone who doesn't talk to you, and don't look at anyone at all if you don't have to. Most importantly, you need to look like you belong here.'

'I look like a guy in a shimmering coat with a bunch of eyes and green demon face. How do I look like I belong here?'

'Learn how to flow from line to line to line.' The Thrice Cursed raised one hand and smiled at him. 'Do as I do, darlings.' She waved and stepped into one line pushing Konstantin ahead, and Adam stuck to her back. Annabelle slipped in behind him, letting Konstantin's bulk keep people out of their way.

It was a strange mixture of strangeness and mundanity. He could see a snake woman with no clothes and no skin on the top half of her body, standing in front of a man in a plain white suit, arguing with him over whether she had the right forms for her expenses, and whether or not she could be assigned more work based on her performance. There were a few hundred blank faced Legionnaires in black and white, performing numerous menial tasks, most of which seemed to be moving pieces of paper to where other pieces of paper were.

Occasionally a portal would open, or someone would appear and join one line or another. To their credit the lines were quick moving and fairly smooth, a grid flowing neatly through the city and Claire ducked, flowed and moved through with them. The others followed her with some sense of vague competence, Claire the Thrice Cursed spat a near constant stream of apologies and excuses as she used

Konstantin's bulk to bully through them, as well as delivering the occasional scolding aimed quite loudly toward Annabelle or Adam. Apparently, she was smart enough not to even pretend to scold the bad-tempered animal.

'So where exactly are we going?' Adam asked. Claire looked back at him with slight frustration.

'Toward the centre of, sorry Ma'am he's new and stupid, town. If these people are hiding and looking to execute their strange plans they're going to do their best to do it where no one's watching. More business gets done the further you get from the centre of town. The centre of town is secure, and isolated, which is exactly what they want.'

'This is going to be a problem,' Adam realised. 'I mean getting in might be one thing, but once we get there there'll probably be some variety of shitshow, and even if we, somehow, find an actual lead, it's going to be merry hell to get out.'

'Once we get closer the Bear and I will earn our keep.' Annabelle looked over at Konstantin. 'I assume you have some ability to detect our quarry?'

'Not until I have a lead or trail of some kind.' He shrugged. 'Find me someone and I'll track you down everyone they've ever touched and butcher 'em, but without that I can't help you.'

'That's okay.' She cracked her knuckles. 'I can do this. Get me as close to the right destination as you can, I'll see what I can do to get us what we need.'

'How?'

'I am currently containing hundreds,' she looked at them all very seriously, 'of spiders.'

'Right.' Claire nodded and lead them through the aisles. 'That's not disturbing or anything.' Steadily the queues started moving faster and faster with fewer and fewer people in them. As they got closer, the buildings got taller and bigger, spires upon spires, walls higher and thicker.

A larger portion of the commuters were Blank Faced Legionnaires, the mindless slaves that formed the backbone of the Legion. They were accompanied by a series of more and more dangerous looking creatures. Where once people could be there for any reason, suddenly there were only a few and everyone was getting more and more scrutiny. 'All right boys and girl, this is probably about the as close to the centre of their operations as we can get without garnering undue suspicion.'

'Then just keep walking around the perimeter like nothing is wrong, like we're walking patrol or doing, normal stuff.' Annabelle shrugged. 'I don't know, you're the expert.' And as they walked Adam tried not to watch the small army of spiders fleeing from her legs, sticking onto the clothes of passers-by when she touched them, and falling out of her skirt in small groups. The four of them walked together, making slow conversations as the little arachnids made their way into buildings and houses, and disappeared down streets. They made a few laps around the city before she stopped, holding a single spider between her fingers. 'These are all that I can afford to give away for now. I can't afford to be away from them all. They'll go everywhere and bring me all the information they can.'

'You animal types are really rather interesting,' Claire commented. 'You could get all kinds of information like that.'

'I do get all kinds of information like that.' She smiled. 'But they're only really useful if no one expects them. Most people don't let people like me into places like this, including your kind of people, who wouldn't let me within a mile of these buildings if they knew, and they wouldn't let me into the buildings no matter what I did.'

'They won't let any of us inside any building without permits, which we do not have,' Claire told her. 'The big complex at the very centre perhaps, if we could bluff and knew where we were going.'

'Not the case,' Konstantin reminded them. 'What do we do while we wait?'

'We keep looking busy,' Annabelle told him. At that moment Adam jostled a man in a suit, who cleared his throat and accepted Adam's apology.

'Excuse me, Sir.' The man put his hand on Adam's shoulder as he made to walk away. Adam took another step, and when the grip tightened he realised that a confrontation would start if they didn't talk.

'What can I do for you?' Adam replied, the man in question had a mask in the same pinstripes as his suit.

'It seems as if you are wearing something I

recognise.' The voice was soft, and inquiring.

'Oh.' He spread his arms. 'Well, I'm afraid this whole outfit is new to me.'

'I would wager it is.' He pulled Adam in close and grabbed his collar. 'See I know that coat of yours, and until recently the owner of that was something of a friend of mine.' He appeared to think a long moment. 'Well, perhaps not a friend, but I knew him well enough. Well enough to know that he would never give up He Who Watches to someone like you.'

'He didn't have a choice.' Adam forced his smiling face into less of a smile. 'I regret to inform you that I had no choice but to take it off a body. The poor man only just managed to hide it from the Lost who killed him. I managed to scavenge it out of the crime scene after the King's Man ran the murderer off.' It was a good lie.

'Really?' The man looked as if he was going to calm down for a moment. 'And the fact that the people who killed him involved a masked man with a green smile and a spider is…'

'Konstantin?' He looked at the bear, who nodded, took a step behind the striped man and smacked him to the ground with one giant paw. He paused for a moment, then stomped down hard on the back of the man's neck, turning and walking out of the line.

'Time to find somewhere to hide, I guess.' Adam looked over at Claire. 'You're the local, any ideas?'

'Well, we need to get off the streets. It doesn't matter where.' She turned and made her way toward a building, darting past the attendant. Konstantin smacked the guard off his feet and pushed his way inside, followed by the other two. 'Now we need to find somewhere out of the way, where no one's looking.'

'And why did we go into a building to do that? A building is smaller than the city around it!'

'What makes you think that?' Claire smiled at him. 'Keep moving. I have a plan, but we need to be concealed before I put it in motion.'

'What's the plan?'

'Run through dimensions until we return here to the sound of Annabelle's spiders having found something. People won't be able to chase us long if they notice and will pass the point by if they don't. We'll go through about a dozen worlds and find our way back here.'

'What?'

'It's one of my standard techniques,' she explained. 'People will assume we've gone further than we actually have, so we'll be in place to hear from your spider pals, and we won't have to deal with minions or numbers.'

'Okay. I mean that's sound thinking but it's not what I meant. I mean we're going to jump through multiple dimensions one after another? That seems kinda dangerous.'

'That is incredibly dangerous,' she snapped. 'But it's a good deal less dangerous than being the one enemy force in an entire city of persistent, organised zealots.'

'What are you getting pissed for? You're the one who was supposed to be able to get us in there!'

'Which I could have done.' Her voice sent chills up his spine and the breath catch in his throat. 'Except for the fact that one of my group was wearing a freshly looted piece of one of a kind armour taken from the body of a Legate!' She grabbed him by the shirt front and shook him. Annabelle moved to his defence, which was ironic since this had been one of their first interactions as well. She shoved the red skinned woman away, her colours shining brighter and brighter.

'Yeah. That's an issue.' Annabelle looked at the two of them for a moment. 'Mistakes were made. Adam, say sorry.'

'Sorry.' Adam nodded. Annabelle fixed her eyes on Claire.

'Apology accepted.' Her voice was grunted and grudging. 'Now, let's go I suppose.' She raised her hands.

'So how exactly does this interdimensional stuff work?' He looked at Annabelle, but it was Claire who answered.

'Weak points can be exploited by certain people and created by certain people or techniques. Thunderstorms are a Legion procedure; the spiders are good at that kind of thing.'

'Pan can weaken the fabric of reality, as you saw once, but it costs him,' Annabelle pointed out. 'Xavier can cut through it at weak points.'

'And luckily for all of you,' Claire slapped down hard on empty air, 'I am quite gifted at it as well. There are plenty of weak points in the city, at least outward and for those with the proper credentials.' She pushed the air and the empty world made a cracking noise, forcing itself open. 'Which, until word gets back that I'm not dead, I still have.'

'Any idea what we're going to be going through that door into?' Claire looked over at him, gave him a small smile, and hauled on the empty sky.

'None at all.' It cracked open and pulled them all inside.

Biting cold hit him full in the face as the group wandered straight into a blizzard. Konstantin took a step ahead of the others and lowered his head, ignoring the fact that they were all shivering.

'Follow,' the big animal grunted, then turned and rumbled away into the blizzard as it slowly turned his fur white. Given that his clothes were currently covering his entire body he took the back position, letting Claire and Annabelle huddle into the fur.

'Where the hell are we?' He could barely make himself heard over the sound of the snow.

'I don't know!' she bellowed. Somehow she could make even that sound scornful, which the Watcher noted was slightly impressive. 'Somewhere cold.'

'Very bloody helpful!' Annabelle yelled. 'What the hell do we do?'

'Make our way to the next weak point!' Konstantin kept moving at Claire's response, a small grunt as he walked.

'Where are you going?' Adam yelled it three times before Annabelle got the hint to tap the bear on the back to let him know they were talking to him. 'Where are you taking us?'

'Cave,' he replied.

'You can see in all of this?'

'No.'

'Then, how do you?'

'It's winter and I'm a bear,' he replied. 'Know where the cave is.' He pushed his way for another, what could have been five minutes or an hour, before the giant creature was no longer shielding them from anything, now there was only snow coming from three directions. Suddenly they were in the cave, and it was only coming from one.

Then Konstantin shook the snow off all over everyone else, made a noise of displeasure, then curled up in a corner.

'Tired,' he grumbled. 'Don't like the cold. Wake me when you find a way out.'

'There's no time.' Claire approached him and, when his eyes closed, made the risky move of slapping the big bear around the head. Konstantin drew his massive claws back to gut her but was apparently too tired to follow up the attack.

'Hit me again and I'll kill you,' he grunted, but apparently, he'd been talked around. He forced himself to his feet and cuffed himself around the head a few times to force himself back into true consciousness.

'Yes, yes, very scary.' She was brusque, that was the word for it, Adam had been searching for it all day. 'But if we don't keep moving, whoever comes after us, will kill us. Plus, we have no idea where we are. There could be ice giants, or demons, or the secret outpost of some death cult. We could end up against anything!'

'Really?' He cocked his shaggy head. 'You promise?'

'Can I promise that I have no idea what's going to happen in this cave?' She threw her hands up in the air. 'Yes. Of course I can.' At that news the big bear shrugged, flashed his teeth in some kind of smile, and wandered deeper into the cave.

Soon enough there was a roar, a crack and a series of squelching noises but by the time the rest of the group got there Konstantin was already sitting in a pile of worm guts, eating a chunk of it with one hand.

'Did you know that these things have teeth all the way down?' He pulled one out of the meat and tossed it.

'I don't know what they are,' Claire told him.

'That can't be any kind of sanitary,' Adam commented.

'Was hungry.' He shrugged, then got up and started walking again. The group followed, each of them shaking with the cold as Konstantin thoughtlessly tore through the local wildlife. He stopped to eat occasionally, pulling pieces off the creatures and consuming them as he did.

'Uhm, Claire?' Adam asked, as Konstantin pulled ahead again.

'Yes?'

'Is this helping us? I mean, is there a weakness in dimensions deeper in the cave?'

'I have no earthly idea.' She shrugged. 'Do you want to tell him to stop?'

'Not really, but, aren't we kind of losing our lead if we aren't going the right way?'

'That,' she thought about it, looking around the cave, 'is an excellent point.' She unfurled her whip, aimed carefully, and lashed out at the roof. After five cracks of the whip the roof rumbled for a moment, then a series of small rocks began to fall. Claire grabbed him by one hand and dragged him away from the area as the rocks increased in size.

'What the hell are you doing?'

'I'm causing a cave in.' She shrugged. 'If I cause too may they'll catch on, but this might make them double back and check another path. If nothing else, they'll at least have to pause to clear the rocks.'

'And if it turns out we have to go back this way?'

'Then we will have a problem.' She shrugged. 'Still, done now.'

'Okay.' He followed her, ignoring the roars of pain and rage from up ahead. 'So, what's with the whole Thrice Cursed thing?'

'Thrice?' She looked at him. 'My name is the Twice Cursed.'

'Not from what I saw from inside your head.'

'Oh,' she sighed. 'That's... difficult. I suppose I've collected another along the way. I'll have to

130

find out what it is.'

'I have no idea what that means.'

'In order to pass me you must answer these riddles, oh god! Oh my god! Violence is not the answer! Violence is not the answer!'

'Violence is always the answer.' Konstantin tossed the body of a small, coal skinned goblin creature behind him. 'Riddle guy.'

'You realise that was a thinking being.' Adam pointed at the corpse.

'Was only a riddle guy. Did the world a favour,' the bear mumbled. 'Hate riddle guys. Which way do we go?'

'I don't know.' Adam made a false, pleasant voice. 'Because the thing that can tell us which one the death trap is, and which one is the path was killed by a giant idiot.'

'All right, all right.' Konstantin grumbled and headed forward.

'What's he doing?' Annabelle looked at them.

'I guess, checking the way forward?' Sure enough Konstantin had rumbled down the path for about five seconds before there was a twang sound and a series of long spears punched into his body. He looked down at them with a little annoyance, before heading back, stumbling a little and lowering himself to his knees in front of Annabelle.

'Spider girl.' He looked up to her. 'You will remove these spears from me and treat any poisons that may be in my systems.'

'Looks like I will.' She nodded, grabbing the spears and wrenching them from his skin. With a disgusted expression on her face she leaned over and bit down into his flesh. After a few moments she drew back, drawing a strange black goo out of the wound which she spat into a vial. She wiped her mouth, stoppered the vial and shook her head. 'That is the most disgusting thing, in the entire world. I hate you, now shut up and take the other path.'

'Right.' He sighed and walked off down the other path. 'Don't like being shot.'

'Then maybe you shouldn't have killed.'

Konstantin raised his hand. 'He was a riddle guy,' he explained. 'I… hate… riddle guys.'

Another ten minutes or so later Claire raised one hand to stop them, and then went about pushing against the sky again.

What followed was a blistering sequence of attempting to travel through dimensions. The next one was scorching hot, making all of them swelter and gasp as they tried to move. Still, at least it woke Konstantin up, the big creature now full of energy once more. This time it was Annabelle who ended up exhausted. She struggled to walk in the heat, and after five minutes Adam had to pick her up and carry her.

The next place they ended up was a swamp, which actually worked out pretty well for Annabelle. While the rest of them were stagging through muck she managed to keep the bugs who flew and crawled off them with the help of the dozen new spiders that slipped into her clothing. The rest of them just did their best not to get the no doubt poisonous muck in their eyes or mouths.

For a second Adam thought the next path they walked through put them back in Legion HQ. They walked across the pure white floor, leaving trails of green and black as they went. Konstantin grumbled and complained as he pushed his way through the crowd of loudly protesting, white clad people. A few security guards came in their direction and Konstantin charged, pulling back his claws.

'Don't!' Adam called. 'They're not Legion! They're just people.'

'Who cares?'

'I do!' he snapped. 'Unless you want to fight me as well as them, you'll either stick to non-lethal or let those of us who know what the words non-lethal means handle this.'

Konstantin let out a roar and barrelled forward, ignoring the people he rammed into as he moved. Adam, Annabelle and Claire moved in his wake, and Adam jumped over his back, landing in front of the rest of the guards.

'Stand down!' he yelled. 'We don't want to hurt you!'

Claire punctuated this threat with a series of sharp whip cracks, keeping the security guards at bay. She pulled her sword for a moment, then, after a stern look from Adam, returned it to the sheath. She locked the sword in place and readied it in her off hand as a bludgeon.

Annabelle, perhaps out of a desire to remain unique, had forsworn her usual whips. She had gathered segments of web and was hurling them at the guards, blinding, paralysing and immobilising any who came close. The webs were a series of vibrant colours, like poisonous animals.

'Konstantin! If you kill anyone we are not stopping for ice-cream.' The fight was joined, the security guards getting up the courage to charge them. Adam smirked as Konstantin barked at him and engaged the enemy. He might have hurt a few people, maybe even broken a few bones but Adam was almost certain nobody died.

'Found a fracture point,' Claire called from the back of the group, landing a heavy hit to a helmeted head that knocked the guard to the ground. 'But you'll have to hold them off.'

'Everyone listen!' he yelled as loud as he could. Claire looked at them, then placed her fingers in her mouth, and whistled loudly enough to cause physical pain.

'Listen up!' she shouted, her voice suddenly undeniable. 'This man has something very important to say.'

'Okay!' he called out. 'I don't want to hurt any of you, and I'm sorry for what happened so far. I regret that it turned out this way and I understand that you're scared, that you're upset, and you have good reasons to be. We just showed up here, and we're going to be just leaving right now. All you have to do is leave us alone, for a minute or so, and we'll be out of your hair.' He paused for a long moment. 'But none of you speak English, do you? You've just been hesitating because I'm yelling.'

The gibbered at him in some language he didn't understand.

'My turn to talk.' Konstantin took a step forward out of the crowd, then threw back his head and let out a bellowing war cry that shook the walls and made the chandeliers shudder. The crowd backed off, and while the security guards advanced, they did go slowly and shakily, slamming bright batons into shields that seemed to make them glow brighter and brighter. 'That only works a couple of times before they get their boys back. There's a good chance they'll keep them this time, unless I do something real.'

'I need time and more spiders to grow any more webs. These interdimensional darlings are doing their best, but there's only a dozen of them and they're exhausted.'

'Fine. I'll do this myself.' He let his claws slip out of his gloves and advanced on them, pulling his sleeves back. Without visible emotion he raised the claws and ran them across his arm. He then turned and did the same on his other arm, then raised his hands and ran the blood across his face. 'Okay. Going to need a cackle.'

'Your wish is my command,' the Laughing One replied. Without any visible movement or thought on his part he threw back his head, and let out a hysterical, ear splitting burst of high-pitched laughter, then lunged at one of the security guards. The man's resolve broke and he retreated from the formation.

'Claire!' He kept his tone sounding hysterical. 'Tell me you're almost done there! I don't want to have to kill what are probably some very pleasant security guards!'

'Almost done!'

Adam let his claws bounce off the baton, his arm bounced back, and he felt a looseness run up the limb. 'Okay, awesome, apparently when they light you up they make your limbs numb, that sucks.' He turned and ran. 'I'm out of ideas. Claire, hurry it up!'

This time when the guards advanced Konstantin took the stage again.

'Killing them,' he decided. 'Can't stop me.'

'And we're done!' Clare called over her shoulder as the air cracked open. 'Move! Move! Move!' Seeing that there was apparently a rip in the world, mixed with all the other problems the guards had apparently decided they were done. No one stopped the four of them from turning and heading through the dimensional portal back to Legion HQ.

CHAPTER SIX

To where there was a small army of Legion soldiers waiting for him.

'Really?' Adam looked around. 'We went through all this crap and they still ended up right behind us?'

'No,' Claire replied. 'The majority of them are in one other dimension or another. These are just he rear-guard they left behind.'

'Big damn rear-guard,' he growled.

'Which is why I'm truly hoping Annabelle's spiders have finished their work?'

'Not quite yet,' Annabelle replied.

'Then again we run.' Claire turned, only to be stopped by Konstantin's paw.

'No way in hell,' he snarled. 'I'm tired of running, and you're all supposed to be warriors!'

'No one ever said we were–' Adam shouted at the top of his lungs, but was cut off by Konstantin's giant furry form, who had barrelled into a small army of the Blank Faced Legionnaires. 'If you don't run with us we're all going to die!'

'I'm not doing that.' Legionnaires had surrounded him, striking him with the whips and clubs that they had made of their limbs as he was slowly but certainly buried under dozens of the Legion's shock troops. Behind them stood a man with a rapier. He wore a plumed hat and his skin looked like it was made of marble.

'You realise that their backup is coming?' Adam

asked no one as he pulled his claws. 'And it might get here long before the job's done?'

'That won't be a problem.' Claire closed her eyes like she was praying, then raised her sword and began to chant. As they watched the Legionnaires stopped fighting and began to turn back and forth from Claire to the rapier guy. 'I can hold them for a while, but you may wish to get rid of the dandy before he gets them back.'

'Couldn't have done that before they whipped me?' Konstantin complained.

'Could have if you hadn't decided to run off half cocked!' she retorted. 'Do you want to fight him or not?'

'I really do,' he decided, then charged headlong directly into the rapier guy. The statue danced quite calmly out of his path, drawing the sword back and plunging it into his side. The Dread Bear snarled, turned and spun with his claws extended, forcing the rapier guy to jump backwards out of the way. As he landed, Annabelle flung a small handful of web at him, but it lacked the mass and she cursed herself.

Adam judged the angle for a moment as the man darted around another of Konstantin's strikes, and the Laughing One's eyes began to track the movements. At the last moment he stepped in the path of the darting dandy and the two of them fell in a tangle of limbs. 'Look,' he told the dandy, grabbing his arms to hold him down. 'I don't want to fight you, I don't want to fight any of you. I just wanted to find out who's plotting against my people!'

'You have come to spy on us!' The French accent was thick and predictable as he raised his knees into Adam's stomach, again and again. Adam slashed at the man's face with the claws, digging shallow gouges into the cheek.

'No! Well, yes, but only a couple of you!' he protested. 'Look, there are people from both the Legion and the Lost doing wrong here. Did you hear about the train massacre? Because we're here to solve that!'

'If you are truly doing the right thing,' the dandy sprang to his feet and retreated at blurring speed, falling into a fencing stance, 'then surrender! You will have nothing to fear from us but justice. Which is no fear at all.'

'Sorry. Authority issues.' Adam was about to re-join the fight when something, strange occurred. Suddenly the Watcher, the Laughing One and Adam just… clicked. The Laughing Man acting in full concert. With an almost tangible click everything fell into place. He ran toward the fencer, and slid low, ramming his feet into the opponent's shins. As he fell Adam caught his sword arm with one hand, and settled the other under the fencer's chin, his claw retracted. 'I could end you with a thought, just relax and let it happen, but I'm not a killer and I don't want to hurt anyone I don't have to. So please, step back and try to understand that I am here to help your people and my own.'

'Your own?' His eyes widened. 'You are Lost!'

''Fraid so.' Adam drew his head back and smashed the point of his forehead right into the bridge of the dandy's nose.

It hurt his head more than he had anticipated, it felt like he was smashing into, well, stone, but the dandy's head pitched back, and he clutched at his face, his sword forgotten. 'Okay. We good to go?'

'I'm in a bit of a bind.' Konstantin's voice was muffled, someone in what looked a lot like black leather was holding Konstantin still in straps around the big animal's legs, arms and in his mouth. As he struggled they tightened around him, holding him still. Adam picked up the Dandy's sword and threw it to Claire, who seized it I her off hand. The eyes of the Laughing One did their trick and the weakest point of each rope began to glow a bright green. Predictably it was just off the giant bear's wrenching body. He cut him free with five swift swipes and Konstantin pitched forward, ramming into the crowd of Legionnaires by sheer accident.

The arrival of the man in leather had apparently switched the authority away from Claire, as she and Annabelle were now in the thick of the fighting. Claire was using her sword to great effect and had tossed the rapier behind her to free up the whip for zone control. Annabelle, without her webs, was ripping into Blanks with her daggers, the hole in the middle turning every stab wound a putrid black.

The man in leather lashed out at Adam and he pitched himself backwards, springing from his hands to his feet and back again like a deranged cheerleader. From his perspective it was like the world's most bizarre game of twister, putting his hands and feet wherever the green points were and hoping that the guidance of his Presences was good enough.

When he reached the others, he did he best to block and slice the leather straps, as they tried to wind or catch around his limbs.

'Now, can we please, please, please go?'

'We can,' Annabelle piped up, sounding very pleased with herself. 'In just a moment. I have to say goodbye.' The dandy had gotten to his feet, he was unarmed, but raised his fists in a distinctly businesslike manner and started toward them. He moved toward Claire, looking across at the leather man, who nodded. As soon as he reached the first Blank, he shrieked and jumped away.

'What's going on?' Adam looked around. The Blanks weren't advancing.

'He doesn't like spiders,' Annabelle spoke, her voice suddenly layered with the sounds of chittering. 'Which would be rude and completely unfounded, if not for, well, what's about to happen next.'

Adam had never been happier to see the creatures, as the flesh of the Blanks started to slough off, falling apart as the colony of spiders crawled slowly but steadily out of the bodies. Annabelle started toward them, a few more of the creatures vanishing into her clothing with every step. As she twirled and pirouetted around the floor, only a few of the arachnids stayed off her person, a small wave of the creatures headed toward the dandy, who was obviously afraid of the creatures. The leather man looked at them but helping would have cost him the advantage over Adam. Left alone, the dandy stumbled away, occasionally stepping on the bugs.

'Guys!' Adam called out, left alone by the distraction of Annabelle. 'I can only hold out so long. I am not that fast!' And as if he'd been speaking prophecy one of the straps lashed around his ankle and pulled him off his feet. 'Konstantin! I'm screwed!' He sat up and started lashing futilely at the restraint.

Watching bears run was strange, it would have been funny if he hadn't been a monster. Konstantin moved with a lopsided, doglike shambling that only became truly terrifying to the leather man once he realised that the creature running at him was surprisingly big and moving terrifyingly fast. He attempted to hold him back, but he was too late to do anything about the third of a metric tonne of teeth and claws running straight at him.

Adam was pulled sharply as the strap holding his ankle pulled taut. He tried to cut it clear as the giant beast smashed into the very human sized Legionnaire and carried him back into the wall. Adam lashed and slashed at the strap wildly as he bucked and bounced across the ground. His strikes were feeble, but after his seventh or eighth attempt he managed to cut it and sawed away until it broke. Konstantin chewed on the black leathers for a moment, and the straps vanished in a burst of light.

'More are coming!' Adam yelled.

'More always are!' Claire looked at them all. 'The blanks that are left are about to come online again, but if you want me to build you an exit we have no other option.'

Annabelle nodded and began to throw the webs that had apparently had enough time to regrow at the blanks' feet. 'You all right, big lad?'

'I'm fine,' Konstantin grunted. 'I'll see what I got from that after we're done. Do I have time to?'

'We aren't killing the other one.' Adam looked at the crowd. 'Konstantin, if anyone advances on us, hit them.' The bear nodded and shifted his bulk into their path. 'Claire, do the "get us out of here" thing.'

The dandy got to his feet, and three more people appeared behind him, a blue skinned woman in a dress in a different shade of blue, and a pair of men who both appeared to be the same man.

'Quickly, please.' Adam stepped up beside Konstantin. 'We don't want to hurt any of you, or at least I don't. We're already leaving, and we don't want any more trouble than we've already had. Please, just let us leave.'

The four of them started to advance again but were interrupted by a sharp whistle from the back of their group. They stopped and looked over their shoulders as a man in a white suit and black fedora advanced past them. The four of them bowed and stepped out of his path, and he tipped his hat to Adam.

'Good evening. My duellist informs that me that you're looking into the train massacre.' And suddenly he was right in front of Adam, his hand still on his hat. 'I am the Lord of the Code, and it is my sacred duty to do the same.'

'Your duellist?'

Code gestured over his shoulder toward the Dandy. 'My duellist. He would appreciate his sword back, if you don't mind.'

'How do we know he won't decide to get revenge for his friend and immediately stab me?'

'They weren't friends.' The Lord turned his head back to the duellist. 'Don't immediately stab him.' He nodded but didn't look happy about it. Adam looked over at Claire, who sighed and tossed the sword across the room. The duellist took a few steps and plucked it out of mid-air. 'Now, you are investigating the train?' After some discrete beckoning from Claire, Konstantin repositioned himself to stand between her and Lord Code.

'We are.' Annabelle stepped forward. 'We already know who committed the murders, and we believe it's a part of the large conspiracy.'

'Ahh, then who was the hand?'

'A mercenary who goes by the name of Six of Nothing. I don't know what his deal is.'

'So the Princess was right. Damn.' He took off his hat, wiped his forehead and put the hat back on. 'It really was only one man. Very well, we allow you to continue your work. Driver?'

'Yes?' Claire's voice from behind Konstantin was embarrassed.

'If you are willing to represent the interests of our people in this, I will see to it that you may be invited back into society one day.'

'I accept,' she squeaked.

'I will know if you lie to me,' he warned. 'I know whenever anyone attempts to deceive me.' Adam wasn't sure if that was true, but he was glad he'd been honest. Claire tapped Konstantin on the side and the bear shuffled out of his position between them, grumbling quietly as he did.

'I understand.' Her entire posture was slumped, her arms hugging herself like a child. 'I don't want to re-join the Legion. I just want you all to leave me alone. I just want you to let me leave.'

'Acceptable, once our interests are met.' He snapped his fingers and, as one, the remaining blanks and all four henchmen turned on their heels and made their way out.

'Who the hell was that?' Adam looked around.

'He's the Lord of the Code.' Claire's voice was soft. 'He rounds people up for the Legion. Does the closest thing anyone can do to secret police in a society where everyone's supposed to be on the same goal and no one's supposed to be able to lie. I worked for him, well, for the people who worked for the people who worked for him, and it's what got me onto the train.'

'Okay!' Annabelle clapped her hands for attention. 'Enough of this! We will talk about this more when we get someplace we might not still be attacked at any second. I have things to show and tell, obviously she does too, so let's get some place safe.'

'Sure.' Claire put her hands back against thin air and began to push. 'But there is something you need to know about him right away. You really can't lie to him, even if you say something you think is a lie, he'll hear the truth and you won't even know for sure what he heard.' A minute or so later she gave a groan of effort and the sky cracked open again, their little crew ducking through one after another.

The feeling of being back in reality was strange. The colours around him felt more vivid, the ground under his feet more solid and the air around him was just… more. He'd done this a few dozen times now and he could never get quite past the memory of the first time he'd come back from another world to be greeted by a small group of monsters lead by the thing that had been pretending to be the bear in front of him.

'Are we okay?' He looked at the rest of the group, slipping off the mask and tucking it into his jacket pocket. He took a few deep breaths and looked around. Annabelle took a spot behind Konstantin, the bear now a large man in a cheap brown suit again. She whispered comforting words to the creatures crawling into her clothes as she did. Claire was back in her dress, tucking the whip away into a bag he hadn't seen before. The sword had just vanished, disappearing into the aether.

'Spider brat,' Konstantin grunted. 'Put your knives away before we head out. No weapons.'

'Weird advice coming from you.' Even as she said it she slid the knives into holsters mounted on the middle of her back under her dress.

'I've been screwed over too many times by you idiots, who don't have powers built in, getting caught up or identified. Makes incidents. Don't like incidents I don't start. Now, let's go find somewhere they won't watch us and see what the spiders have to say.'

'That could be a problem.' Adam's throat was tight, and his hand had balled up into a fist without him knowing. 'There's nowhere I can't be watched.'

'What?'

'People have been spying on me,' he admitted. 'Some crazy sniper guy has been tracking and watching me for weeks. He's been popping up and disappearing out of nowhere, no matter where I am. He could be watching me at any time, and I won't know unless he makes a mistake or I'm searching for him. I only know if he's already there.'

'Then we'll have to just find the safest place we can and do our best to make it work.' Annabelle sighed, took his hand and lead him out of the shopping mall they were currently standing in. Konstantin stole them a car and the four of them packed into it.

Konstantin had a predictably lead foot and wasn't much of a driver, rude and loud, with no problem letting other drivers knowing what he thought of them, even as he made the exact same mistakes they did. Annabelle directed him toward one of the few locations on earth that Adam really felt safe.

'Hey, Sage.' He waved. 'How are you?'

The Sage looked like, and as far as Adam knew was, a massive hippie stoner. He wore a tie-dyed shirt, torn jeans and sandals, and leaned quietly back on a leather chair, raising one hand idly to acknowledge the fact that Adam was there. He was the guardian of the Mercy Theatre, one of the few truly neutral places in any dimension. No matter which side you were on you were welcome there, as long as you didn't talk about the war.

'Passing fair, passing fair.' He smiled, reaching into a bag of pre-rolled joints. 'You want some bud?'

'No thanks.' He nodded at the Shifter, the ticket taking shape changer. She currently looked like a grumpy, acne ridden, slightly overweight, teenage girl who was watching the area with an air of such complete disinterest he was amazed she was awake.

'Doc!' she called out. 'There's some people here to see you!'

Mercy came out the theatre, wearing a doctor's coat and, her blond hair tied up in a pile atop her head. Last time she'd worn underwear underneath the lab coat, this time it was a nightgown, giving her the air of someone who had just gotten out of bed. Or it would have, if not for the makeup and hair being impeccable. She wrapped Adam up in a hug.

'Laughing Man! Look at you, completely uninjured again! Very well done! In another month you'll

148

qualify for my "not a complete moron" package!'

'Which entails?'

'Exactly the same thing as usual except I insult you less.' She shook Annabelle's hand, and then looked at Konstantin, her hands on her hips. 'What the hell are you doing here?'

'I didn't actually rip the gent's arm off you know?' He shrugged.

'You have killed or injured numbers beyond counting! Without rhyme or reason, just because of who you are!'

'You live in a sad and painful past,' Claire piped up, her voice completely monotone. 'When you learn to live for the day you will gain true freedom.'

'And who is this bitch?' Mercy pointed at her.

'Oh, her?' Annabelle smiled. 'She's an ex prisoner of war who has since officially distanced herself from the Legion completely and joined a mission to secure fair treatment for all of those who walk between.' Annabelle smiled as Mercy ran her hand over her hair.

'Really? Very well then, welcome to the tribe. Try not to be as intolerable as you're currently being, the entire time you're here.' She waved one hand to the backstage. 'Theatre four is free. I assume you came here for a safe place to do something? Considering none of you seem to be injured.' She looked at them. 'None of you have any internal injuries, do you?'

'No.' He looked at them. 'Konstantin? Have you healed?'

'I am still in pain, but I will bear it.' He shrugged.

'Good, because treating him would be uncomfortable.'

'Then a room would be great!' Adam cut across the conversation before anyone could threaten, insult or lie to each other any further. 'Please, we only need a little of your time. I know I'm technically Lost but I'm new here and this is strictly Annabelle's business.'

'I trust you.' She kissed him on the cheek. 'Besides, if you break the rules, engage in violence or talk about the war then Sage will throw you through the roof and then the wall.'

'Why does everyone in this community feel the need to threaten each other?' he grumbled. 'Can't we just talk with our words?' He made his way back to theatre four.

Some comedy whose funny parts seemed to resolve around people getting hit in the nuts was playing on the main screen, and several of the seats had been removed and replaced by hospital beds, which currently had no one in them. 'Hey, Shifter!'

'Yeah!' came the call from the distance.

'Can you turn off the movie, so we can use the screen?'

'No problem.' A couple of minutes later the picture went out, leaving the screen white.

Annabelle raised her hands and the spiders headed toward the screen. For a moment the world began to fragment and change, hundreds of different images of floors and walls, roofs and strangers, of places he'd never seen and places he recognised. They saw sex,

150

violence, manipulation and arguments as the hundreds of creatures from all over the world covered the screen with their memories. Eventually the screen finally resolved into a single image.

Three people sat around the room, the spider's eyes incapable of seeing them clearly, but enough of them together built something of a picture. Two of them were women, who were actually physically sitting in the room. On the other side of the room there was a screen, which displayed a man in a plague doctor mask sitting at a desk. The room was black and white, but the ladies' side was split evenly down the middle, while the other was laid out in a random mosaic pattern.

'Is the assassin done with his work?' The women spoke together.

'Apart from the one he let get away.' The man's voice was calm but had a thick undertone of disapproval. 'Which I still believe means he should be killed.'

'That is pointless vanity.' One of the pair of Legion women, dressed in white and sitting on the black side, leaned across the table to stare at him. 'Once the lines are drawn and the war begins again, he will either take a side or die as all will have to. With no shelter to run to, he will either come to us or die in the cold. Either he is humbled or killed.'

'The red coated lunatic will doubtless take him by the hand and drag him into the Lost whether we like it or not,' the other woman sulked.

'Aww.' Adam grinned and put his hands over his heart. 'I'm sure Xavier would be flattered to know he's being hated even when he's not here. We should show him this once we're done.'

'I'll warm the cockles of his... whatever's in his chest.' Claire whacked him on the back of the head. 'Now pay attention.'

'You know Xavier?'

'That is not paying attention,' she scolded.

'But seriously, you know him?'

'Everyone knows him,' she admitted. 'He's had his hat in just about every ring at some point.'

'Does anyone actually like him?'

'A few people, in some world, perhaps? Not me, oh god, not me.' She shuddered. 'Now, eyes front.'

'Now.' The man straightened up. 'Are your sides agents in place? Do you have your hands on the Artificer, is he amenable?'

'Our work on him is almost complete.' The black clad twin smiled. 'The dimensional walls are being weakened as we speak. Soon the pockets, hidden places and worlds between worlds will be where they are supposed to be, and we won't have to deal with the distractions of.'

'Ranting,' her twin interjected, and she nodded, closing her mouth. 'Suffice to say yes, the rituals have taken place on our side. We will be visiting the Artificer post haste. Has your side worked out?'

'We're on it.' He spread his arms almost pleadingly. 'It's not as easy on our end as it is on yours. Legion lands shift by predictable patterns, our weak points could be anywhere.'

'Very well.' The twins smirked at each other. 'But it must be done post-haste.'

'It will be done,' he snapped. 'I have all my people on it, everything will be as it should. Now cease your harping before I–'

'Do exactly what from all the way over there?' One of the twins sneered.

'A fine point.' He nodded. 'Very well. We can get back to our fighting just as soon as every other source of power is removed, and we can focus on each other as nature intended. Until then I expect you to act like professionals.'

'We are behaving like–'

'Behave like professionals who aren't petty back biters,' he rephrased himself.

'Well then, if you have the blueprints, I have the craftsman.' The screen went dark after that, the spiders apparently deciding it had said enough.

'Well,' he sighed. 'That's ominous.'

'Indeed, it is.' Claire nodded. 'Dread Bear?'

He gave a dull grunt in response.

'Can you hunt them down now?'

'Using what?' He spread his thick arms. 'I still have nothing to tie me to them. You'd have better luck finding one of the few people who can make things that would screw with dimensions. Or we could go to the Lost place and find their people, or we could just wait for something else to happen.'

'I have another idea.' Adam thought about it. 'But I'm going to need you all to trust me, because I need sleep before I can act on it.' They shot him strange looks. 'I can't talk to you about it, but once I've slept I'll come back with something. I promise, probably.'

'That's incredibly suspicious,' Annabelle noted. 'Which means I'm going to have to trust you. Hey yo, Mercy! Adam needs to crash for a couple of hours, cool?'

'Back row, and if I need that theatre you all keep your idiot mouths shut. Deal?'

'Idiot mouths will be appropriately restrained.' She nodded. 'Adam go crash.' Adam shrugged, pulled up the mask and the Presence knocked him straight out.

'Hey Katie!' he called out. 'If this is just a normal dream I'm really embarrassing myself right now!'

'Why would you be embarrassed?' she asked from her tree. 'You'd only be speaking to yourself.'

Katie was a strange figure in Adam's life. She'd appeared to him first when he was trying to make up his mind on whether he was going to give up his Presence or not. She'd encouraged him to give it up. It hadn't worked out, but the strange girl living in her own pocket dimension had decided to be his friend anyway, dispensing whatever advice she could and trying to help him get his thoughts together.

Her dimension, in the "moments between moments" allowed her to see everything in the worlds beyond, in spite of her inability to see. Her Presence was an ibis, who never spoke, and she seemed to live in a park in between a bunch of faceless buildings that reminded him of a place he'd liked to go when he was younger.

'So…' He sat down on the only bench, looking up at her in her tree. 'I need your help.'

'As opposed to literally any other time you've been here?' She smirked at him.

'Well, your problem is that you're trapped in another dimension where you can see everything. I have no idea how the hell I would even begin to help you with that.' He looked at her for a long moment. 'If there's anything I can do to help you out of here I'll do it, but I'm not sure.'

'Thank you.' She smiled. 'I might take you up on that eventually, but right now I'm mostly here because I decided to be.'

'Really?'

'There's something I'm going to need to do one day, that requires certain sacrifices on my part, one of which is my presence here.' She spread her arms wide and lay back in the branches. 'There's not a lot to do, but the ability to see literally anything I want is significant compensation.'

'So, what do you have to do?'

'I'm not ready to tell you yet.' She gave him a gentle smile. 'I like you, but this plan is literally my only reason for living and I'm not going to jeopardise it until I'm absolutely ready. If the day comes when you can help me with my purpose, I'll fill you in.' She turned her face toward him. 'Until then, what can I do for you?'

'I need some intel.' He sighed. 'People are trying to unmake every dimension that doesn't belong to either the Legion or the Lost, which, I assume, includes this place.'

'Actually, now I think about it, I'm pretty sure this is Legion territory. On the other hand, I am generally opposed to the wiping out of other dimensions and the people inside. That's a problem and I'll do whatever I can to help. Obviously the amount I can tell you is limited, but I'll do what I can.'

'Okay. In that case I might need to find an artificer.' He had no idea what those were. 'Someone who could build like, really complicated, powerful magic stuff. There's also some people on the Lost side who are weakening the gap between dimensions and we're running out of options. We need to stop them, or at least slow them down until we find where these people are that have those plans.' He'd have to ask Annabelle if the spiders could find those people again. They should have just gone straight to attacking the twins. Stupid, they'd let a good chance slip away.

'Given that you can't currently stop them you need to find an artificer.' She bit her fingers as the ibis picked politely around the park. The Watcher and Laughing One watched it with intense focus. On one occasion the Laughing One advanced, looking almost hungry, and then the ibis fixed it with one empty black eye. The Laughing One retreated back to Adam's feet and curled up, more chastened than Adam had ever seen him. 'I have a shortlist I can give you, but you should be able to have Claire and Konstantin locate the weakest point in the Lost web. The Trapdoor should be able to show you the way into the Lost worlds unnoticed.'

'Awesome.' He nodded. 'Thanks.'

'I'll keep thinking on the artificer.' She jumped out of her tree and made her way over to him, taking her hands in his. 'I don't want to get you into any trouble, but it doesn't seem like I can ethically tell you not to save several dimensions worth of people, kill off all the animal spirits in the world and maybe ruin all of nature just because I don't like the idea of you maybe getting hurt.'

'Yeah, well.' He shrugged. 'After this one I think I'm probably going to slow down a little. I went form upsetting some crazy bear to a quest to save the universe. Konstantin, who I was pants-crappingly terrified of when I met him, is now someone I just comfortably fell asleep in the same room as, which is weird.'

'He's not a bad person.' Katie sighed. 'I mean he's not a person at all really, but whatever, he is he isn't that bad.'

'Coulda fooled me.' That was… interesting. 'First time I saw you you called Annabelle, Xavier and Pan out on being bad people, but the giant rampaging bear gets a pass?'

'No passes, and I never called Annabelle bad. I just told you that she didn't think like we do, and you couldn't know where her loyalties were.' She folded her arms. 'Things that are still facts by the way. His loyalties on the other hand are...' She thought about it. 'Is hungry a loyalty?'

'Okay, so, he's confirmed I guess? What about Claire?'

'Claire's a liar,' she said simply. 'She's also a traitor and a thief. She has turned on almost every cause she's ever taken up with. She would turn on you if she had any other option, which I'm certain she does not. Literally no one else wants her.'

'Helpful. What about that Lord Code guy?'

'He's frightened enough of the situation that he would be willing to accept her, as he is to accept you. He does not want her around, no one does. All of her chickens came home to roost long ago, she's just trying to make a life now.'

'So, how'd she make it through the train?'

'Six of Nothing was ordered to ignore his employer's orders and not kill her, then pretend that he's just done it as a flight of fancy. Before you ask I don't know what the actual reason was, but it was not the "randomness" he pretended.'

'Okay. That's it, I need to find out the deal with those Red people.'

'And I imagine you will soon enough.' She smiled.

'Not at all reassuring.'

'I suppose not.' She sighed. 'Do you want to wake up now?'

'I might need to,' he admitted. 'So, our moment is over.'

CHAPTER SEVEN

'Did you get what you needed?' Claire was the first one to notice Adam sitting up and looking around. The other two had hijacked the projector to watch one of the eight thousand comic book movies which had been steadily coming out over the last few yours. Konstantin had a bucket of popcorn with what appeared to be sliced up hotdogs in it.

'I did.' He pulled himself to his feet and yawned. He was tired, it was only now he'd slept he realised how little he'd slept recently. 'All we have to do is wait.'

'For what?'

'Me.' Leaper the spider stepped into the room and smiled, waving one hand. 'I'm here with news from my father.'

'Okay.' Annabelle looked at him for a moment. 'How did you know when and where to show up?'

'My father knows how to do a great many things.' He smiled and sat down. 'So, what can I do for all of you?'

'We need you to take us somewhere where the line between the headquarters of the Lost and the rest of the worlds is as thin as possible. People are trying to collapse the borders between the worlds. The Legion's side are already done, but the Lost are still locating and working on theirs. Which means we need to show up and stop them from doing whatever they're trying to do.'

'You intend to hunt down and eliminate these workers?'

'Yeah, that's an issue,' Annabelle commented. 'I mean you couldn't kill the Legate of the Eternal Flame, are you going to be okay with what we might have to do now?'

'Well, I'm kinda hoping we can just take them prisoner, or that...'

'That we'll do it for you.' Konstantin loomed over him. 'Sorry. Was that not what you were going to say?' he growled. 'It doesn't make your hands any cleaner to arrange a killing if someone else does the deed. It just makes you a coward.'

'Yeah, well.' He maybe had a point, but Adam really didn't want to think about it. 'Let's just focus on taking them prisoner if we can. It might be useful to know what's going on, and I'd never tell you to kill anyone. It's not my fault I've got to make do with whatever associates the world gives me. I guarantee you if I had a choice of resources the kind of people who kill on sight wouldn't be my choice.'

'And yet between me and Gentleman you've always had one.'

'Life's a bitch.' He shrugged. 'Gotta use the tools god gave me.'

'You calling me a tool?'

'No. Tools do what you make them do. You're more like a runaway truck.' Weirdly Konstantin seemed mollified by that. 'Anyway, so Leaper and Annabelle will take us close, and you two,' he pointed to Konstantin and Claire, 'will find the weakest point. Think you can do that?'

'I don't like the idea of working with him,' Claire sighed.

'Let's not waste time.' Konstantin looked at them. 'How do we get there?'

'All right.' Annabelle nodded. 'I'll put together a web way as soon as I find a suitable basement. We're going to need silk and blood.'

'Don't you guys make silk?'

'No.' Leaper and Annabelle looked at each other. 'We need real silk, newfangled, machine made. My people are becoming irritable. I've accrued some significant debts travelling back and forth as often as I did and I'm guessing Leaper doesn't want to trade on his own reputation.'

'You guess correctly.' He nodded.

'Blood and silk are tributes that work well for spider gods, unless you want to spill some secrets, or you have time to catch a bunch of insects.'

'Okay.'

It was six hours later that Adam, with some trepidation, hung a short bolt of silk cloth on the wall of a condemned building. Spiders began to crawl all over it with seeming delight.

'So?' Annabelle held up one of her knives. 'Who's donating?' Adam stepped forward reluctantly but was shouldered out of the way by Konstantin's significant bulk. He growled when Adam looked at him with confusion.

'I got more than the rest of you.' He held out his hand to the spider, who rolled her eyes.

'Even you need a measure of manual dexterity, dear. Cutting up your hands isn't exactly a great idea.' Konstantin sighed and took off his jacket, undoing the top three buttons of his shirt to expose the top of his hairy scar covered chest. Annabelle approached him carefully.

'Now don't freak out and tear my limbs off or anything, okay?' she grumbled. 'I'm trying to help here.'

'Oh, just shut up and do it!' he dismissed. She pushed the knife quickly into him, not deep, the knife began to drain the blood out of him quickly. She pulled back and whipped the knife across the silks, a long line of red. She began to paint in those lines, putting together a crude web. The carpet of spiders came thicker and thicker until they almost covered the silk entirely until they, and it, vanished.

Annabelle began her work, straining laying and building her own silks, humming to herself pleasantly as she did.

'Hate spiders,' Konstantin grumbled.

'Not exactly your biggest fan either.' Leaper's hands spun, the webs coming thicker and thicker.

'I didn't like them at first either, but they're not so bad once you get to know them.' Adam leaned down and picked one of them up, who seemed to have a couple of missing legs. He muttered a short reassurance and placed it gently on the silks. 'There we go little buddy. You're fine.'

Adam spent the next ten minutes trying to make conversation with Claire and Konstantin, which didn't work out well. Once the web was done the two of them put their heads together for a moment, then began to walk through the webs. Annabelle took the rear-guard position and the two of them followed into the web.

'You coming, Leaper?'

'I'm afraid not.' He shook his head. 'You can handle it.'

The first time Adam walked out into the web he'd been terrified, and honestly, he was still a little anxious. After all, they were all still currently standing on what looked like a white high wire, over a bottomless pit full of spider webs. Some supported buildings, or colonies, some supported what looked like entire small cities. As Adam looked up and to the right he thought he might even be able to see the carnival he spent most of his time at.

He knew he couldn't fall off the line. He knew he could probably fall and hang off just by the soles of his feet without risking falling over, but it was still a long drop into nowhere. He picked up the pace, not speaking and trying not to attract too much attention.

The pair leading the group steadily picked up their pace, Konstantin moving at a loping barrel, Claire never seemed to run or even jog, the same dignified stride never changing its tempo but somehow speeding up. The others all ran after them as fast as they could, or at least as fast as Adam could. Wherever the lines met Claire and Konstantin conferred for a brief moment, before turning one direction or another.

Eventually, after spending almost an hour wandering through the darkness, the two of them looked at each other for a moment, Konstantin nodded, and Claire took a swan dive off the web.

'What the hell?' Adam reached out to try to catch her, and missed completely, only to watch her turn in mid-air and land on her feet on the roof of a building. Annabelle looked at her for a moment and then began to weave in her hands. She handed one part of the length each of the others, and then tossed it off the side.

'Claire!' she called. 'Catch!' Claire snagged it out of the air with one hand and placed it on the ground. Annabelle wrapped the other end around the line of web, then jumped, only for the web to arrest her fall right before she hit the ground. After a couple of moments Konstantin looked at Adam and motioned for him to go. He shrugged, slipped the loop of silk he was holding around his waist and jumped off.

Adam remembered flying from a vision once, and this was close but not quite the same. He fell, and just short of a plummet the string pulled tight and caught him, driving the breath out of his lungs. As he struggled for it, Annabelle tapped the rope, letting him drop onto his ass. He took a couple of deep breaths and pulled himself to his feet, enjoying the adrenaline rush.

'Clear the bloody path!' Konstantin's voice came from above him and Adam set off at a run toward the spider, as the Dread Bear landed in a messy heap just short of running into him. He pulled on the string and fell onto his feet, tossing his head in both directions. 'Hate this.' He looked at Claire. 'Let's keep moving.' The group headed off at a fast walk, ignoring the annoyed noises coming from Konstantin as he tried to raise the pace.

When they reached the end of the city that occupied its own island in the sky, Claire and Konstantin looked at each other and nodded.

'This is the spot.' Claire looked at them. 'I'd be happy to get to work, as long as you're all ready?' They sounded off, and she began to push against the sky again. After around ten seconds the sky began to crack. 'All right everyone, move, move, move! Haste is required!'

Konstantin, in full bear form, charged through the hole with a roar, pushing Claire aside to slam through the break in worlds, quickly followed by Claire, Adam, and Annabelle.

Sure enough, standing right in front of them, at the other end of the portal were a group of people, each one glowing a different colour. The world around them glowed with all of those colours, light coming off what would otherwise have been a mirrored room.

Konstantin was already standing on top of two of them, the red one having been knocked down and stepped on, and the yellow clutching a broken leg. He was locked in combat with the green one, who was four times bigger than any of the others, armoured in glowing green plates. As the two pushed, the green being got the advantage, picking him up and throwing him across the room. Konstantin's body hit the wall with an unpleasant crack.

The two injured parties retreated quickly behind the green creature, in a sudden blur of blue light.

'Okay, tellytubbies!' Adam popped his claws, facing off against the group. 'Any chance you're willing to come peacefully?'

'Please say no,' Konstantin growled. Annabelle and Claire took their places beside him. Adam smiled to himself; it struck him as funny that the two men in the party were the best and worst fighter in the group.

'You broke our legs.' All six of them spoke at once but it was the yellow one who motioned at their own legs. That one crawled to the back corner, but the red one had dragged himself to his feet and squared off. Suddenly the colours stopped radiating, and the other five looked at the yellow one.

'I'm sorry, York.' The red one's voice was soft. 'We can't be distracted by the pain.'

'I understand,' the yellow one grunted. 'Kill them all.'

'Rude,' Adam pointed out. 'You know I told my people not to do that? You're officially the bad guys right now.'

The group transformed in front of his eyes, all but the green one who was already an armoured hulk.

The blue one turned from a person to a streamlined creature, with blades on his arms, skull, torso and limbs. The red one's hands lit up in flames. The purple one took on a set of scorpion claws and tail, and a monster's face with gnashing teeth. The orange one manifested a sword and shield out of nothing.

Adam took a moment to be suitably intimidated, the rest of the team apparently did not. He'd expected Konstantin to charge straight into the green one, but to his surprise the giant creature lowered its shoulder and smashed into the one with the sword and shield, pitching him backwards into the wall, then laying into it with claws and teeth. The big one charged at Konstantin, only to be pinned to the ground by Annabelle's webs around his legs. As she wrapped his legs up spiders poured off her. The green one ripped the chords with every step and pull, but Annabelle had the time and the skill to say ahead.

Claire danced with two opponents, the blue one with the terrible speed and the purple one with his claws. The whip cracked in the purple creature's face, keeping it at bay with strikes to its large, sensitive eyes, and managed to barely hold the blue one with her sword. It was faster than she was, and she was losing, already her red skin was stained with black blood.

Adam was rapidly alerted to the fact that he was in this fight when a fireball came flying at his face. Even as he rolled, he turned for the blue one, it was only a matter of time before one of those blades found its mark on Claire.

'Mistake.' The Watcher's tone was dispassionate. 'Go for the red one, he's the weak link and once you close, one of the others will be forced to engage you in order to defend the red, keeping him on your terms.' Adam sighed, took a deep breath through the mask and charged for the one throwing the fireballs.

As usual the Laughing One's instincts took over from his. As the fireball thrower began the process of launching fists of flame at him, the trajectory appeared in green in front of his eyes. He rolled on the ground, sprang out of the path of a fireball and kept his forward momentum going. He could see the self-satisfaction turning to uncertainty, and then to fear as Adam moved like he knew what the man would do before he realised it himself. It must be terrifying, he realised, to have someone able to read your every move.

'Hit the deck!' Watcher called, and Adam fell onto his face as the blade slashed where his head was. The blue one swerved suddenly at the last moment. If the enemy hadn't been perfectly cohesive, the blue one would have had his face scorched off. As it was it gave Claire a clean chance. She laid into him with the sword, cutting him open in a few places.

Adam grabbed the red one's hands around the wrist and placed them against his own face, pinning them close. 'I don't know if this'll burn you or not.'

'I'll kill you!' The red one screamed. 'We will tear you to pieces. We will cook you alive and eat your corpses!'

'They might.' He shrugged. 'But you won't.' He drew the man's hands back for a moment and then smashed his forehead into the bridge of his opponent's nose. He intended to keep it up until the man lost consciousness but was plucked off his feet before he had a choice.

'Konstantin!' he called, looking into the blank mask of the bright green creature. 'Konstantin, if you don't do something I'm going to die!' The green man brought his fist back to drive it into Adam's face.

The big man started the swing and then stopped, the arm locked and unable to move. As he looked around with confusion he saw a whip curled around his wrist. Adam lashed at any weak point he could hit with his claws. He couldn't get close enough to hit the body and the claws couldn't even scratch the armour.

'What, you thought he was the only one who could help?' Claire called from her position behind him, slamming her sword into the crack in the green man's armour and slamming her hand against the pommel to drive it home. The giant creature slammed Adam twice into the floor, before finally toppling backwards, clutching his sides.

Adam was busy trying to regain his ability to think, stumbling to his feet. He watched the scene unfold around him, unable to do much more.

Claire was squaring off with the blue one, as the green, bleeding badly, got to his feet again, struggling just like Adam. Now she was dictating blue's movements with the whip. She kept him from running or dodging as much and probed him with her sword for a place to stick him.

Annabelle squared off, spider against scorpion. The bigger creature apparently wasn't poisonable, so she was making do with blades and webs. His massive claws were stuck together, so he wielded them as clubs.

Where was Konstantin?

He was down, dammit, slumped over the unconscious or dead body of the orange one. He needed the help. Adam supposed that fighting four of the other side and beating three of them was more than he could have asked of even the Dread Bear.

The guy with the flames was getting back up.

'Get up!' he ordered himself. 'Get up now!' Slowly but surely, he forced himself to his feet. 'Annabelle!'

'Yeah?'

'Send the sisters after red and blue. I'll handle the scorpion!'

'Handle me, will you?' The creature spoke through the pointed mash of teeth, his voice distorted as he advanced. 'Come on then, handle me!' Adam advanced on him. He couldn't run, his head was swimming and he figured it was probably taking everything his Presences had to keep him moving.

No. He realised the fact suddenly. It was taking the Watcher to keep him upright, but he could still use the Laughing One's abilities. He could still use the sight and speed, just not to the usual levels.

That was fine, the sight would be all he needed.

He advanced on the purple creature and the world turned black and green. The creature in front of him became his only focus as he moved toward it. His eyes scanned its striking patterns, checked every movement, examined its entire body for weak points. Only the obvious one appeared.

Strikes with the claws around the head and neck

would maim or even kill this scorpion creature. There was no way to just knock it out, and its arms and body were too thick scaled to be vulnerable. In that second the entire Laughing Man had to agree to go for the head. He took a deep breath and charged at the creature.

Even now he had no idea if he could do it, but he had to try, he had to commit to this strike. He stepped on the scorpion's claw, bounded off it and struck for the monstrous face.

He had no idea if he could go through with it or not, but he struck, swinging with all of his strength at the creature's face. At the last moment, the only thing in the world he wanted to do was pull the claws back, even if it means he lost for good.

The choice was taken away from him by a long pair of yellow tentacles, which caught him out of the air and tossed him into the roof. He felt his bell ring, then tumbled through the air and landed on the ground. He set his hands on the floor and pulled himself to his feet.

'Sound off!' he called, his voice groggy. 'Anyone on my side still up?'

'Down to one arm.' Claire called. 'But the green one isn't getting up.'

'The others are all poisoned,' Annabelle called. 'Just purple, blue and yellow left.'

'I thought we beat yellow already?' He rolled out of the way of the tentacles, then slashed at one as it wrapped around his neck.

'You thought wrong!' she replied. 'I'll handle yellow.'

'Blue's mine!' The sound of sword clashing against carapace hinted to the truth of that statement.

'Which means,' he rolled back and got to his feet, 'that he's still my problem.' He faced off against the purple one. The spiders had done their work, they'd kept anyone who fell down out of the fight. He hoped Annabelle had stuck to knocking them all out like he'd asked her to, but he wasn't her boss and he couldn't make her do anything.

Just as he was thinking that he'd had a lot of time to recover he fell back onto his ass and scrambled to his feet. Apparently the purple one had taken the time to get the web off his claws, and they now snapped at Adam's face.

'That's quite enough.' He turned away from the claw with a twirl he hadn't done. He realised that he was no longer in control of his own body and mouth. 'I hope you understand, that if you do not surrender we will have to kill you. I suggest you turn back to your native shape and come peacefully.'

'Killed my family!' it roared.

'No. We didn't.' Annabelle's voice was quiet. 'The bites I gave them were paralytic. They certainly won't enjoy the next few hours, but they aren't dead or dying, yet.' The fight had slowed to a crawl, Claire and the blue one squaring off, waiting for opportunities.

'Which will have to change,' he admitted. 'There is

no way for us to render you unconscious. Which means I will have to go for the kill. This is our last chance to all walk out of here alive.' With an agonised scream of fury, the purple scorpion monster slid back into a brightly coloured human body, followed by the blue and yellow.

'Well.' Claire made a grunt as she forced her shoulder back into place. 'That was bracing.'

'Can someone check the bear, please?' Adam mumbled through his own fog. 'I'm kinda groggy. I think I should stick to the parts that are mostly watching.' He watched Annabelle toss webs around the limbs of the rainbow men who were trying to break the world.

'I'll do it.' Claire turned toward the mass of fur, and with a mixture of kicks and cursing managed to rouse the shaggy creature, who answered her offensive with curses and an attempt to murder the woman. Claire was far too fast for him, especially in his current state, and he returned to his senses before the got a paw on her. Konstantin mumbled insults and threats as he braced his bulk against the wall.

The second the webs were around them all Adam felt the power leant to him temporarily, by the Laughing One, disappear and Annabelle had to catch him before he hit the ground.

'It's okay babe.' Her voice was soft and comforting. 'It's all right, I'll get everyone together and then I'll open a path back to the carnival. I'll take you home and we'll be fine. I'll take care of us. She took his weight easily with a smile on her face. Konstantin and Claire piled the bodies onto the former's back, all but the green one who they would have to leave. They carried the bodies through first, followed by Annabelle, with Adam at her side.

'So,' came a voice from the other side of the portal. 'This is, quite awkward.'

Konstantin and Claire were surrounded. Claire had her sword drawn, but Konstantin looked like he could barely stand up on his own.

'Stay down. big lad.' Adam put one shaking hand on Konstantin's shoulder. 'I know you might be able to make it out alive, but the rest of us won't be so lucky if you decide to go teeth and claw.' There was no price to spare the big creature's ego.

'Right,' his half-conscious form grumbled and dropped the pile of bodies onto the ground. 'I'll stay down.'

'That's a wise choice young man.'

Adam looked around to the army of spiders that surrounded them, led by a pale woman in a floor length black gown. She waved at them and smiled. 'If you all wouldn't mind surrendering your prisoners, and yourselves, I'm certain we can come to a peaceful resolution.'

'What's going on?' Annabelle stepped up and fixed the woman with a glare. 'Why are you getting in our way? We have important work to do! We're trying to save your people as well as our own!'

'That is enough,' the woman snapped. 'Annabelle,

you are coming with me and I will have no argument! We need to talk, and you are doing to do as you are told.'

'Auntie, I don't have time to.'

'This is not a discussion!' the woman snapped. 'You are coming with me right now!' With that Adam felt a short sharp sting on the back of his neck and fell on his face.

CHAPTER EIGHT

'Hey.' Adam's head hurt, and the hand on his face was cold and smooth in the hot environment. 'Wake up sleeping beauty. You're all right, and I'm really sorry my family is so shitty.'

'Annabelle.' He pulled himself up into a sitting position, as his head began to spin he lay back again and closed his eyes 'What's going on?'

'So, Aunt Wolf kinda knocked us all out. She poisoned all of you and hit me over the head with a hammer,' she grumbled. 'Well, she had me hit over the head with a hammer. Spiders don't exactly do blunt force trauma most of the time.' She climbed up onto the bed beside him, wrapping her arms around his chest. 'And I would totally understand if you want to leave me forever and never deal with this again.'

He pulled her closer to him and twined his legs with hers.

'I'm sorry, but as much as I would love to have this complete and total analytical breakdown of our lives, both separately and as a couple, I don't have the mental fortitude for it right now. I was poisoned, and I literally just woke up. Can we have a slightly easier conversation. Please?'

'Okay.' She thought about things, running her hand idly through his hair. 'What do you wanna talk about?'

'I have no idea.' He thought about it for a moment. 'Tell me how you were adopted?'

'Okay.' She thought about that for a moment her hand moving down her face to his chest.

'Wait?' He was suddenly frightened. 'Am I not wearing my presences?'

'No.' She didn't sound bothered, that made it okay. 'They're on the other side of the room. Don't worry, they only took them off you to stop them from waking you up. They weren't trying to rob you.'

'Anyway.' He tried to clap his hands for attention, managed to get them halfway up from his body and let them fall again. 'Story time! Story time!'

'Okay.' She laughed. 'Once upon a time, there was a little girl whose parents abandoned her at a carnival and ran away forever.'

'That is not a fairy-tale beginning.'

'Look more carefully at most fairy tales,' she disagreed. 'Anyway, while the vast majority of missing children are kidnapped or murdered, this one was taken in by a kindly group of strange women, who just so happened to be spider spirits.'

'Is that a common thing?'

'Spiders specifically? No. Spirits? More than you'd think.' She shrugged. 'Being taken in by spirits isn't exactly an everyday affair, but the human ability to step between dimensions and exist within most of them with a measure of safety is a trait that makes you very valuable. You'll find a lot of adopted half breeds in our world, of which Raven and I are only two.'

'Raven? Really?'

'The name didn't tip you off?' She sounded pleased

with herself. 'He's a bird, I'm a spider. That's why he couldn't come with me into the Web. Spiders and birds don't exactly get along.'

'And Konstantin?'

'No. He's just a bear spirit who's old, smart and powerful enough that he can live in the centre world.'

'Centre world?' He let his confusion show in his voice.

'Picture a diamond. At the top is Seraph, at the bottom Eldritch, on the left Lost on the Right Legion. If you drew a line from each point to its opposite, you'd get what will still exist if our enemies succeed in their crazy ass plan. At the exact centre of all of it is the centre world. Our world, exactly neutral between light and darkness, order and chaos. It has no native magic of its own, and if you go too far from your native world, it becomes inhospitable.'

'Inhospitable?'

'Too hot, too cold, too dark, too bright. Too in or out of line. For example, if you walk into the Seraph world at the top, it would seem so rigid you would have no idea how to do anything. If you went to Eldritch you would find it almost, but not quite impossible, to figure out where the hell you are, what you're doing or how you exist, but you can go everywhere, we all can. That's why we're so valuable.'

'I mean, that's very important but we're off topic.' There was something ruminating in the back of Adam's mind, something about the time he'd had his mind taken over by the King of the Eternal Flame, but it would take some thinking in the background first. 'What happened to you?'

'I was essentially their pet when I was younger. I was cute and useful and nice.' She shrugged. 'We played together, me and the young spirits, who had enough individuality to think. Scarlett and I have been close since you were children. This is part of why I can't tell you how old I am. We, they, spiders, don't think of time like you do. I aged differently there and after a while I got to know the other spirits in the spider world. Eventually I moved to the carnival and became a performer.' She pointed at her dress. 'Alone, I'm quite a dancer, and a passable acrobat, but with my partner I was quite capable. My real gift was gathering intel, out thinking my own people. I built my web like we all build our webs, and I mastered being a spider. I learned to think in secrets and resources, in what's good for the colony, the species and myself. Over time I learned how to take things apart and put them back together. I learned schedules, resources, I learned to work people and most importantly I learned to put on a show.'

'And in the end, they let you take over the carnival?'

'In the end they didn't notice I'd taken over the carnival until it was far too late to stop me. I'd set things up with my sisters, cousins and aunts in order to make sure that no one could dispute my right to run the show. The carnival is the centre of our civilisation, and a few others besides. It's a neutral place for us to meet with representatives of other groups, which secured my position of importance.' She kissed him on the forehead. 'And now I do my best to make a society that spins.'

'So, do you have a mother?' He couldn't not ask. 'I mean you talk about sisters and aunts and...'

'Hell no.' She laughed a little. 'That would mean picking a favourite of my aunts, in front of all the others, which is a terrifying proposition.'

'Okay, so how'd you end up with the Lost?'

'It makes it easier to build webs on their side. The Legion might be more orderly, which we might think helps us find somewhere to hide, that would be wrong. See, the Legion doesn't allow corners, it doesn't leave dark places unscrubbed. They wash out the places where we could belong. While the war endures, the Lost being in the lead is good for us.'

'And if they win?'

'They won't.' Her voice was kindly amused. 'Only delusionals like Xavier think the war is ever going to end. They're going to fight, and one side is going to be winning, but neither side is ever going to win.'

'Nothing's ever going to change?'

'Things change all the time, and something major might.' She thought for a long moment before she continued. 'But if they do, it won't be as a result of the war. The only way the war ends is if both sides lose.'

'Wow. You realise I was trying to stay off serious matters, right?'

'You realise you asked a question that had a serious

answer, right?' she retorted. Finally, he felt ready, so he opened his eyes and tried to sit up again, clenching his fists and setting his jaw. He waited for the rush that would come as he hit his feet. He managed to, barely, stay upright, and Annabelle propped him up, helping him make his slow, partly staggering walk over to the table.

'So…' His voice was shaky. 'What's going on right now?'

'One of my aunts has kidnapped us, either because they sold us out to someone else, or because she doesn't like the new independent streak I've been showing by getting a boyfriend and spending time out of the world not on business.' She thought about it. 'Or she finds you interesting and has decided to kidnap you to chat with you.'

'Okay.' He sighed. 'That's screwed up. So, what do we do?'

'First I go talk to Aunt Wolf.'

'As in wolf?' Adam gnashed his teeth, growled and made a bad fake claw gesture.

'Spider. Wolf spider. She's not an actual wolf, don't be dense.'

'Yeah, well I was unconscious recently.'

'Yeah, anyway, we have a chat and find out who or what she has up her ass. Then we either negotiate or stage a break out, depending on how well this goes. We'll need to get our allies back, unless you feel like feeding the Legion brat to my family, and either way we need to secure at least one of the other prisoners.'

'She kept them?'

'She did. She never lets what's hers get away for free. They're probably still unconscious. I'll happily leave them with her as sacrificial lambs as long as we get to talk to one of them first.'

'That's, a little brutal.'

'They tried to murder us,' she reminded him, then lifted him gently over to the mask, and held him up while he pulled it onto his face.

'Welcome back.' The world went dark and the panther appeared behind him. 'I need to speak with you before you do what you do next. I need to make certain that we both understand the terms on which we are operating.'

'I'm not on anyone's side but mine,' he made it clear to the creatures. 'And yours, and maybe Annabelle's. Pan and the others I'll help out if I can, but I'm not taking part in any war. It's stupid.' He leaned down and petted the creature. 'That what you had in mind?'

'No,' it replied. 'But I understand.'

'If you have any interests you want to express, feel free.' He looked the creature in the eyes as he scratched it under the chin. 'We're a team here; if you want to direct us one way or another I'll certainly consider it.'

'No.' The creature had a soft purr in its voice, it was still a cat after all. 'I'm fine with us against the world for now, but I'm part of a greater whole and if the greater whole decides it has a problem with me, things may become complicated.'

'We'll deal with that when it comes.' He nodded. 'I have a few more immediate concerns. Are we still being watched?'

'We have been in the recent past, but not at this exact second.' Suddenly he was back in the world and with a little more ease he reached down for the Watcher's coat and pulled it on.

'Flushing the poison,' the Watcher reported. 'You'll be fully operational soon.'

'Good job both of you.' He leaned over and kissed Annabelle, then returned himself to speaking aloud. 'So, do I get other clothes? Or am I rocking the flasher look?'

'Actually, it's about time I taught you something anyway. Now this will be harder to do the closer you get to our world, so don't count on it.' She cupped him under the chin and fixed him with her eyes. 'Close your eyes and think about what the three of you make together, what you would look like combined. Then simply impose that will onto your outfit.'

'Okay.' He thought about the three of them, and then combined his image of the three of them. It would have to cover him almost completely, and he couldn't lose the white coat or mask. As he thought about it he felt things change on his body, the sound of cloth shifting and moving over his skin. After a few moments he heard Annabelle make a noise that he hoped was approval.

'How do I look?'

'Badass.' She took his hand and lead him, her free hand covering his eyes. 'Don't open your eyes, okay? I want you to see it. Hey!' She called outside. 'Can we get a mirror in here?' A few minutes later, and with her permission, he opened his eyes to reveal what he'd made.

The coat was long and white, and sat over black pants, black boots and a tight black shirt. The coat had a hood, which he could pull up over his head. The trim of both outfits was bright green and of course, looking back into his face, was the ever-grinning commando mask.

'I could have looked like this the entire time?'

'Yeah.' She had the decency to look shy. 'We just forgot to teach you.'

'And after all the time worrying about how I was going to prevent my wardrobe from being ripped apart every time.' He chuckled. 'It's kinda funny. All right, let's go.'

The woman at the head of the banquet hall was just as tall, thin, pale and imposing as she'd been last time. Her long black dress fell to the floor as she swished into the room. She flashed them all a welcoming smile and spread her arms wide.

'Welcome, Anna darling!'

'Don't let the fact she's being friendly fool you,' Annabelle spoke without moving her lips. 'This is the centre of her web as fully as Trapdoor was at the centre of his.' Then she ran across the room and launched herself into Wolf's arms in a bear hug. 'Auntie Wolf! It's a pleasure! A rather rudely conducted pleasure, but a pleasure nonetheless.'

'I know, darling and I'm so very sorry. I really am, but I had to make sure you'd come and stay. There's no way to do that without an element of force. You see, you've been keeping everyone out of the loop. You've all been keeping us guessing and now, all of a sudden, you turn up in my territory with that bloody great bear!' She released Annabelle and sat down. 'That thing has killed many of our people. This is becoming deeply concerning to us!'

'There are more important things going on than family business, Auntie.' Adam could see on her face that Annabelle realised she'd said the wrong thing as soon as she said it.

'I'm afraid that's simply not good enough, darling.' Wolf's voice went cold. 'There was a time when nothing was more important than the family business.' Annabelle lowered her head and sunk into her own chair.

'You're right, Auntie, and I'm sorry.' She reached out to Wolf Spider and took her hand. 'I'm sorry you don't think I'm good enough. I'm doing the best I can, for all of us. Sometimes that means building the web in directions I can't quite explain sometimes.'

'I am uncertain as to how exactly going off galivanting with strangers and killers benefits us.'

'Because you aren't aware of the whole picture, Auntie.' Her voice was soft and kind. 'Someone working on the web can't always see the whole structure until it's done. You just have to trust that it's there.'

'I fear you have used up your store of trust, my darling.' Wolf shook her head. 'You're going to have to explain some things to me.' So, Annabelle did, breaking it down easily and quickly as best she could. She told the entire story of the people weakening the barrier between dimensions that would collapse upon the universe, killing or forcing out everyone inside. Wolf was understandably humbled by the story and applauded at the end like a child.

'Well then you must go of course!' she agreed. 'I'm certain the three of you can manage nicely. You can take a couple of the units charged with weakening the boundaries with you for intelligence purposes as well.'

'Thank you, Auntie. I'm so glad you understand.' The entire speech sunk in. 'Wait, three?'

'Yes, dear.' She nodded, getting that "aggressively reasonable" look the elder always give to the younger. 'I'm afraid the bear can't be allowed to go with you. He's been evading our teams, our assassins and our agents for decades. He's dangerous, clever and insane and we won't be responsible for letting him go again.'

'Please, you must understand, as dangerous as he is we need him. We need that brute strength and ferocity. It will be a good deal more difficult for us otherwise. He comes in very useful.'

'If you can't complete this without that kind of main force, then you really don't deserve to be doing it at all. We're spiders darling. We don't rush in and brutalise our way out of problems. Frankly I'm surprised with you.'

'Understood.' She nodded and took her aunt's hand. 'This disappoints me, but I'll see you seen, Auntie. I promise when this is done I'll come by and tell you everything that's been doing on. I think it's been far too long since we got the whole family together.'

'Agreed.' The two of them air-kissed and the meal was completed with a measure of calm. They chatted about family matters while Adam ate.

By the time they got to the end of the meal it seemed like nothing was wrong, and Annabelle made her apologies before she headed off, collecting Claire before heading off into the darkness together. The three of them picked up two of the colours, orange and yellow seeming like the smallest threat, and carried them toward the exit. They'd almost reached it before something raised its pesky head.

'Guys, I'm sorry.' Adam's voice was soft. 'But I can't do this.'

'You can't do what?' Annabelle looked behind him, a confused expression on her face.

'Leave Konstantin behind.' He turned around and started heading back, stopped when each of the women grabbed him by one shoulder.

'The man is a murderer,' Annabelle snapped.

'The lady is right,' Claire agreed. 'He's quite mad.'

'Not to put too fine a point on it, but so are the rest of you. So is just about everyone I've met since all this started. I think the only person around here who isn't, is me.' Annabelle stepped away like he'd hit her. 'I don't like him any more than the rest of you, but he's part of my team. I agreed to him being with us, I convinced him to join up with us and that makes him my responsibility! He's on our side because of me and I'm not abandoning him.'

'He's a violent animal!' Annabelle shrieked.

'He's on my side!' He'd never yelled at her before, but it was too much; he felt so full of something he couldn't even describe. He forced it down, forced his voice back to normal. 'Listen to me. I can't save the world, I can't protect everyone. I'll do my best, but how can I even begin to know what that means if I can't protect the people I take personal responsibility for? I asked him to come with us, we got him arrested and you want me to turn my back. What kind of person does that make me?'

'The kind of person who can see the bigger picture.' She folded her arms.

'Yeah, well. I was never much good at that.' He turned away from her and looked at Claire. 'What do you think?'

'I'm not interested in risking my own life to save the bear.' She shrugged and stepped over toward Annabelle. 'You're on your own.'

'Yeah.' He shrugged. 'All right. Annabelle, if you can keep the way out open as long as you can, I'd appreciate it.'

'What if I say no?' Her eyes locked with his and she sounded hurt. 'What if I tell you you're on your own?'

'Then I guess I'll know I'm on my own.' He felt a

stabbing pain in his gut.

'Goddammit, Adam. This thing isn't even a person! It's an animal! It's a hungry, pissed off, stupid animal!'

'That's not a choice you get to make for me,' he replied. 'If I'm doing this alone, that's fine by me.' He shrugged. 'See you when I see you.'

'That is a profoundly stupid thing to do!' Annabelle called out at his back. 'If you get caught. When you get caught, I'm not sure if I can protect you!'

'I'm not asking.' He looked over his shoulder for a moment, then pulled up his hood. Once he was away he turned his focus inside.

'You two with me?' If the demigods in his own body were going to turn against him, he had no idea what he'd do.

'Nothing you said was exactly untrue.' The Watcher's voice was dispassionate. 'If we cannot protect those we are charged with watching over I fail to see where the line of those we protect should be drawn.'

'Sure. Let's go against an entire army of venomous creatures to save someone you don't even like.' The voice had some amusement in it.

'Are you making fun of me?'

'Even I don't know anymore, but I'm in. It sounds like a laugh.'

'Okay.' He nodded, letting out a sigh. 'I'll meet them once we get out.'

'I am uncertain you will be welcome.'

'If that's the way it has to be.' He didn't want to show how much that hurt, but he'd liked how this was going, he'd even begun to see a future. A slightly screwed up future, but still a future. He hoped this wasn't the end of it.

But he couldn't leave someone to die if he could do something about it. Especially if that only happened to a person because of him. He couldn't give up on that level of responsibility. He'd rather be wrong doing what he thought was right than be right doing what he knew was wrong.

He took a couple of breaths and moved back to Wolf Spider's camp. The wolf lived in a mismatched ramshackle settlement, an archipelago of web suspended islands, each one with a different kind of construction. They went form things as simple as yurts, to skyscrapers. He even saw a small castle on top of the islands. On each of those facilities was a range of people who Adam suspected either were spiders or served them. Anyone who saw him and figured out that he hadn't left would probably ask questions or raise an alarm. He'd seen enough spider magic to know a simple tug on the end of the web would alert everyone.

Which meant Adam couldn't be seen, couldn't fall off the islands and couldn't make too much of an impact on anything.

'Either of you have any idea where to start?'

'As usual, you may rely on me.' The Watcher took command. 'I will audio map your ears to the Bear's specific voices and noises. Keep moving, I will let you know when I hear something.'

'What if he's not making any noise.'

'Yes. What if our giant raging bear is making no noise at all at any given time? We shall just have to hope.'

'I'd figure the odds of that are about one in one,' the Laughing One quipped.

'Is there anything I can do to make this easier?' he asked them.

'Keep mobile and, if possible, get high.'

Adam sniggered to himself in spite of the seriousness of the situation then looked for the biggest skyscraper he could and made his way straight toward it.

'Okay. We can't go through the inside, there are too many people there. So, I'm going to climb up the side. Do we have the strength for that?' Of course, they did. 'Also, can we change our colours?' They could, not much but they could keep the glow down and mottle the white enough to make it look natural. He looked up and down the building, planned out his route and began to climb.

Even with an enhanced physique and claws it wasn't exactly easy to make his way up a sheer wall. After a lot of thinking, and a fair bit of effort he managed to stick his claws in and brace his knees against the wall. This allowed him a slow shuffling gait up the side of the building.

He ground his way up, stopping at the occasional window to rest for a moment. He did his best to keep quiet, though an occasional grunt of effort slipped out. He'd made it mostly to the top of the building when he felt his supernatural strength beginning to fade.

'Any chance we're going to make it before you two give out?' He shuffled up another agonising step, letting out a growl. 'Because if you two are holding something back now would be the time to tell me.'

'No.'

'I'm afraid not.'

'So, you two can get cocky.' He thought about that. 'That's something worth knowing, provided I don't die horribly. Okay, so I'm going for a window. I'd rather have to knock someone out or deal with an alarm than fall twenty stories to my death.' He pressed his ear to the window, standing on the narrow ledge.

Balancing lightly on the narrow sill he reached out and cut a hole in the piece of glass with one green claw. As it started to fall he caught the glass in one hand and, since there was no way to get it down without it breaking, he tossed it off the outside of the building. It shattered on the ground, but he didn't hear it.

'Hope no one heard that.' He sighed and began to slowly and agonisingly contort himself through the hole in the window. He lost his balance half way through, slipped and fell, landing on his hands on the office floor. He managed to turn it into a clumsy roll on the floor and pulled himself slowly and staggeringly to his feet. 'Any idea where the stairs are?' He looked around the corners and closed the door behind him. 'Okay, gotta find an exit, exit exit

exit.' He slowly but surely made his way through the rooms, keeping his senses open for the sounds of people or spiders walking.

He was on the stairs when he heard it for the first time, running up the wells because he couldn't trust the elevator. He was pretty sure he could climb back down, he just needed to get up there, give himself the room to see and hear everything around him, allowing him to find the bear. As he heard the door opening he leaped over the side of the stairwell and caught himself a floor down, pinning his body to the wall.

'What was that?'

'Door slamming?' The second voice had a chittering quality to it. 'You'd think the civilians would have the courtesy to appreciate that some of us have sensitive ears.' Don't breathe, Adam, don't move and don't breathe. Trust the Presence to mask you, keep the claws ready.

'You really need to get past this.' The Watcher's voice was in the back of his head. 'Going for the incapacitation will make it almost impossible to get them both without raising an alarm.'

'That's something I'll just have to live with.' He waited until the two of them turned the corner, then snapped out and slammed his face directly into the nose of the human, spreading it across his face. He lifted him as he started to run, stepping on the head of a hairy brown spider as he slammed the human into the wall.

'What are you doing What's going on?' He threw

the barely conscious human down the stairs and then drove his knee into the spider.

'Help! Help!' Came the chittering voice as Adam drove his knees into the furry body. He slammed his fist into the creature's head as it crawled and thrashed, trying to knock him off.

'If you throw me I'll have to kill you. Stand still and go to sleep.' The spider stayed still, and Adam slammed both hands into the green point the Laughing One put on the creature's head. It passed out and he made his way up the stairs. From that point on, whenever he heard people on the floors above him, he ducked through a door and waited til they passed, then picked up his pace again. It was only a matter of time before someone raised the alarm and Wolf sent her people, so he'd have to be elsewhere.

'I'm not going to get to rest at the top, am I?'

'Of course you will,' the Panther replied. 'Perhaps as much as five entire minutes.'

'I hate you. Okay.' He slashed the lock on the roof door and dragged his way up. 'All right Watcher, my senses are yours, do your thing man.' He made his way over to the side of the building.

'Pace a circle around the roof, move slowly and try to relax. I will be your eyes and ears.'

He felt everything around him growing dim as he walked. There was no colour anymore, the noises of the world around him, spiders chittering, electricity humming, there has been music coming from an island a long way away that he could no longer hear.

He could no longer see lights or make out distinctions in the things around him.

'Kill you!' The voice came into focus in the distance, the only thing he was noticing, clear and sharp. It as a half growled, half spoken tumble that was typical of the bear. 'I will rip each and every one of you limb from limb as soon as I get out of here.' There was a break before the bear let out a roar, and Adam's head jerked to the side. He ran over to the east side of the building and every time he blinked he got more and more long sighted. It was as if a computer was using his body to scan the world.

'Got it,' the Watcher reported. 'I am mapping your route.' As he started to mark green paths Adam felt a rush of pain through his head. He stumbled forward and looked behind him. He spied four men with weapons he couldn't identify, except for the fact he'd been hit with something that looked like a hammer. They spread out, giving him nowhere to run.

'I can think of somewhere we can run.' The green path was a short one.

'You want me to jump off the building?'

'Or you can fight four superior combatants.'

'I hate my life.' He looked at the four men facing him and let the feelings of panic and desperation come into his voice. 'You want to get your filthy poisons into me!' He screamed as loud as he could, then threw himself off the side of the building. It was a weak bluff he knew, but if it bought him a few minutes that it was a few minutes he could use to run away. 'Okay!' he called inside his head. 'Puny human wondering what the two outer gods are planning here!'

'Slow the descent with your claws?'

'That is not a plan!'

'It's the best I've got.'

'I hate both of you,' he let them know, then reached out and slammed his hands as hard as he could into the wall. It felt like his arms were going to rip out of their sockets.

'Your arms have been pulled from their sockets.'

'Less than thrilled to be right. Would you fix it?' Adam managed to go through an entirely singular experience. Over the next few seconds his shoulders were pulled out of and replaced in his sockets dozens of times. He pushed his hands in as deep as he could and allowed the walls to cause him the pain that meant he might survive. He even stuck his feet against the wall when he could for tractions sake. His claws slipped out a half-dozen times, leaving deep gouges broken up by feeble scratches, which turned back into holes as he managed to catch his grip.

He broke through a window, his claws ripping the glass and his chest and arms on the sill. He felt his breath leave his chest, let out a gasping cough and tried to catch onto the sill to break his fall a little, only to realise he'd moved too late and ended up scratching and fumbling his way back down.

'Well that was the worst thing I've ever done.' He avoided windows for the rest of his trip down, he was having enough trouble breathing as it was.

He began to seriously slow down just a few stories from the ground, but still ended up hitting it harder than he'd have liked. His legs jarred and collapsed under him, planting him on his back. He lay very still on the ground for a while and did his best to get his breath back.

'You need to be moving.' He heard the voice in his brain and gave the finger to his own mask.

'I need you to understand.' He said it softly. 'That during my short life I have been mind-controlled, imprisoned and tortured. I have had multiple parts broken and almost had my lower jaw removed. I have dealt with some of the most fantastic and miserable experiences a being is capable of. So, when I tell you that this was the most unpleasant thing I've ever done it isn't from a place of ignorance.'

'Be that as it may, you need to move.' The Laughing One was trying to be reasonable, but Adam could tell for right now even it didn't see anything particularly amusing. 'People will be coming to fetch the body eventually.'

'All this,' he grumbled darkly, 'for a bear I don't even like.' He took a few more steadying breaths, then hauled himself slowly and painfully to his feet. 'I'll handle this on my own for now. You two focus on healing me and getting your strength back. I'm going to need to be at 100% next time they find me.'

'You don't have any knowledge of stealth. At all.'

'Stick to the shadows, don't move when someone's looking at me. If anyone bothers me hit them as hard and fast as I can.'

'It will have to do.' The Watcher cut off its counterpart's objections. Adam's vision blurred for a moment, then showed him a green path to the bear. 'You are correct, Adam. We have no time to hesitate.'

Adam's world became a strange place, his own natural wonder tempered by the absolute desire to get the job done. He set off at a run, moving to the outskirts of the island. He couldn't quite risk jumping off and taking the web like the spiders did. There were usually bridges across the structures that connected them but most of them had too much web for him to take, so he had to make leaps and cling to the sides of structures before he could make slow, agonising progress back to the top.

Every time he heard people he went by the simplest plan he could think of, hiding behind whatever was close. He ducked behind tents, slipped into houses, and on one notable occasion he spent ten minutes hanging off the side of the island by his claws, waiting for a trio of gossiping spider women to pass him by.

'Please tell me I'm healing quickly.'

'Indeed, you are.' His body had a series of strange tingles running up it at various moments. The feeling grew more intense and disorienting during times when he had a few seconds to stay still in, as well as a few random moments which sent him stumbling.

His best chance was the fact that they didn't know he wanted to rescue the bear, or that he knew the way there. Even if they knew that they wouldn't know the route he was taking They'd have to waste time looking for him. They would likely fan out steadily, giving him time to craft a lead.

As long as–

'Hey!'

As long as he didn't get seen. Dammit.

'Yeah?' He turned around, pulling the mask down with one hand and slipping it into his jacket. 'What can I do for you?'

'You can tell me what you're doing here.' He was big, a little bigger than Adam, and showed no visible sign of spider parts.

'I'm on an errand.'

'For whom?' His eyes narrowed. He'd likely work for Wolf and know that Adam didn't. Just say something quickly, you don't have time to pause.

'Scarlett,' he blurted. 'From the Carnival. She said she had word that the Queen was here and wanted to send someone to ensure she as being treated well.' He advanced with a smile, realising that his shirt had vanished with the mask and he was standing in pants and a jacket.

'Really?' *Don't blurt, don't say anything, wait for him to make a move. Guilty people ramble so you can't.* 'Well you're out of luck.'

'Oh?' *Claws draw fast enough that you don't need them out in advance. Keep them inside.*

'She's gone. She left a couple of hours ago.' A couple of hours ago. That was disturbing, had he been here that long? He must have taken a long while climbing up the side. Adam sighed and ran his hands up his face, leaving him with a sad smile.

'Aint that always the way.' He sighed, then shrugged. 'Still, knowing her she'll have other business to settle and won't get back in a while. Maybe I can at least get credit for the message.'

'Wait a minute, that's not the way to Lady Wolf.' The man's eyes narrowed, and Adam forced out a very real noise of frustration.

'Seriously? Dammit I was sure I had this all figured out. Where did I get turned around? If Scarlett found out about this she'd never let me hear the end of it.'

'Next time tell her to send someone else.' He grabbed Adam by the shoulder and he supressed his natural urge to jump. 'That way, straight on and don't let anything slow you down or turn you. It's not that hard.'

'Thank you.' He nodded. 'Sorry, Sir.' The man, mollified by his submission, patted him on the shoulder.

'Just go.' Scorn entered the voice, but that was okay, if they were laughing at him they weren't suspicious. Adam set off at a jog to a rope bridge, or what seemed like one anyway. This time if he announced his presence they'd dismiss it. They'd have the report. He returned his mask to his face and set off, heading back into the shadows.

'The errand boy trick?' More scorn came from inside his own body. 'Really?'

'Oh would you shut up?' he snapped. 'It worked didn't it?'

'Only because he wasn't very bright and hadn't heard of you. If he encounters any of her servants they'll know where you are.'

'They'll know where I was,' he corrected. 'You know for a guy called the Laughing One you are not a happy go lucky soul. Will you stop taking what tiny amount of fun I was having in this situation out of it?'

'My dearest apologies, of course.' He felt a smile in the back of his head. 'Away then?'

'Away.' Adam, with renewed energy, began to jump from one small island to another on an ocean of debris over an abyss. He jumped and bounded from place to place, then made to last leap that would take him to one of a couple of dozen small islands that sat around his goal.

'Chances are this is where it'll get rough.' Pattern recognition was doing its happy work. He lowered himself to the ground and made his way slowly.

'You know,' he said as he took his place behind a clump of rocks. 'I really should count my blessings. Without you two to take care of this for me it'd be a real challenge finding all the guards.' As he spoke the two of them took his senses again, each of the guards and defences lighting up bright green. 'No wonder they use the island as a prison.' There was nothing around the large island that contained the prisoners. From those islands there were a few bridges, each one manned by dozens of guards.

'This could be complicated,' the Laughing One sighed.

Adam clapped his hands. 'On the contrary, my internal companion, this couldn't be any simpler; it just isn't going to be easy.' Finally, Adam got to have a plan all his own. Shame it was the exact same unpleasant thing he'd had to do last time.

As he approached the bridge and heard the guards chattering, Adam made his way to an island beside the one with the bridge. Slowly but surely, he made his way around the side, clinging to the edge of the island by his claws. He kept his face turned toward the wall, so his smile didn't show and used the Watcher's strange, other senses to know his surroundings. When he knew no one was around for a good while he climbed up and waited a moment, getting his breath.

Finally, he'd made his way to the side that was closest to the bridge and slowly, agonisingly, made ready.

'Okay kids.' He grinned under his mask. 'Now it's time for the stupid part.'

'Look at it this way,' the Laughing One taunted. 'Compared to the last plan this part is essentially sane.'

'That is not as reassuring as you might think.'

'Just trying to be happy go lucky.' The taunt didn't miss. Adam took a breath and swore under it as he jumped, slamming both of his claws into the side of the bridge without the expected sparks or rock cracking.

This would be so much easier if Annabelle was here, he grumbled to himself. If she had been she could have just webbed them across rather than making him hand over hand his way across solid stone. If only she hadn't been so stubborn about leaving him. Why couldn't she have understood? Why couldn't she have just stuck by him. Why couldn't she show some loyalty?

Sure, he was being stubborn, but she could have seen his side. She could have at least tried, just this once. He wanted this relationship to work, but he was trying to be part of her world and keep his principles as well. What was he supposed to do when she was willing to just up and leave?

'This is not helping.' The Watcher put an end to his self-pity like a door slamming in his face. He took the scolding, forcing Adam to concentrate on making his way slowly and certainly across the side of the bridge. 'Besides, if she was here, they'd detect the lines of silk and catch you immediately.'

Once he got up on the other side of the prison it was easy enough. Given that the island was practically impregnable they hadn't bothered to put a proper guard on the prison itself, there were a couple of them guarding a few dozen prisoners. As he walked, he kept his head down and moved at a sprint. If it was obvious to the prisoners he wasn't a guard and wasn't there to help them, hopefully they'd just leave him be.

'Dude!' someone called.

'Hey!'

'Over here!'

'What's going on?'

So much for that. Ignore them, keep your mouth

shut and just keep running. There's no need to bother with them. He slipped through the cells and moved to the side of the bear's cage. He began to climb up the thick mesh that surrounded him on every side.

'I'll kill you!' the bear bellowed. 'Whoever you are I can smell you! I'll kill you!'

'Would you shut the hell up for a minute?' Adam growled in the back of his throat. 'I'm here to get you out, you big oaf.' He thought for a moment. 'Actually, you know what? Go ahead and keep yelling threatening stuff, just don't aim it at me. Don't give any sense that anything has changed. Are you poisoned?'

'Not anymore.' He grunted, then raised his head, returning to the intimate and expansive vocabulary of threats. Inside the mesh cage he was held by webs. Adam moved to the door and examined the lock holding it shut carefully.

'On three, roar as loud as you can,' he muttered. 'One, two, three.' On cue the ear-splitting roar rang out. Adam slammed his claws through the lock and caught it as it fell through the air. He slipped it into his jacket and climbed inside, heading over to the webs. 'Now hold still'

'Where are the others?'

'Sorry I'm all you get. The Wolf Spider refused to let you go, so the others all left.'

'Then what's your game?' The bear looked up at him, his yellow eyes flashing. 'Why come back?'

'That's not what we call holding still,' he grunted,

sawing through the webs. 'Besides, we had a deal. You agreed to stick with me til this was done, remember?'

'You made no such agreement.'

'It was an implied agreement.' He slit the web. 'When you joined the team, you became part of the team.'

'I owe you.' The bear seemed decidedly displeased about it. 'You let the rest of the team abandon you because you were not willing to abandon me.'

'Yeah well, life's a series of cruel ironies.' He dismissed it. 'Go back to threatening the guards, will you? Not too much though, we don't want them to actually come over here to shut you up.' The bear did so, returning to threats. This time he went with anatomical specificity, informing them of his plans for everyone around him. After a few more minutes he'd hacked the webs to pieces. 'Okay.' He smiled. 'I think it's weak enough that you should be able to muscle your way out as soon as we have a plan.'

'A plan?'

'We don't have a way out of this dimension,' he whispered. 'The spiders aren't exactly friendly, and I can't cut my way through dimensional barriers. Can you?'

'No,' he growled. 'First things first, we get out of Wolf's territory. Once we're clear I'll be able to scare someone bad enough to get us out of here.'

'How exactly do we plan to get out of her territory?'

'I can move fast enough.' He pulled himself to his paws. 'As long as they don't web me too bad.'

The man on guard duty was a consummate professional. He was clever, disciplined and capable, and had a trio of associates who were also clever, disciplined and capable. They were ready, they were prepared for any event. They were fearless and absolutely devoted to their cause.

So they thought, anyway.

That adaptability, capability and fearlessness were all tested that day, when a creature from the nightmare of someone with a crippling phobia of bears came barrelling across the bridge. A human, with a bright green smile clung to its back, letting out a sharp peal of hysterical laughter that split the air. As he prepared his weapon, the bear's massive bulk smashed into the gate, bringing it down with a thundering boom. The man with the smile jumped from the bear's back and cut the guard's weapon in half, picking him up and pushing him into the path of his comrade's gun. Three bullets thudded into his back as he was pushed into his compatriot. The two remaining guards put a few shots at the bear, but never got close to anything important.

'This is awesome!' Adam yelled, settling onto the bear's back.

'This is humiliating,' the bear complained.

'You want to be dignified and dead, or humiliated and alive?'

'Right.' He careened into a pair of spiders, doing

their best to hold the line, and Adam, with one hand bunched in the flesh of the bear's neck, swung down and hacked away at the webs. 'Alive it is.'

'Then shut up and haul ass!' He jumped off Konstantin's back, knocked a shock trooper aside, punched him twice in the face and jumped back on. 'Left here!'

'What?'

'My Presences know the shortest way out! This way!'

He picked up the pace, knocking a tent aside and stepping on a pair of people who were in the middle of some inappropriate act which will only be alluded to here. He built up his momentum and jumped as far as he could, landing in a shambling heap on the next island. Adam leaned back and clenched his legs tightly, swinging his claws to cut balls of web away. They ended up coating Konstantin's fur, and Adam's chest and arms.

'Do I fight these guys or?' Adam addressed the Presences

'Just hold them off.' The Laughing Man rolled off the Dread Bear's back, launching at the guards who were following him. He saw the venom spit coming from one of their mouths, and turned, billowing the coat behind him and letting it get hit. He looked the two of them in the eyes and glowed his mask.

'You realise if you slow him down, he'll turn around, and if he turns around you both die?' One of them hesitated and the Laughing Man tackled him, shoving him off the side of the island. It wouldn't really hurt him, since his partner was a spider, and sure enough a web was already coming down to catch his falling comrade. Adam jumped back onto the bear, yanking himself up the fur without a word of protest from either side.

Konstantin kept running, smashing through a house wall, his head and shoulders tucked in as he charged his way through doorways, walls and people alike. It became a game of follow the lights, as Adam jumped to, slashed and kicked whatever the Presences told him were the right things to go after, as Konstantin followed the path he laid out. He sprang, tumbled, launched, whirled and hung from various parts of the giant creature's body to deflect incoming webs, avoid enemy attack and not get sent sprawling off the bear's back by the remains of the structures they were going through. Occasionally they ran into issues, a wall or person Konstantin couldn't immediately break through, or something that knocked Adam off the bear's back. It only held them for a moment before the other found a way the first couldn't create.

Adam didn't want to kill anyone, and as far as he could tell he didn't. To the best of his knowledge the people Konstantin trampled underfoot didn't die, probably, but he couldn't worry about that. There was no time. He just had to keep moving.

'Do you have a plan?' the voice cut through his moralising.

'I thought we were doing your plan.'

'I mean past the next few minutes.'

'With any luck we'll hook up with Annabelle and the others.'

'And if they don't want the trouble we provide?'

'Then I'll think of another way to do this,' he snapped. 'Maybe I'll get Xavier or someone on my side.' He sighed at the gruff laughter that came from the running bear.

'You, me and the Red Gentleman? What a merry time you'll have trying to keep the chaos and carnage reigned in.'

'Yeah. That's why this isn't exactly plan A.' He laughed in spite of himself. 'Look, I'm Lost for a reason. I'm not a great strategist, I mostly just do whatever seems a good idea.'

'This seemed like a good idea?'

'It seemed like the right thing to do.'

'Even that seems unlikely.'

'Oh, shut it!' he snapped. 'We're running out of time. They're gaining on us!' It was true, everyone had realised that the bear was free, and they were no doubt even now figuring out what they were planning. Soon enough there'd be obstacles the giant creature couldn't push through.

'We're getting close.' Somehow the big creature could sense it. 'Once we're in someone else's territory they'll need to get permission to follow. It'll give us time to get clear.'

'They'll be waiting for us at the border.' He leaned

down to look the bear in its bright yellow eyes. 'Talking works faster than moving.'

'Should we turn?'

'No point.' He shook his head. 'That'd just give the ones behind us time to catch up'

'So, our choice is between letting an army catch us, and running right into their ambush?'

'Yeah, spoiled for choice, aren't we?' He was used to laughing when no one else was, so he was pleasantly surprised to hear the bear's dark chuckle mirror his own.

'We go through then,' the giant growled. He smelled like blood and hate, debris, web and cloth sticking to his fur. Despite that, or maybe because of it, his muzzle was tilted in something Adam almost imagined was a smile.

'Did you decide that for a reason? Or just because it'd be fun?'

'Both.' He picked up his pace further. 'And since I'm driving, I suppose you're out of options.'

'I was going to say charge anyway.' He held on for dear life and ducked as a figure that had inspired such fear in him, who even Xavier had been afraid of taking on directly, barrelled straight into the trap they'd built for him. 'In about ten seconds slam to a halt and throw me forward with your head.' He heard no confirmation as he counted off the time, but nine seconds in he felt the bears muscles bunching beneath the fur, and the bear threw him clear.

The webs in their path would have been invisible

to a normal eye, they'd been made that way by a master, designed to be strong enough to slow down the bear a little without ever being visible. Unfortunately, the Laughing One's eyes had come into play. He flew, tumbled head over heels and began to lash out at the strands. He couldn't cut through them fast enough to avoid being caught in them, but he managed to hack through in a few more seconds. By the time the bear got there he was sticky and stiff, but able enough to jump onto his back. As he landed he saw the ambushers moving, bewildered by the interruption, but determined to do the job nonetheless. 'You ready, big lad? This could get ugly.'

'I like ugly.' He chuckled.

'You are ugly.'

'Beauty is only skin deep.' He picked up his pace.

'I strongly suspect you're ugly on the inside too.'

'Yeah well, it's also subjective.' He slammed into the first layer of the ambush.

Behind a dozen soldiers stood the Lady Wolf Spider herself. She was as beautiful and imposing, as pale and uncompromising as death. On either side were a couple more of her people. The dozens of them would have been quite a spectacle, given their colours sizes and species varied wildly, if only they'd stopped to appreciate it.

'You have decided to disobey me after all,' she began, obviously expecting there to be time to make speeches. 'You have disobeyed me, and my niece and made the stupid, desperate mistake of–' The words broke off into a scream, as they refused the expected speechifying and barrelled straight into her at the surprising top speed of the bear. She was knocked flying for a loop, both metaphorically and literally, sprawling out of their path as the dozen moved in. Adam readied himself on top of the bear, his eyes sharp for the attack.

The spears came first, and Adam swatted most of them out of the air, the others digging into the bears bulk. The webs slung at him and he took the brunt of them, only to have his arm pinned to his side by the white. He guarded the bear as best he could with his one remaining hand, parrying without reprisal as the bear ran.

It was the Wolf Spider herself that finally got him, a close fist strike to the Dread Bear knocked him sprawling tail-over-head and Adam toppled off, rolling twice to get to his feet and trying to free his webbed arm.

'What do I do?' Konstantin locked eyes with him. He knew already that the bear could only kill so many. Only momentum was keeping them safe.

'Go!' He lunged for the Wolf spider, his claws making a desperate strike she deflected with almost contemptuous ease. 'Get help!' Being Annabelle's boyfriend should buy him a few days, he hoped.

Konstantin grunted, gave a nod and ran out of her territory at a full tilt, the few webs clinging to his body breaking on his feet as he moved. Adam grabbed Wolf with both hands and held her still as best he could.

'I'm under arrest, aren't I?' He commanded the

Watcher and the Laughing One to stay on him when he passed out, no matter the cost to his body. He'd need them.

'I believe so dear.' Then she smashed her forehead into his face.

CHAPTER NINE

'I really need to stop waking up here.' Clearly, they had started the attempt to remove his Presences, and ended up tearing away his skin. They'd clung to him as ordered, and as a result as he flicked open his eyes he almost screamed with the pain. 'You both okay?'

'Stayed on as ordered,' the Watcher muttered. 'Spent some time healing. Well enough now.' Its voice was pained, but strong.

'How long has it been?'

'Twelve hours or thereabouts.' Adam scowled and tried to pull his way free. 'Don't bother. We already tried.'

'While I was out?'

'Had to be done. We would have woken you up once we got through.' The Laughing One's voice had a shrug in it. He didn't know what he'd expected, remorse? It wasn't capable.

'Guards come in three times an hour, except for the last two hours, in which they came twice each.'

'Is that relevant?' he addressed the Watcher.

'Not at the moment,' it conceded. 'I have not yet factored in all the possibilities, so it could eventually be vital in our escape, should you desire.'

'Why would I not want to escape?'

'Because the last time you escaped you only survived the experience due to the Wolf Spider's decision not to kill you?' It was a suggestion they both gave, the Watcher matter of fact, the Laughing One

214

full of scorn. 'Or because last time you had a rampaging bear and still failed to make it out?' That one was just Laughing One.

'Yeah, but I might be able to escape on my own.'

'They will be familiar with our paths now,' the Watcher informed him. 'There is very little chance that stratagem will work again.'

'Okay, so what do I do?'

'Negotiate, stall and hope that you put your faith in the right people.'

'You mean Konstantin?'

'Or your actual allies and friends, if he can get hold of them.'

'He knows where they are.' He closed his eyes and let his body relax. 'I guess I'll go back to sleep for a while then. Are you two okay to keep watch? I need to waste a bit of time and I see no other reason to stay conscious.'

'Get some rest.' He closed his eyes and another six hours disappeared like that.

The next time he woke up it was in the presence of the Wolf Spider, who looked down her nose at him. She let him clear his head for a moment before she spoke.

'Why would you do this?' Her voice wasn't accusatory, just honestly inquisitive.

'Which part? I've done a lot of stuff recently.'

'Why would you risk a mission you described as crucial, that you seemed to truly believe was the end of several dimensions, not to mention attacking and badly wounding several of my men and yourself just to save a savage creature you have known only days.'

'Because everyone has to draw a line somewhere and I made a deal. That moment he became part of my team. Whether I know him or like him is irrelevant. We agreed to stop this together, and he would have done the same for me.'

'He left,' she pointed out.

'Right. Let me rephrase; he is currently doing the same for me.' He made a show of relaxing and closing his eyes again. 'The way I see it, everyone can choose to be part of the solution or part of the problem, and Konstantin chose to be part of the solution.'

'So, what does that make me?'

'Maybe they'll get it done without me, maybe we'd have gotten it done without him. Either way, when you decided to get in the way you became part of the problem.' He opened one eye and fixed it on her. 'I'm sorry, but your lack of foresight is going to cost everyone something, including you, unless you wise up.'

'How dare you?' She took a breath to continue her tirade and he laughed.

'Sorry, it's just, I've always wondered if people actually said that and it turns out someone does! How dare you? Seriously? Okay, I dare because you took away a resource from someone trying to save your entire dimension because of the past.' He sighed.

'You have no idea what that thing has done!'

'Yeah well, I can't look backward. Makes us a pair

since you can't look ahead. So, what now?'

'What now?' She seemed taken aback. 'What do you mean what now? After what you just said to me?'

'Well, I'm mostly bored at this point so let's move on to the next thing. Move onto the torture, or interrogation or hostage situation or whatever you're doing. Annabelle would probably pay to get me back if you care, but there's no one else and I don't really know anything So unless you're going to be torturing me for fun there isn't much good I'll do you.'

'Perhaps I should simply kill you.' She placed one hand on his neck.

'Maybe you should, but that'll piss off Annabelle. Possibly Xavier and Pan as well, that's the Lost Soldier and the Red Gentleman to those who don't know them well. Oh, and the Dread Bear says he owes me, but he already doesn't like you much so the risk there is negligible.' Once he was thinking it was hard not to keep talking. It was how he flowed.

'Why won't you cooperate?' She seemed to be close to a tantrum.

'I thought I was.' He let the confusion into his voice. 'I told you your options, tried to figure out how to facilitate your motivation. What am I supposed to do? Beg?'

'Well.' She paused for a moment. 'It may help a little.'

'If I thought there'd be any tangible result, I'd give it a try.' He really would, he wasn't too proud. 'What do you want from me. I don't know how to help you!'

'Why did you have to free the bear?' She pouted, the floor cracking as she stomped her foot. 'He was supposed to face justice! You stole my justice!' '

'And you stole my ally.' He sighed, he would have liked to run his hands through his hair, but they were tied down. 'Well, with any luck he'll be back in a couple of days and one of us can get what we want.'

'Would you stop being so damn, cooperative?' She was angry now, clutching her clothes and stumbling her words. He was stalling quite well he thought.

'Weren't you upset with me a moment ago for not cooperating enough?'

'Yes, but, no. Cooperate better!'

'How? What am I supposed to do?'

'Give me something worth having!'

'The best thing you can do is call Annabelle or wait for the bear. Or, better yet, just let me go. I'll leave, and we can part friends!' That was not likely.

'You wounded my people,' she snapped, turning away from him. 'I will ask the rest of the family what to do and we can act from there.'

'You know I'm going to get out eventually, don't you?' he called out. 'These claws aren't just for show!'

She thought about this for a moment, turned around, walked back to him, and bit him hard on the arm. A few seconds later he was out.

The Wolf Spider was feeling frustrated, but essentially pleased with herself for yesterday's antics. She was certain one of her cousins would know what to do, and if not, she could certainly wring some concessions out of the Carnival in exchange for the return of the Queen's pet human.

'Excuse me, Miss?' One of her white tails returned to her, looking up into her eyes. The poor wretch was physically shaking as he looked at her, and no wonder. She knew full well she did not take bad news with restraint.

'Speak boy! Let's have it out!'

'The Dread Bear is on the border of your territory.' His voice wavered. 'He demands the release of the Laughing Man, immediately'

'He demands?' He winced at her words. 'Under what authority does he demand?'

'He claims if you do not there will be immediate and violent retribution.'

'From whence will this retribution come?'

'Presumably himself. There is someone with him, a small white clad man with a firearm but I am uncertain what use he would be.' Poor boy thought he was supposed to think.

'An assassin with a plan perhaps?'

The boy thought about this. 'His associates have included assassins thus far.' He nodded. 'So, will you be going in person, Madam?'

'Yes.' It was a frustration to go to this much effort just for one idiot human, but she had committed to this course of action, and she could at least bring the bear back to his cell. 'Bring me my personal guard. If they would care to attempt violence I will not be found wanting.' It was, with a measure of confidence and a small army of her faithful enforcers, that she made her way to the entrance.

She watched the two of them for a long moment, one was the Dread Bear, in his human form. There he was, a large, ugly, squared jawed fellow with a brown suit and too many teeth. The other man was slight and pale, dressed all in white and holding a gun with a scope in both hands. Surprisingly it was the man with the gun, who she had never seen before, who seemed to be most at ease. The Dread Bear clenched and unclenched his fists, twitched and paced. She watched the two of them for a moment before allowing herself to be seen.

'You have a prisoner. I need him back. Made a deal,' he grunted.

'You are very impolite.' She looked at the calm one. 'I know the Dread Bear, and I am the Lady Wolf Spider. I do not know you.'

'I am known to some as the Knife from Nowhere.' He smiled. 'And others as the Forgotten Eye. It is my current job to facilitate the return of the Laughing Man.'

'And if I refuse to return him?'

'The methods will change, the objective will not.' His gun hummed softly, and he pointed it at her.

'That shot will not land.' She was absolutely confident.

'Problematic.' He yawned. 'But not insurmountable. Now, kindly release the prisoner.'

'I will not. Now, are you finished threatening me? Because I have things to do.'

'No.'

'Thank you, now can we get to...' She paused. 'I'm sorry, what?'

'No, I am not finished threatening you. On the contrary I have only begun.' He put his fingers in his mouth and let out a wolf whistle that split the air. From behind him came a small army of Blank Faced Legionnaires. The faceless black and white figures fell into line behind them.

'Not bad, but not nearly enough.' She smirked.

'Seriously?' He snapped at the world in general. 'I gave the signal!'

'I am not your minion,' came the voice from the shadows.

'Well, no. I appreciate that, but it's less a matter of authority and more a matter of using planning and effective communication for maximum effect.'

'Oh. Right.' The voice sounded embarrassed. 'We're sorry.' Two figures stepped out of the shadows.

'Are you?'

'Yes.' The man in the red coat tipped his hat.

'And you are?'

'Six of Nothing.' He bowed. 'Yes indeed.'

'How?' She turned to the Dread Bear, tearing at her hair. 'How did you, you of all people, with no friends in the world, manage to compile an army of Legionnaires and the two finest agents of the Red Ladies?'

'Well, as it turns out,' the Dread Bear cleared his throat awkwardly, 'they like the kid.'

'Okay.' Adam took a deep breath, looking from one face to another. 'How the hell did you get this together?'

He was back in his own world, standing beside the four of them and their small army of black and white monsters. Where before it had been frightening to see them, since they wanted to kill him, it was far more disturbing to be standing among these strange twisted creatures when they weren't even reacting. There was a small army of the faceless creatures, their limbs and torsos twisted and distended. They just, chilled, swaying and shifting in formation.

'Truthfully, wasn't even hard.' Konstantin shrugged. 'He was there waiting for me when I stepped across the barrier, with that rifle of his pointed at my face.'

'That's how he opens most conversations as far as I know.' Adam shrugged. 'It's how he opened all the ones we've had so far.'

'Only with people who have good reasons to kill me.' He thought about it. 'And, as I am technically your enemy and I've been spying on you, I'm certain you all qualify. I don't actually want to fight any of you, I simply wanted to be certain none of you would immediately kill me. Which, since none of you have thus far done, has a one hundred percent success rate as a conversational gambit.'

'So, we got some troops together and came to get you back.'

'And you picked him?' Adam pointed at Xavier.

'Well, you did suggest it.'

'You laughed it off!'

'When I thought we had other options. Now we don't.' He shrugged. 'I found the Red Gentleman and his weird little friend there. The gunner over there got a little army together to make up the numbers.'

'And I agreed to assist you out of a deep personal affection for…'

'Pan blackmailed you, didn't he?'

'…my deep personal affection for not being blackmailed by Peter.'

'And what exactly is that guy doing here?' He pointed to Six of Nothing, who wasn't paying attention.

'I felt bad about killing all those people.'

'That's no truer than his first answer is it?'

'No, indeed it is not,' he agreed. 'I want to abuse their methods for my own purposes.' He looked around. 'I was not supposed to admit that.'

'That is not the case!' Xavier seemed appalled. 'We are only here to help!'

'You're lying.'

'Yes,' he admitted. 'I thought I was better at it than that.'

'So, what the hell is your actual game?'

'I am not going to tell you that.' He smiled. 'Suffice it to say, as the dimensional barriers become thinner, interesting things will happen. I would like to take advantage of that eventually, if that's at all possible. To that end, I need to examine how they do it.'

'So, you want the bad guys to win?'

'On the contrary!' He raised one finger. 'If you don't succeed, all of my friends die. All my vested interests are in this! I also intend to take advantage, so do your best. I have the utmost confidence in you.'

'Really?'

'Not even a little.' He smiled. 'If you fail I have another half dozen plans in place.' He patted Adam on the back. 'But you're my first resort, so do your thing!'

'Okay.' He turned away and looked over at the guy with the gun. 'What's your deal? You shoot at me, then try to start a reasonable conversation with me at gunpoint, and now you come to my rescue. Would you like to make an abundance of sense to me very quickly?'

'I absolutely would.' He smiled at Adam. 'But you don't have that kind of time, or context. The best I can do is tell you that I have been tasked by a very intelligent being with a unique perspective to keep you safe and operational if at all possible.'

'So that's how you always seem to know where I am?'

'It's part of it,' he admitted. 'Part of it's my own rather unique set of gifts.'

'You know I haven't actually seen you do anything to protect me.'

'No.' He flashed a smile. 'You haven't'

'Then why are you helping me? You're Legion, and I'm Lost.'

'Technically in both cases you are correct, but as I said to you last time, it's much more complicated than that.' He sighed and waved one hand, like he was swatting a fly. 'In the meantime, you need to go back to the Carnival and speak to the Queen.'

'There's going to be some problems there.' He cleared his throat. 'We didn't exactly part on the best of terms.'

'Well then, by all means allow that to collapse the dimensional boundaries and kill millions of people, because heavens forbid you should feel awkward.' Xavier put his hand over his heart.

'Well, fuck you very much.' He sighed. 'I'm going.' He looked over at Konstantin for a moment. Was this really the ally he'd chosen? 'Can you get us there the same way you got us there last time?' The big man thought about it, shrugged and wrapped an arm around Adam's shoulders, dragging him away from the group.

'You smell foul,' Konstantin informed him.

'Like you don't.'

'Yes, but I'm used to my stink, and my nose is better than yours. I'll take you somewhere you can shower and eat before we go.'

Adam had been expecting a flop house, what he showed up to was a hotel that looked way too expensive and exclusive to let either of them in. Surprisingly they nodded to him and let him head to

225

the elevator.

'You have a room here?' he guessed.

'I have suites here and a few other places. Also have standing reservations at restaurants nearby, paid for by your kind to keep me happy.'

'Man, they never bought me anything,' Adam complained.

'You don't turn into a half tonne killing machine.'

'I do not at that.'

'Well, when you figure that one out you might get yourself paid.' He headed into the suite, collapsing into a leather armchair. The place was opulent beyond opulent, with sheets that had a thread count that was probably a very high number that Adam didn't understand. The view was nice, and the furniture was cosy.

'Ordering food, you can have whatever you want as long as it's meat.'

'Rib eye, medium rare, fries on the side,' Adam grunted.

'You like whiskey?'

'Don't hate it.'

'Good enough!' He placed the order, then lay back down in his chair

'You're being surprisingly pleasant.'

'Hungry,' he grunted. 'Besides, don't get to eat with people. Like it.'

'Thought you hated people.'

'The ones who talk too much.' He bared his teeth and Adam shut up, heading for the bathroom and taking a wash. After a dozen none too subtle hints about his own body odour the Dread Bear made his way to the shower and emerged ten minutes later muscular, scarred, hairy and complaining as he scrubbed himself with a towel.

They ate together, watching something on TV neither of them was particularly invested in. It seemed like the big man could understand the need for a moment's peace. The two of them got a steady stream of meat dishes brought up to the room as they filled their bellies with about ten people's worth of food between them. At the bottom of the bottle of whiskey the hotel had supplied him with Konstantin slapped his knees and got to his feet, cracking his neck back and forth.

'Okay! Transport should be here any second now.'

'Really?'

'Why do you think I turned on the TV?' Adam had no idea what the hell he was talking about until the television in question began to blur into snow. The static began to blur, ripple and take on a variety of vague shapes that reminded Adam of one of those magic eye puzzles. After a few more minutes the screen solidified into something he could start to recognise.

It turned into the outline of a person, that seemed to be walking toward them. The shape became clearer and clearer as it filled the screen. As it got closer the static started to leak through the screen, spreading into a head, shoulders and legs out of the screen. He started to push further and further out of the screen until it was a complete man, who tripped and landed on all fours.

He shook his head and began to solidify, his body turning into a black and white blur, then into a man whose entire body was laid out like a checker board. He looked at them, cracked his knuckles, tossed his head and turned into a pale man in a black suit. He looked around for a moment and his eyes widened.

'Konnie!' He sounded like an excited child, running up and wrapping his arms around the big man's shoulders. 'Konnie! How are you?'

'Not in front of company!' He pushed the smaller man away. The man in the suit looked around for company for a moment, saw Adam and waved excitedly. 'Boy, can you at least try to act like you have some professional discipline?'

'Right, yeah right!' He clapped his hands, then straightened up and presented his hand for Adam to shake. 'I am Traveller Vanish.'

'Your name is TV?' He chuckled.

'That is a thing that people call me for short!' The little man seemed excited.

'Short is also a thing people call you.' That inspired a slight pout, and a shaky chuckle.

'I'm the Laughing Man. Nice to meet you.'

They shook hands and Konstantin nodded. 'Well, now we've all had our fond hellos can we please get to the Carnival and stop the world from ending?'

'You know, normally this would be where I

complain about you wasting our time showering and eating.'

'But you just realised that we were waiting for TV to show up?'

'That's right.' He nodded. 'Let's go.'

'Okay then.' TV clapped his hands. 'Here's what needs to happen. All you gotta do is take a hand and walk with me. Keep walking mind, no matter what, just keep your head forward, and ignore everything you see.'

'What am I gonna see?' He understood, spider dimension rules.

'No freakin' idea.' TV shrugged. 'Television is a big place.'

'What do you mean?'

'Just do as you're told.' TV nodded. 'We are not, as I understand it, blessed with some grand abundance of time.'

'You are correct.' He nodded. 'All right.' He took the man's hand and followed him. He felt the static rush in to fill his senses as they walked toward the TV. As they moved the screen grew larger and larger, their senses filling with the equivalent of white noise. If you don't know what white noise feels like, well to Adam it was like having his skin rained on by rain that wasn't wet.

'Already hating this!' he called.

'This is the easy part!' TV replied at a shout. 'The hard part's coming up, so just keep moving, okay?' Adam took a deep breath of flavourless air and strode out into the nothingness. As they walked through the static it began to slowly clear and he was in a world.

'Okay. So, the hard part's coming?' That had been a little too easy.

'Yes indeed.' As he said it Adam was bombarded with images from every perspective. Celebrities danced and argued, fought and screwed, they laughed and cried and did a thousand other things around him. Monsters from the imaginations of the greatest minds of cinema and television slaughtered people in front of his eyes. As he watched a serial killer from the golden era of film lunged at him, knife drawn. Adam drew up his free hand to block it, but TV pulled him forward and the image changed to the most beautiful woman he'd ever seen, naked in front of him. He watched her for a moment, his mouth agape and tried to keep moving while every emotion in his body begged him not to.

The next fifty steps were pure sexual bombardment, a rush of screaming, lights and gunfire. He refused to stop moving, but he dearly just wanted to just fall on his face and clutch at his ears, screaming.

'Don't... lose... my grip!' The boy seemed to know what he was feelings and somehow, through the Watchers intervention he didn't doubt, he was able to hear his voice even over the din. He just kept walking forward, closing his eyes and trusting his feet.

He opened them again after a moment because he simply couldn't imagine his eyes being closed as any kind of good idea. For all he knew, all the things he was seeing were just as solid and dangerous as they would have been in real life. If that was the case, he didn't want to be eyeless as well as everything else.

Konstantin wasn't doing much better than Adam by the looks of it. He salivated and snapped at creatures only he could see, lines of drool falling from the sides of his mouth. TV kept up a steady stream of encouragement as he led them through, calm as if he was talking to a spooked puppy. Adam couldn't hear the exact words, so he just kept his head down and kept focused on the peaceful voice in his ears. Monsters reared up in front of him, then the world went into monochrome for a while and for a few steps Adam could have sworn he'd turned into a cartoon.

He had a gangster's bullet flying right at his face and had to duck as he lunged forward out of sheer terror, he almost lost his grip on TV's hand as the bullet whizzed past where his face had been. As he tugged, TV tripped and fell, pulling Konstantin with him. The big man secured a grip with both hands, yanking them back. As they sprawled in front of him he lifted the two of them gently off their feet, with exaggerated care, like he was doing his best not to break something fragile, then put them back down.

The images got more and more regular as time went on, images often flickering into different things six or seven times a step. Gangster, kiss, monster, murderer, giant bug, lizard, corpse, car speeding directly at his face. All he could do was keep moving.

God, he needed to be out of this. He needed to get out, he needed, he needed, what did he need, where was he? What was going on? Why was he here?'

And then he stepped out of the TV in the manager's office in the Carnival.

The manager was a large man Adam knew as Max, who never went outside because his human form wasn't quite human enough. His limbs were longer by half than any human arms could be, and he still had four segmented eyes. At the moment he held a pistol in each hand, covering TV and Konstantin. 'Laughing Man. What are you doing in my television with a young man and a bear?'

'Point that at him one more second and I'll wear your goddamn guts,' Konstantin growled, and the man turned the other gun on Konstantin as well.

'I needed to talk to Annabelle,' Adam explained.

'And you had to break into my office to do that because?'

'She's busy, and I'm not completely sure she wants to talk to me right now.'

'If you aren't sure she wants to speak with you, may I recommend you honour those wishes by leaving?' His tone was aggressively reasonable.

'Look,' Adam spoke through gritted teeth. 'Can you just ask her? Please? If she doesn't want to talk to me that's fine but I didn't have time to wait for Scarlett or one of the others who can be bothered talking to me to show up!'

'Very well.' Max nodded his head just a little

further than a human would. 'I shall contact the queen. Please wait outside.

'Umm, Konnie, can I?' TV tugged on Konstantin's sleeve.

'Yeah, kid.' He nodded. 'Head out.' He tousled the young man's hair and TV nodded and walked back into his namesake, disappearing from sight. Adam and Konstantin looked at each other for a moment, then headed out into the carnival grounds. Konstantin sat down at a table and Adam sat across from him.

He wasn't usually comfortable with silences, but the knowledge that Konstantin didn't really want to talk, and the Laughing Man's sense of opportunity meant he knew for a fact there was nothing to be gained from conversation.

'So, who's TV?' And yet he still wasn't comfortable with silence for some stupid reason.

'None of your goddamn business.' Adam raised his hands to motion that he was backing off and went back to staring into the distance. Konstantin let it stand for a few more long moments before he spoke. 'He's just some kid I know. I don't know if he can grow up, or just doesn't, or if he just does it real slow but he's been a kid for decades. We help each other out from time to time.'

'And why does he call you– '

'Nothing good can possibly come from you repeating what he calls me, ever, for anyone.' Konstantin's voice had a growl in it.

'Got it.' Maybe he wasn't such a monster after all.

Then he looked over to the cart where Konstantin had threatened to murder his way through the entire carnival, got up, and walked away to wait elsewhere.

CHAPTER TEN

Annabelle didn't make any effort when she came out. She didn't, as he had feared, send someone to come with an entourage to throw him out. She didn't, as he hoped, come running into his arms to apologise for ever doubting him. She just walked over and sat down beside him. They looked at anything but each other for a good, long time.

'I'm glad you made it out,' she told him

'Yeah, right, thanks.' He smiled a little and looked at her, then looked away again. 'Did you guys handle everything all right while I was gone?'

'Yeah.'

'Good. That's good.' He sighed. 'Is everyone all right?'

'Yeah, everyone's fine. You?'

'A few of the guards got hurt,' he admitted. 'No one died according to the Lady Wolf. Konstantin got out just fine, but I got caught.'

'Oh?' She smiled and cocked an eyebrow at him, and he sighed.

'Turns out you were completely right about this whole thing being a stupid plan.' He could at least give her that. 'Or, a stupid idea. Anyway, he had to go get help from outside and come back to get me. It's a little embarrassing, but apparently he and Xavier both liked me enough to come save me.'

'Or Pan.'

'Blackmailed him? Yeah, that's what I was

thinking too.'

'How'd you know he'd come back to get you?'

'I didn't.' He shrugged. 'Just thought it was the right thing to do.'

'You know that he's…'

'I know full well what he is,' he admitted. 'But hell, who isn't?'

'What?'

'I'm not sure where you expect me to draw the murder line here. Am I supposed to go back for Xavier? For Pan? For…' He paused a long moment.

'No, go ahead.' Her voice had daggers in it. 'Say what you were thinking.'

'Are you telling me you haven't killed people?' She was silent for a moment after that one.

'Only in self-defence.'

'How many of the fights you were defending yourself in did you absolutely need to be in?' She looked at him like she'd forgotten how to hold her mouth closed. 'I had to draw the line somewhere, so I picked my own team. Whoever I'm with, as long as they stick by me, I stick by them, stand up for them. The people helping me, the people I care about, which is you in case you were wondering. You and Pan and maybe Wraither and Xavier as well. I don't know, maybe Konstantin too? I don't like him, but he didn't bail on me, so I won't bail on him.'

'I have no idea what to do with that,' she admitted. 'You could have cost us the entire mission, and you could have cost me you, and I don't know if I can accept the idea that you'll do that for just whoever you team up with.'

'I'm not asking you to be okay with it.' He spread his hands and gave her an appealing look; this time she was willing to meet his eyes. 'I'm telling you who I am, how I feel. I'm not asking you to accept it. That's your choice.'

'That's...' She sighed. 'Surprisingly realistic.'

'Yeah well, knowledge of self is a divine virtue.' He smiled.

'I'm not sure I can be okay with that.'

'Then I suggest you take your time and think it over.' Adam got up 'Let me know when you're ready to get to work. I can put our stuff on pause until then.'

'You can be surprisingly cold sometimes.' She sighed. 'You hurt me, you know.'

'Yeah, and you hurt me.' He let it show on his face for a moment before chasing it off. 'But we have bigger things to worry about right now. Like the rest of the worlds. We'll have time for hurt feelings later.'

'All right.' She nodded. 'Let's go.'

Claire waved idly from the corner to Adam as he walked into where they were meeting, a small smile on her face.

'It's been a few days,' she observed. 'Way not to die I guess.'

'Thanks.' He smiled. 'You two done anything but waste your time while I was away?'

'Yellow guy's in prison,' Annabelle explained. 'I

dosed him variety of truth serums, because we were more or less out of time, and we got a bunch of names Claire tells me are very important, and a few I know are important.'

'He named a number of high-ranking people within the Legion and Lost alike,' Claire briefed him. 'Apparently, the one thing they can agree on is the fact that the lines of fire have to be clear for them to fight. There are four of them in total, any one of whom would have been problem enough. The Shatter Twins, The Skeleman and Six of Nothing himself.'

'Yeah, I may have some good news on that!' He thought about it for a moment. 'Actually, it's more of very neutral news. One problem replaced with another slightly better problem. Does that count as good news?'

'How about you tell us the news, and then let us decide?' They were all becoming impatient with him.

'Right, yes, that thing. I will do that. Six of Nothing and the Red Gentleman are involved, and friendly. They aren't on the other side exactly, but they're not on ours either. They're on their own tiny side.'

'Right, of course.' Claire ran her hand through her hair and scowled. 'Because why would a battle to secure the fight only has two sides have only two sides? That would make far too much sense.' She thought about everything for a long moment. 'You are correct. I absolutely cannot decide whether this is good or bad news. I feel as if it should be, but the knowledge that there are a pair of Reds running around with their safeties off is not quite the reassurance I was hoping for.'

'So...' This was his team. Not exactly reassuring, but he could work with it. 'Is the yellow guy being treated okay?'

'He's in a cell, but as cells goes it's fairly nice. I would advise you not to worry about it, we will only keep him until we figure out what to do next, after we foil whatever insidious plan our enemies are hatching.'

'Okay.' It was best to figure out what they were doing next. 'What was the plan if I didn't come back?'

'Well, I presume Annabelle would have asked after your wellbeing again in a day or so.'

'That's not what I...' He thought about it, it made him stop a moment. 'Oh, she sent people to check on me?'

'She sent an official petition for your release, which was denied, and then sent someone to check on you.' Well, that made him smile a little, though Annabelle looked embarrassed for him to know it.

'Anyway, that's not what I meant. What were you guys planning for saving the dimensions?'

'Well,' Annabelle took over the conversation. 'We've probably held them back for a while, getting rid of the guys who were doing the breaking. I suppose our next plan involved figuring out who was designing whatever device they intended to use to finish this plan of theirs. Or we could just start hunting the people in charge.'

'That does not sound like a great plan.'

'Well, we were going to go after the Legion side first.' Her voice was a little defensive. 'That way if all else failed we could always just claim it was an act of war and hope they fought each other.'

'Okay.' He thought about that. 'That sounds like as good an idea as we've ever had. So, what? We just go all bounty hunter on these four guys and finish this that way?'

'If that's what it takes.' Annabelle's tone belonged to a soldier in camo, not a sweet looking young woman with coloured hair. 'It won't be easy though, like, covert ops into enemy territory where everyone wants to kill us not easy, but I'm prepared to go for it if I need to.'

'Very well.' He thought about it for a moment. 'Between the spiders, and you and Konstantin's talents you could probably get there in a couple of days. I mean we'd have to walk through an army of minions and assholes and take on, uhhhh, hey, Claire?' He looked at her. 'How badass are these Legion sisters?'

'I believe you know of a person named the King's Man?'

'Yeah.'

'Roughly equivalent.' With those words Adam felt what little confidence and hope he'd had fall out of his stomach, and dread settle like a lead weight in his gut.

He remembered his fight, if you could call it that, with the King's Man. He'd lunged feebly at the

Russian giant and been thrown across a room into a wall. Trying to get by him, not beat him, just get by him had cost him broken fingers and the man had held him there until the King of Eternal Flame had taken over his mind and made him hurt his own people, and he'd been holding back.

He remembered that Pan and Xavier, the most dangerous people he knew, fighting in perfect harmony had managed to get the giant to a standstill.

He sat down on the floor.

'He frightens you.' It wasn't a question. 'Is he really that bad?'

'If there's two like him we can't beat them both together. Hell, we probably can't beat them apart. The guy didn't just beat me, he crushed me. If they have access to the same kind of power he has, or equivalent...' He shuddered. 'He changed my mind, against my will, by sheer force of his.'

'Okay, that is not a small problem.' Annabelle put her hand on his shoulder and looked at him with honest concern 'Are you okay?'

'Yeah.' He got up and stepped away from everyone, he needed a moment to think, and get his head right before he spoke to the others.

'I do not wish to harm you.' He heard the Russian voice in his head. He really hadn't, he hadn't wanted to hurt Adam he just could barely help himself. He'd barely cared about anything that was going on and he'd still beaten most of the team handily. He'd just, done it because someone had asked him to.

If these people had power and actually cared?

'We're so screwed man.' He held his face and freaked out in private for a few good long moments, before he was interrupted.

'We have a problem.' Konstantin spoke from a respectful distance. Adam couldn't help himself, he started to laugh.

'Of course we do, what now?'

'Someone's shown up demanding we release our prisoner.'

'Did you try telling them he's dead?'

'We already confirmed that he was alive.'

Adam groaned at the news.

'Well, looks like I now have to go pretend I know something about something.' He got to his feet and pulled out the mask, latching it over his face and running his hands through his hair to smooth it down. 'Did we see the guy?'

'Not yet.'

The two of them made their way out to the fairground, and saw Annabelle talking to a man, he was tall thin and appeared to have a plague doctor mask for a face. He wore a black suit and a gold watch and seemed somehow familiar.

'I'm afraid you had no right to take our agents prisoner. They were performing clandestine operations in the best interests of our people I demand their immediate release.'

'Oh crap.' It wasn't just because he was demanding something they weren't going to deliver.

Adam knew that voice.

He'd heard it in that film the spiders had taken.

'What's up, Sister?' Adam made it look like it was the most natural thing in the world to sit down at the table beside the arguing pair, flanked by Konstantin.

'Make sure Claire's hidden,' he whispered to the big bear as Konstantin fell back.

'Laughing Man.' She gave a very brittle smile. 'This is the Skeleman. Skeleman, the Laughing Man. The Skeleman thinks he has the right to a prisoner we're holding.'

'Really? Which one?' He locked eyes with the Skeleman's empty sockets.

'His name is Weaver York. I believe you encountered him and several of his compatriots going about their business?'

'Those weird colourful guys?' He looked at Annabelle. 'Is he talking about the weird colourful guys?'

'Yes, he is.' She sounded less than pleased about the direction Adam was taking the conversation.

'You know it was the strangest thing,' he told the suited man as if he was sharing a secret. 'We were just running an errand for the Carnival when we came across the most delightful thing! These people were making a room into a painting with lights. It was the most darling thing in the world! So obviously we thought we'd stay and watch, and then out of nowhere they attacked us!' He put his hand on his chest. 'Attacked us, can you believe that?'

'I cannot.' He made it clear that in this case cannot meant do not.

'Well, apparently they found my friend over here,' he pointed to Konstantin, 'was scary looking. Truthfully, he was in a bad mood, so perhaps they were frightened? Either way, we won the fight and took one of them with us. We would have imprisoned them all, violent dammed madmen that they are, but other than the big one none of us could carry them home. We hope they haven't caused too much more trouble for you.'

'Frankly they seemed insane,' Annabelle backed up his story.

'And what exactly, are a member of the Lost, a spider and a bear doing out for a stroll together.'

'On our own business.' Adam folded his arms. 'We were taking a stroll, and unless you want to prove we report to you I'm not sure we have to tell you.'

'I am your superior.' The Skeleman mirrored his movements.

'I'm not sure the Lost works that way.' Adam shook his head.

'I am sure I can make it work that way.' That was the cordial tone gone.

'Not without bringing the full wrath of my kind down upon your head.' Annabelle glared at him. 'This is sovereign territory and your rules do not apply here.'

'Again.' This time he stepped backward and raised one hand. Seven dark eyed men with hooded cloaks made their way up behind him, gnashing their teeth and twitching. 'I daresay I can make my rules apply here.' Annabelle raised her own hand and a few dozen spiders surrounded the unit. The Skeleman lowered his hand and the men returned to a state of calm, sitting on the ground with no expressions on their faces. 'I do not wish to harm you, or this place, or your people. I entreat you, simply release your prisoner to me, so that he can return to his duties. You will be compensated for the attack, of course'

There was a tense pause for a moment.

'If I could discuss things with my partner?' Annabelle grabbed Adam's arm and started to drag him off.

'By all means take whatever time you need.' He looked at his watch. 'So long as that time is measured in minutes, not hours.'

She took him away from any observers, and Annabelle wrapped one arm around him, pulling him further and further until they reached a small tent. She opened it, pulled him inside and turned to him.

'He's totally threatening us,' she informed him.

'Yeah, that seems clear.' Adam nodded.

'I don't like it, but if he's willing to outright threaten me here, he's not going to make it empty. He'll send everyone after us to get what he wants.' They looked at each other for a moment and she spat it out. 'So, we have to release the prisoners.'

'He's going to get the others back from the Wolf Spider.' It was just a fact. Lady Wolf Spider had proven herself short-sighted enough that she could be bribed or threatened into giving up the prisoners. 'That means if we release yellow we're back to square one.'

'These are my people.' It was all she had to say. He understood, you had to draw a line somewhere, and the Carnival had trusted her to look out for their interests. If this Skeleman decided to invade the Carnival they'd fight for her, but it was her responsibility not to make them. He shrugged, forced a smile and cracked his neck each way.

'All right then, guess we've got work to do.'
'What?'
'Well, we should use the minutes we're allowed to mobilise the others and get ready to leave.' Adam shrugged. 'As soon as we return yellow we should make ready to go straight into Legion territory.' He thought about things for a moment and got up. 'Actually, I also need to message some people. Have someone watch over the waiting guy and send someone out with yellow when his patience is just about to break. In the meantime, we can work against whoever this is'

'What exactly is the plan here?' She looked at him, her eyes were desperate, she needed him to know what he was doing.

'The plan here is to go after the Shatter Sisters, kick their asses somehow and use that to find out whatever their plan is, where it is and how to screw it up. Hopefully there's something that needs to be handled on the Legion's end and we can stop them by kicking these chick's asses or breaking stuff.'

'That is a nebulous plan at best.' It looked like he'd let her down.

'I am more than open to input, that's just what I have. Find out what they did, and break it, then break the next thing and the next thing until something breaks that can't be fixed.'

'Fair enough.' She nodded. 'Are there people you need to call?'

'Yeah. I don't have his phone number or anything, but I know how to find him.'

'Scarlett will take you where you need to go.' Adam took a deep breath, collected his thoughts and drew some conclusions.

'I really hope you won't hate me at the end of all of this.' He sighed. 'I never tried to hurt anyone, I just...'

'Didn't you say we had to put this on hold?' She raised an eyebrow and he nodded.

'Yeah, sorry, I didn't mean to.' He forced a smile. 'Even I'm not that cold I guess.'

'Good to know.' She nodded. 'I hope we don't hate each other too.' With that she headed out. Adam was re-joined by Scarlett, who regarded him significantly colder than she had in the past. She took him on a walk, without so much as sparing him a word, helped him relay his message and returned him to the Carnival.

'Thanks.'

'Welcome.' She shrugged. 'Don't get Her Majesty killed.'

'Yeah, I'll do my level best not to.'

'We count on her.'

'I understand that.' He nodded. 'And she's doing her best to live up to that trust right now. So, if there's any way to make sure she gets out of this okay, I'll do it.'

'Take me with you instead.' She fixed him with a glare. 'I can do everything she can do, and I'm a lot less necessary to the Carnival than she is.'

'I mean, that's up to her.' He sighed. 'You wanna convince her of something go ahead and try. All I've done so far is go along for the ride with all of you. I can't tell anyone what to do.'

'You do realise,' the Laughing One spoke up in the back of his head, 'that everyone around you has followed almost every direction you've given since this whole mess started?'

'Yeah well, none of this was my idea,' he muttered.

'Sorry, what?' She glared at him.

'None of this was my idea!' he repeated. Well he might as well complain to everyone since he was going it.

'Oh, grow up and take some responsibility for your actions!' she demanded. 'Talk to her, convince her to let me.'

'She is no longer my goddamn responsibility!' He turned on her. 'I'm starting to think this whole relationship was a huge goddamn mistake.' With that he turned away and headed for the door. 'If you want her to do something, you make her do it.'

'So,' Konstantin rose to join him as he headed back

to the others. 'What's next?'

'Someone else comes up with a plan for once is what's next!' He walked past him, and when Konstantin stood in his path he tried to shove him out of the way. Konstantin moved as far as a brick wall would and glared down.

'You wanna rephrase that?'

'I do.' He nodded. 'I really do. I don't know what we're doing next. We'll be heading out soon. I hope someone thinks of something by then.'

'You want to tell me why you're suddenly throwing attitude everywhere?'

'Do you care?'

'Not really.' He scratched his ass and yawned. 'But I get the feeling this is going to get in the way, unless you talk about it so I'm gonna pretend to listen.'

'I'm tired of being the only one who comes up with things and having them criticised when I do.' They paused and looked at each other for a few long moments.

Then Konstantin burst out laughing, his deep booming voice split the sky with uproarious guffaws. He reached out and slapped Adam on the back, driving the breath from his body, then held his knees for a few moments. He balanced himself as best he could, laughing and laughing.

'What's so funny?' he wanted to demand but the knowledge that the guy he'd be demanding from was an insane mass murderer he settled for repeating himself. 'Come on, why are you laughing?'

After a minute Konstantin looked over at him.

'What did you think being a leader was?'

'Hold on!' He raised his hand to ward the words off. 'Hold on, I am not, I repeat not, anyone's leader.'

'Really? Cause you sure as shit act like it.'

'Annabelle has more experience, she knows what she's doing. Why isn't she leader?'

'Why would she be? She's a spider, they don't do this kind of thing much. They tend to build things gradually, not, whatever this is.'

'It's not my area of expertise either!'

'But you sure act like it is.' He shrugged. 'You might whine a lot, but whenever you have an idea you say it with determination. You demand action and when someone criticises, you demand input. The reason you're in charge is because in the situation you're in, no one knows what's going on, and you're crazy enough not to let it stop you.'

'Really? That's all it takes to be a good leader?'

'Oh gods no.' He laughed some more. 'A responsible person would make plans, gather intelligence, in absence of that though, doing the obvious thing with determination and taking advantage of opportunities as they come a long is the best you can hope for, and you don't suck at that.'

'Is that what you do?'

'No. Roar a lot and kill people is most of my plans.'

Adam laughed a little until he realised Konstantin wasn't joking. 'And all the damn criticism?'

'Have you not met people?' He laughed again.

'Bitching, moaning and running away is about all you humans do.'

'Wow. Rude.'

'You want to hear a story?' Konstantin looked at him.

'Sure.'

'Well, once upon a time, I used to know a weedy little shite who ignored the fact I'm twice his size, didn't much like him, and regularly considered eating him with one bite. In spite of all these facts he couldn't resist the urge to question, second guess and criticise everything I do.'

'Really? What happened to him.'

'I ate him.'

'Oh. I thought he was me for a second there.'

'He is you, now piss off before I eat you.'

'Fair enough.' He got up and headed away. 'We're heading into Legion territory for the purposes of violent assault and kidnapping, soon.'

'Good plan!' He clapped his hands. 'Finally, I get to do my thing.'

'Roaring and violence?'

'Roaring and violence!'

CHAPTER ELEVEN

'So,' Adam looked at the room full of his allies, as dubious as they were. He wasn't sure he could trust any of them, not even Annabelle anymore. He'd believed in her, and knew she was tough and clever. He cared about her, and knew she cared about him, but it was hard to imagine her ever choosing him. Her loyalty to was to her people, and it would be stupid and selfish to want it otherwise. 'Are we going by thunderstorm again?'

'If only.' Claire held out her hands. 'I may, possibly, be able to keep us moving in Legion territory without raising alarms, but the people manning checkpoints will know us now. There's a chance Lord Code could get us in, but not without having us seen.'

'Can TV help us?' He looked at Konstantin, who thought for a moment before shaking his head.

'It'd be too dangerous for all of us to go through and I won't risk his life. He went with two of us and we almost got us all lost a dozen times. Doubling that number halves our chances.'

'Could your people help us?' It was Adam's last option, far from ideal, and when he saw Annabelle's jaw tighten he could see she didn't feel any better about it than he did.

'One of them could.' She nodded. 'A few of them have webs that link to the Legion places, the places we can't go, but the majority of them I couldn't get to in time.' She thought about that a moment. 'Only one ticks both boxes.'

'Anything we should know about that one?'

'Oh, come on.' She gave him a slightly condescending look. 'Seriously dude? With our luck? Who was it ever going to be?'

'It's Widow then?'

'Widow indeed.' The Black Widow was one of the most powerful and dangerous of the spiders. She was strong, clever and was known to have webs and influence that reached wherever she cared to.

She had also once tried to seduce Adam with her mind controlling beauty to stay with her forever. The only reason she'd failed was the fact that Pan wasn't interested in women at all. He'd threatened the spider queen into letting Adam go, and none of them had parted on good terms. She had offered Adam a place at her side but had asked them not to come back for any other reason for a good long while. That had been months ago, and that didn't feel like long enough.

'She's not going to like that.' He muttered. Annabelle gave him a "no duh" look.

'No, she is not, we're going to be at her mercy.'

'And we'll have to bring a gift.' He thought about that for a moment. 'They like rare things and clothing, right?'

'We.' She glared. 'We like those things, yes.'

'All right, we'll have to stop by home before we go. I have a plan. I have no idea if it'll work but it's worth a shot.'

They took the journey down the coast to Widow's territory again, as they had the first time Adam journeyed into another world. They made their way to the same ruined house, and this time Adam made his way up the stairs with caution, avoiding the spiders who crawled in the corners as they made their way to Annabelle. He was in their house, and he didn't want to risk hurting them.

'Excuse me?' When he reached the top, he bent down and looked at one of the arachnids. 'When I was last here I tried to hurt one of your kin. I wonder if they would be willing to come out and accept my apology.'

Annabelle looked over her shoulder and gave him a ghost of a smile as she worked on the web.

'Seems you can learn.' She smiled. 'Slowly but surely.'

'Thanks a bunch.' He rolled his eyes, then bent down at the yellow back spider who had crawled out to stand in front of him with a vaguely expectant air. He'd never seen a spider look expectant before, but somehow it managed. He bent down and offered his hand to the creature, which placed one of its legs on it for a moment and withdrew. 'I'm sorry. I didn't understand back then what I do now and if I'd known I would have left you alone. Maybe I said I was sorry before, but that was just because I was afraid. Now I'm actually sorry, so, sorry.' He shrugged. It wasn't exactly elegant, but it was the best he could think of. The spider looked at him for a moment, then tapped his finger with one of its legs and ran back into the woodwork.

'Does that mean he forgives me?' He looked over at Annabelle.

'He forgave you the first time.' She smiled. 'But it's nice to see anyway.'

'What's his name?'

'You really need to get over that.' And her smile turned to eyerolling. 'Individual spiders don't have names unless we gain the correct intelligence. Now let me work.' He did so, going back to the others. 'Are you two going to be all right in the spider realm?'

'I've rarely encountered them.' Claire shrugged. 'Shouldn't be a problem.'

'They don't like me, but they'll tolerate me.' Konstantin nodded.

'If either of you are attracted to women I'd advise you not to look at her directly, she has kind of an influence on people.' Konstantin nodded again, and Claire shrugged, returning to sitting on the ground muttering to herself. Probably meditating.

'We're ready.' Annabelle had built the lines again and this time she took the lead. She walked calmly through the wooden hall, and as the rest of them followed one by one they ended up back in the black void full of webs that was the spiders' world. Adam always thought he'd gotten used to doing what was essentially standing in empty space.

It was still goddamn weird though.

'So where do we go?' Adam looked at Annabelle

and she looked back over her shoulder with a smile on her face.

'This time there's no tricky navigation or attempts to dodge notice.' She raised two fingers to her mouth and let out a piercing whistle which sent the spiders, who hadn't been doing anything, crawling toward her. After a moment all but one stopped, one the size of a small bus that looked like it was falling through the air. It wasn't falling down though, it was falling sideways, right through the sky. It spiralled softly toward the people, a soft but regular corkscrew that trailed a thick web from its hindquarters.

Adam looked at the creature as it arrived, then shrugged and began to climb its body, crawling over its head onto its back then sitting down on its abdomen, waiting for the others to climb up.

There was no point in worrying now, he had his gift and his plan and just maybe it would work out all right.

'I only wish for you to know the name of the king.' He heard the words in the back of his head, and as he remembered it all the confidence was knocked out of him. Two people with the strength of the King's Man. What the hell was he going to do with that? God what was he doing?

Not the issue right now, push it away, be rid of it, shut up and enjoy the ride Adam. By now the others had climbed up, and the spider was falling back toward where it came from, turning around and letting another thread spool from its back. This time it didn't spiral, keeping a single consistent fall toward the destination.

It was just a large pagoda, with a series of hammocks, suspended platforms and places for the Widow's servants to rest and lean, to preen themselves and prepare to guard her if anything should go wrong. There were a few pieces of real furniture there as well.

Adam kept his eyes away from the large, hanging construction in the centre, keeping his gaze on the ground, on the guards, on his friends. He knew he was susceptible to her charms, if that if he so much as looked at her he'd be sucked into her thrall again. He knew what she looked like, or at least what she looked like to him. She was a shapely, almost naked woman with dark skin and long red hair, she wore a dress made of spiderweb that served more to draw attention to her nakedness than obscure it.

He wanted to look at her, with a basic instinctual desire that was almost impossible to think or logic his way out of. Luckily it was only almost, and he managed to keep his eyes on the ground.

'Not happy to see me this time?' Her voice was soft, but it carried. Every word was spoken like a confession, like she was telling some secret desire only to you. 'Or have you decided it's time to come back and live with me after all?' She laughed, and he flushed at the memory. The truth was it wasn't so far from tempting, she'd offered him a peaceful life, a quiet, pleasant existence with her in this place. His wiser voices won out though, and he kept his head down.

'I'm sorry, but no. I'm here on a crucial mission from–'

'You said you wouldn't be back for a while Anna.' Apparently, her conversation with him was over. 'That you would give me time to cease being upset with you. I am currently upset with you.'

'You said that if we were to come back, we should bring a very nice gift.' With that Adam took a few steps forward, planning to walk until he detected someone who would come to take it from him. When no one came he just kept walking until he hit the edge of the web structure she rested on, and a hand entered his field of vision.

Oh, damn it, even her hands were perfect. How could he be so interested in a hand? She had long slender fingers, with perfectly manicured nails and a single golden ring on her middle finger that looked like a fang. He stared at it for a few moments, until she clicked her fingers and his attention was snatched.

'Gift!' she demanded, like an impetuous child. He reached out and deposited it in her hand.

'A suit jacket made by the Red Gentleman himself, it's merest touch can burn, cause pain to and on occasion even scorch or incinerate creatures of the Eldritch or Seraph. He sewed it by hand himself, and as far as I'm aware he's the only one who makes them. Gave it to me personally.'

The Widow held it in one hand for a moment, and then pulled it back sharply, Adam stepped away.

'Annabelle,' he called out. 'Any chance you could let me in on her reaction.'

'She is… reluctantly and faintly pleased,' the Widow answered for herself. 'Does the Red Gentleman know you're giving away one of his coats?'

'He doesn't.' He shrugged. 'But I'm sure he'd understand, and I don't care if he doesn't. This is important.'

'And how about the rest of you?' Adam could feel the scrutiny shifting and the tension left him, letting him put his eyes where he cared to. 'Anna dear, I was almost certain you had sided with the Lost, and yet somehow you find yourself with at least one Legionnaire! One admits to a certain curiosity.'

'Oh. She was recently broken out of prison, after serving a sentence for treason,' Annabelle informed her, and Adam heard the sounds of applause.

'You bring me such interesting dining companions, and the bear?'

'I go where I want, do as I please, and answer to no one.' Konstantin's already deep voice as deep enough to shake the web.

'Rude.' She sighed. 'Well, now we're all introduced more or less politely.' She sounded casually pleased, as if bad weather had cleared up. 'So that seems to be all my questions but the big one. What exactly are you doing here after I warned you all off.'

'We need your help, everyone needs your help.'

'Oh everyone!' Her hands clapped again.

'Everyone needs me? I am rather excited. What exactly does everyone need from the likes of me?'

'We need you to sneak us into Legion territory.' Annabelle spoke without giving too much away, but the entire pagoda already burst out into gasps and muttering. Black Widow waited until the noise had died down before she spoke.

'That would be taking a side in the war.' Finally, she appeared to be taking something seriously. 'That would be violating one of a very small number of rules I currently possess. I do not get involved in conflicts between the sides.'

'This isn't a conflict between the sides,' Adam spoke up. God, it felt like he was breaking the rules by just speaking.

'Really?' He could feel the eyes on him. 'Because you and my dear Anna, along with a traitor to the Legion are making their way into Legion territory. No matter your reason, no matter what you decide or what you want, I am still making a move against the Legion.'

'It's a coalition attempt by both sides to eliminate the neutral parties. There are people on the Lost and Legion sides planning to get rid of us.'

'Well, then you don't need me!' Her voice was cheerful. 'You can just go to the Lost side and solve things there. Isn't that lovely? Good day.'

'It's not that simple!' she protested. 'The best way for us to–'

'It seems we have a misunderstanding.' The Black

Widow was suddenly in front of Annabelle, forcing Adam to look away before he fell back under her spell from a glance at her ankles or something like some kind of weird 1920s guy. 'I am not here to present you with a convenient option. I am not here to facilitate what you would find easy. No, if you want my help this will require a significant concession on your part.'

'Right.' Annabelle sighed, like she was about to do something which would cause her very real pain, and then leaned up to whisper something into the Black Widow's ear.

'What is she saying?' He advanced a little, trying to seem quiet.

'I have no idea,' the Laughing One sighed. 'Too quiet even for me I'm afraid.'

'That is quite an offer.' The Widow's voice was a little horse. 'I accept.'

'Annabelle?' Adam felt a little ill and wasn't sure why. 'What are you volunteering to do?'

'None of your business,' she snapped at Adam. 'I do what I have to for my people.' She turned to the Widow and gave what he imagined probably wasn't exactly a pleasant look. 'Now take us where we need to go.'

'This will have ramifications, for me, for all of us.'

'I know that!' And her voice was as cold as cracking ice. He heard the sound of feet leaving a floor, and the crack of flesh hitting flesh.

'How dare you?'

Adam looked up, seeing the Widow reeling,

looking more shocked than upset.

'Because I'm the only one who pays attention you spoiled, arrogant child of a woman!' Annabelle was crying now. 'I've been taking care of our people, in spite of you! I'm the one who watches out for us, not you, not the others! I've been paying attention while you all become selfish and petty and short-sighted. So don't you dare ask if I understand the ramifications of anything I do, since I'm apparently the only person who actually gives a shit!'

'Well.' Widow's composure broke completely, and she finally sounded like she was feeling something, a small tone of hurt in her voice. 'Perhaps you are ready to grow up after all. I will convey your concerns to our people. I apologise, if we have made things hard for you.'

'Apology absolutely not accepted. Now, open the gate!'

'Very well.' She looked at Adam and there she was again, tall and dark and beautiful, but she had a few little flaws, and her hair was no longer so vibrant.

'Thank you.' He nodded and looked at the others. 'Are you all ready to go?'

'Ready.' They sounded off.

'Yellowtail will take you.' And she was back, that bored, unaffected voice as the giant spider from before landed back in front of them. 'Stay safe little man, and bring my niece back, or I shall liquify you from the inside, slowly and over a number of years.'

'Understood.' He climbed back onto Yellowtail and

looked down at the creature. 'Are you related to the one I apologised to?'

'The one you apologised to is part of me,' it replied. 'Now come along and stay low.' The group clambered onto the back of the spider, who began to make his way slowly and ponderously through the web.

They passed through a dozen different realms as the spider clambered through webs so thin that Adam found it hard to see them unless he stared. They crawled across the sky, seeing what looked surprisingly like Paris, then under a city where everyone flew through the sky on the back of what looked like bears. They flew through a world that seemed to have no light at all, operating on faith that they were going in the right direction. After this and a half dozen other worlds Adam finally returned to the world the Legion owned. As he crawled through the sky he finally lowered himself down on top of an office building.

'So.' Adam looked to the others. 'Do you have a plan?'

'I do.' Surprisingly it was Konstantin who spoke. 'Give the spiders who watched the meeting to me, and I'll find my way.' Annabelle smiled and held out her hands, a dozen or so spiders crawling onto the ground. Konstantin picked up one of the spiders, sniffed it for a moment, and then popped it into his mouth, chewing it with a speculative look on his face. 'East.' He nodded. 'Follow me.'

Following the tracker while keeping up the illusion

that they belonged there wasn't easy, especially knowing that everything he was wearing made him identifiable. He kept the Laughing One in his pocket, at least the Watcher was only obvious to those who had known the Legate, and stuck to the centre of the group. Konstantin lead the group, beating a simple direct trail, stopping every couple of minutes to isolate the next path. Annabelle kept her colours muted, and Claire kept up their image of being Legion. As soon as they got attention she would become an imperious, ranting creature that no one wanted to look at for too long.

Adam had to appreciate the overtime Claire was putting in, she danced through the arcane series of lines the rest of them could barely see and wrangled a series of unreliable strange people who didn't understand their situation on a path that occasionally required the group to turn or move suddenly. The rest of them barely managed to follow her lead, and she still managed to cover their dismal attempts to look like they belonged.

'So, Annabelle.' He had to ask.

'No,' she replied.

'What?'

'No, I'm not going to tell you what I offered Widow, and I'm not talking to you right now. I need to keep my head on straight and you'll only confuse me. You told me to keep our stuff on pause, and I'm trying. So now you need to trust me when I say worrying about it's only going to get in the way.'

'Would you two shut up and stop distracting our tracker form his work?' Claire snapped.

'Work's almost done.' Konstantin pointed one claw at a large spired building. 'Who we're looking for is in there.'

'That's operating centre 31C in the fifth square of the third quadrant,' Claire informed them. 'Some of the major players operate out of there.'

'Does that help us at all?' Konstantin snapped.

'It lets me get my bearings,' she retorted. 'Don't be a dick about it. Any idea where in this building we're going?'

'Up?' Konstantin shrugged. 'Long way up, one of the top floors maybe. Can you get us in?'

'I'll do my level best.' Claire cracked her knuckles and brought her hand to her whip, twirling it in her hand. 'Do we need a code word or gesture for you to attack.'

'Yeah, wiggle your ears and say kill that guy,' Adam joked, Konstantin snorted with laughter.

'You people really need to work on your procedures,' she scolded.

'I hate you,' Konstantin replied. 'And your procedures, and your idiot face.'

'Well, that was pointlessly hurtful,' she reproached, but she was smiling, and he seemed less than entirely contrite. She approached the two men on guard duty with a smile on her face, gently twirling her whip.

'Excuse me, Miss, what are you doing here?' One

of the guards held out his hand to stop her moving by hand, she paused a moment but refused to stop.

'We are with the Son of the Golden Smile's delegation,' she snapped. 'You are interfering with important business.'

'I was not informed that.'

'There is a meeting! Now! He requires logistical support and enough data to support his understanding.' Her tone grew aggressive. 'Unless you would like to be personally responsible for the Son of the King being forced to make concessions! Tell me, would you like to disgrace my cause, a king and yourself with a single act of obstinance?' This time she did push the armed guards out of her path. The two guards behind him braced their weapons and made to strike. 'Gentlemen!' Claire didn't look behind her. 'I am being obstructed in my duties, should this continue, remove the obstruction!'

'Yes, Ma'am.' Adam nodded.

'I will have to message his representative in the tower.' The guard scowled.

'Good man, you do that!' She patted him on the chest and the entire group poured past the guards and into the elevator. As soon as the door closed Claire braced against the wall. 'Well, that was mighty bracing.'

'Good bluffing,' Adam approved. 'Who is that Son of the Golden whatever?'

'The most out of touch, inattentive and essentially useless of the direct servants of the various Kings.

Anyone lower they would have questions, and there's almost no chance he'll be here.'

'So why did they think he'd be in a meeting?'

'Would you question the movements of a man who you could have killed without so much as a word?'

He had no idea what was going on or what that would be like, but he shrugged and took a few breaths to steady himself. 'Ready to go?' He looked at Konstantin. 'Let me know when we're high enough and I'll hit the button. Claire, talk us as close to the enemy as we can and then, I guess we just rush 'em.' Not that he had the first idea what he'd do once he started. Two King's Man level people could rip this entire team's lungs out. 'Someone tell me you guys have a plan for actual violent, because if we're using mine all we'll be able to do is hold the line until my backup gets there.'

'Then we shall stall for a while,' she shrugged. 'My people are almost here as well.' Claire pulled her hand from her neck and pulled out what looked like a white grub. Adam knew it, one of them had once been stuck in his neck to spy on him.

'That guy in the douche hat?' Adam pointed to the grub and she nodded. 'He's been able to see and hear everything we do.'

'Indeed he did.'

'I thought you said you were going to report back in spider world.'

'Yes.' She straightened her outfit. 'That was less "report in" and more "build a safeguard against your inevitable mishandling or betrayal".'

'Oh goddammit.' Adam held his head and looked over at the grub, then leaned over to talk into it. 'You're going to get some support from across the aisle. Try not to be too big a prick about it.'

'You know I can't actually communicate a message back, yes? He doesn't actually talk through the bug.' She thought about that for a moment. 'It would be difficult, but not impossible.'

'Yeah, well.' He sighed. 'Now I just have to hope your ambush doesn't step on my ambush.'

'Can you cancel yours?'

'No, and I wouldn't if I could. I trust my guys, and I don't trust yours which I know is exactly the same reasoning you have.'

'Quite.'

'It's now,' Konstantin spoke, and Adam hit the button to get off at the next floor. As the door opened they stopped and looked at each other.

'Ready?' They sounded off in the affirmative and set off at a "we have important things to do" strut as soon as the doors opened. They'd made it halfway down the corridor before a trio of guards got in their way.

'We are representatives of the Son of the Golden Smile.'

'The Son is not on this floor.' They glared at Claire.

'Well okay.' She shrugged. 'I guess it's violence.'

'Well finally!' Konstantin started his charge. 'Haven't killed anyone since this whole mess started!'

'And you still shouldn't kill anyone now!' Adam tried to yell it, but he realised there was no point. At this point stopping Konstantin at present would be next to impossible. He was, unfortunately, entirely correct. The bear had been holding himself back by conscious and extensive effort, due only to his professionalism and his small, but not inconsequential appreciation for the fact that while he and Adam may have saved each other the smaller, younger, weaker man had risked far more to do it.

He had hit the limit of his ability and desire to hold back. He charged all three of the guards, ignoring the bullets they sent in his direction. The bullets hummed into his bulk and he slammed right through them, biting into one and tossing him like a ragdoll into the wall.

'Should we be helping him?'

'Why would we need to?' Adam calmly jumped over Konstantin's bulk, knocking the door the guards were protecting down. 'Besides, no time, we can't let them call for backup!'

Sure enough, inside the room, looking like Adam expected them to, were the twins. They watched him for a moment, looking him up and down as the rest of the group formed up, then looked back to the screen, looking at an old man.

'We'll be sending our agent to collect your delivery soon, dear. I'm so very sorry but we have an unexpected guest.' The twin in white picked up a remote control, hit the button that turned the screen off, then turned around and looked at their enemies.

'Good day to all of you.' She smiled. 'In the few minutes before our people arrive and horribly murder you, would you like some tea?' The twin in black got up and headed to the other side of the office space they were in. Inside was a simple kitchen setup, a conference table and a couple of cubicles. The walls of the room were covered in mirrors, dozens of them up and down the walls. They reflected everything in an infinite pattern.

'By the authority given me by the Lord Who Watches the Code and as a duly appointed member of his inquisition, under special circumstances act 38B I hereby place you under arrest for your conscious attempt to interfere with the fabric of universes without full understanding of the consequences.' Claire drew her sword and whip. 'In doing so you have committed crimes against servants of the Kings and Queens, Sons and Daughters, Gods and Goddesses and the other beings which we all serve and are empowered by. Furthermore, should you choose not to acquiesce to your arrest I have full authority to use any method to restrain and retrieve you, up to and including ceasing your respiratory and cognitive function and retrieving the spirits within for appropriate punishment.' Well, Adam reflected, nothing stalls quite like official procedure. 'Do you intend to come quietly?'

'I'm afraid we cannot do so at this time.' The twins, no doubt thought they were being neutral, not displaying emotion, but after spending months dealing with spiders, who were subtle by nature, and his time in forced conversation with the King's Man during his imprisonment, Adam had learned to pick up on the smallest of expressions. Something Claire had said had rattled them, gotten under their skin.

He saw the attack coming as soon as the white twin had the idea, jumping to knock Claire to the ground as a glass shard spun toward her face. To the twins it must have looked like he was precognisant, or impossibly fast. That was good, overestimation could buy him time. He rolled to his feet and set the mask of the Laughing Man onto his face, and the world was prioritised once more.

He could finally see how someone could end up like Pan or Xavier, well, not Xavier, but Pan maybe, with his Presence on and engaged all the time. The clarity they provided, the simple sense that ninety nine out of every hundred things didn't matter was almost intoxicating. He squared off in a defensive stance, his claws long and razor sharp.

'Why do you have to be lethal?' he asked his other half.

'Because if there's no stakes there's no drama, and without drama there's no comedy,' the voice piped up. 'Watching someone who has a staunch objection to killing make do with a lethal weapon? That's hilarious.'

'That's not even a little funny.'

'Yes well, all humour is subjective, and so much harder to appreciate when the joke's on you.' As they spoke he watched the twins transform. Usually he would have attacked during the transformation, just to be unsporting but there was no point if he was supposed to be stalling. As he watched, they grew more angular, larger, their arms turning to blades and their skin gaining a black and white swirling pattern. They were now, Adam realised, exact mirror images of each other.

They spread their hands wide, and the mirrors began to warp and twist around the room. Two of them were suddenly four, eight, sixteen

'Are you outnumbered here or not?'

'No idea!' Claire replied, her whip already blurring in the air, striking out at the mirror figures. 'I'm not sure if we try to figure out the real ones, or just hit everyone?'

'Konstantin! You have the best chance of finding the real one, go for it. The rest of us, screw it, get everyone!' Adam tried to focus, realised he couldn't tell the difference between the figures, and set off at a run. With any luck these guys weren't nearly as good at pattern recognition as he was. He figured the best attack plan as drive by. He needed to give them something to look at, to give Annabelle's spiders time to do their job and let Konstantin find his quarry.

'What's the plan here, boss?' Claire called out. She'd fallen into a defensive stance, her sword held point out as she fended off the copies with the whip.

'Start by seeing how solid these things are.' He slid across the ground and struck for one's ankle. The creature jumped over his strike and he brought the other claw up, hacking between the creature's legs. As the claws bit deep the creature let out a short scream, a shattering noise, and vanished. 'Okay, they're solid but not too solid, we don't actually need to kill the copies!' A blade swung at his face and he barely managed the catch it, all six of his claws catching the arm blade. As it hit the obstruction the blade fractured and shifted into a different shape, a hook flying at his face. He pushed with all of his strength and hit the deck, rolling away.

Two or three of them he could have handle, six, was a bit of a problem, so when the number of opponents reached nine he realised he was going to die. He felt the Watcher's pain as blades slipped through the coat, and his own as edges and points bit into his chest.

He tried to predict the patterns, to dance through the maze of limbs, weapons and monsters. Occasionally he managed to break apart one of the doubles, but it was quickly replaced with a new one.

The spiders were doing more than their share, the bites, venoms and acids they could deliver tearing through whatever the copies had instead of blood and sending them falling apart, even as the little arachnids fell apart by the dozens. The only problem was that the twins could copy themselves as fast as the little creatures could break them. Annabelle covered more with her webs, usually giving her or one of the others time to finish them off.

'Laughing Man!' Claire called out, and hearing the name, Adam felt himself growing colder, the world slipping out of his reach and his understanding of the situation growing. 'Block for the bear!'

Konstantin had one of them pinned and form the fact that all of the copies were suddenly making their way toward him he'd picked the right one. As they all began to launch themselves, Adam stepped in their path, holding his claws up to block.

His hands moved faster than he'd ever moved before, blocking, deflecting and shifting weapons as they developed against his arms. As he pushed them with all his strength they piled weight, and piled weight and piled weight on him. His arms were pinned, the blades were biting through the armour, seeking his flesh slowly but certainly.

'Please tell me someone has a plan here!'

'Oh, not to worry Laughing Man,' a familiar voice came from the distance. 'I'm here to protect you, as per usual. Knife get the mirror!' Suddenly the weight started to lift as the creatures atop him fell apart.

'Xavier,' he called as he looked up from the pile of broken things. 'Good to see you again.'

There was a high-pitched hum that rang through the room, followed by the noise of glass cracking. The noise grew louder and louder, and the glass shattered over and over. Even as the copies started crawling out they were deformed and twisted as they crawled out of the shattering glass.

Xavier looked, different, but Adam couldn't

exactly tell how. He had the same red coat, same hat, same sword, but he looked off. He still only had the one arm; the other one he'd given up for a con to foil the King of Eternal Flame.

That was it, Adam realised as he fell back into his old patterns, blocking and dodging around Konstantin's body as he fought the Shatter Twin. Xavier wasn't displaying like he usually did. He moved quickly and quietly, his head down avoiding staying anywhere or looking at anything for too long.

The rapier in his cane was poised to strike as soon as Konstantin moved from his path. The big bear was fighting what appeared to be both the real mirror twins, pieces being hacked from his bulk as he wrestled and bit at one. As the other moved to strike his blind side it screamed and fell on its back, its leg suddenly a twisted mess, this allowed to bear to toss her away.

Xavier took his chance and pinned her to the wall with his sword like a butterfly. He left the sword in her, tipped his hat to Konstantin and smiled. 'Dread Bear, nice to see you still get about in your twilight years.'

'Wanna lose your other arm, little man?' Konstantin retorted from the ground. The big creature wasn't letting the fact a quarter of his blood was currently on the outside of his body, and that he'd almost lost his last fight, distract him from his eternal goal of getting into another fight.

'Not on your best day.' Adam had one of its arms

pinned, and Konstantin was currently lashing out for her throat as she struggled to kill him.

'Hey, Legion!' Konstantin yelled. 'Where's your backup? I thought you had people coming.'

'I did, I do, they're currently holding the floor to ensure the twins agents and reinforcements won't attack, changing this situation from impossible to apparently winnable.' Claire had finished off the last of the copies and was now aiding Adam in holding the other one's arms down. Konstantin bit down, ripping a chunk out of her throat and watching as she ceased her struggle.

The one stuck to the wall was attempting to warp, twist or improvise something to get off the blade, trying to grow its way out. Whenever it got close Annabelle would web it in place, and Xavier would reinsert the sword somewhere non-lethal but painful.

'Nice of you to come.' Adam got to his feet. 'Do we have a way out?'

'Out?' Xavier sighed. 'Yes indeed, out with a struggling demigod? That would be a no.'

'Claire? Any chance your boss will allow us to leave with her?' The devil woman began to pick up the pieces of her sword, which has apparently been broken in the fight.

'I would advise you not to ask.' Claire shrugged. 'There's an off chance you'll be allowed, but with the cards in his hands he will likely keep her.'

'All right!' Adam looked around. 'Plan, Annabelle, tell me you have a huge number of webs within you right now.'

'Define huge.'

'Enough to cart a bear, a checkerboard chick, yourself and Claire down the side of a building.'

'Probably not.' She ran her hand through her hair. 'I'll give it a shot.'

'Gent, Knife, hold the door!' He sighed. 'Dammit, I hate climbing down the side of buildings.'

'That won't be necessary,' came a voice from the doorway. 'Please call off your sniper my dear boy, I do find getting shot rather inconvenient.'

'We just beat down the Shatter Sisters,' Adam informed him.

'I have an army around this building.' The man in the fedora walked across the hall 'You are impressive, but not that impressive.'

'Hold fire.' Adam raised his hand. Mikhail gave him a wave from the building adjacent and put his gun up. Adam turned back to the guy in the doorway. 'You know you look like a detective from a 1920s noir movie, right?'

'You know you look like the villain from a 1980s slasher movie, right?' he retorted. 'On the understanding that none of you are under arrest, and you are all free to go at any time, I would like you all to speak with me. If you do so willingly and without more violence you may leave freely or interrogate the remaining Shatter Sister.'

'I want you to swear.' Adam folded his arms, locking his eyes with the so-called Lord. 'To

Annabelle, not to me. Claire works for you and I'm Lost so you probably don't care about keeping promises to us.'

'Untrusting, but in the case of some of my people quite astute.' He curled his lip like the fact was distasteful. 'They are not all, by their nature, entirely trustworthy. They are honest, but untrustworthy.' He turned to Annabelle 'I hereby swear that, at the end of a series of short but insightful conversations you may have access to the Shatter Sisters, only restricted by the fact that you may not murder them. Upon the end of that conversation you may depart in peace. I shall see you to the exit of your choice myself.'

'I hear your oath, Lord, and it will bind you.' Mikhail climbed over the windowsill, apparently his gun had a grappling function. He reached out a hand and Adam shook it.

'Better late than never.'

He shrugged at Adam's criticism.

'You didn't exactly leave much of a trail to follow.'

'I need a word with you.' Adam looked at the Lord. 'Can you take us to somewhere we won't be watched? Knife and I need to talk.'

'Why don't you talk with me first?' The Lord smiled. 'Then he can, and then the two of you can hold your private conversation whilst I chat with your friends.'

'Seems fair.' He took a deep breath and looked at the fedora guy. He followed the path down the hall and walked in. He'd been expecting an interrogation room, metal chairs, welded down table, a single bare lightbulb hanging over his head. What he got was a room with cushioned chairs, paintings on the walls and a hardwood table. Code put his fedora on a hat rack and collapsed into a cushioned armchair, pointing to the one across from him. He'd expected at least to sit at the table. As Adam landed in the chair Code ran his hands up his own face, taking a few deep breaths.

'You'll forgive me, I do not generally display emotions in front of my historic enemies, but I am beginning to, what the word? Blow my composure?'

'What do you mean?'

'The only person who is not in the dark here is your little group. I have monitored you. It gives me some intelligence, but all I truly know is the fact that a train under my supervision was invaded and my prisoners were murdered. A member of the Lost pulled an undercover operation in my territory and I had to let you go and trust a traitor. I do my best to keep up, and I know the Shatter Sisters' partners need to be removed.' He sighed. 'I feel... out of my depth and for a being who thrives on information that is the single most unpleasant feeling a being can have.'

'Look, I think I can help. I know there's a war going on, but I think the war's stupid so I'm happy to reach across the aisle to help people who need it.' He took off the mask and relaxed a little, then began to relate what had happened to his would-be interrogator.

'Do you need a drink? I need a drink,' he said once

Adam was done, having not interrupted a single word. At Adam's nod he picked up a bottle of whiskey and poured them both a glass. 'You know, I've been trying to quit. Every year I begin saying to myself this is the year I take my last drink.' He shook his head and handed Adam a glass. 'And every year I find another good reason not to. They say promises to yourself are the easiest to break.'

'So they say,' he admitted.

'Control,' he revealed. 'That's why I do this. I like doing the right thing, I like helping people, but my motivation is control, and this, is not controlled.'

'Why are you telling me this?'

'Running out of other options.'

'I understand,' Adam admitted. 'I don't think I've been in control of anything since all this started.' Lord Code physically shuddered at the notion.

'From what I hear you've been in control of your own people this entire time.'

'Doesn't seem that way from the inside.' He tapped his head.

'Seeing and being are very different.'

'Truer words never spoken. So, what do you really want to know?'

'Excuse me?'

'No one who craves control makes the same declaration every year, it doesn't happen. You would have either adapted or quit by now, or just stopped promising yourself. You're working me, and I don't begrudge you, but I'm easily bored and would rather get to the point. What do you really want to know.'

'Are you certain your side is working with mine?'

'Oh yeah, those two and one on the Lost side, and a bunch of minions. Seven I know of and probably plenty I don't.'

'I can't think of anything that would make the Shatter Sisters cooperate with the Lost, unless they were ordered,' Code finished and poured himself another drink.

'So, who could order them?'

'The entity known as the Queen of Reflection, one of the spirits that governs the Legion.' He rolled his eyes.

'Like the King of Eternal Flame?'

'Just the same,' he admitted. 'I will admit if they have the guidance of a Queen this is an issue, but I will not be daunted from my task. I shall assist as best I can.'

'Why would you help me? I'm Lost.'

'Because it is not in the best interests of the Legion as a whole to have the war only two sided. Many of our more problematic members thrive on intrigue. Without independents to focus on they will turn on their own. Besides, it's impossible to truly predict the repercussions of a move like this. Would it successfully wipe out the independents? Only some of them? Would it destabilise connections between the worlds? It is impossible to be certain, so what do you need in order to get this done?'

'I need to know who's building that device they're going to be using.' Adam sighed. 'I also need to know exactly what they're using it for.'

'You don't know that?'

'I have zero operational intelligence!' he snapped. 'None whatsoever. I only even know that's a concept because of TV. You guys probably have spies, operations teams, budgets and shit. I have none of those things. I have whatever I can pull together. If you want my help, get me some actionable, operational intelligence and I will act on it!'

'Oh thank the gods above and below.' Code leaned back in his chair, looking like he was about to cry. 'Finally, something I can actually do. I will get you any information I can as quickly as I can. I'll be in contact with the traitor and will feed you information through her. Anything else?'

'They have their own people weakening the borders to make ready for the device. They've done your side, they need to do ours. They were well into it when we kidnapped them, and once they're free again, which is likely nowish, they're going to be back at it.'

'I can't do much about that.'

'Neither of us can.' He sighed. 'The guy in charge is called the Skeleman, and he has seven people at his back. They're gonna lock this down airtight. The only attack vector is the artefact they need. So, you get on that and I'll try not to get us all killed.'

'May I make one more request?'

'Sure.' He nodded. 'I'll handle it if I can.'

'Get the Red Gentleman out of my universe as soon as humanly possible. Please.'

'Soon as I'm done talking with the Knife, I promise.' Adam got up. 'That all?'

'Yes.' He raised his glass. 'But I wasn't lying. I actually am an alcoholic, I've just given up trying to give up.'

'Okay, well, thanks for that.' Adam got up and walked out of his office. He didn't have the first clue why this guy was telling him that, but it was done now.

He took Mikhail by the shoulder and lead him into a nearby stationery closet, then looked around.

'Are we being watched?' he asked his Presences, after they both responded he looked at the young seeming sniper. 'So, how's your sister?'

'Well enough.' Mikhail's eyes widened as he cleared the gun, small surprise, but visible. 'How'd you figure it out?'

'A few things that took a while to add up. You look similar, you both have the same accent, and a few other things, but it mostly came down to the watching. It didn't matter where I went, what dimension I was in, what I was doing. Not many people could watch like that.' He tried not to look awkward. 'Even then I probably wouldn't have got it if everyone hadn't told me how hard it was to get strange information. There's only one person I know who can watch anything, anywhere, and the only time I knew I was being watched was when you were watching me. The other times I had no idea. Then it clicked that the only person who could see whatever she wanted happens to look a lot like you.'

'Well, given that Katie is a prisoner in a pocket dimension who may only speak to people every few days... On the other hand, she is as well as ever she is.' He gave a slightly bitter chuckle. 'Yes, for the record Katya, or Katie as you know her, has been spying on you.'

'For you?'

'For herself.' He didn't look the least bit embarrassed. 'She spies on me too, she spies on anyone she's interested in. It's the one privilege she still has. So, what do you need from me?'

'I wanted to thank you first, for showing up I mean. If you hadn't gone to Xavier and thrown down for me, I don't know if I'd be alive right now.'

'You would not.' Mikhail shrugged. 'It's fine. You're helping me and saving my sister's life, so it was the least I could do. I wanted to help.' He finished reloading his weapon and put it away.

'So, back when we first met?' Mikhail had shot at him a lot. 'You were trying to scare me off too?'

'We were,' he admitted. 'If it hadn't been for that stupid bear and his stupid plan we would have had a hope of it working. We could have scared you out of this. With her scaring you intellectually and me scaring you physically we would have been done.'

'Weren't you trying to kill me?' Mikhail shook his head.

'The setting I had it on would have hurt you badly, perhaps injured you permanently, but it never would have killed you.'

'You were willing to maim me?' he growled.

'I will not apologise,' Mikhail retorted. 'You were on a road to danger for which you are not and will never be prepared. I wanted to save you, even if it meant hurting you.'

'You wanted to save me?' He paused for a moment. 'Oh shit, you mean?'

'My family is unique, all three of us have gifts. You've met the whole family I believe. Myself, my sister Katia, and our bother Alexi. I suppose you would know him better by another name.'

'Don't say, don't say it, if you don't say it won't hear it and won't have to be true.' It didn't have to be a fact that his strange eyeless friend and his misguided guardian angel were connected to.

'My brother is better known as the King's Man.'

CHAPTER TWELVE

'What, do I do with this information?' Adam asked the universe in general, then turned on Mikhail. 'No, seriously, that's not a rhetorical question.'

'Accept that things are not as simple as you thought. My brother got in over his head and due to his lack of caution he learned the name of the King. Unlike you, by the time anyone knew what was happening to him we had lost the chance to bring him back. He had gained three more Presences and something about the King forced them to work together. That's all I can tell you for now. Things are in place and there may be a part for you if you wish to play it. Let's not distract you from your current business.'

'So, you weren't working for him?'

'I was trying to minimise his impact, sometimes that means working for him, sometimes against him. I'm sorry that we didn't try harder.'

'It's okay. Pan and Xavier took care of it.' He smiled, but Mikhail was unconvinced.

'No, they didn't. They stalled him but did not stop him. He knows you now, and the only way you could be safe from him is if you don't catch his interest again.'

'He's that dangerous? I just fought two people who everyone said was compared to him.'

'If any of you believed that, then he was holding back.'

'Holding back, seriously?' Adam was shaking, and he had no idea how to stop it. Once again, he felt that overpowering strength on his body. That surprisingly gentle unstoppable touch that accidentally broke and concussed him. 'Okay.' He got up and clenched his fists, pretending he wasn't terrified. 'Do you want to go back to what you were doing, or come cover us when things go down?'

'I will cover.' He nodded. 'I'll go speak to Code now.'

'I'll meet up with you in the real world,' Adam told him. 'I've been told to take Xavier out of here.'

'That's good sense.' He nodded. 'I'll find you soon.'

'Wait, one more question.' He raised one hand and Mikhail stopped. 'That place she lives, is that part of your plan to protect people from your brother?'

'No.' He smiled a little. 'That's part of another plan, to free my brother from the king.' He closed the door with a smile.

Adam headed back into the conference room, to see the rest of them nervously stirring and plainly uncomfortable, except Claire who seemed at ease, making everyone a cup of tea with a smile on her face.

'Xavier,' he called, heading over to the tall man. 'You're with me.'

'Am I just?' He raised one eyebrow. 'And why exactly is that?'

'Because no one wants you here. I had to promise to take you off their hands in order to get their cooperation. You want to come with me or do I have to pretend I'm capable of forcing you to do anything?'

'I shall spare you the humiliation.' Xavier got to his feet, tipped his hat and smiled. 'This place makes me physically ill anyway.'

It was as he headed for the door Adam saw it in a shattered piece of mirror, a reflected picture of Xavier's face.

He looked burned beyond recognition, his eyes almost but not quite falling out of his head. His skin was blackened and red, his lips burned away to expose his teeth. Adam tried not to jump as he felt the Laughing One slam the door on his emotions, suppressing all reactions and feelings until he could recollect his composure.

The two of them walked together, once they got to the elevator he dropped the impulse to pretend to be in charge.

'You got a way out of here?' He looked at Xavier, who flashed a smile, leaning back against the mirror at the back of the elevator.

'Of course I do.' He nodded. 'Happy to help.'

'Is it selfish that I'm kind of hoping the interrogation takes a few days?' Adam asked. 'I could really use a couple of real night's sleep.'

'My week has been quite restful.' Xavier gave a theatrical yawn. 'Other than being called to save your giggly behind twice.'

'Yeah well, I'm the only person who laughs at your jokes,' he retorted. 'I'd say we're even.'

'In what twisted world?' Xavier threw up his hands and shook his head. 'You people make no sense to me.'

'Can you not tell the difference between me being facetious and me being genuine?'

'Not even a little.' He sounded pleased.

'Okay, so you've been hanging out with this Six of Nothing guy?' He switched conversational topics.

'I rarely get into contact with my own people. There are very few of us and we're sent all over the worlds. It's a rare chance to be among my own people.'

'And where's Pan?'

'Peter is taking some time off from his warden position to be in love.' He seemed pleased by that. 'If his relationship is going to survive then he can't be watching me every day of his life.'

'Which you're exploiting?'

'Honestly, no. I would likely be doing this anyway. I wouldn't risk Jeremiah's happiness by stepping too far out of their control unless I had to.'

'There's actually a person that you like?'

'I told you already, he's a darling. Anyway!' He clapped his hands. 'Are we going to be killing people together again?'

'I don't kill people,' Adam protested.

'Still?'

'It has been like, days since I last saw you.' When Xavier said nothing, Adam rolled his eyes. 'Yes, still. Anyway, we're going to be stealing some important gadget that's being built by bad guys and beating down the people involved.' He put his hand on Xavier's shoulder. 'Have you heard from the Little Bear? Is he okay?'

'He and Raven are both fine. Little Bear is currently in hiding, doing some recovery after our little psi op. Being the Dread Bear for a good long while is a problem, and he still has something of a heart. Raven is currently off exploring options after that transformative experience of his.' The two of them had been involved in, and partially casualties of, a plan Xavier had started. Raven had been turned into a Blank for a while, and the Little Bear had done a number of unpleasant things, including, as far as Adam knew, permanently crippling Xavier by tearing off his left arm bare handed.

'And you are?'

'Passing fair.' He shrugged. By this time the two of them were walking through the streets of the Legion city, causing the others to gather around and watch as they completely ignored the organised lines of the world, pushing and shoving as they needed to in order to make it where they were going. 'The arm is something of an inconvenience, but one adjusts. Besides, this brings the number of foiled members of royalty this year up to two.'

'One day someone's going to fill me in on who the hell these people are.'

'Remember the chessboard?' He smiled. Adam had been shown a chessboard with dozens of creatures on it, and himself as a piece while he'd been under mind control.

'I do.'

'There are a number of players from outside the world, you have one playing alongside you right now, called the Laughing Man. The kings and queens are another side, each of them more or less working with the others. I work against them, with the lords and ladies.'

'I don't even a little bit understand.'

'The imperfection is yours, of that I assure you.' Xavier smiled. He stopped at a seemingly random door, pushed his sword into the lock and turned it. It ground and clicked for a long moment, then slid open. 'Don't tell anyone about this. The Knife said it was a secret, and I would prefer to keep him as an asset for as long as I can.' He pushed Adam through the door. 'Besides, a way in and out of the world owned by my enemies is an intriguing prospect.'

'Okay.' They stepped into the real world and again, Adam smiled as his feet hit solid ground. 'Well, unless there's something else we need to talk about I'm going to go home and get a solid eight hours. Okay?'

'It's morning.'

'I can't think of a single thing I actually want to do other than go to bed.' It wasn't as if he'd made a lot of friends since this mess had started and now that he and Annabelle were in whatever pattern they were in, he couldn't go see her. He did have some friends in the circus, but he wasn't sure if he'd be welcome there. 'God that's depressing. I well and truly need to get a life.'

'I suggest you ask Peter. He's one of the few I know who manage it.' He smiled. 'Perhaps you need to settle down with a pretty patron of your own.'

'Thanks, but I'm hoping my relationship with Annabelle isn't dead yet. Unfortunately, all of the friends we had are friends she had.'

'Well, best of luck and get some rest then, my good man.'

'Wait, no, first food.' Once again interdimensional transportation had led to his body catching up with him. It was now immediately demanding large amounts of sustenance. Xavier facilitated, leading him to a place that would serve him food as quickly as possible. After eating three times his usual he made his way home and waved to his housemates on the way in.

They didn't expect him to be social anymore; they didn't seem to expect much of him at all anymore. Not many people did in his real life.

Had they ever? Had anyone really expected anything of him? His dad maybe, before he'd died, maybe a couple of teachers. Now, not so much. That's what he now realised had been going on with his life, no one to point him anywhere. There'd been no pressure because not only had people expected him to fail, no one even expected him to try.

'And who's fault is that?' he asked himself. Few days' rest, then back to work.

He spent the next three days jumping from frustration to frustration as he ran back and forth trying to find something worth doing. As he searched for opportunities to refine his few and limited skills he came up empty time and again. It turned out there weren't many places among the Lost you could just walk up and into.

He started spending time at the café he'd met Xavier, Annabelle, Pan and the Little Bear in. Unfortunately, this was also the place he'd snuck into and robbed while he'd been under mind control, so he still got the occasional look. Still, it was a place to get coffee in the morning and beer in the evening, or beer in the morning if he really felt like it and people didn't look at him strange when someone at the bar asked what he was up to and he told them his spider girlfriend was upset in another dimension. Instead they looked at him like a sad case who had nowhere to go, which he was.

Once he got bored he decided to go elsewhere he headed home and gamed or binged one show or another until he got bored. This would normally have taken him weeks, but he'd become accustomed to his new life and now needed excitement.

Adam was almost grateful when new trouble came along.

'My brother is coming to see you tomorrow.' Katie spoke to him from her tree when he woke up once more on the bench in the space between spaces. 'He tells me you had a conversation I would have preferred you not have.'

'I tend to stumble into those situations I guess,' he

admitted. 'Besides, I figured out the first part.'

'So yes, I have a pair of brothers,' she admitted. 'Alexi is the elder, the King's Man, and the younger, Mikhail became an operative for the Legion to act to limit the King's impact on the world while pretending to be allies. In the course of that I ended up here, with him.' She wrapped her arm around her ibis, who gave Adam a blank, fish eyed look. 'For my work to continue I need to survive, and for that to happen you need to succeed. So,' she clapped her hands, 'let's focus up, shall we?

'The Lord of the Code has discovered that the Skeleman is coming back into the real world, your world, tomorrow. He is attempting to gain some intelligence. Apparently, the Legion's side of this involved obtaining an artefact. According to him they didn't get around to it before a gang of...' She looked down at the Ibis. 'What were the Skeleman's words? Pissant, goddamn, psycho killers without morals, ethics or understanding of how things are done, came along and screwed things up for them. Did I get that right?'

'More expletives were involved,' the ibis replied. 'Other than that, you are correct.'

'Wait a minute!' Adam looked down at the bird. 'He can talk?'

'I am a Presence,' it croaked. 'We can all talk.'

'Then why didn't you talk to me before?'

'Because I'm not fond of you.'

'Well, fair I guess.' He looked back at Katie. 'So,

he'll be in Brisbane?'

'Briefly.' She nodded. 'There will be a window in which you can strike.'

'Then I'll have to get Konstantin, Claire, Xavier, Annabelle, Pan... think we can call Wraither and Raven? We'll need everyone ready.'

'Slow down,' she snapped. 'A full-frontal assault will attract attention. Go with the bear Annabelle and Mikhail, with Xavier in reserve. Follow him, let him lead you to the artefact, and then let him go to where they keep it. They know someone is on their trail, so they don't have a lot of time. Killing one of the instigators will do well enough, but there is at least one Shatter Sister and the Seven Breakers to finish the op.'

'So, we have to secure the artefact.' He nodded. 'Okay, I'll rally the troops. Get me my sniper, I'll bring Xavier for when things go wrong, Annabelle for access.'

'You have to take the bear.'

'Konstantin? Are you sure? I wouldn't call him discrete.' She sighed in frustration.

'Trust that I know things you don't and take the bear. You can manage him. It'll be fine.'

'You think I can manage that thing? He's insane. He doesn't listen to anyone!'

'He listened to you. Perhaps he didn't obey but he listened. He owes you, and you can hold that over him.'

'That makes me uncomfortable, like, colonoscopy uncomfortable. My two partners,' he pointed to them, 'might be opportunistic by nature but the idea of exploiting someone sits wrong with me.'

'That weakness may kill you,' the Laughing One interjected, before curling up in Adam's lap. He was too big and far too heavy to do it for long, but it was rather nice for now.

'My inability to exploit and destroy others for my own wellbeing will eventually lead to my downfall?' The creature nodded.

'Could not have said it better myself.'

'Yeah well, I think I'm more comfortable with that fact that the idea of leading someone around by their guilt.'

'Noble,' the Watcher observed.

'Thanks.'

'It wasn't a compliment. Nobility means reminiscent of the behaviour of the noble classes, and the noble classes were stupid inbreeds who lead their people into the ground.'

The panther cackled so hard he fell out of Adam's lap and rolled around on the ground like a puppy. Adam blushed and held his hands over his face.

'Either way!' Katie raised her hand for silence. 'You need to bring the bear. He'll be a lot more use than you'd think.'

'Why do I feel like I'm getting my own Xavier here? Someone I hate but I'm developing a working relationship with, whether I like it or not?'

'Well, do your best to avoid that if at all possible. That dynamic does seem to be horribly unhealthy for them both.'

'I don't know. Xavier seems happy with it.'

'Yes, he's quite good at seeming,' she replied. 'Now go get your crew and get on your way.' They stood there and looked at each other for a moment.

'You have to wake me up before I can do anything.'

'Oh, yes.' She shook her head. 'Apologies. I shall end our moment.' She gave him a gentle shove with both hands and he pulled the mask off his face, springing awake and heading for the attic.

CHAPTER THIRTEEN

'Anyone here?' He bent down and looked around the corners. 'Any of you? I need a spider, and a way back into the Carnival. The moment is fast approaching that I'm going to need your help.' He headed to every corner before a small spider with orange markings came out of one of the cracks in the wall. 'Good evening, little one. Are you here from Annabelle? And why do I ask you questions when most of you can't talk?' It reared up and extended one of its eight legs, and Adam put his hand down. The creature tapped it like yellowtail had done and he nodded. 'I need you to take me to the Carnival. People are trying to kill us all and we need help.'

The creature didn't move, its eight eyes blinking rapidly. 'Okay. There's an ant colony under my housemate's floorboards. Three rooms to the left and one down. He doesn't treat his room all that well and the ants spread like the plague. Eat away.' There, spiders would do what he wanted if he paid them.

As he watched some spiders headed down the stairs, while others came out of nowhere and began to make their lines. This time he didn't have time to hesitate and set to the wall at a run. He wasn't sure if he had time, or how far away he came out. He headed for the staff entrance, only to be stopped at the door by a security guard named John.

'Come on, Johnnie.' He stared down the big man. 'I have important things to do.'

'Line's over there.' He didn't know the big guard very well. He'd spoken to the grunt from time to time and he was clearly loyal to Annabelle. He'd apparently decided to have a problem with Adam.

'John, you know you can't keep me out of here if I decide to walk in, so why don't you just tell Annabelle I'm here and let her make her own choice.'

'Fine.' His muscles clenched and unclenched. 'In the meantime.'

'I know where the damn line is!' he snapped. He didn't move toward it, leaning calmly against the entrance. 'And if Konstantin is here, get him for me too!'

They kept him waiting and he didn't have a choice. Well he did, he could cut through the bars or scale the fence, but they'd likely decide to start a fight and that would get bad. No, he'd let this petty crap play out. There was no sense in wasting time or getting hurt. He sat down and leaned against the door frame, his eyes half closed.

'What do you want?'

'To save the world?' He looked up at Annabelle. 'Also to stop wasting time sitting outside a circus waiting for you to get ready.'

'I assume that means you have a lead?' Her tone had that careful neutral quality to it that it only had when she was trying not to sound angry.

'I need everyone. The Skeleman is coming into town and we're going to stalk him on his rounds. Which means I need you, Xavier and Konstantin.'

'I don't like the idea of bringing Xavier in on this.

He is clearly and presently aligned with the Lost.'

'Yeah, but like you saw on the screen, his people exist in another world just like yours. He's not going to risk losing his home and hurting his leaders.'

'How do you know?'

'Because of something he said. He loves the time he spends with his own people because they're the ones who come close to understanding him. Unless you've heard that those Red, whoever they are, are on one side or the other, he's with us.'

'Do you know where the Dread Bear is?'

'I thought he was here.' He thought about it for a moment. 'I know the hotel in the real world he says at. Can you get Xavier? I don't know where he goes, and I don't wanna bother Pan.'

'I'll find him.' She looked at him for a moment, her eyes suddenly serious. 'Are you ready for this?'

'I'll have to be, won't I?' he snapped. 'Come on, I'll get Konstantin, you get Xavier and the fifth will be waiting for us.'

'Who is he?'

'My guy among the Legion,' he admitted. 'It's a little complicated, but we're working together on this. Remember how I said someone was following me? It was him.'

'You're friends with your stalker now?'

'Needs must when the devil kicks you in the junk.'

'That is not the original quote.'

'Well, I don't know the real version.' He shrugged. 'Are you okay?'

'I'm fine. I just have a lot of work to do, taking care of the Carnival you know?' She looked over her shoulder. 'Did you like it here?'

'Huh?' That was, unexpectedly friendly.

'The Carnival,' she explained, frustrated. 'Did you like the time you spent here?'

'Yeah. It sucks that they seem to hate me now, but they're cool. I had a good time being one of them. I miss them.'

'The kind of place you could see yourself ending up? If you stayed out of your own world I mean.'

'Yeah.' He nodded. 'I could see myself doing something like this. I went home for a few days and was bored out of my skull. I liked going on adventures on Carnival business. I liked talking crap and watching shows and solving trouble. I hope I get to come back.'

'Trust me, this place will always be a home for you.' She looked around. 'Okay, maybe not for the next couple of weeks but after that, always a place.'

'Thanks.' He nodded. 'Okay, shall we go?'

'You go ahead. I'm going to have to talk to the family about rounding up Xavier without bothering Pan.'

'Okay.' He nodded.

'Sister will take you home.' The spider in question didn't take a human form, just the slightly spooky appearance of an orange backed spider the size of a small dog. The creature led him home, and he caught a bus into the city.

Saviours of the world, he reflected, should not have

to ride the bus. He made a mental note to ask Jeremiah to hook him up with supplies, at least enough money to get him where he wanted to go. It was a short hike to get to the hotel, and the way into the hotel tested his capacity to tolerate human scorn as everyone around him glared. He knew he didn't fit in here. Once he got to the room he smashed his fist on the door.

'Hey yo, Konstantin!' He called up. 'Get your fat ass up!'

'You have no respect for the mood of this place,' came the grumbling voice from behind the door.

'You have no respect for literally anything that isn't you. Now open the door before I kick it down! We have things to do!'

'Okay.' He opened the door and looked Adam in the eyes, wiping sleep from his own. 'Where are we going?'

'Actually, we're kinda waiting for this guy to show up in the city.' He looked embarrassed as Konstantin's face grew thunderclouds.

'Then why you kickin' down my goddamn door?'

'I'm not.' He paused, remembering he'd literally threatened to do that. 'Sorry. I'm kinda' not great in the head right now.'

'Don't care about your feelings,' Konstantin replied. 'Just knock next time.' He turned away and Adam took that as invitation, heading inside. 'So, who are we waiting for?'

'Some guy called the Skeleman is going to be in the city very soon, recovering some vital artefact or another. We don't want to lose him, but if we do I'm going to need your nose and if I run into a roadblock I'm going to need your… everything else.'

'Sounds good.' He shrugged. 'When do we go?'

'You might have to be ready at a moment's notice at any point tomorrow. I don't want to be that hurry up and wait guy, but at this point I don't have much of a choice. We're all on eggshells til then.'

'That's fine. I'll stay ready.' He shrugged and pointed to the door. 'Feel free to head out at any time or stick around. I don't much care.' Adam made to leave, and Konstantin made yet another show of how little he cared, so Adam decided to stick around, taking a seat and turning on the TV.

'Let's fight,' Konstantin said, after a couple of hours of companionable silence and a meal.

'What?'

'You and me are gonna fight,' Konstantin decided. 'I'm going to have to figure out how good a fighter you are, and it might help you improve. So come on.'

So that was how Adam spent the rest of his time. He dodged, ducked whirled and spun away from Konstantin's surprisingly fast hands. The big bear wasn't nearly as disposed to charges and lunges when he didn't need to be. Adam thought finding blind spots would be easy, considering his bulk.

It should have been less surprising than it was he supposed. Konstantin had been aware of the limitations of his size and bulk for a long time, of course he'd learned to predict attempts to take advantage of that. Adam did his best to dance around him, but he was barely faster than the bear was and every time he seemed to be making progress he ended up backed into a corner with nowhere to go.

'What am I doing wrong?' he asked after his tenth bout, and it was clear this was what the bear had been waiting for.

'You focus too hard on your target. You focus on your strikes and mine, which is good, but you focus so intently you have no idea of anything around you. It's called situational awareness, and you seem to have next to none. It's not enough to have Presences to do that for you. That'll turn you into a decent fighter, but not a dangerous one.'

'Okay.' He thought about that. 'How do I work on it?' Konstantin hesitated for a long moment and headed around the room they were training in. He began to haphazardly place and shove dozens of stacks of chairs, tables and equipment around the room.

'There you go.' Konstantin squared off again. 'We learn the same way we learn everything. We learn by making mistakes over and over, until we stop failing. We make a dozen, hundred, thousand errors and pay the price again and again.'

'For someone who hates people so much you're a surprisingly good teacher.'

'How do you think I came to hate you all so much? I've been teaching your kind to fight before what you are as even a kind. Since your biggest cities were things you'd see barely more than a small town now.' He yawned and squared off again, then charged at

Adam, who rolled out of the way under the table. Konstantin went through it and Adam used the opportunity to jump on his back. Konstantin saw this coming and lashed out, so Adam jumped back and crashed into a stack of chairs, going down hard and landing on his back.

'Dammit!'

That was more of their night, Konstantin pushed, ran and guided Adam around the room while he crashed into obstacles, made a fool of himself and failed again and again to anticipate the moves. Whenever he managed to figure out where or how Konstantin was trying to lead him he ran into Konstantin's actual attacks, slammed down by sheer bulk or gashed by claws.

'We're done.' Konstantin turned away and headed for the door. 'Any more and you'll hurt yourself.'

'What's the time?' He looked around, then went over to where he left his phone. 'It's half past midnight. I can't get home.'

'There's another room in my suite.' He shrugged. 'A couple, but one has a bed.'

'You sure? I don't want to be all up in your space.'

'I don't care.' He shrugged. 'I'm used to sleeping with humans around anyway. It'll be like the old days.'

'What old days?'

'My old days.' They got into the elevator. 'I'll tell you the story in the morning if you're interested.'

Interlude, The Story of the Dread Bear.

In the ancient times no one could challenge the bear. He was the most dangerous creature in existence. Buffalo, bison, wolf, all were helpless against the bear. On occasion they were lucky, ten, fifteen to one would give them hope.

Man too was helpless to resist bear once he had a mind to destroy, but man had something the other beasts had not. Man was clever, he hid from bear behind his walls, in tens and twenties and hundreds he opposed a single bear, and when winter came and bear needed to sleep groups of men would sneak into his home with spears and axes and butcher the bear.

Among all bears there was one greatest, one strongest and largest, one cleverest and most feared and he kept all men at bay, but he too needed to sleep and while man had not yet risked waking him, he knew it was only a matter of time.

One tribe of men was wiser than the others, and they sent four of their best and brightest to the bear's cave, joined by another the tribe had not sent. The five of them stood outside the bear's cave, and when he stepped outside and roared at them to go away they all bowed before him.

'We have come to see you,' the leader of the group told him. 'If you train us while you are awake, to fight as well as your kind fight, in exchange we will guard you while you sleep, from other creatures and our own kind.'

'What makes you think any of you are worth teaching?' the bear demanded.

'I am the strongest of my kind my tribe has ever met.' The woman who stood in front of him was a giant, with a bald head and muscles like stones who could hurl men who should have been stronger than her, like rag dolls. The bear fetched *a boulder he himself could barely lift and rolled it to her.*

'Lift this above your head and you may train with me.'
She set herself against the boulder and strained, pulling and
heaving upon it with her entire body. She struggled for
hours, lifting the boulder a little higher each time. First to
her knees, then her shoulders, then finally with a grunt of
effort she pulled it over her head. She held it up for almost a
second before springing backwards and dropping it to the
ground, almost crushing herself in the process.

The bear allowed her inside, and then made his way
down the hill to where the rest of the group camped. 'Why
should I train any of you?'

'I am the fastest of all my kind.' The man who spoke
stretched his legs as he looked at the bear. 'I cannot lift a
boulder, if that is your test.'

'There is a hart in the next field. Young and strong, with
white hair. He is clever, and swift and aware. Fetch me some
of his hair.' The man looked at the bear for a long moment
and stood, brushing his long hair from his face and striding
into the distance.

For days he chased the creature; he attempted to ambush
it, attempted to block it, attempted to keep the creature's
options limited. He grew smarter and smarter, raced faster
and faster. For days he tracked and stalked and planned.

For two days the fastest man in the world did nothing.
He rested quietly by the camp fire, slept like a child and just
when the bear began to suspect he had given up and simply
could not face the humiliation of heading back down the
mountain, he returned to the field

It took hours, even then of sprinting, guiding, scaring

and bolting but finally, with a desperate lunge he managed to pluck a few strands of white hair from the very tip of the hart's tail. He opened his hand, lying there in the grass, breathing hard.

The bear allowed him into the cave and returned to the others.

'I am the greatest hunter in my tribe,' the third man barked, refusing to even wait until the bear spoke. 'The greatest tribe in the world! Test me in whatever way you see fit, I will do this!'

'Shoot the moon,' the bear retorted.

'Excuse me?'

'Shoot the moon,' the bear replied, returning to the cave. The man knew it was impossible, but he took a few shots at it anyway, studying the problem from every angle. Eventually he developed a plan. He stepped into the darkness, demanded the bear stand beside him and tied a white band around the base of the arrow. He smiled, drew back the bow, took aim and fired. After a moment, when the arrow was out of sight he smiled.

'I hit it.' He pointed up.

'No, you didn't,' the bear retorted.

'Find me the arrow, fetch me the undamaged moon, or admit that I have done what needs to be done.' The bear searched for the arrow with the white band for some time, but when he couldn't find it in two days and two nights he admitted he could not prove anything.

The man had fired the arrow to where he knew it would be and had the fastest waiting in hiding to untie the white band from his arrow. The bear knew he had been tricked, but not knowing how, he had no choice but to admire what had been done. He went down the mountain and spoke to the next in the list. He didn't speak, just sitting and looking at the bear as the bigger creature loomed over him.

'Why are you worthy of my training?'

'My mind,' he replied. 'My body may not be special, but my mind is. I can plan, track and execute to any purpose.' He got up and looked at the bear. 'I need to be able to fight if I am to defend my people.'

'There's a rabbit warren to the east.' He peeled back his teeth. 'There are black rabbits there, and they are faster and smarter than any other rabbit in the world. I have never managed to eat even one.'

'I could crush that entire warren right now!' the strongest snapped.

'I could run them down,' the fastest suggested.

'I could simply pluck one on the run.' The hunter raised his arrow.

'I'm not asking any of you!' he snapped. 'I'm asking you.' He poked the claw into the smartest's chest. 'No weapons and no assistance.' He turned away.

The smartest watched the warren for a few hours, marking entrances and exits, comings and goings He set traps and watched the rabbits jump, avoid and slip through them. They were clever and swift.

He went to the surrounding areas, gathered supplies, and blocked the exits and entrances with rocks, ignoring the creatures attempts to dislodge them, and resetting them every time the creatures succeeded. Then he went down to the river, filled a cauldron with water and heating it over a *fire until it started to boil. He set a dozen traps outside the last exit and poured the cauldron into the last entrance.*

In the end he returned with three badly scalded black rabbits. The rest of the warren set up a new warren, but he got the one he needed, and two more.

'What about you?' The bear looked at the last person at the fire. She had not been sent by the city, she had chosen to come on her own. Even among the others they had not treated her as company.

'There isn't anything special about me,' she said softly. 'I'm not, any of the things those people are. I'm just a person. I just want to help my people. I'll do anything, whatever I have to, in order to prove myself. I'll find a way to do any of the things they did, or something else, whatever it is you need.'

'I can't use you.' The bear turned away.

'Please!' She looked at him, almost begging. 'I'll do whatever it takes.'

'Stand guard at the cave.' The bear turned away. 'No food, no rest, no sitting, for three days at guard.' It was impossible, of course it was, but she did it anyway.

On the second night, the smartest and fastest of them slipped out with some food.

'Come on,' the smartest urged. 'He's sleeping, and he doesn't care. You can rest for a few minutes, get something to eat. He takes plenty of time to wake up, you will have more than enough warning.'

'Thank you, but no.' The other one smiled, bracing herself against the wall, holding her spear to her chest. 'I was given a task, and I will complete it.'

On the morning of the third day the bear decided he was not without mercy, he questioned each of them, and they revealed that for those two days she had no so much as closed her eyes for longer than a blink.

'All right.' The bear looked at her. 'Come in.'

'Sorry.' She slammed the spear butt down on the ground as best she could. 'But I was given a task and I will complete it.'

'I'm telling you I'm satisfied!' the bear snapped. 'You can come inside, I'll train you!'

'I'm sorry. I was given a task and I will complete it' Though her body screamed its objections she stood straight backed and stared ahead.

'I gave you the damned task!'

'Be that as it may. I was given a task and I will complete it.' She glared.

She lost consciousness around sundown on the third day and fell slumped against her spear.

'No one tells her she fell asleep,' the bear growled.

So, the bear trained them for many days and nights, in the summer, autumn and spring he trained, and in the winter, they guarded his sleeping form. When he finished training them, they returned to their home and guarded their town. For years it was the same thing, the village sent the best of their people and he trained them in exchange for protection in the winter.

At first they sent only their best and brightest, only a few a year, but as time went on they sent more and more, less and less skilled who showed less and less deference.

Eventually he lost his temper and refused to train the next group, demanding they come back only when they learned some respect. By this time the first guards, who had greeted him with such awe and determination, were old and could not fight. They refused to teach the bear's secrets to others, as did all of those who had mastered his teachings.

Eventually, after years of the bear's ignoring their increasingly frustrated requests, the men decided they would be finished with this creature once and for all. They went up the mountain with dozens of their warriors and demanded that the bear begin taking their soldiers for training again or leave their valley. The bear flew into a rage and killed several of the men who came for him.

When he came down to the city, it was as a creature of pure wrath, and his students made choices. Some chose to fight beside the bear, others chose to side with their own kind. Mother killed son, brother fought brother, daughter murdered father, and the greatest city of men fell apart.

And the bear was Dreaded ever after.

End Interlude.

Adam awoke with the Dread Bear's story in his head.

With very little else to do, and understanding that he needed help learning to fight, he stayed with the Dread Bear for the rest of the day. He trained with the strange, aggressive giant as hard as he could, working on his situational awareness, understanding and physicality. He knew this guy knew how to train people, and as strange and standoffish as he was, he obviously knew what he was doing.

Unbeknownst to Adam, he was improving at a frighteningly rapid rate. Every time he hit a wall the Dread Bear pushed him straight over it. He improved more in hours than most people would in years by the power and magic of the bear's chosen training.

He got a message from Mikhail letting him know the Skeleman would be passing through at around midnight, so the bear closed his training at ten.

'You're still absolute dogshit as a fighter.' The bear looked at him on the night of the third day. 'Against any real opponent you'll die in a matter of seconds without pulling out more power and it'll be good riddance to bad rubbish.'

'Thanks.' Adam glared at him. 'Tell me there's a but there, please?'

'Yes, yes.' He waved a paw. 'But you're much better than once you were, and you show some distant, slight potential to be something that vaguely relates to special. Currently, if you're up against an idiot who has some power but doesn't know what to do with it, and you get lucky, you might end up on top.'

'That's pretty much how you'd describe me, isn't it?'

'I'd probably swear more.' He smirked. 'For what it's worth, I would have tested you if I'd had the option, and there's an off chance you might have passed.'

'You're not a nice person.'

'I am not nice, nor a person,' he agreed. 'You should head off and get some rest. Tie up any loose

313

ends you may have before what happens next, happens.'

'Don't really have anything to tie up,' Adam admitted.

'That's dangerous.' The bear looked at him. 'My people, the humans, they trained with me, all had something to hold onto. Something they believed in. It might have been what broke 'em in the end but it also stopped them from doing those silly little things like snapping and killing all their own people.'

'Then I guess it's lucky I'm not one of your students.'

'Still dangerous.' The bear scowled. 'Someone like you, with all that violence in you and that thing in your head. Find something worth fighting for or you'll end up fighting for fighting.'

'You mean like you?' Adam snapped, and Konstantin let out a growl, suddenly appearing twice his size.

'You have no idea who I am or what I fight for, boy. Given a hundred years you could not begin to understand what I have done, and what I still do! I gave up so much, suffered so much, surrendered so much for you petty little creatures and you will never show me so much as an ounce of–'

'You're right.' Adam took a step forward and snarled back into his face. 'I have no idea who you are or what you did, or anything else. So until you've got some reason to expect I should, you have no right to expect my faith! You want my thanks? Fine, thank you, you've stuck by me since we met, and it's given me a chance to survive but you don't get to tell me how to live!'

The stared at each other for a few long moments, then the bear turned away.

'You remind me of the boy.'

'What?'

'The boy with the rabbits. He was the least loyal to me, not because he was any less trained or believed in me less, he just asked more questions. Wanted explanations and wouldn't do anything if he didn't know why he should.'

'Thanks? I think? Was that a compliment?'

'No, it was a commentary, you're a stupid child, but you're all stupid children when you start. One or two of you, if you're lucky, earn the title of stupid adult.'

The clock struck eleven, and Adam took up two spiders. 'Go get your queen. She has work to do, we all do. Tell her to come find us and we'll get this done.' He looked over at Alexi and Konstantin. 'The Gentleman and the Carnival Queen will be by soon. In the meantime, Dread Bear, Knife, Knife, Dread Bear.' He'd go by codenames until someone said otherwise. 'Knife, do you know exactly where he is?'

'I will, in about an hour.' He untucked a set of three earrings and pushed one of them into Konstantin's ear and the other into Adam's. The mask quieted the pain and Adam felt some kind of connection 'We'll connect through these if we need to split up. Until then I have a nest waiting. I'll need the two of you on the ground.'

'Got your back.' Adam nodded 'You know one of the biggest problems about this whole "gods in clothing" thing is we all have signature looks. I glow, and Konstantin stands out a mile away on account of the whole "huge guy in the same suit" thing. He'll recognise us.'

'You'll have to follow him without the Presences then. I'll keep him in my sights from the rooftops but if he moves too far, too fast I'll need you to follow him while I reposition.'

'Okay. I'll need a bag to keep my stuff in while I trail him. Konstantin, stay close. I might need you for if I lose them.'

'You mean for when you lose him.' Konstantin ruffled his hair, then reached under the bed and pulled out a ragged old blanket. 'Don't worry about it, I have procedures for this. Let's get to it.'

So it was that when the tall, bone pale man in the suit, his bird mask packed away in his gear, appeared Adam discretely followed him, keeping more than a street away from him at all times as Mikhail tracked him through a scope. Whenever he needed to move Adam moved in, following the pale man quietly through the crowd. He carried his bag over his shoulder, grumbling as he made his way.

At one point the thin man walked past a homeless man who was hidden under a blanket. He smelled like whiskey and something rotten, and sniffed the air as the pale man passed, holding his hand out for money. Once he turned the corner Konstantin waited a few moments, then rose, tossed aside the whiskey bottle and the rotten blanket, then sniffed the air and headed off.

'Got him.' Konstantin smiled his too full smile. 'I'll stay on him as best I can.'

'When the hell is my backup getting here?' Adam grumbled. 'If this guy decides to skip dimensions on us, we're all screwed.'

Mikhail watched the Skeleman through the scope, calmly keeping a running commentary on how many times and all the different ways he could have killed or seriously maimed the Lost elite by now if they weren't in a crowd.

'You realise he's an incredibly powerful being and there's a decent chance your shot would bounce off him and hit someone else, right?'

'That is an issue,' the sniper considered. 'I'm pretty sure I could break through it, given enough time.'

'Because giving someone time to shoot them is exactly what leads someone to the heights of the Lost. Now shut up and focus, please.' Konstantin grumbled. Adam changed position again, slipping behind a wall to wait for the Skeleman to pass.

The white spider crawled up the side of Adam's neck, and he let out a sigh of relief.

'Our interdimensional backup has arrived, and I really hope Xavier has the brains to hide.'

'He does,' Mikhail replied. 'He's with me. Your

spider should be close enough, soon enough.'

Annabelle tapped Adam on the shoulder, and as he turned his head he saw she was wearing far more muted colours than usual. She wore her hair a deep blue-black that had seemed just black, though as the wind blew her hair back it revealed a shock of pink underneath. She gave him a small smile and took the white spider back from him, plucking it gently from his shoulder.

'When does he leave?' she asked.

'I have no idea,' he replied. 'We're going to just follow him until he steps through, and then slip through after him.'

'You realise if he makes us he'll have ample time to build a trap for us between him leaving the dimension and us making it in after him?'

'You realise that if we don't follow him and he gets this thing, all the life in like… hundreds of worlds will be completely wiped out?'

'Why would you bring that out?'

'To stop you worrying about things you can't change.' Adam shrugged. 'If he has a trap we have to spring it, if he makes a break for it we have to chase him. No matter what we track him until he returns with the artefact or one side dies.'

'Well, that is both well-reasoned and incredibly disturbing.'

'Think of it as my version of that weird ass thing Xavier and Pan do.' With that he returned to tracking the Skeleman.

Eventually the target made his way into a building, and Mikhail kept watch on the elevator.

'Thirteenth floor, seven rooms across on the left, he's vanished, we'll need to follow him. We'll be there soon.' Once they made it up and the others made it across, Xavier and Annabelle got to work, Annabelle's spiders weakening the gap in the world enough for Xavier to cut through it. Normally they'd go in together for security, but Konstantin was the kind of person who didn't do 'together'. He barged in, without ceremony, once the hole was open, and the others slipped through the gap behind him.

The world was dark, and Adam focused and listened to the world for any available details. The floor under his feet was some kind of stone, and everything was hot and close. It was like being in a stone, heating vent How the hell could he find anything in this darkness? He reached out and fetched his phone out of his pocket, taking a couple of deep breaths and trying to quiet the claustrophobia that was slowly but certainly developing in his gut He slipped out his phone and turned on the torch function to get his bearings.

Then Konstantin came shattering through the wall with roughly the speed and enthusiasm of a locomotive. He growled and looked at Adam for a moment, then sniffed the air.

'Good thinking, kid.' The bear nodded. 'I can't track shit right now, there's too much energy all around, but there's not a lot in the way of technology here.'

'Yeah.' He nodded. 'That was absolutely my plan. How do we find the others?'

'Not easy.' He shrugged. 'I can move freely through the realm, walls are thin, but no one else could.' Adam reached up to the communicator.

'Knife, the Dread Bear and I are together, are you there?'

'Yes.' To his credit he sounded almost completely calm. 'I'm currently in a very small space and I am not entirely sure how to get out. I am retaining my calm breathing patterns and attempting to gather my composure, but I fear I will soon run out of air. I have resisted the urge to blast my way out on the grounds that I didn't want to risk a cave in.'

'Well, that's an interesting factor that Konstantin didn't consider and apparently isn't much of a risk. He put his face through the wall.'

'Konstantin?'

'The Dread Bear.' He was not good at this whole covert op thing. He needed to get his composure back. 'Anyway, we need to get you some room to breathe, so would you put a hole in that wall with that weird cannon, so we can trace the damage?'

'That'll blow our attempt to follow him discretely.'

'So will you suffocating in a small room while we search blindly for you.'

'Your point, while callous, is well made. Watch your six, I will attempt to only shoot through the rocks without blasting what is behind them, but I can make no promises.' There was a crack and blast in the distance and Adam climbed onto Konstantin's back as the big creature barrelled through rock walls. Every few seconds he stopped to listen to the sound of sonic cannon blasting through rock. 'Okay, I think we're almost there, and you can stop shooting now. Konstantin, you have found him, right?'

'Him and only him.' Konstantin's head cocked. 'I can hear screaming, not his screaming, different, unrelated screaming.'

'Unrelated screaming is not nearly as reassuring as you seem to think! We're going to need to pick up the pace!'

'Knife, pin yourself against the wall and fire at the opposite one, then stop when I tell you to stop.' Konstantin rumbled.

'Got it.' The gun began to fire, the sonic cannon ripping through the rock almost as fast as the bear did.

Adam, following behind him, noticed fourteen solid rock walls, all of which seemed to have been more of a momentary irritation to the bear than a serious problem.

'Stop!' Konstantin called, and the gun powered down as he made his way through the wall, it had been weakened but not broken by some of the sonic blasts, and Konstantin took a moment to rest against the wall, rubbing its furry head.

'You okay?' Adam looked at him, and he pulled himself to his feet.

'Yeah.' He nodded. 'Do we head toward or away from the screaming?'

'It could be Xavier.'

'Screaming?' Konstantin didn't sound convinced.

'Causing the screaming. The Red Gentleman in a confined space with someone for this long? He could have just been speaking and they would have started that.'

'Right.' That apparently seemed much more believable to Konstantin. 'Knife, soften up the wall for me.'

They made their way through the walls that way, Mikhail shooting small holes in the walls to weaken them for Konstantin's way through. The two of them made good progress, and even better once Adam used his own abilities to pick the best fracture points in the walls.

The good news was the source of the screaming was Xavier.

The bad news was he was in fact screaming.

Xavier faced off against the three of them, drawing his rapier and facing off against them like they were his enemies, his composure was blown, his usual smiling face replaced with an ugly snarl, his eyes wide with animal fear.

'What's going on?'

'You!' he snarled. 'You put me here! You did this to me!' He lunged, almost blurring with speed as the blade swung at Adam. Konstantin managed to match him, swatting him out of mid-air with one paw. 'How dare you put me here?'

'Xavier!' Adam called out. 'We didn't put you here!

You volunteered, you're okay! Annabelle! Is Annabelle here? Is she hurt?'

'No.' From behind them came Annabelle's voice. 'I'm fine, spiders manage mazes of labyrinths pretty well. What's going on?'

'Xavier's lost it!' Adam jumped forward and caught the sword between his claws, locking it up with his other hand. Xavier still pulled the sword out and made to strike again. Konstantin hit him with his shoulder and he tumbled backward, landing on the wall with his feet and striking hard, sticking the sword right into the bears side. 'What the hell do we do?'

'I finally kill him!' Konstantin clawed at Xavier's chest, tearing the skin.

'No, you don't.' Annabelle stepped forward and tossed a web out. 'Red, if you come back without us the Soldier will never let you forget it. He'll tell the whole world what you did, who you are!'

'He put me here!' He pointed his sword at Adam.

'I don't care what he did!' she screamed at him, throwing another web. 'I know what your problem is, and I need you to think anyway! It's only a matter of time before the thing that owns this place shows up and kills us all, and if you let us die, you will have failed your mission! You will have failed the Ladies!'

'Can't fail the Ladies.' His voice was soft, almost woozy. 'Can't fail the Ladies.'

'Then quit acting like a psycho and soldier up! I know you're getting twisted right now but you need to take a deep breath and act like a person wo's done hard things his entire damn life!' Her tone moved from comforting to authoritative, the last syllable like a whip crack in the air.

'I need to get out of here.' He was still panicking, but more or less had a hold on it. 'I hate this place and everyone in it.'

'We're moving!' Annabelle gestured for the rest of them to follow her. 'We need to go quickly, or we'll be in a lot of trouble! Things that live in places like this will generally be sensitive to the smallest vibrations. I thought we'd be cool as long as we didn't bother them, but something's been putting holes in the walls, which has probably riled them up.'

'Yeah, we were doing that.' Adam looked at her, and she let out a series of curse words worse than any he'd heard her say in her life, including several in languages he couldn't identify.

'So you're all stupid,' she concluded. 'Grats. Now we need to haul ass even faster! I don't know what calls this place home, but whatever it is you have almost certainly provoked by smashing pieces of its home! If we're very lucky we–' The walls began to rumble. 'Get into the place Xavier was stuck in, now, now, now, go!' They, grumbling primarily out of confusion and fear, piled into the room where Xavier had been imprisoned.

The thing that came screaming through the tunnel was grey and silver, covered in mouths and gnashing swirling teeth.

'What is that thing?' Adam screamed.

'Train worm,' Annabelle told him.

'What the hell is a train worm?' He looked over at Konstantin. 'And have you picked up that guy's trail yet?'

'A train worm is an analogue of trains, and dragons, and other, slightly weirder stuff. They run like trains, but they're living beings and they eat people and anything else that gets in their path. The good news is they have set paths they operate on. The bad news is when they break those patterns they go insane and attack everything in the vain hope of getting rid of whatever is ruining their home.'

'Which we've just done?'

'Which, as you said, you've just done.' She turned to Konstantin. 'I can make my way through this place without getting eaten, probably, maybe.' She directed them backwards and another worm smashed through the holes that Konstantin had made, turning them into a new, bigger than bear sized tunnel. 'But I don't know where to go! I hope you've still got the trail!'

'I hate this place.' Adam informed no one in particular.

'All the holes have cleared something of a trail.' Konstantin sniffed. 'It's fading but I have one, I can go the easy way or the long way. I don't know the long way, but I can tell you when you're getting closer.

'How's your head?' Adam put one hand on the bear's head.

'S'just a skull,' he grunted. 'I'll tough it through.'

'Let's go the long way.' He looked at Konstantin.

'Which direction are we going now?'

'That way.' He pointed north-east and Annabelle began to move, setting off at a run. As they came to forks, T-junctions and off roads she made turns according to Konstantin's knowledge and her own instincts. It seemed like she understood the entire place and how to get through it.

'How are you doing this?' Adam asked.

'Please,' she scoffed. 'I ran through more complicated labyrinths than this when I was twelve. Spider magic is all about the complicated patterns and, excluding the holes you guys made with your blundering, these things seem to have an internal logic to them. Left, now, fast!' They jumped to the side just in time for the gnashing, rumbling monster to head by them.

'What the hell do we do to get by those things?' Adam yelled after the worm went by.

'They'll go by the same route every time. I can steer clear of them as long as we don't run into any unexpected complications.'

'Unexpected complications like?'

'Here.' Konstantin pawed at the ground.

'What?'

'Trail ends here, meaning the dimensional gap he went through, also here.'

'Where the worm blitzed through at a hundred K's an hour with its teeth gnashing like a goddamn meat grinder?'

'Yeah, complications exactly like that.' Annabelle

sighed. 'I hate complications.' She cracked her knuckles and closed her eyes for a moment, pressing her hands against the rocks.

'Annabelle?'

'We're going back into the nearest side tunnel and waiting until the next worm comes When it's gone by, I should have maximum time to get the job done.'

'Anything any of the rest of us can do?'

'Try not to make any more messes or get me killed,' she snapped, waiting against the wall for the creature to pass by. Sure enough, it rumbled, screamed and ground down its path as she slipped out to get to work. She weaved with her web covered hands as the spiders joined in to make a path. The rest of the group stayed behind her, and Xavier waited with his sword drawn for the exact moment the path was ready.

'It's coming,' Konstantin muttered.

'What do you mean it's coming? I'm almost done and if it gets by we'll have to start over!'

'What do we do?'

'I don't know, slow it down somehow! I'll be finished soon.'

Adam looked at the situation for a long moment and snapped into order mode.

'Mikhail, burn a pit into the ground, Konstantin help him widen and deepen it!' Adam set to work cutting pieces out of the ground, he couldn't do much but better that than doing nothing. The three of them dug the deepest ditch they could, but it wasn't much, and it'd probably only slow it down a bit.

'Fall back.' Mikhail looked at the two of them. 'I have this.'

'Are you certain?'

'Not in the least, fall back anyway.' He set to work on his gun, pulling switches, switching scopes and racking slides into place, the gun seeming to grow in his hands. 'I have a plan.'

'Which is?' Xavier smiled.

'Shoot it, a lot.'

'Peter would doubtless be gratified to know someone on the other side is capable of the same near fatal levels of stupidity he is,' Xavier commented. 'Everyone who isn't planning suicide by death worm, stand behind the spider girl.'

'Pay attention!' Mikhail boomed, glowing a pure white. 'I can only do this once.' As the worm barrelled toward him he got to work calculating something, even as the spinning, tearing, grey maws bore down on him.

The sound of the worm was overpowered by the sound of a thousand choirs screaming in agony. The world around them began to shake and the roof started to collapse as the entire corridor filled with a strange wavering in the air. The worm didn't stop but it began to slow down, teeth flesh and steel beginning to bend, break twist and snap. As the creature got closer it slowed down more and more as things ripped and tore from the creature. It wasn't moving slowly, but it was buying the seconds.

'Done!' Annabelle called out.

'Hold fast!' Xavier hacked at the air and a portal split open.

'Knife, through the portal and jump to the side, everyone else behind me!' Konstantin barged in front of them and everyone took their places behind him. Maybe the giant bear could grant them some measure of protection, but it wasn't likely.

Adam thought for a moment that he might have been completely wrong, but as what looked like the lacerated insides of a worm screamed past them, all logic left his world and he closed his eyes and curled into a ball, screaming and hoping everything would go away.

'All right, Gent,' the Dread Bear called out. 'That was hateful, even by my standards.'

'I will admit that this was more visceral than I'd liked, far from ideal.' Xavier spoke from the other side of the portal. 'I would say watch your step but, well...'

'What's going on?' Mikhail looked around holding what appeared to be a pistol, walking behind Xavier.

'It went through the portal.' Xavier clarified, looking around. 'Well, some of it did anyway.' Adam stepped around him and looked through the rip in reality. Sure enough on the other side was a few hundred meters of leaking worm guts and metal. On both sides of the portal was even more.

'Are you okay?' He looked at the bear.

'Just a few layers of skin.' He looked down at himself. 'And a bit of muscle.' The group walked through the portal, every one of them looking just a little disgusted at the spray of guts. They moved to the side and waited with the rest of the group. As soon as he stepped through, Konstantin took a couple of breaths and fell on his face. Annabelle began to wrap the injured bear as Xavier closed the rift.

'This,' Adam looked at the others, 'was not exactly low key.'

'Oh, don't whine at me!' Annabelle snapped. 'I did what I could. You all made this next to impossible. If you wanted me to be quiet about it, you shouldn't have knocked in the goddamn walls!' She scowled and shook her head. 'Come on Dread, you got a trail, or don't you?'

'I do.' He set off at a loping run down the path. 'Stay on my back. If you slow down, I'll leave you behind.' The bear was much slower than usual, moving only at Adam's usual running speed. The bear charged through the jungle, ignoring the path in favour of crashing through the underbrush. Adam moved beside him, cashing on the left.

'You realise there are probably snakes and wolves and whatever else in your path? Not to mention the fact we're supposed to be–'

'He's getting away!' Konstantin replied.

'Stop! Stop!' Adam tried to pull him back. Konstantin ignored him completely and continued barrelling through the growth. Adam stayed on his right, lashing out at anything that looked like it might attack the bear and startling it away.

Annabelle had taken another approach, and was

currently swinging through the trees like Spiderman, which Adam supposed she kind of was. Mikhail sat quietly atop the bear's bulk, checking every direction with his comparatively little gun. Xavier reappeared occasionally from the undergrowth, but the sounds of beast murder echoed in the distance, so Adam assumed he was probably killing interdimensional monsters just for fun.

'Excuse me,' The voice came from a fair distance away. 'If no one minds and if it's not rude to ask can you please stop tearing apart my home?'

'We're in a hurry,' Konstantin replied. 'We're looking for the guy who made a mystical artefact designed to make a hole between dimensions.'

'You have found him,' The old man standing in front of him, folded his black clad arms. 'What do you want?'

'The artefact, well, I want to rip your throat out with my bare teeth, but the Laughing Man here wants the artefact of yours to save everyone. One of us is going to get what we want.'

'I'm afraid it's going to have to be you my large friend.' The old man smiled. 'The Skeleman has already been here, he has already taken the artefact with him.'

'Konstantin keep moving, if he doesn't get out of the way run him over. Follow the trail and follow this asshole back to the real world so we can rob him.' The old man folded his arms.

'I am an artificer, Sir' The old man shook his head. 'I can protect myself. I would not advance upon me if

I were you.'

'Konstantin. Why are you not charging?'

Konstantin thought about this for a moment, snarled, and charged at the old man.

The ground formed a wall in front of them, and the old man turned around, vanishing from view as Konstantin shot a hole in it. 'You are welcome to attempt to break through if you like. I would advise you to look out for the traps though.'

'Tell me where he was going.' Adam looked at them for a moment. 'Tell me where he has to be to use that artefact of yours and I'll leave you alone. Won't break up your stuff or kill you or burn down your house. We'll leave you be completely.'

'You are a determined little man.' He smiled.

'And that invisible wall will break if struck exactly there.' Adam pointed to it. 'The explosive traps on the ground trigger there, there and there, some kind of monster will be released if we go there and,' he looked the old man in the eyes, 'I can do this all day. Granted I might have to, but I can make it all the way there.'

'How do you do that?' He looked at Adam, surprise breaking his composure a little.

'I have very good eyes.' He watched the guy for a moment. 'Wait a minute! You're the old guy the twins were talking to in their lair!' he realised. 'You're the dude in the screen! Man, we could have saved so much time if we'd thought about this! Of course that was going on. Man, I'm so glad the last of them is going to die in prison!'

'Oh.' He smiled. 'Well, I'm so sorry to have taken up your time. No harm done I suppose. Anyway, the artefact can only be used from the exact dimensional centre. It can only work in proximity to all four sides, hitting the line dead centre.'

'So it has to be used…'

'In the real world.' Annabelle finished the thought. 'We'll have to get a dimensional centre point in the real world.'

'Meaning we came all this way, just to have to go back home?'

'I'm afraid not.' The old man looked apologetic. 'You see the only traversable paths in and out of this dimension are the one the Skeleman just took, closed by him, and the one you took to get in here closed by,' he chuckled, 'me.'

'What the hell are you babbling about?'

'I have closed the only gate out of this dimension and do not intend to open it until long after the detonation. I apologise for keeping you all here and will gladly offer you my hospitality once you've had some time to rest.' He smiled.

'What did he do?' He looked around at all of them.

'He trapped us in here with him until after the bomb goes off. He'll be protected here, and by the time we make it out it'll be done. I think he's hoping we'll give in.'

'So, what do we do?'

'Well, honestly.' He drew back his sword and slammed its point into the most breakable point in the wall, shattering it in a blow. 'Even if I thought this was entirely futile I would almost certainly do everything I could just to spite him. No doubt he is keeping the world closed by force of will, so I shall have to go through him to the goal.'

'I can smell the trail, but I can't see the way out,' Konstantin growled. 'I can find where it was, but I'll need one of you to open it.'

'Feel free to try.' The old man sighed, heading into his hut.

'Annabelle.' Adam looked at her. 'Either way we need to find our way through these traps. Let's get on it!'

'All right, let's get at it!' The two of them spread out, blanketing their awareness over the traps. Between Annabelle's understanding and Adam's eyes the two of them worked their way around the circle, figuring out what all the traps were. They slowly but certainly began to chart a path of traps they could deactivate.

'You realise that even as you do all of this nonsense I can quite easily design more traps as you disassemble them, keeping this exercise going indefinitely. Honestly, settle, get some sleep and you can come inside tomorrow.'

'You're absolutely right!' Xavier smiled. Everyone seemed surprised at that, and he laughed. 'No, you're right that this is taking too long. I'm already bored.' He walked up to the edge of the wall he broke. 'If you wouldn't mind, choose me the most direct path which will take me through the smallest number of traps.'

'I mean even the shortest path still trips like, five or six of them.'

'Good enough!' He went to clap his hands and then sighed. 'This would be easier if I had both arms.'

'You complain a lot about something that you literally brought upon yourself,' Annabelle criticised, Xavier gave a shrug and a smile.

'All right.' Xavier took off his hat and held it out to Adam. 'I need you to throw me down the most direct path.'

'Throw you?' He thought about it. 'Oh, right, that.' He took the top hat and clenched it in one hand, then twirled twice as if he was throwing a discus, trailing Xavier's entire body with surprising ease, then released it, hurling hat and man into the air.

'That is,' Mikhail watched the red jacketed man fly on the brim of his hat, 'the strangest being I have known.'

'Stranger than the train worm we cut in half with a portal?'

'Much.'

As Xavier flew through the air, forces detonated, explosions went off, lights and gasses filled the air and a number of wild beasts were released into a strange maze of monsters, several of which killed themselves as they moved through the artificer's other traps.

In the end it was another wall that caught him, swatting him out of the sky. He didn't see it coming and his face slammed into the wall. As he tumbled he landed on his feet with a wince, wiping blood from his face.

'And the hard part begins!' As Annabelle and Adam kept a running commentary of the traps he was about to encounter he made his way through, sword drawn with his cane in his teeth. He stepped on a rune that made a blast of force and leaped, letting it carry him high into the air. For a moment he stood perfectly still, taunting the beasts on the other side of a field of traps, which killed them all instantly.

He began to probe the wall, darting backwards and forward across it.

'Hey, Carnival Queen, what's your range like?'

'You mean can I throw webs onto the invisible wall? Yes.' She started to walk through the path of detonated traps, avoiding the ones that recurred, until she stood within her throwing range. 'Gent. You can walk up a wall, right?'

'For a way, yes.' Annabelle began to throw webs up the invisible wall. 'Won't be easy, but it should be doable.'

'If this doesn't work I will almost certainly fall to my death.' Xavier took a short run up, got stuck, and slowly, agonisingly slowly, began to walk up the wall.

'Well,' he called out when he reached the top. 'That was unpleasant.' He jumped down, and his coat began to billow like a cape, slowing his descent.

'Why didn't you do that when you hit the wall?' Adam asked, as Xavier drifted down.

'I wasn't thinking clearly, I'd just hit my face, going

very fast, on the wall.'

Soon after, he kicked down the door and made his way into the hut.

The screams that rang out through the hut made Adam want to try to brave the traps himself, if not to save the man, at least to put him out of his misery. Only the knowledge that it would take him hours to get through the traps without killing himself kept him still, waiting for the old man to die.

'This is sick,' he muttered. 'I need to stop hanging out with you people, you disgust me.'

'He's tryna kill us!' Konstantin growled.

'No, he's not!'

'He's tryna kill… oh who gives a shit what you think? Gent! Hurry it up, we're on a clock!'

'As you say.' Xavier emerged from the hut and spoke a few quick words, the traps disappearing in front of him. He smiled and strode across the path, retrieving the cane end from where it had come loose from his mouth. 'Still have the trail?'

'Yeah.' Konstantin nodded. 'Can you open the world?'

'Not yet.' Xavier shrugged. 'I can do it soon enough. I believe a little research may be in order, if my new friend would care to join me?' He gestured toward Mikhail, who nodded and quietly strode into the hut.

'That's concerning.' Adam shook his head and lay against the wall of the hut, not game to go inside. 'No more quests for a good long time. I'm going to find somewhere quiet to crash for a year or so.' He closed his eyes.

'I thought you loved this stuff deep down.' Annabelle sat down beside him.

'I do, just not the part where everything is wrong, everyone around me is monsters and I'm pretty sure I'm gonna die.'

'Admittedly that's not my favourite thing in the world but you kinda have to take it with everything else.' She tousled his hair. 'You know for someone who says he enjoys this stuff you sure do complain a lot.'

'Yeah, well.' He shrugged. 'That's just my style I guess. Bitching about stuff lets me deal with the hard parts so I can enjoy the good. Besides, I like the cool stuff and the adventure. The violence, not my favourite thing in the world but the other half seems to like it.'

'The other half?' She watched him tap the grinning tac mask. 'Man, what's it like to have a Presence separate to who you are?'

'Yours is really so much a part of you?'

'I mean the new one is settling in a little, but he's already more of an influence than a separate identity. The original one has been part of my life since I was knee high.'

'It's like...' He thought about it for a few moments. 'It's like having voices in your head who want to help you and have very definite ideas about how to do it. He and Watcher don't seem to like me, or each other very much, but they need me to get what they want. We chat sometimes, and they're occasionally helpful but I can seem crazy when they're talking to me.'

'That's not fair!' the Laughing Man interjected in his head. 'I like you just fine. You're funny and only slightly annoying. Besides, I need you for the punching part of the punchlines.'

'See, right now I want to remind him that punchlines don't have to involve actual punching and respond to the objection he just raised, but that would make me seem profoundly crazy if I said it aloud.'

'Are you profoundly crazy?'

'I don't think my amount of craziness is particularly profound. I think I'm probably just regular crazy, but the voices in my head are telling me things that are actually helpful, and they give me claws and cool eye stuff. He thought about it. 'I guess what it actually is, is the difference between it happening automatically and doing it manually. You just know what the Presences are thinking, they're part of your thoughts and instincts. I have to hear mine first, and the instincts only cut in when things are vital.'

'I mean that might be the case.' She shrugged. 'You're gonna be okay, you know. I know it doesn't always seem like it, but you have your head on straight.' She reached out and tousled his hair. 'I know you don't think you know what you're doing, but you're handling all of this pretty well.'

'Okay.' He got up and headed to the house, his eyes firmly closed. 'Any progress?'

'Some.' Xavier nodded. 'I have plenty of research

here, but I can't make any of it make sense. I am not, when all is said and done, a researcher.'

'The Watcher might be able to help.' He opened his eyes as he faced the desk, keeping them fixed on the papers. He only looked at each page for a couple of seconds, ignoring the actual content and letting the Watcher do its job.

'So, in the meantime,' he spoke as he skimmed, 'what's a Legion assassin doing hanging out with a Lost, whatever Xavier is?'

'My sister told me I had to get him onside, so I approached him and told him that you would die if he didn't help. He threatened to stab me in the eye if I didn't leave him alone.'

'His lack of fear in the face of an eye stabbing piqued my interest. We had a short conversation and he told me what was going on. He told me that you couldn't ask for our help because you didn't want Legion or Lost hearing about this. His willingness to ignore your wishes and do what he thought as a good idea anyway, also appealed to me.'

'So, we arrived just in time to do what we had to and meet with the Dread Bear.'

'Got it.' He started to collect everything. 'I'm not sure what any of it means, but I've been told that this is the relevant information. Go do important things related to interdimensional travel, and violence.' Xavier looked at him for a long moment as he closed his eyes again.

'When did you get competent?'

'After the Little Bear murdered that one guy and you put two pieces of gods in my head.' He thought about that. 'Is that actually… wait, do I really have a piece of the King in my head? Cause that's terrifying.'

'Only technically. Once they're in, they have to be loyal, or you have to be loyal to them. They split off and take their own identity, incorporating who they were and their new circumstances. It would be more accurate to say that you have a piece of a god that you cut off and used for your own purposes.' Adam followed him out of the hut holding Mikhail's hand.

'That's a disturbing thing to think about.'

'Really? I find it rather comforting, like the idea of putting to use the trophy you took from something you hunted.' He smiled.

'That is not comforting.'

'We'll agree to disagree.' Xavier's smile widened. 'Now, spider girl, I will need webs in certain places; sniper, shoot a thing when I say shoot a thing. I'm going to be stabbing a dimension now, which will please me in a way that is only a little visceral and almost entirely nonsexual.'

He drew back his sword and began directing things by the centimetre. They began their detailed intricate work, piece by piece, to destabilise the dimension. Adam was acutely aware that he was running out of time with every moment and that he had no idea what the deadline was. After a few minutes of work Xavier asked him if he had any important "not getting in the way" to get done, so he went into the distance to chat with the voices in his head.

'You two have anything to say?'

'We are almost certainly going to have to murder Xavier one day,' the Watcher noted. 'It's not among our chief concerns currently but I thought you should know that this is a matter we should consider. While killing people is not beyond me, a mass murderer or torturer is not something we can tolerate.'

'Okay,' he accepted. 'Good to know we're all in agreement there, apart from the me murdering him thing. I don't want to kill anyone, I've been clear about that.'

'And by no means should you until it becomes entirely necessary.'

'No. No killing!'

'You're yelling quite audibly.' The Laughing One's voice was frustrated for once. 'You understand that every person with a Presence or Presences manages to keep their conversations internal, resulting in never seeming even remotely insane?'

'I did not.' He nodded. 'Good to know. I must have a particularly annoying pair to be cracking up like this.'

'So you're taking no responsibility for your own mental state at all?'

'None.'

'Excellent strategy.' The laughter echoed.

'We're done,' Xavier called from his position. 'We can go now.' Adam got up, walked out into the field and watched Xavier cut the portal open.

'I expected this to be harder.'

'I blew up, fell several hundred feet, got attacked by monsters and tortured a man.' Xavier glared at him. 'Is there some level of difficulty you feel this has not reached which you would like to subject me to.'

'Right, sorry.' He nodded. 'Let's go.'

CHAPTER FOURTEEN

They arrived back in the world, all of them now looking entirely human. Adam and Xavier still looked odd, and the thought of this particular group spending time together was a slightly strange sight.

'Ready to go?' He looked over at Konstantin, who closed his eyes for a long moment, took a deep breath, flexed his hands and nodded, then almost collapsed. 'You okay?'

'Just need a minute to get steady.' He tossed his head and straightened up again, clenching his fists. 'Need a minute to…'

'He's in incredible pain,' Annabelle pointed out. 'Remember, not all of him was behind the portal when the worm came through. It tore away a significant portion of his body, then spent hours at a run.' She reached out to steady him and he pushed her away. 'He's strong, but no one can handle that.'

'I'm fine.' He shoved them away from him and started to walk again. 'No time to heal, got work to do.'

'Knife!' Mikhail looked at him. 'Can you get us a car?' He looked at Konstantin. 'You can track from a car, right?'

'Don't need a damn car.' His voice was slurring.

'Stop being an ass.' Mikhail slapped the bear in the face. Konstantin let out a growl but made no further offense. 'Can you track from a car or not?'

'Yeah,' he rumbled. 'Gonna kill you for that.'

'Yes, when you can stand I imagine you'll give it a

344

try.' He didn't sound intimidated.

'Can stand just fine,' he grumbled. Adam dragged him out of sight of the public, and they waited for the car to arrive.

'You'll need to follow on your own.' Mikhail looked at Xavier. 'My driver will be amenable to a lot, but he won't take you with him, and it'll raise a good deal too many questions.'

'Understandable.' Xavier bowed. 'I mean why on earth should I travel in comfort? I was only blown up and fell three stories.'

'I fell down a fifteen-story building and ran through a dimension and I didn't complain.' Adam folded his arms. 'Harden up.'

'Aww.' Xavier hugged him, he smelled like blood. 'You absolutely did complain, it's virtually all you do, but the thinking cap is proud of you anyway.'

'Stop hugging me.'

'Ahh, yes.' Xavier withdrew. 'Cannot undermine our great warrior's image! Someone fetch this man a horn of mead and a trumpet!'

'What?'

'I don't know,' Xavier admitted. 'I'm not sure what warriors do other than screaming and dying and setting fire to things. They tend to set fire to things rather a lot? Should we be setting fires?'

'No!' Adam snapped. 'I am explicitly stating that we are not setting any fires. No fires!'

'Understood.' He nodded. 'Very well, I shall away and see you again soon.'

'First, since when do you talk like that? Second, I need to hear you say the words "no fires".'

'Since I felt like it, it comes and goes with my whims, and I understand, no fires.' A second later Xavier was gone. Soon enough a white town car pulled up to the alley and Adam and Mikhail managed to barely drag the half-conscious body of the Dread Bear into the vehicle and belt him.

'Sir?' The driver was a thin man with skin that somehow seemed to lack something, like a guy who had died ten minutes ago.

'You will follow the directions of the large, tired looking man,' Mikhail snapped at him from the front seat. 'He is attempting to track an enemy agent.' Adam wound down the window on Konstantin's side and the big man took deep breaths.

'Go straight,' he mumbled.

They followed his directions as Adam kept Konstantin awake with words, shaking, the occasional shove or slap which lead to more threats of horrific violence. Adam had no idea if that was a genuine threat and no time to wonder. He figured it didn't much matter until they were done. If this guy was petty enough to start a fight after that, then he'd deal with that then. He gave direction after direction, leading them through the city with a pained expression.

'Is he okay? Do we need to get him to a healer?'

'No,' Annabelle shook her head. 'And none of the nearby healers would treat him if he did.'

'Not even Mercy?'

'We stretched Mercy's hospitality allowing him to stay there for a few hours. She won't help put him back out on the street.'

'Why not?'

'Because Mercy's goal is to limit the amount of pain in the world in whatever way she can. Konstantin is one of the few people in existence who quantifiably hurts to the world every day.'

'And yet she didn't kill me when she had the chance,' Konstantin spat weakly from his position, red flecked saliva staining his lapel. 'Difference between me and them, when I decide someone needs gone, I actually go them.'

'Save your strength and stop talking unless you're actually giving direction, how about that?' Annabelle snapped. Konstantin let out a laugh and Annabelle turned back to Adam. 'He just needs to sleep it off. The Dread Bear has walked off worse.'

'You two know each other?'

'Only by reputation.' She shrugged. 'I don't think anyone actually knows him.'

'What about the kid?'

'What kid?' As she asked the question Adam felt Konstantin's large sweaty hand on his wrist, claws digging into the soft skin.

'The Little Bear,' Adam lied. 'I mean surely he had to know the guy to turn into him.'

'Having met the real Dread Bear, do you actually think if he'd actually known anyone the Little Bear would have fooled them for an instant?'

'Then why go to so much work to seem like him if it wasn't a good job anyway?'

'Because the Legion has hundreds of ways to check if you are who you say you are. Shapeshifting is redundant if they can read your mind, soul, location history and fire out where you're pretending to be is. If I understand right, that little con was pretty much the only way to fool all of them.'

'Seventy-nine,' Konstantin mumbled.

'What?'

'There are seventy-nine Legion checks for identity.'

'Actually, there are one hundred and twenty-three,' Mikhail chimed in from the front seat. 'Can you please stop talking about this in public and act as if you're something close to professionals?'

'Right. Then why didn't anyone know?'

'Shut up!' Mikhail snapped. 'These questions can wait for a better time.'

'May I ask what business brings Sir on such a circuitous route with such... interesting people?' the driver spoke with a raspy voice, looking at the group.

'The bottom of the barrel,' Mikhail muttered darkly. 'We are following a man who is acting against Legion interests. This has necessitated the assembly of this motley crew of thugs and miscreants.'

'He's the thug.' Adam pointed to Konstantin. 'I think that makes us the miscreants.'

'Hard to argue with,' Annabelle commented.

'Right.' Konstantin pointed in the direction and the

driver turned. 'We're getting close.'

'That's a problem,' Adam commented.

'Why?' Annabelle looked around and it dawned on her. They were right beside the Queen Street Mall, the area in which hundreds of people walked the streets, shopping, eating, thoroughly ignorant of the world around them.

Everyone, as Adam understood it, had a spirit along with them in the worlds of the Eldritch below and the Seraph above. The spirits did not, as a rule, like their humans being dragged into matters involving Presences against their will and would often respond by manifesting violently. This wouldn't be so bad if not for the fact that people could have spirits who were the size of large trucks in another world.

If the group did anything magical here, they were risking nothing short of hundreds of angry spirits in the middle of the city. Adam put the mask away, hiding it inside his coat.

'What do we do?' He looked at them. 'We'd have to go on foot from here, and Konstantin can't walk. They'd notice him immediately.'

'I have a plan.' Annabelle tossed Konstantin her phone. 'Have the driver take him around the mall, make sure that our guy's in there. If he's not, give me a call.' She pointed to Mikhail. 'You go do your thing.'

'Yeah.' He nodded. 'I'll go get high.'

'I did that joke already.' Adam informed him smugly.

'It's a good joke,' the sniper defended. 'It bears repeating.'

'It does not.'

'Get out of my car.'

They spent the next half hour pacing around the mall looking for the Skeleman. Since the only thing they knew about how he looked was the fact that he usually dressed well and wore a plague doctor mask, there wasn't much they could do to identify him, since taking off the mask worked as well to hide his identity as it had Adam's. After having it confirmed that he was in the mall, the group split up, checking shops, businesses and thoroughfares. They didn't know exactly what they were looking for, simply hoping there was something which would tip them off.

In the end it was Annabelle who found him.

'He's sitting at the bus stop with a suit case,' she observed. 'I sent a spider into it, but whatever's in it, I can't identify. It doesn't look like anything from this world though. It glows and spins in its case, some pieces are even entirely separate.'

'Where's he going with it?'

'No idea. He's been waiting here for hours.' Xavier joined the group from a distance, keeping back for when he was needed.

'Xavier?' he asked. 'Can you take it off him?'

'Provided he's alone, and is not willing to risk using his abilities, and provided I am.' He thought for a moment. 'Which I am, I can probably do it. Knowing he has some backup waiting and assuming he is willing to use the full extent of his gifts to strike me down? No chance. I am willing to risk a lot for your goal, but I need a chance of success.'

'Fair.' Adam looked at the others. 'If the rest of us surrounded the two of you so you could make the grab?'

'Again, he would likely use his abilities to attempt to stop us. We need something we know would oppose him if it manifested, something dangerous enough to get his more extravagant powers out of the equation.'

Adam thought about this problem for a second. It was likely that if he was fully aware of the potential ramifications of his next action he would have been far less likely to suggest it.

'He's Lost right? So completely Lost he's willing to wipe people out to pursue his goal of spreading freedom across the universe?'

'Universes?'

'Whatever?'

'Absolutely.' Xavier nodded. 'What's the point?'

'I have a plan.' He paused. 'Okay, maybe that's overstating it. I have an idea.'

The security guard hadn't taken much persuasion. The knowledge that a strange old man had just spent hours wandering around a bus terminal carrying a whirring suitcase had just enough of a "terrorist attack" vibe that he could be encouraged to call the police with ease.

The police officer, confronted by a small well-dressed young man in white, was something more of a challenge. He didn't really want to bother people just going about their days and it wasn't illegal to hang out at a bus top with a suitcase, even if it was a strangely sized one. It wasn't until he could be persuaded that Mikhail had seen the suitcase buzz and vibrate that he became amenable to the idea of having a chat with the old man. He still made no promises, and indeed had no intention of doing anything more than talking, but it would cost him nothing to have a conversation.

'Excuse me, Sir.' The officer made his way over to the old man as the rest of the team gathered around, watching from a distance.

'Yes?' The old man looked up at the policeman, his face shifting into a wide, entirely insincere smile.

'May I ask what you're doing here?'

'Waiting for a bus,' The man gestured toward the terminal he was sitting at.

'According to security you've moved from stop to stop over the last three hours and haven't caught a bus.'

'I'm sorry, is that a crime?' The smile didn't move, but the Skeleman was looking around, probably for whoever planned this.

'No, Sir.' The officer was becoming annoyed. 'On the other hand, you are carrying a very large briefcase, that you've been steadily shifting around an enclosed space for a number of hours. That's not illegal, but it is suspicious behaviour. If you don't mind, I'd like to see what's in it.'

'And if I do mind?'

'Then that would be even more suspicious behaviour. May I see some identification?' The old man rolled his eyes and reached into his pocket, pulling out a wallet. Adam knew this guy wouldn't ever open that case, but they had a few ideas on how to make things worse.

Annabelle started it by sending a small cluster of spiders into the pants of the Skeleman, it was possibly the most childish plan they'd had, but since he was too busy to notice what the little creatures were doing she'd put them in place for when she could mess with him.

One of her more special sisters crawled up the case and into the lock, manoeuvring the tumblers of the lock into place, and webbing them there so she could get to work. As the old man became more annoyed the officer looked like he was losing interest in keeping this going any further, so Adam sighed, took a deep breath and made his way up to the meeting.

'Excuse me, Officer?'

'Yes?' The cop was either tired or annoyed.

'This guy was behaving weirdly, and I didn't think about it until I saw you over here, but I think it might help. I just don't wanna seem, uh, controversial or anything.'

'Yes?'

'I don't know what exactly it was, but he was talking to some guy on the phone, it sounded like Russian or something Arabic or something.' He winced at that, it was tacky, low brow and frankly idiotic, but he needed to push the cop from tired into interested.

'If this works,' the Laughing One commented, 'I am going to lose all faith in your people.'

'What are you talking about?' The old man looked at him, their eyes met, and he scowled. 'Oh, you little bastard.'

'Excuse me?' The cop looked at the two of them. 'I'm going to need to talk to both of you.'

'Oh really?' The Laughing One sighed. 'This is just sad.'

And with almost perfect comedic timing the suitcase fell open, the device falling out.

'What the hell is that thing?' The cop jumped back. The device that fell out didn't look like a bomb, it didn't look like anything he could recognise, but it didn't have a timer or visible wires or anything. On the other hand, it did have a range of moving parts, things that whirred and beeped and the entire effect was strange, confusing and not unthreatening.

'That is an experimental propriety piece of technology!' Respect to the Skeleman, he adapted quickly. 'You even viewing that is a breach of my confidentiality clause! This could cost me my job!' He bent down to lock up the device, only to have the briefcase fall open again immediately because the spier had broken it. Judging from the expression of pain on his face, the spiders against his legs had started biting and he was trying not to freak out.

Adam gave the old man a smile and stepped

quickly between him and the cop. 'What's going on?' he yelled as loud as he could. 'This man has a bomb! We're all going to die!' Even as he yelled it, he hated himself a little. The more he did this, the more he played upon the weakest parts of human nature, but he knew it was the easiest way to create enough confusion to take advantage. As the Skeleman stepped forward, ready to grab the case and move, to take advantage like Adam had, Adam took two steps, slammed his head into the bridge of the man's nose, and shoved him out of the way with his shoulder.

The Skeleman turned with the shove and was knocked off his feet by what sounded like a gunshot. If he'd stayed down and they'd checked the body they would have noticed there was no bullet, but the confusion was too great. Adam reached back and pulled hard on the power of the Presences, his eyes growing sharp and the world around him predictable. He struck out at the cop, hitting in the throat just hard enough to cost him his wind. Adam turned and ran into the crowd, shoving people as he moved.

As he did he saw a blur of fast moving red, Xavier doing his part, picking up the strange device and bolting away. The Skeleman got to his feet and made ready to chase him, but Adam kept pointing and shouting as Xavier widened the gap and vanished into the distance.

Keep all the attention on the Skeleman, don't let them notice the impossibly fast guy in the red.

Eventually Adam slipped away into the crowd and

re-joined the world, taking a few minutes to seem like a regular person before heading to the park down the street. Annabelle had switched her colours again, and Adam and Mikhail were in street clothes, carrying their gear in bags as not to be visible in their white coats.

'Okay.' Adam looked around. 'Everyone okay?'

'I suspect a security camera may have noticed me carrying a gun,' Mikhail sighed, brushing his hair out of his face. 'My people will no doubt be upset with me, as it will be a drain on resources.'

'I'm fine.' Annabelle shrugged. 'No one even bothered me. What about you?'

'The plan went off pretty much without a hitch.' He paused for a long moment. 'Except I'm pretty sure Xavier just betrayed us.'

'What?' Annabelle looked around. 'What are you talking about?'

'It's the punchline.' He looked at them like it was self-evident. He couldn't believe for a moment that they somehow hadn't grasped this, it was all laid out so clearly to him. 'Everything so far up to this was difficult, almost impossible and potentially lethal. We only succeeded through a mixture of luck and taking advantage of every opportunity. This time we made it out fine, we didn't even have to fight.'

'So?'

'So, what made it so easy?'

'I mean your plans, us working together, and Xavier, but making things easier is his job, he did it on our last little adventure too.'

'He was planning a betrayal then too! Not necessarily betraying us, but betraying! The man who made it suddenly too easy just happens to be an expert in cons and betrayal.'

'That doesn't mean he betrayed us.'

Adam sighed and sat down at the park table. *It was so obvious! Why was no one else seeing it?*

'Fine. If you're going to be obtuse about it we'll give it another ten minutes, but I'm telling you he betrayed us.'

'Okay.' Annabelle looked at him for a moment. 'Are you okay?'

'No, I'm frustrated, because you're not even trying! Honestly, it's entirely obvious. What's your...' He sighed. 'Xavier, who worked his way into the crucial role of fetching the machine, is suddenly the only one who doesn't make the rendezvous. With his history, and his pattern of behaviour thus far, what are you...' He paused, something dawning on him. 'This isn't actually a logical train of thought, is it?'

'It is not.' They all seemed to agree with Annabelle's perspective.

'Okay.' He stopped to think. 'I don't know what's going on with my head, but I know for a fact he betrayed us!'

'Okay. Give it a few minutes, and then if he's not here we'll look into the possibility.'

'Okay.'

Annabelle looked at the group a few minutes later.

'I'm not saying for sure he really did betray us.'

'He did.'

'But if he did!' She held up a hand to stall him. 'Who could he possibly have betrayed us to. He only actually likes, well, no people. He tolerates Pan, but he can't have betrayed us to Pan because that's not how betrayal actually works.'

'Either way we need to contact him.' He pulled out his phone and dialled Pan's number.

'What do you want?' He sounded annoyed.

'Have you heard from Xavier recently.'

'No.' The annoyance grew thicker. 'I'm on vacation, what do you want.'

'He betrayed us.'

'May have!' Annabelle corrected.

'He betrayed us and no one but me seems to realise it.'

'Okay, he what?'

'Betrayed us and stole a superweapon capable of destroying entire dimensions.' He thought about it for a moment, his voice eerily calm. Why was he so unemotional about this? 'Actually, you know what? Reverse those two. He was supposed to steal it and give it to us, instead he ran off and gave it to someone else. Do you have any clues as to who?'

'Wait, I'm sorry, he fucking what?' Pan bellowed into the phone.

'He…' Adam paused. 'Oh, you heard me and that was an expression of frustration. Yeah, any idea who he might have sold us out to. Was it you?'

'No, it wasn't me, you idiot. Give me a minute.'

Pan hung up.

'Pan believes me,' Adam observed.

'What the hell is up with you?' Annabelle glared at him. 'If you're right, this is a disaster. Why are you so calm?'

'I don't know.' He shrugged. 'It's like, suddenly I can see how everything is going to work out. Besides, it's not like it's going to happen to us.'

'What?'

'I mean think about it.' Adam shrugged. 'It's Xavier, he's devoted to the Lost. He's not going to wipe out anything that belongs to us, if anything he'll go after something ruled by one of the…' He froze.

'No, say it.' Mikhail's voice was cold. 'Say it. One of the kings. He's only my brother after all.'

'What?' Annabelle's eyes were wide.

'I didn't mean,' Adam stammered.

'Put the mask and coat down.' Mikhail's voice was calm as he took Adam's hand. 'They're affecting you deeply, and unhealthily. Put the Presences down and step away.'

'No wait, seriously, what did he say?' Adam ignored her as he put the garments and their bag onto the ground. Suddenly everything was less bright, less sharp, less clear and obvious. Oh my god, he'd actually just said it was okay for a dimension to be destroyed because no one he knew was there.

'I'm sorry.' He ran his hands across his face. 'You're right, of course we have to stop him.'

'It's fine.' It was not fine. Adam could see in his

eyes and posture that it was not fine. 'What do we do?'

'You fill the others in on your situation, while I answer my phone.' He pulled it out. 'Please tell me you have some good news.'

'I can't contact him.' Pan bit off the words. 'He's off the grid. Xavier is not allowed to be off the grid. In the event that he goes off the grid for more than three hours I'm legally allowed to kill him. Goddammit, I'm on vacation!' There was the sound of breaking glass and words of reassurance from Jeremiah. 'Okay, has Xavier been talking to anyone lately?'

'No one except...' He scowled down at the bag with his Presences in it. 'While you idiots were noticing everything, why didn't you think of the assassin guy?' He put the phone back to his mouth. 'It was the assassin guy.'

'Who?'

'Six of Nothing, the assassin. He came with Xavier to help me, and Xavier was talking about how good it was to be with his own kind again.'

'He's off with another servant.' He let out another frustrated growl. 'So, they're off on the Ladies' business.'

'The Ladies?'

'That damn death cult he's a part of. He's gone completely off the rails. So, this thing can destroy a dimension?'

'So we've been told.'

'Okay. You need a way into the Land of Eternal Flame. It's a battleground on the outskirts of the

King's Land. If he puts the bomb there it'll cascade and kill the King, at the cost of several dimensions.'

'What do you mean we need? You're not coming?'

'I wouldn't be able to get there in time. I'm sorry, but you're gonna have to sack up and do this yourself. I'll get you a call as soon as I can and try to find you a path into…'

'Mikhail!' Adam called out. 'Do you know a way to get to the Land of Eternal Flame?'

'Yes, several.' Mikhail nodded. 'It is my second home.'

'Okay, Pan, we've got a way in. Now what do we do?'

'Find Xavier and tell him that my hand is on the button and I will spill his secret across every world if I have to. I don't mind the idea of getting rid of the King of Eternal Flame any more than he does, but destroying an entire dimension is going too far. Several of our own people share a realm with him because they're trying to kill him. You have to get there and find him now. If he doesn't listen, you might have to break his stuff or beat him down.'

'Okay.' He shook a little at the idea, and picked up the Presences again, he needed their calm. 'Mikhail, take me to your brother.' He paused as his guts twisted. 'Take me to the world your brother lives in and help me find Xavier. Do not actually take me anywhere near your brother.'

'How do we suggest we find your runaway? It's a

world, as big as yours.'

'Yeah but Xavier will be at the most delicate point in the dimension.'

'That's...' Mikhail held his head and took a deep breath. 'In the middle of a battlefield, in which there has been a battle for a hundred years.'

'Awesome!' Adam clapped his hands. 'We're gonna die!'

'Find him!' The man known as the Skeleman was not having a good day. He had been bitten dozens of times by spiders, had experienced the failure of a carefully made plan, lost two allies and been robbed, using a childish ruse of all things! The humiliation was almost too much to bear. What on earth was he supposed to do? Without the twins he'd been reduced to operating on one side of the equation, and not the side he was used to!

Luckily everyone knew about the Red Gentleman, everyone knew how he was, and more importantly everyone knew who and what he hated most. He would go immediately and without hesitation to the Land of Eternal Flames. Which meant this was where the Skeleman would be going as well.

He took the Seven with him. He'd trained them personally, and though they had been taken by surprise once, there would be no such problem this time. They would act together, as a unit, and they would not fail again. In the confusion he could truly thrive.

'We need to think about this, Sir.' Breaker Vain was a good compatriot. The young man wreathed in violet had aided in this plan from the ground up, but he possessed no real skill in violence. He was easily frightened, often hiding behind his shell and claws

'No, we do not!' The Skeleman kept his voice hollow and empty. 'We do not have time. We cannot afford to hesitate! He will be going to the Land of Flame and we need to be there when he arrives! We must take our equipment back, even if that means losing everything.' He took a long deep breath. 'Even if it means we all die.'

That was the core of the issue, that was what he had made his peace with. Nothing was more important than getting this done. Nothing was more important than unifying his people.

'Let's go!' Breaker Battle already had her armour and blades in place. She was about as smart as a brick, but she could fight and would do so for him. He would bring all he could, field his own army as a distraction, and leverage his power to his own advantage. It would be enough to defy the reds and get him alone with that little pack of rabble lead by the grinning imbecile.

Who was he anyway? The Skeleman had not heard of him, and he figured that was something he should have figured out. He would need to do some research once he was done with this. His finger had doubtless left the pulse.

'You will lead my people.' He put his hand on the

shoulder of the remaining Shatter Sister, her face set in a deadly rictus. She was unburdened by pain, fear or doubt anymore, nothing left but vengeance for her sister. She gave a nod and a smile.

Sometimes he felt so weighed down by his own fears and doubts that he couldn't move anymore. That getting out of bed had become like carrying a car on his shoulders, so weighed down by his losses, by pain and fear. Not fear for himself, he had outgrown that long ago. His fear was for his people, that they would fall to infighting, that they would fail because they had no clarity of vision. They were a rabble of children, they were the Lost! They were supposed to thrive on the chaos! They were supposed to unite into a horde to swallow their enemies! They should not be a pack of fools who fought themselves!

Drive and clarity of vision! That was what his people needed! Not laws, or government as such but the drive and ambition to finally win this war! He would give that to them, that would be his gift to the worlds.

'I will lead the Breakers to retrieve the artefact!' He looked out of them, the seven glowing, soon to unify. 'Do not move until we are ready and remember who our enemies are. You are not here to win a war we cannot win, we are here to win a very specific battle. Seek out the Reds if you need to and keep them busy until we can retrieve the device, then we shall pull out. Do not fall to infighting or lose track of your goal. You are strong, you are capable, and I need you all to think!'

'You need us to think.' They nodded together.

'Keep your temper.' He looked at the Shatter Sister. She wanted to snap at him, he could see it. She wanted to demand that this little lecture end and that she already knew what she was doing.

'I shall.' She kept her voice calm and forced a smile.

'Make your preparations!' he demanded. 'We leave immediately!'

He would be ready to unleash his powers, and he would save the Lost once and for all.

CHAPTER FIFTEEN

'Everyone make ready, this will be unpleasant.' Mikhail loaded his gun, now a rifle again.

'That's not exactly a surprise.'

'You cannot lie to the fire.' His face and tone were intense. 'You shall confront it and it shall test you. It may make you stronger, or it may break you. Show it no fear, show it no hesitation and hold nothing back from it. It will frighten you, it will test you and there is only one punishment for failure.'

'Yeah, I get it.' Adam nodded. 'If I panic I get burned to death. Let's get this started.'

'Very well.' Mikhail looked into the fireplace of the church they were standing in. It was a nice building, brick spires on the outside, frescoes of virgins, great deeds and saints, the whole deal. 'I warned you.' He grabbed a handful of incense in his hand and threw it into the empty fireplace.

A dozen fires lit at once inside the single fireplace, together and yet somehow sperate, each one carrying something with them. The comfortable fire of a hearth burned in the centre, bringing comfort. A bushfire burned around the outside, bringing the desire to consume, destroy and rebirth. A cooking fire, simple and utilitarian, a chemist's flame that turned one thing into another. All danced, burned and twisted around each other, each one changing all the others.

'What do we do?' Adam looked over at Mikhail, his eyes reflecting the fire.

'Walk in.' Mikhail raised his hands and the fireplace coalesced, somehow all the different fires at once. He smiled, spread his hands wide and walked into the fire. He displayed no pain, not even discomfort.

'Why do you fight?' The voice wasn't a voice as such, it was crackling and burning and the spaces between made somehow into words.

'For my family.' There it was, no hesitation, no holding back, didn't even sound like he had to think about it.

'Why are you here?'

'My presence is required.'

'Who are you?'

'I am Mikhail Donjevic, to the Eldritch the Forgotten Eye, to the Seraph the Knife from Nowhere, and I am in a hurry.'

'So be it then.'

He disappeared into the fire, leaving no trace.

'I still want to go,' Konstantin grumbled.

'You passed out an hour ago!' Adam snapped. 'You can't come.' He turned to Annabelle. 'You next or me?'

'You afraid?'

'Oh, hell yes.' He nodded.

'Then I'll go.' She took a deep breath, closed her eyes for a moment, then rushed into the flames.

'Why do you fight?'

'To protect my people and our way of life.' There it was, only a little more hesitation than Mikhail. She winced like she was in pain but kept her eyes up and her jaw set.

How could he see her from that angle? He was behind her, and yet he could somehow know the expression on her face.

'Why are you here?'

'To neutralise a dangerous rogue element,' she screamed in pain.

'Why are you here?'

'Because people who matter to me need me to be here.'

This time there was no scream.

'Who are you?'

'My name is Annabelle.'

She screamed again.

'Who are you?'

'The future Queen of Spiders!' she yelled, and the fires retreated.

'Why should we let you pass?'

'Because of a simple question. In the future am I going to be in a position to hurt you or not?'

'Understood.'

The fire let her go

'Did she just threaten the concept of fire?' He jumped a little as he received a message on his phone. Not a text message, the phone just went black and white writing flashed up.

'We are in place. Code.' He nodded. That might be helpful. 'So, she just threatened fire. How do you threaten fire?' He sighed and took a deep breath. 'I'm going to need you two to help me see to the heart of things here. I'm not sure what exactly to do.'

'Pretend you have some actual dignity and walk into the fire.'

'Right.' He laughed and strode inside.

For a moment it hurt worse than anything had ever hurt before. He almost let out a scream before the mask kicked in. He gritted his teeth, locked down his emotions and did his best not to show a break in composure.

'Okay,' he yelled out. 'This sucks, so let's get it over with!' The fire was painful, now hot, now uncomfortable. He could feel the breath and strength draining form him, but it was only a trickle. He could hold on as long as he needed to. He'd be okay.

'Why do you fight?'

'To protect people.' The pain ran up his body like, well, like someone had set every part of his body on fire. He pushed down on it with all of his strength, tried to hold it back, tried not to think about it even as it bleached his mind clean of everything else.

'Why do you fight?' the crackling voice asked again.

'I don't know.' The pain came again. 'Look, I have no idea what the answer is here! I don't know what you want from me! I don't know what I'm fighting for, I just do it because it's what in front of me and it seems like the right thing at the time!'

'Do you enjoy it?'

'Oh, come on, why do I get more questions?' The pain

was inside him now, searing away at his very soul.

'Because you understand less. Do you enjoy it?'

'Of course. No one does anything they don't like forever. It's weird and bloody and fun and sometimes I hate it, but all I've ever wanted was to wake up every day and not be bored. I have been so bored my entire life, and then this happened.'

The pain was gone, he stood in the fire now, uncomfortable once more.

'Why are you here?'

'Because Xavier screwed me.' He would have liked to pretend a more noble motive, but he knew what the truth was. 'I might have come anyway, but I trusted him. I treated him like a friend and he screwed me, so I want to see him fail.'

That made the voice inside him laugh.

'Who are you?'

'Adam.' He shook his head. 'Sorry, I don't have a good answer. I'm still lost right now. I have some work to do before I can answer that question.'

'You simply don't know?'

'That's how it is,' he admitted.

'Why should I let you pass?'

'Because if you don't it'll be boring, you'll be bored, I'll be in pain and they'll be dead, which I'm not sure but may be boring? The world will go on as it was, the same boring endless war made all the more boring for the fact that one of the few interesting elements has been removed from it.'

'Very few people would find eternal war boring.'

'They lack perspective,' he pointed out. 'Short answer is, if I don't go it wouldn't be fun.'

'And what does fire care what makes you laugh?'

'I don't know.' He shrugged. 'I think you do though.'

What came next was agony beyond agony, but it only lasted a few seconds then the world was just very hot. The environment was slowly but surely draining every piece of moisture out of his body.

'It's hot,' he observed.

'Well yes, did you expect the Land of Flame to be otherwise?' Mikhail rolled his eyes. 'Come on, enough time has been wasted already.'

'You know,' Adam looked around as they started to walk, 'by videogame rules we are definitely going to fight someone badass here. There's always the most annoying bosses on the fire levels.' It did look almost exactly like a fire level. All around wild fires blazed out of control, seemingly immune to the fact that there was no fuel to burn with. There was lava in the distance, and rocks were everywhere, covered in cracks and breaks filled with burning material of some kind or another.

In the distance there were stone fortresses that appeared to have naturally grown out of the ground, and between them were armies. Things that looked human fought beside things that looked decidedly inhuman, marching in lockstep and formation with armies aligned slightly differently.

Adam couldn't tell exactly what was going on,

371

except for the fact that one of the armies was marching in an actual formation, while the other resembled a screaming horde of barbarians. As he watched, the horde fell back, and then charged, a few people with incredible powers knocking a hole in the formation.

'And that just keeps happening?' He motioned across the armies.

'Legion pushes, Legion gains ground, Legion starts winning. Lost regroups, Lost pushes back, Lost breaks through. Legion falls back, Legion recovers, Legion pushes. I don't think more than a kilometre of ground has been made in the last decade.' Mikhail looked out at them, his face sad. 'It's like that, metaphorically or otherwise, across all dimensions, including our own.'

'Really?'

'For eternity, unless something changes.'

'That's... existentially terrifying.'

'Don't worry, my sister has a plan.' Mikhail put a hand on Adam's shoulder. 'In the meantime, we have to stop someone else breaking the system before we break it in a different, better way.'

'Let me guess.' Adam pointed to the middle of the battle, the front line. 'That's where we're going?'

'Point of lowest dimensional stability.' He thought about it and pointed. 'Right in the middle of the Legion line, right there.'

'I hate life.' Adam looked at them. 'I think we can count on Claire and Code to interfere on our side. Do we have a plan here?'

'The good news is we don't need one.' Annabelle

pointed to the line. 'Xavier already has one of his own, we just need to abuse that.'

'Isn't our plan just to rob him?'

'Exactly'

'Okay, but how are we going to do that? Isn't the entire point of Xavier that we can't beat Xavier?'

'I'm hoping once we send him Pan's message he'll at least slow down.'

'And the other guy we can only assume is exactly like Xavier?'

'I suppose we improvise and hope we don't die.'

'No!' Mikhail snapped. 'This time make a plan!'

The world slowed down, suddenly charging men were running through mud, a leaping beast hung in the air. Adam sat down and thought.

After a few minutes he got up, and the world sped up again.

'Okay!' He grinned 'Wait until the most important part of whatever ritual is going on starts. That's when it'll be most vulnerable. Make sure everyone has laid out their cards, all of our enemies, and then we attack. All we have to do is clear Mikhail a space and let him shoot the device until it breaks.'

'Simple.' Mikhail nodded. 'But possibly effective.'

'Is it really that easy?'

'His primary skillset seems to be breaking things from a distance, your skillset is untangling complicated situations. Taking advantage of other people's skillsets seems to be mine.'

'You said the word skillset way too many times in

that sentence.'

'Is that really what you want to talk about right now?'

'Until I see Xavier or something else that I think is relevant to our interests, so...' She pointed into the Lost army. 'Now.'

Sure enough, the latest Lost pushback seemed to involve a group of people who looked like a rainbow and a man with a bird skull for a head. On the Legion side was the familiar image of one half of the shatter sisters, both sides marched with, 'An army of skeletons,' Adam observed. 'Why is there an army of skeletons?'

'What did you think the guy called the Skeleman did?'

'Mikhail go be a Legionnaire for a while and get into position for when the time is right.'

'Will there be a signal?'

'I trust your instincts.' He nodded and then looked at Annabelle. 'You and I have to get toward the front of the Lost lines and as close to the facture point as possible. It's okay if we get seen, as long as Mikhail doesn't.' The little Russian looked at them seriously for a moment, and then ran off. They lost sight of him quickly, becoming just another face in the ordered lines that constantly formed and reformed. Adam had to trust that he'd do what was best, he seemed closer to being in control of himself and his situation than anyone else he'd met so far.

'Okay then.' He took Annabelle's hand and looked

her in the eyes. 'For the horde?'

'For the horde.' She grinned, and they joined the Lost side of the battle. They stayed off the battle line as it moved slowly but surely onward but kept close to the front. 'You really think it is the way the Knife says it is?'

'You'd know better than I would I guess.' He shrugged. 'You're smarter than I am, and you've seen more than I have.'

'Seems like things are about to stop going our way.' The line started to form up again, then burst open in a blur of red. 'Or not.'

'Forward!' Xavier shouted, and the five people in red behind him went with him. No sooner had he charged than hell broke loose. The Lost and Legion sides both deployed skeletons to isolate the small patch of red. As the battle joined all around them, that small section became almost peaceful, the shock troops securing it as the Reds faced off with the Skeleman's men.

Xavier was being kept more or less at bay by three of the coloured creatures, purple, yellow and orange. The purple kept him pinned down with its claws, while the whips and fireballs from the other two kept him off balance. He danced around them, waiting for his chance, his jacket burning a bright red. At any given moment Adam knew, he could kill any of them, one moment of lapsed defence, but he looked like he was losing for now.

The other four Reds were engaging the Shatter

Sister and those skeletons that weren't being busied holding the circle for them. They all seemed to have some kind of weird ability, as well as sharing Xavier's knack for sudden blurring speed. Only one of them wasn't in the fight, the one setting up the device, the smallest of the group by far, his hand occasionally flashing to protect the prize.

The Skeleman and Six of Nothing were firmly entrenched in a fight all their own. Six's hands moved in chops and strikes, designed to tear through a body. He saw the strange assassin engage a Skeleton that struck at him with a sword, his arm blocked the blade and his other hand smashed through the skull. Whenever he struck bones splintered, but the Skeleman had more, and fought with a terrifyingly fast whirl of what appeared to be some kind of double ended scythe.

'Time to move,' Adam decided, seeing the little guy step up to engage the Shatter Sister, belching fire into her face. 'Code, fire away, Annabelle, block for me.'

'The hell do you mean block for you?'

'Stop people from killing me while I'm working!' He set off at a run, heading straight past the fight toward the device.

Predictably Xavier almost blurred to appear in front of him, the bloody rapier held out in a duellist's stance, a smile on his face.

'As lovely as it is to see you, I'm afraid I can't let you go any further.' He dodged a fireball with a twirl. 'This could be the ultimate realisation of my greatest ambition.'

'Pan knows.' Adam tried to go around him, only to be blocked with almost contemptuous ease. 'Once this is done you're done. Whatever he has over you, is about to fall on your head. This is it, last chance.'

'Oh, don't be melodramatic.' Xavier waved one hand, the conversation pausing for a moment so both he and Adam could run from the scorpion man, both with one eye on the device. 'Peter will get over it. He's been upset with me before.'

'He told me to tell you his finger's on the button.'

'Oh.' Xavier appeared to be having an actual human emotion for a moment. Sadness, or guilt or something flashed across his face. 'Sacrifices must be made.'

Adam took immediate advantage of the moment's opportunity he'd been afforded. 'Code! Get in here if you can!' Before the half an emotion had left Xavier's face he bolted for the device. Xavier took a single step to block him, and Adam sliced for his throat. It was the first killing strike he'd ever attempted.

It fell pathetically short of the mark of course, but Xavier had to actually dodge, rather than flicking it aside. Xavier made to head him off again, only to be pulled off his feet by the yellow one's whip.

Adam jumped back as a solid wall of green armour almost smashed into his face. As it was, it smashed him backwards, sending him pitching onto the ground. He rolled, took a few steps and bolted, his mind entirely on his goal.

Which is why he didn't see someone step up

377

behind him, kick out his legs with one foot and pin him to the ground by the shoulder. Pain racked Adam's body as a spike went right through him.

'Sorry,' Xavier spoke from above. 'You are a valuable person and I don't actively want to kill you, so don't make it hard for me not to.'

'Did you just stab me into the ground like a goddamn butterfly?' Adam called out.

'I already apologised.' Xavier left the ground and from the sound of pain Adam guessed he'd thrown his hat into someone.

'I hope whatever Pan does to you gets you killed!' he called out as he reached back for the swords hilt with his free hand. Pain racked his body as he bent his knees under himself, then pushed up as hard as he could, pulling the sword free of the ground.

'Why the hell aren't you blocking my pain?' he asked.

'It doesn't work that way!' the Watcher screamed. 'He's hurting us too!'

What he said next was mostly swearwords, three of which he invented on the spot. The other words were a number of inarticulate noises that would have been swear words if he could have articulated them.

The sword eventually came loose, falling to the ground with a clatter. He needed to keep moving. He needed to get Mikhail his shot.

He flew backward suddenly, a strike from the front of him sending him pitching back, rolling twice, and dragging himself back to his feet.

'Dammit'

'You really don't think before you act do you?' Annabelle picked him up.

'What happened to me?' He shook his head, trying to clear it.

'Six of Nothing backhanded you.'

'Seriously?'

'Yes, we are drastically outpowered. Now, will you listen to me? I have a great idea.'

'Okay, hit me!'

CHAPTER SIXTEEN

'That is a terrible idea.' He looked at Annabelle, who was running a long cord of spider silk. Adam looked out over the battlefield. The Lord Code had broken the isolation of the battlefield, Claire was currently reading a declaration that seemed to be charging the Legion forces with treason, and the rest of the Legion's loyalists had joined the fray. The Lost, not to be outdone, had centred their attack here and now the gap of empty space was closing by the second.

'Oh, shut up. It's a perfectly good idea, as long as you land properly and don't scream.'

'I have no idea how I'm possibly not going to screw those things up.' He sighed and held up his left arm, the web wrapping around it once, twice, three times, then around the other.

'This is worse than any of my ideas thus far.'

'Did you not hear me when I told you to shut up?' she snapped. 'Brace yourself and get ready. This is going to hurt a lot.' She spun her arms, there was a sound of rustling silk and Adam was hurled into the air.

Not screaming was harder than he thought it would be. It began with the fact that he felt like his arms were being ripped out of their sockets again. Then there was the fact that he was flying through the air again. Only this time he didn't have the magic hat or something else that could keep him from shattering his bones on impact.

'I believe I can help, if you will allow it.'

'Then do it.' Adam felt his emotions back off a little further as the coat he'd been wearing began to billow and shift into some kind of wingsuit. 'Can we make it to the thing?'

'No.'

'Oh, I have an idea!' the Laughing One piped up. 'This is going to be hilarious. Turn when I tell you to turn!' He did so, following the path laid out for him by the Laughing One and directed toward an unlikely and unwilling ally.

Annabelle had grouped up with Claire and a pack of Legionnaires, making a loud and obvious charge right into the Reds. As the green guy in the massive armour turned to block her, Adam turned down to a swoop, heading straight for him.

The Watcher cut the wings, sending him plummeting down straight onto the green man's shoulders.

As Xavier blurred toward Adam he was knocked to the ground by the purple scorpion man. The others all caught what Adam was doing just too late to do anything about it. As the Skeleman noticed, Six of Nothing smashed him in the face, as one of the Red Men on the permitter turned to face him, his face was sheared in two by the Shatter sister.

That was how the chaos worked. He'd seen it before, he'd seen it the first day in the alley. He'd seen the causes and effects and order in the chaos that made this war so hilarious because neither could exist without the other. He could see the intricate web of a thousand tiny factors that could cause an error. He could see it so much more clearly now.

He knew the Skeleman wasn't in this fight, he just wanted to get past Six of Nothing to the device, and that Six of Nothing was too focused on violence to do contribute anything but violence begetting violence. He knew that Xavier didn't want to kill him but would if he had to. He knew that the rainbow men were only doing this because they had to, and Claire would do anything for anyone who offered her a home.

He also knew that he wouldn't be able to make it in time. Even with all these advantages at least three people would make it there before he did.

Fortunately, fetch was not the game he was playing.

'Mikhail! Pull!' He didn't want to use the young man's real name, but he couldn't risk his yell getting lost in the battle. The web stuck to the device and Adam turned and whipped it over his head, sending the artefact flying forward and up in an arc.

Xavier leaped for it. To his credit he launched himself as fast as his hat could go.

Which was not faster than the speed of sound, that burst of screaming noise drove some of the fighters to their knees as Mikhail's cannon blasted the device, holding the distorted air on it as it bounced and shook with impacts before it finally shook apart.

'If you say that was too easy I'm going to have my sisters eat your balls.' Annabelle and Claire wrenched on his arms, pulling Adam back as Blanks rushed in to guard their retreat. Lord Code gave him a tip of the hat from his spot facing off with the blue and orange fighters.

'How dare you?' the Skeleman roared. 'How dare you! How dare you lesser minds destroy my years of hard work.'

'Yes, yes, we've all been very defied.' Six's voice was happy, but his eyes were full of hate. 'Now stand still so I can crush your ridiculous skull.'

'Traitor!' the Skeleman yelled. 'You are a disgrace to your own order! To your people!'

'Well, technically I didn't betray you.' He leaped, kicking the suited man in the chest with a foot that sharpened into a blade, the weapon cutting through suit and flesh. 'I just ended my contract early and spared the Thrice Cursed.'

'Which is absolutely against the rules,' Xavier pointed out. 'That was treason.'

'I sincerely regret doing that.'

'Because it was against the rules or because she's now ruining our plans?'

'The second one.'

'Well then, apology accepted.'

'Excellent. Now go kill your little friends for ruining our plans.'

'I suppose I must.' Xavier took off his hat and aimed what would doubtless be a lethal shot.

'Xavier, if you stop now I'll tell Pan you turned on your own people at the last moment and destroyed the device. Keep him from blowing your secret.' It was a desperation move, but it was all he had. 'All you have to do is get us out of here!'

The yellow man pitched backward as a burst of sound hit him in the head. The hum of a sonic rifle was accompanied by a meaty thud, and the colours all turned, suddenly looking confused and lost.

'Time to go.' Xavier smiled. 'I'm sorry Six, no hard feelings?'

'None at all. Going to have to race you to the prize though.'

'Sister! Sword!' Xavier called. She tossed it to him and he plucked it out of the air, blurring as he ran.

Fast as he was, Six of Nothing was faster. His hand swung for Adam's face, who barely got the claws up in time to block them. The claws shattered against Six's skin and he fell back, taking a moment to get his breath back as the hat scythed for Six's head. The assassin ducked, and Xavier vaulted over him.

'You two may wish to vacate the premises with alacrity!'

'He missed me with that one,' Adam noted.

'Fucking run!' Annabelle simplified the message and Adam eagerly obeyed, dancing through the horde as he ran away, twisting ducking and lunging beside Claire and Annabelle. Luckily the Legion seemed to be treating them like friends for now, so the occasional flash of white was safe.

Adam kept his eyes on the two assassins moving with abnormal speed. As Xavier's blade broke the skin it sizzled, but Six of Nothing didn't appear to be hurt.

He snapped out one hand, aiming at Xavier's throat only to have it catch fire in mid-air as Xavier's coat wrapped around it.

'Is this guy indestructible or something?'

'All but!' Xavier replied.

'Do you have any special powers you've been hiding?'

'Several! But I have the wrong outfit for most of them. Now fewer words, more fleeing!'

Adam ran as fast as he could through the swell of bodies, keeping one woman to each side of him.

'Follow me!' Claire called. 'I have an exit!'

Xavier whipped his hat off his head and threw it with visible spin on his wrist. The magic hat appeared to gain a life of its own, slashing cutting and hacking into Six as it danced through patterns

'This is very rude you know!' Six complained.

'You broke the rules; therefore, I'm allowed to.'

'Is that a rule?' He stopped for a moment.

'No,' Xavier admitted. 'But it makes sense to me, turnabout being fair play and all.'

'I could quickly come to hate you and your silly hat.' Six caught the hat, the brim ripping through his hand and coming to a rest in his arm. He tossed the hat on the ground. Xavier ran to get it and Six was on Annabelle, cutting through web and cloth with his bare hands. She tossed a ball of webs into his face and as he pulled it off Xavier's hat cut off his head.

'This should probably be a bigger impediment to me than it is.' Six caught his own head and put it back on. 'I love being me.'

'We're not gonna make it,' Claire muttered.

'Xavier, if you have a way to open the portal you should do it.'

'I need a moment.'

'You understand that this guy could kill me in one punch, right?'

'Be that as it may,' he snapped, 'I need a moment!'

'We can save you.' Time slowed down again, the Watcher's voice filling the air. 'But we will need something in return.'

'What?'

'Your absolute trust.'

'All right.' He didn't have much of a choice. 'You've got it. Have at.'

'I'm afraid it's not that simple.' Now Adam was looking at the inside of his own mind. It was like a vehicle, himself driving the consciousness, while the others stood behind him, buried in the subconscious. They could give him advice, guidance, help him, but he was in control, he was in command, and they could give him only a little of their power if he kept it that way.

Just like that, with a simple effort of will, Adam took his hands off the controls. He took a step back, put a hand on each of their shoulders and pushed them forward.

'Get 'em boys.'

The thing that emerged from the whirl of cloth didn't look like Adam. It wore a white coat and mask that covered his head, with black eyes, a black shirt and pants, a twisted pitch-black smile. In each hand he carried a curved green sword.

He bowed as he faced Six of Nothing, spreading the swords wide. As the assassin charged he parted and shifted the swords, each one biting deep into meat. The Laughing Man's movements seemed slow to his eyes, but everyone else's were slower still. As the blade of a hand bit into his clothes he turned to the side, then leaned forward to whisper into Six's ear.

'You aren't nearly so indestructible as they think, are you, little Nothing?' he asked.

'Closer than you.' Six caught the blades inside his body, his own meat regrowing to hold them in place as he slammed his face into the Laughing Man's. He pitched backward, flipped in mid-air and landed on his feet, his hands blurring as shards of green crystal thudded into his enemy. 'The funny part is it's right in the pattern.' His voice was chuckling, as if they were friends sharing some gag over a pint. 'Your attempts to seem invincible are what ultimately gave the game away.' He tossed a shard at Six's left leg and, unexpectedly to Adam, but predictably to the Laughing Man he danced away, rather than just allowing himself to be hit like every time before. 'You can put yourself back together, but…' He swung a new sword he'd made from the air. Again, Six of Nothing jumped away from the swipe rather than taking it, as was his pattern.

'What's so funny?' For indeed and of course through all the blood and pain the Laughing Man had not stopped laughing.

'I've been watching.' He laughed 'Watching has always been a flaw of mine, but lately I found a friend with the most magnificent eyes.' He jumped back and aimed the sword at his leg. 'It's in your left calf isn't it? The one vulnerable point you have, the one I can't puncture or break without killing you.' Six's eyes widened for a moment, then he concentrated.

'Not anymore.'

'It's only a matter of time.' He thought about it. 'Nothing isn't what we thought was it? It's not that you don't want anything, it's that you actually want Nothing. That's why you want to tear a world apart, just, because it's there'

'It's true.' He flashed a grin. 'And now I have to be rid of you.'

'It's open!' Xavier called.

Six of Nothing made a move, what had once been a blurring pace now positively predictable. He wasn't as fast as the assassin was, but he could see it coming. He drove the sword forward, and, as it penetrated the flesh, tossed man and sword away.

As Six pulled himself to his feet the Laughing Man unleashed one of his missing tricks. It was one that Adam may learn one day, once he understood the joke. Once he understood how funny this broken twisted world was.

He pushed his laughter into the other man. He pushed the knowledge, understanding and futility of it all, feeling himself begin to glow.

Six of Nothing smiled. He had less far to go than most people.

'Shall I tell you a secret?' he spoke. 'Between you, me and the boy?'

'Sure.' The smile spread, and he chuckled a little. 'Before you die.'

'I chose him because he understands. He understands that the only point of the world is to experience it. That's the only joy of the joke, the telling of it and understanding. Things aren't funny if you don't play your part, if there's no stakes. He understood that sometimes the joke was on him and didn't mind if it was funny. If there was anything in him that he held sacred, he would have crippled me. Somehow, he ended up where I needed him. A person with all the questions finds a spirit with all the answers.'

Six shook with laughter, but he could see the hate in the man's eyes.

That was all he had. All the chances in the world and all he had was the desire to make nothing.

'That's not funny.' He laughed.

'Of course it is.' The Laughing Man struck thirteen times, watched the pattern of each flinch and pivot, found the weakness.

And cut it in two.

Likely Adam Westbrook would remember this. Likely he would not understand.

They would explain it, he would grow to comprehend.

'Problems?' He looked at Xavier, who tipped his hat.

'That was one of the few people in existence I actually liked,' he reflected. 'Oh well, easy come easy go.' He pushed the Laughing Man through the hole.

The Laughing Man, on the other side of the portal, awakened on a chessboard. He'd been there before, once, while Xavier had been freeing him from mind control imposed by the King's Man.

'Xavier!' he called out. 'Am I in the hat again?'

'Yes, you are.' This time it wasn't the hat himself that spoke to him, it was Xavier. He didn't look exactly like himself. His skin wasn't skin, it was covered entirely in cloth. The hat lead into a mask over his face, then into the collar of his coat, then jacket, gloves, pants and shoes. Not a piece of his skin was exposed.

'You have both your arms,' he observed.

'Yes, believe it or not I did notice that.' Xavier smiled and flexed his hand. 'In this world you are who you know you are, and I know I am this.'

Adam looked around, then, seeing no mirrors, held up his hands. They shifted from black to white, to veins of green, the claws grew and faded.

'Why am I so weird?' He looked down at his outfit, all of it was changing and shifting.

'Because you have no idea who you are.' Xavier shook his head. 'Adam, I have brought you here to stop you making a horrible mistake.' He thought about it. 'Until the appropriate time to make a horrible mistake of course.'

'So basically, going counter to everything else you've ever done?'

'You mean the opposite to your usual actions.'

'Granted but I'm here to talk to the other two. Yes, you two.' They appeared. 'We all need to have a conversation.'

'About what?' The Watcher was perched on his shoulder, its claws digging a little into his shoulder

'Well, about you giving him his body back for one.' He folded his arms and glared at them.

'I thought you liked us better?' The Laughing One strode between them, moving with its usual sinuous grace.

'Oh, I do, but it's not all about me. Things need to get done and the two of you are no use at all, other than my personal amusement.' He chuckled a little. 'Which was tempting, but I decided against it.'

'It doesn't matter what you want!' the Watcher snapped. 'Adam needs us in command to protect him.'

'From what?' Xavier looked around. 'The battle is won.'

'Well, you for one.' Which Adam had to concede was a pretty good point.

'Oh, yes, right, me.' He thought about that for a moment. 'If I promised not to kill you?'

'We would have no idea whether or not we could trust you,' the Laughing One pointed out.

'I'm going to, or at least pretend to. Pan will screw him if he kills me.'

'Unless he kills both of you and pretends

something went wrong.'

'It's okay.' He stepped past the cat, pushing its head away. 'I trust him. It's okay.'

'Candour compels me to admit that you probably shouldn't,' Xavier pointed out.

'Besides, while we're talking Annabelle is probably doing more than enough to stack the deck against you. If your betrayal turns out to be inevitable you'll wake up with like, spiders in your eyes or something.'

'That is an annoyingly good point,' Xavier pointed out. 'Now, as for you two, please release my acquaintance from your mind control or I shall murder at least one of you inside his mind. This will likely be traumatic for everyone in here who isn't me. I haven't done it before and it will be something of a novelty.' He paused. 'Despite that I find myself not actively wishing you pain.' He smiled. 'That's a nice thing. I have had at least one nice thing happen today. Also, I got to kill several people. You know this would be a very good day if you hadn't killed one of my friends and foiled my ultimate plan for killing the greatest of my many enemies.'

'You seem remarkably cool with that.'

'I didn't really have time to get attached to the plan.' He shrugged and reached out, tousling Adam's hair. 'Besides it's hard to be mad at you. You're like a stupid child or puppy. You have no idea what's going on and you just do whatever feels right. Even if it means you urinate on the rug now and again.'

'I mean, thanks, I think?'

'And if we decide not to give up control?'

Xavier went to speak, but Adam raised one hand to cut him off.

'Allow me, if you please.' The gentleman tipped his hat and Adam turned to the owl. 'If you refuse, we'll kill you. Some of the magic is mine, and I'm pretty sure I can handle this.'

'You would threaten us?'

Adam whirled and caught the Watcher around the neck, the claws digging into his shoulder.

'You threatened me first, and you are goddamn right I am willing to kill you. I'd like to be friends but if you want to be adversarial, I'm willing to do it that way.' He looked down at the Laughing One. 'You two used my body to kill a person, and now I have to live with those memories. I have to see that behind my eyes for the rest of my life.' He looked at the Laughing One. 'I'm in charge. Problem?'

'It's your joke.' The panther smiled. 'I'm content to tell it. For now.'

'I let you kill someone,' he admitted. 'I can't let you do that again.'

'You let everyone else do that!' the Watcher protested.

'Everyone else isn't inside me!' he snapped. 'I can't control Annabelle, or Pan, or Konstantin or that.' He pointed to Xavier. 'But I can control you two.'

'Yes, you can.' The Watcher's voice was cold. 'As the Laughing One said, for now.'

'Okay.' He looked at Xavier. 'We good?'

'We are.' Xavier bowed, and the chessboard faded away, replaced with the church they'd come out of. Xavier paused for a moment looking around the place and shuddering a little.

'You okay?' Annabelle spoke from the pew she was laying on.

'Yeah, though do you mind if we get to a minimum safe distance before you withdraw whatever anti-Xavier countermeasures you prepared?'

'Will do.'

'Fare thee well.' Xavier waved. 'Shall I could to one hundred before I leave?'

'That would be ideal.' Annabelle smiled at him and turned to leave.

'But not necessary I'm afraid.' The voice from behind them was familiar. It made Adam think of red velvet and silk. It flowed through and filled the chapel, forcing everyone to notice.

'I was hoping to have a little more time, Auntie.' Annabelle looked at Adam, then the Black Widow.

She was wearing more than usual, meaning actual clothing: a long white dress slit up the legs, cut low in the top and had cut out sections around the hips. She looked decidedly less than pleased.

'That was not our agreement, dear. The terms were simple, once you were done with your current business you would come with me for your formal training.'

'What?' Adam snapped.

'Understood.' Annabelle ignored Adam. 'Give me

a moment to put my affairs in order?'

'But of course.' She bowed her head slightly. 'Hello, darling.' She blew Adam a kiss.

'You know you don't have to do this right?' Adam demanded. 'We can stop her, we can talk to Pan and do something about it. We can–' She cut him off.

'Even if we did that It'd cost me my family. Spiders have no time for oath breakers.' She smiled. 'Sorry Adam, but it seems our fledgling relationship is at an end. I'll be gone for a couple of years.'

'I can wait.' It felt like a kick in the gut, but he looked her in the eye.

'If you did I'd appreciate it.' She smiled, her many times pierced lips glinting a little in the light. 'I'll understand if you can't. I release you.' She tapped him on the lips. 'But I am going to have to add just a little to your pain. I have a favour to ask.'

'Bad timing,' he observed.

'That's the theme of our relationship, you grinning idiot.' She gave him a hug. 'I'm sorry, but I need you to take care of my carnival for me while I'm away.'

'What?' He jumped back. 'I have no idea how to take care of a damn carnival!'

'The place runs itself day to day.' She put her hand on his shoulder. 'I need you to keep them straight, keep the ship moving in the right direction and manage their egos. Most importantly, keep them neutral.'

'How would I do that? I'm Lost remember?'

'Doesn't matter.' She smiled. 'I trust you. The

people who ended up in the Carnival did because they wanted to be beautiful, they wanted to be great, to entertain and be entertained. They're dreamers, and they need someone who understands their dreams, but has their feet on the ground. I want it to be you.'

'I have no idea what I'm doing.'

'You haven't had any idea what you were doing this entire time, and you helped me save the world.'

'Twice.'

'Twice,' she allowed. 'Please Adam, I need this, my people need this.'

'Okay, but if I suck at it I'm giving the job away.'

'Deal.' She shook his hand and turned around. 'I think you're awesome, just by the way. Any girl would be lucky to be with you.'

'Back at ya.' He smiled. 'I mean, guy, not girl, or I guess girl too if that's how you swing. See you when you get out.'

'See you then.' She took a step away, then turned back for a moment. Without thinking he lowered his mask and pressed his lips against hers.

'Come along, dear,' Widow pointed out, tapping her wrist. 'We are on a clock.'

'You're right, Auntie.' She took the Black Widow's hand and they turned away, heading for the door.

'So, does this mean I can finally take all that shit out of your face?'

'Only if you don't mind losing a finger or two,' Annabelle responded. 'Can you send someone to take Adam home?'

'Back to the Carnival? Certainly.'

Scarlett joined him a few minutes later, crawling out of the woodwork as a small spider, before turning to her human form.

'Hey.' She waved. 'Welcome to the team, new boss.'

'I have no idea why she picked me for this,' he admitted.

'It's okay, I do.' She smiled and took his hand. 'I'll show you the ropes, don't worry.'

'Xavier,' he called over his shoulder. 'Tell Pan what happened, I'll back you up if you keep your lies reasonable.'

'Divine!' He grinned. 'Farewell!'

'Okay, Scarlett.' He took a deep breath. 'Take me home.'

EPILOGUE

'Sir?' It took a moment for Adam to realise that the strongman was talking to him. The squat pack of muscle and bulk had been given to Adam as a bodyguard when he wasn't training or performing. He had a rotating list of personal servants and bodyguards, which the Watcher took care of, so no one lost time from more important things.

'Troy.' He nodded. Troy Mangakhia was his favourite of the bodyguards so far. He had some spider magic Adam didn't understand, but it made him stronger and tougher than hell. 'I told you not to call me Sir.'

'Yessir, you did.' He nodded. 'There's a large man at the gates. He's a member of the Lost who came here without permission or aid. He says he knows you personally, but we can't let him in without risking our neutrality.'

'What if I go out to him?' He thought about it. 'He has the word lost tattooed in all caps on his head, right?'

'Yes, and that would be good.' He thought about it. 'Not in that order, flip those.'

'Right then, let's go.' He pushed aside the papers he couldn't understand that seemed to have something to do with money. He knew Scarlett had already handled them, but he wanted a chance to understand what was going on, He was already reconsidering that.

People treated him differently now. Despite the fact they didn't know him, the great and good of the Carnival knew he was in charge here and wanted him to know their names. They needed to make a good impression. This was working so well that Adam had no idea, and he legitimately thought they were just lovely people. The Laughing One thought it was too funny to let anyone correct him.

Adam saw Pan leaning against the gate, the Lost Soldier was looking twitchy. He fixed Adam with a look and then held out one hand, which Adam shook.

'How much of what Xavier told me was lies?'

'I don't know what he told you.'

Pan thought about that for a second.

'I'm gonna guess all of it then,' he decided. 'Don't worry about it, you're not going to get into trouble and neither is he.'

'Oh?'

'He's too valuable.' He shrugged. 'X is one of the few people who have access to just about every world. He protects our interests and I can only get so angry. If you hug a rabid dog, you can't get pissed when it bites you. You decide whether or not to shoot it, act accordingly, and move on.'

'So, his secret's safe?'

'Always and forever.' Pan ran his hand across his scalp. 'You're in charge of the Carnival now. How'd that happen?'

'Because for some stupid reason Annabelle trusts me.' He shrugged. 'From what I can tell it's mostly going to be keeping them satisfied and neutral.'

'Fair enough.' Pan stared him levelly. 'The Lost won't like it if you do.'

'Yeah well. I probably will anyway. I like you guys but it's my job, and I feel like I owe it to Annabelle.'

'Fair enough, kid.' Pan put one big hand on his shoulder. 'Well, if you ever need any advice...'

'I'll give you a call.' With that Adam turned back to his carnival. He had strong men to manage, two of the acrobats were refusing to perform until one of them was chosen as the official star. Three of the spider queens were settling issues in one of the tents, the fire twirlers had been making problems and everyone knew the clowns were up to something though no one could quite agree what.

Still, he thought, as a real smile slid out underneath the mask, just for himself, at least he'd never be bored again.